Nigel May is an author, TV and radio presenter and a journalist. He has been described as "the UK's male Jackie Collins" and has written six page-turning glamorous blockbusters. As a showbiz journalist, he has interviewed countless celebrities around the world for magazines and newspapers. His TV work has included appearances on ITV, BBC, Channel 4 and Channel 5, as well as broadcasting from America. He is one of the UK's most popular crafting personalities through his work on Create and Craft TV. On radio he is a proud member of the Gaydio team. He lives in Brighton and is obsessed with all things '80s, flea markets and the Eurovision Song Contest. *The Girl Unknown* is his seventh novel.

To Michelle Cooke, the strongest girl I know.

Nigel May

THE GIRL UNKNOWN

How Do You Rebuild a Life You've Never Understood?

AUSTIN MACAULEY PUBLISHERS™

LONDON • CAMBRIDGE • NEW YORK • SHARJAH

A CIP catalogue record for this title is available from the British Library.

ISBN 9781528918176 (Paperback)
ISBN 9781528962216 (ePub e-book)

www.austinmacauley.com

First Published (2019)
Austin Macauley Publishers Ltd
25 Canada Square
Canary Wharf
London
E14 5LQ

Welcome to my darker side. A million thanks to "Team Unknown" – to the people who have seen this thriller through, from conception to completion. Eternal gratitude to Alan and Lottie, my utter soulmates. I love you both so very much. To David Lever, Andrew Carter and Mel Brown for being divine playmates. To Chris Meyrick, for his total strength and joyous friendship. And to Louise Porte, for being there for everything. To Helen Jenner, for initial book shaping and to all at Austin Macauley, for launching it to the world. To Gaenor Davies, for her loyal support, and to every person who has bought any of my books – whether it be for the glam or the grit. And finally to Jimmy Sutton, for his 'shimmy', without which life would be a much less thrilling place.

Prologue

Peru, Now

Even the smell of the room seemed different to Lucie Palmer. As if already impregnated with the sweet, anticipatory joy of freedom. She scanned her eyes around the room, taking it in, the stale drabness of the cold white walls and the softness of the cushion placed on the chair she was seated at. A comfort she had almost forgotten about. She tapped her fingers on the surface of the wooden table in front of her, listening to the sound they made. Melodic and somehow upbeat, despite a lack of tune. Her nails were bitten and worn away, the clean, colourful manicure that had once lived there now a thing from another life. If she closed her eyes, she could see how they had once looked. The pride she felt. Colourful and bright. Pristine. Before any hue of happiness had been snatched from her.

She opened her eyes and focused on the door on the far side of the room. Solid and strong, yet the small square window towards its top allowing her a view beyond that represented all that she had craved for so long. A corridor. An escape. A return.

After that, a light. Daylight. One with no boundaries. Something unimaginable since what seemed like an eternity.

Lucie allowed the corners of her mouth to spread into a smile. An action that had become alien to her. The sensation felt good yet full of fear. A fear of what was to come. Despite her longing. A chill spread across her back, at odds with the heat of her surroundings. She'd never become used to the stifling blanket of air that had wrapped itself dangerously around her for so long.

She closed her eyes again and breathed in deeply through her nostrils, the hiss of the air passing into her body, the only sound occupying her mind. She let the breath back out through her lips and pushed her hands down on to the table as she did so, enjoying the feel of the surface against little finger to thumb. She tipped her head back and only then opened her eyes, her attention immediately caught by the fan circling overhead. It moved slowly, inefficient in its duty. She didn't care. Nothing mattered any more. Not now that the end was finally in sight. She watched the arms of the fan spinning, their movements as irregular as they were slow. Her mind drifted, hypnotised by its spinning. Around and around, a groundhog motion that quickly became mind-numbingly repetitive. Like so much of her life had been recently. For longer than she cared to remember really. One thing aimlessly looping into the next, its purpose forgotten yet accepted as how it had to be.

The sound of the door opposite opening brought her thoughts back. A man entered; his uniform horribly familiar to her. She shuddered as she thought about the first time she had seen it. The depth of the petrol blue material, the badge on his chest, the weapon at his side. It was as menacing now as she had found it then. But today, there was a difference. An accessory that had never been there before. A smile painted across the deep tan of his skin. His seemed alien too. It was their only connection. Lucie couldn't remember when she had last seen such a welcoming, if somewhat stained, smile. Especially from someone dressed like him. She couldn't help but respond. In his hands a backpack, another added and unaccustomed accessory.

'Are you ready?' His tone was as deep as his skin colour, his accent strong.

'I'm ready,' she replied. She had been for an eternity. Not just for the hour or so she had been left in the room where she was sitting, but for a lifetime before that. Ever since the confines of her surroundings had been initially placed around her. An entrapment that she would never forget, no matter how much she cared to.

'Then come, Lucie Palmer. It is time.' He used her full name, an action that took Lucie by surprise. It represented an individuality that had been unknown before. She had been one of many, a statistic.

Lucie rose to her feet and walked towards him. He opened the door and handed her the backpack.

'Your belongings. Do you know what you're going to do?'

It was none of his business but yet, his friendliness warranted an answer.

'Go home, I suppose. Not that I'm sure where that is anymore. It's been a while.'

'Good luck Lucie, and I hope we never seen you here in Peru again. We see many girls like you here and it never becomes easier to see young women throw so much of their life away. How old are you now? 24?'

'25. Last week. A quarter of a century, and this is where I spent it. Happy birthday, huh?' Her voice a mixture of sarcasm and regret. 'That was not what I had planned when I was growing up.'

'It is never too late. Today is your day to celebrate. Finally, you are free. To escape this…' He waved his hand in the air searching for the right word before deciding on '…madness.'

'Madness. That's one word for it. I can think of many others but I need to go. To leave this behind. I shouldn't have been here.'

The two of them were now at the other door at the far end of the corridor. He drew back the large metal lock on its frame and pulled it open. A rush of heat hit Lucie's skin from the outside air. Once more, she shut her eyes and breathed in through her nose, enjoying the moment. It felt different to any other air she had ever inhaled.

'You shouldn't have been here, Lucie. You are different to many of the girls here, there is a softness about you.' Words of compassion from one of the many who had been turning the key on her existence for so long. For a second, Lucie was able to catch sight of the human behind the uniform. It seemed odd. She'd been so used to hating him. All of them. For no other reason than what they represented. Her captivity. 'But you shouldn't have messed with the drugs I guess. You've learnt your lesson.'

The smile was replaced by a downward turn of his mouth. To Lucie, it screamed smugness. All traces of human disappeared and she didn't even say goodbye as she stepped through the door and into the open air. Why was she spending a second longer there than she needed to? As the door shut behind her, she turned her head to the right and then to the left, deciding which way to go. For once, there were choices.

Choices that had been missing from the moment she had been imprisoned in the Peruvian hellhole of a jail six years ago. Her life snatched from her after being charged with the possession of nearly £2 million worth of cocaine. Her life thrown away and tossed inside a stinking cell with nothing but iron bars and smashed dreams for company. Nineteen to 25. Years when she should have been experiencing what the world had to offer. The ways of love, travel and wanderlust. Finding out who she was, what she wanted. But in such a short space of time, control of her own life had been ripped out of her hands.

'Learnt my lesson?' mused Lucie, as she stared across the busy street in front of her, the cacophony of motorists shouting directions and beeping horns an almost new sound to her. 'Shouldn't have messed with the drugs? I've told you so many times. I'm innocent.' Her words for her and her only.

The stabbing of a tear threatened the corner of Lucie's eyes but she fought it back, refusing to let it have its way as she moved down the street. Unsure of where she was going, but knowing nevertheless that it had to be the right direction. Away from prison, away from captivity and away from a life ruined by drugs yet again. They'd always been there, a presence in her life. A bruise that she always seemed to sport. The irony was tangible. Her life ruined by narcotics.

Even though she had never taken any herself.

Chapter 1

Brighton, 2004

Another knock at the door caused 11-year-old Lucie Palmer to lose her concentration again as she tried to complete the word search puzzle she'd been poring over sitting on her bed for the last half an hour. Even though she was hidden away in the sanctuary of her bedroom, the knock on the front door of the fifth floor flat she shared with her mother, Ruby, was loud enough to be heard from her bedroom. Not even the closed door of her own room and the stretch of hallway between her room and the shabby paint-chipped front door could blanket the urgent knocking that sounded with increasing regularity.

Lucie scanned her eyes to the Justin Timberlake calendar hanging on the wall. She loved him. It wasn't the official calendar like some of her friends owned, this was a cheaper one from a bargain shop in town, but it still had photos of Justin looking super cute and that was all that mattered to Lucie. She looked at the date. Saturday 14th August. Saturday. Always a busy day at the flat. More visitors than ever. Both on the doorstep of her mum's flat and inside its four walls.

Lucie tossed the puzzle book to the floor and listened to the familiar sounds that always followed a knock at the front door. It would always be one of three things. Sometimes it would be one of Lucie's school friends seeing if she wanted to play. It wasn't often and seeing as it was now the summer holidays, most of her friends were away with their families sunning themselves somewhere tropical around a swimming pool as blue as Justin's eyes. Lucky them. Lucie was spending her summer playing outside the flat on the swings that occupied the patch of grass in front of where they lived. She'd not even been to the beach this summer yet. A wave of hope hit her as she heard the door open, hoping a familiar voice would sound. Unsurprisingly, it didn't.

Sometimes, the knock would be followed by the opening of the door and then a hushed, muffled conversation. Lucie knew by now that it would last no longer than a minute. Her mum's voice clipped and to the point, the visitor's just the same. She'd seen it in the flesh too, not just heard it through the hollow wood of her bedroom door. Her mother would disappear into the front room leaving the visitor awkwardly staring into the hallway and fidgeting nervously, an impatient dance from side to side. Some of the visitors would spot Lucie and give out a clumsy "all right?" in her direction. Others would look right through her, almost as if their jittery eyes couldn't see her, looking everywhere and nowhere at the same time. Then her mother would return and a package of varying sizes would be handed over. But never before the visitor had offered a handful of money, notes scrunched together underneath tight knuckles that her mother would always count before offering up her prize.

The third post knocking scenario was the one Lucie dreaded most. As she tuned her ears to the action at her front door, she suspected that it might be the case for this one. It was the fifth visitor so far today and it was only mid-afternoon – it was always the same on a Saturday. The weekend seemed to make their flat a very popular destination. The door would open and her mother's voice would suddenly fill the air with an excited screech. This meant that whoever was visiting was a familiar and welcome face. It would normally be a man. Sometimes the same one. Maybe more than one. Sometimes a mixed group. Some of the faces Lucie recognised as they lived in other flats on the same estate as her and her mum. Some were new to her. Her mother would invite them in and they would all then group in the front room of the flat.

As Lucie listened to the action, she heard the visitors, this time it seemed to be two, a man and a woman, enter into the hallway of the flat and as ever, the voices faded somewhat as they went into the front room and the door was closed behind them. They could be in there for hours, her mother only reappearing to answer another call at the door.

Lucie hated those hours. It was during those hours that Lucie didn't exist. As if she no longer lived in her own home. Her mother would become so lost in her own world. The world behind the door of the front room. A world where curtains would be drawn, no matter what the hour of the day, smoke would circulate in the air, its scent heavy and cloying and Lucie would never be welcome. It was a world where her mother became even more of a stranger to her.

Lucie had learnt with experience that behind those doors was a place that made her invisible. She'd ventured there before. Having no choice when hunger made her question what time dinner would be. Or when she needed to tell her mum that the fridge was empty.

Her skin would become clammy as she left the safety of her own bedroom and gingerly tapped on the front room door. When no answer came and as her throat dried with nerves, she would turn the handle and push the door. It was then that she'd seen into horrors of the world beyond. Her mother and her "friends" dotted around the room. Sometimes screaming and dancing, bottles of beer and God knows what littered across the floor and virtually every surface. Surfaces where piles of white powder seem to sit. Lucie didn't know what it was, but she knew that it was often there. Little bags of multi-coloured tablets, sweet-like in appearance were sometimes visible too. Ashtrays, beyond full, spilling their contents.

For as long as she could remember, Lucie had witnessed scenes like this. For her, they were the worst moments. Staring into the room and feeling her lips begin to tremble as she attempted to form the words asking her mother for something. And then watching as her mother walked towards the door and without saying a word, silently shutting it in Lucie's face. That was the worst moment of them all. The moment of rejection from her own mother. Lucie knew that later her mother would be a different person, a person who would actually speak to her and maybe, if Lucie was lucky, hold her in her arms or read to her in bed. Those were the moments Lucie lived for, the moments when Ruby became her mother again in the true sense of the word. The moments when she wasn't behind the closed front room door.

Lucie knew that she had no desire to knock on the door again today. She couldn't face having the door shut on her yet another time.

Sliding herself off her bed and grabbing the puzzle book from the floor, she opened the door of her bedroom and headed past the front room moving as quickly as she could to avoid the pungent, sweet smell filling the air. She opened the front door and stepped out onto the mat on their doorstep. It said "WELCOME" in big black letters. It always made Lucie a little sad as she sometimes knew that her mother's "friends" were a lot more welcome than she, her mother's very own flesh and blood, would ever be. At least it felt that way at times. Lucie stepped forward and looked over the fifth floor balcony, down at the stretch of grass below. A dog, one of the many strays that seemed to roam the estate, was attempting to dig into the hardened, parched soil, burnt dry by the summer sun, at the side of the swings. Running to the staircase, she headed off to climb down the five flights to the swings. She might as well. She'd already spent most of the summer holidays there. When her mother was "busy" and her friends were AWOL, sadly there wasn't really anything else for her to do.

Chapter 2

Now

The first night of her freedom was not as Lucie had expected. After six years of sleeping in the most basic of conditions inside her Peruvian jail, Lucie had assumed that by booking herself into a hotel she would have had the best night's sleep in a long while. She couldn't have been more wrong. How could it be that soft white cotton sheets and a room with air-con and an en-suite made for a more restless night's sleep than a mattress as hard as floorboards and a metal toilet within reaching distance?

Lucie sat bolt upright in bed, torn from the worst nightmare, her entire body covered with a layer of sweat. The sheets, soft though they were, were now soaked too. The sound of her own breathing, fast and loud, scared her with its own ferocity.

She reached over to the bedside table and grabbed a glass of water. She downed it in two large gulps, the liquid feeling good against the heat of her throat and the volcanic thoughts racing through her mind. Her head stung with the images of what had been galloping through her brain whilst she slept. Explosions, faces, carcasses, bloody fights, images of those she had loved, those she had lost. Things that would never be the same again. But then after the last six years of her life, Lucie knew that nothing would ever be the same again. And that was part of the problem. Lucie had no notion of what her future would hold. She may not have had the most conventional two and a half decades on planet earth – in fact, she had dealt with more than most people had to cope with in a lifetime of three score years and ten – but all of a sudden, she was lost. Lucie Palmer didn't have a clue what was to happen next. Everything she had known or experienced was out of reach. She was alone. In control of her own destiny, and after six years of being told exactly what to do for virtually every minute of the day, the thought obviously terrified her more than she cared to admit. And judging from the vivid nightmares, she had just been experiencing, a heck of a lot more than she actually realised. There was no way in hell that she would ever want to step back inside the confines of her Peruvian prison cell but somehow the rigid structure and discipline of others ordering her around had become second nature to her and in some bizarre way almost a comfort. Enforced structure meant never having to make any decisions for yourself and as Lucie placed the glass back on her bedside table and walked to her hotel room window that strangely seemed like a good thing. At least she could never make any wrong decisions if she wasn't allowed to make any decisions for herself at all.

'Wrong decisions. Christ knows I've made enough of those already,' sighed Lucie to no one but herself as she stared out of the window, the sky now tainted with the first streaks of early morning light. Her room, on the twelfth floor of the hotel, looked down onto the street below, a criss-cross of vehicles going about their business. The streets were always busy. It was one of the first things she noticed about Peru when she had first arrived there. That seemed like a lifetime ago now. Somebody else's lifetime. One full of strangers. People she had thought she'd known. Including herself.

Lucie bit her bottom lip in confusion as she tried to focus her thoughts on all that had happened to her. How things had come to be. Nothing still made sense to her. Not really. She was an intelligent girl, strong at both school and college so how had she been so stupid, how had she let herself become so vulnerable? Even though her heart knew the answer, her brain still refused to believe it.

She could feel her lip begin to tremble as a glaze of tears warned of its arrival. She moved her eyes away from the street and looked up to the skies above her. They seemed almost as hectic, the thin white wisps of plane trails embossed across the sky as people flew away from the country. A country that she had wanted to leave so long ago. And she almost had. But it was never to be. The aeroplane had been so close yet so far. She might even have seen it, one of the many she'd spied through the taxi window as she made her way to the airport that day.

Lucie had thought about that day a lot. Relived the horror time and time again. It was a day that she would never forget and never be allowed to. It was embedded. She had hoped that the thoughts of it would fade with time, especially now that she had escaped the confines of her captivity. But as she gazed up at the aeroplane lights plotting their way across the sky above Lima, she knew that it was an experience that would never stop piercing her to the core with razor-sharp severity.

Thoughts of the airport filled her mind. She closed her eyes, but the images still remained as clear as ever for Lucie...

Lima Airport, Peru, 2012

Lucie wound down the window of the taxi carrying her to the airport and relished the cocktail of cool breeze and Peruvian sunshine that embraced her skin. Earphones in, she wallowed in the joyousness of Taylor Swift's *We Are Never Ever Getting Back Together*, one of the many tunes that epitomised the euphoric few months she had just spent working in Peru. All thoughts of life back home in the UK and her troubled upbringing on a council estate on the south coast seemed literally a million miles away, not just whatever distance it really was between where she was now and where she had been back then.

Peru had given her all that she had dreamt of and more. Experiences that she had never even thought she deserved and emotions that she hadn't even known existed. It had been a hot few months and that wasn't just a weather report.

Her attention was torn away from Taylor's anthem as her cab driver turned to face her and ask a question. Unable to read his lips, she removed her earphones and smiled, asking him to repeat himself. Oblivious to the fact that he was driving in one direction and looking in another, a fact that seemed commonplace for many of the taxi drivers Lucie had used over the past few months, he kept his eyes firmly on his passenger as he asked again.

'What airline is it?'

Lucie told him. The next 36 hours would be mainly spent in the air. Lima to Amsterdam. Amsterdam to Madrid. Finally, Madrid to Ibiza. And another dream waiting to happen. Finally, after everything that she had endured in her short life, things were playing pretty smoothly for her right now.

She closed the window as the car pulled up outside the terminal and checked her mobile. No messages. Strange but maybe not that surprising. Busy times. Should she ring now or wait until she was all checked in and enjoying a glass of something fizzy in the airport lounge? She decided to wait. It was much easier to speak when the only thing to contend with was the effervescence of bubbles as opposed to a suitcase that seemed to be so much heavier than it had been when she'd flown into Peru months earlier. That's what a long, hot summer of gift-getting and souvenir shopping did for your luggage she guessed. Even the taxi driver appeared to wince slightly as he hauled the heavy case from the boot of his car and placed it in front of Lucie.

She paid the man and lifted the extension arm on the case before pulling it inside the terminal. She slipped her mobile into the messenger bag wrapped over one of her shoulders as she did so. Calls could definitely wait until she was luggage-free.

The queue at check-in for her flight was much longer than Lucie had hoped. Despite arriving at the airport with time to spare, it seemed that most of the people on her flight had shared exactly the same idea. That it paid to be prompt. The line housed a mix of ages and looks – from young summer revellers like herself through to more mature couples in their retirement years who had evidently now ticked off Peru on their bucket list. Lucie joined the back of the queue and reinserted her headphones into her ears.

She was just reacquainting herself with another of her summer tunes when she felt a hand on her shoulder. She span around to see who it was. The man was heavy set and uniformed. Airport security? Lucie wasn't sure. The look on his face was not a friendly one and Lucie, as she had in the taxi just minutes before, pulled her headphones from her ears to hear what he had to say.

The man asked Lucie to accompany him. Lucie was about to ask where but decided against it when she spotted another two uniformed men in her peripheral vision. Something told her that remaining silent and complying with the man's wishes was probably the best thing to do. Thoughts of what could be happening bounced in her brain. Perhaps, it was just a jobsworth of a guard doing a security spot check, or maybe there was a problem with her passport, or maybe something had happened to someone she knew back home. All sorts of irrationalities echoed inside her. If there was a problem, then maybe she should steel herself accordingly.

'Is something wrong?' she asked, as the man escorted her away from the line of passengers waiting to check in. Her question was met with silence. A creeping of dread started to move its way across her body. Lucie could see that the man with her, and the two she had spotted moving as one a few steps behind her, were all carrying weapons. Airport security being what it had to be in this day and age, she could understand why, but the thought of the guns in such close proximity to her only seemed to escalate the cauldron of fear brewing inside her. She was suddenly aware that all eyes seemed to be upon her. As she scanned around the airport hall, she could see the inquisitive looks of people close by spearing in her direction.

People moving out of the way as the trio of security advanced to their destination, as yet unknown to Lucie, in an ominous triangle of power with Lucie and her case at the centre. Something told her that this was so much more than just a routine check. For the first time, a total sense of dread washed across her. Goosebumps spread across her flesh. All eyes seemed to condemn her, but for what she had no idea.

The next few moments seemed to pass in a blur, as if she was dreaming, a vision lacking clarity that she would never fully be able to recall. Doors were opened, white-walled corridors walked, more people coming into view. Again, their eyes slicing into her.

Lucie found herself in a room. There were no windows and the air hung heavy with anticipatory apprehension. She was told to sit down by the man who had escorted her. She did so. Her case was lifted onto a table by two officers. Lucie watched as they opened her luggage, her mind immediately thinking about when she had packed it just a few hours earlier. A smile of recollection involuntarily showed itself on her face. It vanished immediately as the present replaced it. Was everything clean? Would they be rooting through her smalls? Was there anything in there she needed to worry about? For a second, embarrassment mingled with fear as she contemplated the personal items they might come across.

She watched as they meticulously started to remove her belongings. The T-shirt she'd been wearing on arrival in the country, the shorts she'd bought for her first day at the beach, the multi-coloured sarong that had been ripped passionately from her body on that night not so long ago that still seated itself beautifully at the forefront of her mind. For a moment, she was no longer in the room with its oppressive air and ominous expectancy. Instead, she was transported back to a pivotal moment of life-changing bliss that would forever have top billing in her memory bank.

The memory shattered into a million shards as she refocused on the scene literally unpacking itself in front of her again. There amongst her belongings, the two men began to pile up package after package of carefully wrapped white parcels. Each of them like bricks of alabaster building her demise as they continued to grow higher and higher.

Shock smothered Lucie. 'What the…? I didn't pack those. I have never seen them…' Her words trailed away into nothingness as one of the officers at the table took out a knife and ripped into the lining of her case. More of the packages followed.

Why were they there? How had this happened? She had no answers. Which meant she couldn't give any. All she could do was listen and wonder, her mind a ticking bomb of confusion, as she heard those in front of her make their accusations against her and escort her heavy-handedly from the room. She took one last look over her shoulder at her belongings lying on the table and the packages scattered there as she was man-handled through the office door and away to a destination unclear. Her clothes so familiar, but everything else so conflicting. How had this come to be?

Chapter 3

Brighton, 2006

Lucie's bags were packed. Her pretty pink backpack and her favourite leopard print case. She sat on the end of her bed staring down at them. She wasn't sure whether what was inside the two pieces of luggage was enough for her needs, enough for where she was going. Where was she going? She had been told to pick out her favourite things. The dresses she liked to wear, the toys she liked to play with, the photos she liked of her friends and family. Actually, make that friends and mother. There was no other family. It had always been her mother. A father was an entity that had always remained unknown. And she had never had the luxury of a brother or sister. Which had always saddened her and still did at the age of thirteen. Sometimes she pretended she had a brother. Just in her mind. She would have conversations with him and he would always give her the answers she wanted to hear. Be the perfect brother that she had always wanted. Sometimes when she first woke up in the morning, she believed that he really existed. In those dreamlike seconds before reality would hit.

Lucie was well aware that her family make-up was not like the other girls she knew. How she envied their talk of "Daddy did this…" or "I was staying at my grandparents…" It was something so little and commonplace to them but to Lucie, it was the world. A world she didn't seem to have.

She could hear her mother in the front room of their flat. She was crying. She had been all morning. Lucie looked at her watch. Just after midday. She'd been ready since 9:30 a.m. She thought she had to be. If she was heading off on an adventure then surely it was sensible to be ready to go at the earliest hour.

She scanned her eyes around the bedroom. They felt a little stingy and she squinted and blinked a few times to try and make them feel somewhat better. She knew why. The air in her room still smelt of smoke. It permeated throughout her home. Sometimes she could cope with it, the smell as familiar to her as a pizza delivery to her front door or the soft scented goodness of her fruity bubble bath. But some days, the irritating pecking at her eyes caused by the acrid clouds that wafted through the house itched at her features. It was a smell she never missed when outside the house, even if sometimes it appeared to follow her wherever she went.

The wallpaper in her room, red and flowery, had begun to peel at the edges and a patch of damp in the far corner above her bed appeared to be bigger and more creeping than the last time she had looked. She would have to ask her mother to fix it. Maybe her mum could ask one of her many friends to fix it. Perhaps if she stopped crying for a moment.

Lucie knew why she was crying. She knew why there was no point in asking her mother anything. After today, Lucie wouldn't be coming back. The nice lady in the white blouse with long straight hair like Hannah Montana who came around to the house and wrote things in her special book had basically told her that. She said that it was necessary and for her own good. That it would help both her and her mother. Lucie's mum hadn't cried then but obviously now she was. Now that she knew that Lucie was being told that she had to go away. Leave her behind. The lady had said that it might not be for forever. What was the phrase she used? 'Just until mummy got better.'

Lucie didn't really know what was wrong with her mother. She'd heard other women on the estate say that "Ruby Palmer was a sick individual" and that "that poor child should be taken away". Her friends' mothers had said it in front of Lucie. As if she wasn't there or was unable to hear. Well, now the nice lady was going to take Lucie away and her mother could get better and that was what was important, wasn't it? If mummy was ill, then she needed to see the doctors and maybe go to hospital and suddenly, everything would be better for both her mother and for her. Then she could come home. Then Lucie could ask about new wallpaper for her bedroom. She stared back up at the stain of mould in the corner where the wall met the ceiling. She'd tried to calculate how big it would be by the time she came back. She had no idea. How long would it take for her mum to get better? Sometimes the nice lady didn't have any answers either.

She could still hear her mother crying as a knock sounded on the front door. After waiting thirty seconds or so and hearing another knock, Lucie guessed that her mother must be too upset to answer it. The thought made Lucie sad too. The thought of her mother being both ill and upset. That didn't seem fair.

Lucie went to the front door and opened it. Her eyes spiked with pain again as the bright light of outside mixed with the smoke inside the flat. She looked up and saw three figures silhouetted against the sky beyond their balcony. She instantly recognised the middle one as the nice lady with the long hair.

'Hello, Lucie. May we come in?'

Lucie opened the door and allowed the woman in. She was followed by two men. They both had uniforms on. Lucie didn't know who they were but they looked official and a little scary. As if they sensed her apprehension, both men smiled as they followed the lady into Lucie's hallway. The action made Lucie feel instantly better.

'Is your mum in, Lucie?' asked the lady.

Surely, she didn't really need to ask. You could hear her through the front room door sobbing.

'She's in there,' stated Lucie. 'She's upset about me leaving and about being ill too I guess.'

'You understand what is happening, Lucie, don't you?'

'Yes.' Even if she wasn't a hundred per cent clear, Lucie didn't want to appear stupid in front of the lady.

'Are your bags packed? Do you have everything you need?'

Lucie nodded. 'My bags are in there.' She pointed to the bedroom. The woman indicated to one of the men to go and fetch the bags. He did so.

'You fetch your coat, Lucie. I'll just try to speak to your mum.'

Lucie went to grab her coat. It may have been sunny outside right now, but she would need it if she stayed away until the winter. As she did so, she could hear the woman knocking on the front room door.

'Ruby, it's Georgina Waters, the social worker. We've come to take Lucie with us. You know this is for the best?'

'Piss off.' Ruby's voice was angry and raw. The door didn't open.

'Ruby, we need to leave with Lucie. Do you want to say goodbye?'

Lucie had re-joined the men and the nice lady in the hallway, her coat draped over her arm. Despite her mother's swearing, she couldn't help but smile at how silly the two grown men looked carrying her pink rucksack and leopard-print case.

The woman smiled at Lucie and spoke again at the door. 'It's time for us to go, Ruby. It's your last chance to say goodbye.' She tried the door. It was locked and the sobbing continued behind it.

The social worker turned her attention to Lucie. 'Okay Lucie, it's time for you to say goodbye. Your mummy is too upset to see you so if you have anything to say, then now is the time to say it. Do you understand?'

Lucie did.

As the woman and the two men ushered her towards the front door, Lucie shouted in her cheeriest voice "bye mum, get well soon, I love you". Her voice cracked slightly and let out a wobble as she did so. She was determined not to cry. Leaving her mum to become better was the best thing for everyone. She shouldn't cry about it. That wouldn't help anything, she knew that. She'd discussed it with her imaginary brother and he'd agreed.

At first, the door didn't open. It was only when Lucie was virtually out of the flat door that the door swung open. She span around to look at her mother. Ruby was crying and two of her friends were sitting on the sofa in the room behind her.

Lucie waited for her mother to reply, to say something. To tell her she loved her too. Her mother said nothing and shut the door again, her sobs once more audible beyond it.

'C'mon Lucie, let's go.' It was the woman speaking. Lucie didn't really hear her, suddenly deafened by her own sadness. Her mother had watched her go and said nothing, obviously too upset about Lucie leaving to be able to say what she really felt. The thought made Lucie sad. Her mother loved her, she knew that. How sad that her tears stopped her from telling her. That misery drowned her.

Lucie's heart was still breaking for her mother when she climbed into a car with the nice lady and the two men five stories below and sped away from the flat.

Chapter 4

Now

'Welcome to London where the local time is…'

Lucie zoned out on what the in-flight attendant was saying as she touched down at Heathrow Airport. The air outside seemed grey, late afternoon showers and a blanket of cloud painting the sky into a shadow of sombre, grim realism. So, this was it. Her homecoming. Back to the land where she grew up. Back to whatever was waiting for her. Her future as unknown as the last paragraph in a book when you're still delving into the prologue. The next chapter, no matter what it was, would be back in the UK. What money there had been left in her bank account when she'd exited the stinking hellhole of her life in prison had been used to buy her ticket home. Home. The word meant nothing to her. It had no tangible meaning. To others, it would be cosy comforts, a sanctuary, a place to escape the world and bathe in the harbour of the warmth within, but to Lucie, there was nothing. There was no home. There was nothing. Just bricks and mortar. The news she had received a few weeks earlier whilst still inside had put pay to that.

She stood up and released the catch on the overhead locker above her seat, reaching inside to locate her backpack. Her worldly possessions, it would seem. She tried to imagine what she still had left at the house she had shared with her foster parents Roger and Tanya Grimes. Seeing them seemed so long ago now. It still hurt to think that she would never see them again. Their lights permanently extinguished. Her one piece of certainty in life removed to bring her entire existence crumbling down.

A mist of cold caused her to shiver as she recalled the moment she learnt of their deaths. The guard at the prison informing her that there was news from home. Bad news. Her foster parents, the two people who had showed her more love than her own flesh and blood had ever managed to, had both been killed. Their car found upturned in a ditch on a remote country road, the shell crushed out of shape, their lifeless bodies within. At least they had died together. That had been Lucie's first thought. They had been so in love. It only seemed fitting that they should both be taken from life together. Spared the agony of one having to witness their own heart breaking with grief as they mourned for the other. Her second thought had been to try and remember the last time she had seen them. They'd wanted to visit her in prison, but she had been so aware of the disappointment she had caused them by being there in the first place that Lucie had requested that they stay away. She couldn't bear the thought of their own disappointment adding to her own already mountainous misery. Plus, she had always believed deep down that her innocence would be proven, that sense would prevail and it would become clear that the drugs in her suitcase did not belong to her. That way when she saw Roger and Tanya again, it would be with a backstory that didn't scream guilt.

She would head back to their house in the north of England. It could no longer be her home, not with such an aching gap within, but she could collect some more of her things. Try to rebuild. The house would be sold. She had already instructed that. Once the initial horror of losing her foster parents had subsided to below hysteria, Lucie had been informed that she was the beneficiary of the Grimes' wills. The couple were affluent, or at least they had been. They had spent a small fortune over the years trying to provide Lucie with the best things in life, and another small fortune attempting to secure the best defence lawyers cash could buy when the news of Lucie's arrest had broken.

Lucie had been informed that there was money left. Despite her current bank account looking far from glowing, she'd been told that soon funds would be released to her. She would not go short, that was clear but the selling of the house would allow Lucie a clean start. Away from everything that had gone before. Away from her own life. A somehow cursed life so far that was unable to stray too far from the continual black path of heartache and tragedy.

Having cleared passport control, Lucie walked through the "green" channel at customs. An unexpected wave of nausea hit her as she did so. Would that always be the case when she walked through such a place? She suspected it would be. A surge of unwanted, undeserved guilt hitting her like a battering ram. Expecting the unexpected and the worst case scenario every time.

She hesitated momentarily as the electric glass doors separating her from the arrivals gate whirred into life and began to slide open. Afraid of what might be beyond. Would there be photographers, reporters and a barrel of questions ready to be fired her way? For a second, she realised how totally unprepared she was. She had just spent hour after hour on planes. Long, endless, listless. She could have worked out a strategy but instead, she had just stared out of the window, lost in her own confusion.

'Move it, will you?' A voice from behind her, gruff and impatient as she realised she was blocking the door. Without thinking, she stepped forward through the doors and out into the unknown. A life unknown, as it always had been to be honest. Just now, more than ever.

A vacuum of air seemed to surround Lucie as she took in the wall of people in front of her. But they were no questions, no flashlights, no dramatic running towards her with microphones in hand. There was nothing. Just a line of people waiting for their loved ones or their clients. A mix of emotions washed over Lucie as she realised, both gladly and strangely a little sadly, that she was yesterday's news. A silly girl from days gone by who had no doubt gotten just what she deserved in the eyes of the masses. If only they knew.

So, this was it. No triumphant return. No fanfare. Just indifference. Just Lucie, the few belongings that had survived her Peruvian ordeal and an as yet vague appointment to settle the financial dealings of her dear departed foster parents. Not the average day-to-day existence of a 25-year-old, but then Lucie was far from average.

It was as she began to make for the exit that she heard the voice.
'Lucie…'
It sounded familiar yet ominously out of place.
'Lucie, it's me.'
Lucie span to face to voice. She dropped her backpack from her hand as she took in the person before her. Smartly dressed, make-up immaculate, head to toe designer if Lucie wasn't mistaken, not that she was actually sure what was in fashion anymore. Hair a little grey around the temples, older than she remembered, but now styled into a neat pony-tail. The overall effect was one of style, grace and affluence. A woman with taste. The complete opposite of what Lucie had always associated with her.

'Lucie, it's me, darling, welcome home…'
The words were dry and barely there, but they came.
'Mum?' Disbelief despite the vision before her.
'Yes, I had to come. When I knew you were out.'
'But…how? Why?'

There were other questions firing around Lucie's brain but too many to verbalise.

'I'm so sorry about everything, darling. Everything. But you're home now. You're here with me and we can be together. A family. Where you belong. I can make this better.'

The words may have been a decade or so too late but they still spread a warmth through Lucie's heart. Home. Family. Words that meant so much.

'Come with me, Lucie. Let me explain.'

Lucie didn't know what she was to do but as her mother, Ruby, moved towards her and took her in her arms, the subsequent connection between them as they hugged made her realise that she had no choice. Being in her arms felt good, despite everything that had passed before. Maybe there was no other choice right now, but holding her mother's hand as they walked from the terminal out to the airport car park felt like the best thing in the world. A perfect moment. And there hadn't been many of those lately.

Chapter 5

Now

'I blame myself for everything, of course. It's no wonder you became mixed up with all of that...' Ruby searched for the word as she continued to hold her daughter's hand in the back seat of their taxi. She settled on "badness".

'I didn't do it,' stressed Lucie.

'I know you didn't, darling. I bet those drugs were put there. Planted on you. Shoved in the case when your back was turned. It's always the same story, isn't it? Some naïve, silly girl being turned into a drugs mule for some big time wannabe gangster wanting to spread their nasty vile trade worldwide. I'm so glad my own dealings with all of that nonsense are behind me. It's time to start again.'

Lucie was struggling to keep it together. Her life ahead was a blank page. It certainly had been for the last few days since her release. But never had she ever considered the story now being written in front of her. One starring her mother. This was a tome in which she never expected to star. Wondrous and bewildering and a wrecking ball to her senses all at the same time. Yet one from which she had no desire to escape even though Ruby's unknowing chastisement suggesting that she was some "silly girl" transported her back 15 years.

'I know who planted them. I was duped. I should tell the world. Share my story.' There was defiance in Lucie's voice. It felt good to talk. Since her release, most of her conversations had been with the voices inside her head.

'Do you really want to, Lucie? To drag it all back up, to relive it all. To haul your horrid story through the papers for a few measly pounds. That seems kind of tragic. Beneath you.'

'It wouldn't be about money. It would be about justice. I don't need the money.'

'The papers would blame me of course, say that drugs were something that you had always been faced with. My name would be dirt. Do you really want that to happen? Especially now that we've found each other again. It's been too long. No amount of money should spoil that.' There was a hint of cracking in Ruby's voice. She reached down into her handbag and pulled out a packet of cigarettes. She lit one and wound down the window of the taxi, the gust of air from outside a welcome relief on her face.

'I've told you it's not about the money. I don't need money. I have some of that coming from...' Lucie stopped, unable to continue. Unsure what to say. Her foster family and her blood family had always been two separate things. Now to potentially hear them in the same sentence felt more than a little odd and off-putting.

'From your foster parents. You can say it you know. I don't mind. I'm not proud that you were taken from me and I'm not exactly thrilled about our lost years, but I will always be grateful for what they did for you. They obviously turned you into a fine young woman...despite your recent accommodation.' Ruby took a deep drag on her cigarette and blew the smoke in the direction of the open window. 'But that's over now. The years of us being apart I mean, not the fact that your foster parents are no longer...' It was now Ruby's turn for her words to peter out, the horror of realising how her last few words could be callously misconstrued dawning on her.

For a few seconds, there was silence. Neither mother nor daughter knowing what to say next.

It was Ruby who eventually did.

'I'm so sorry about your foster parents, Lucie. I heard that they were killed. I read about it online.'

'How did you know it was them?'

'I know more about you than you realise, Lucie. You may have been taken from me Lucie, ripped from our home, but you could never be ripped from my heart. There will always be a connection. Even when we're not together.'

Lucie contemplated the words and watched as her mother finished her cigarette, flicking the butt out of the window with an expert action and an immaculate manicure. As the wind caught hold of it, the still smouldering butt disappeared out of view.

'You still smoke, then?'

'I do. Allow me some pleasure in life, Lucie, even if this one is giving me daggers.' Ruby indicated the man driving their taxi who had been staring at Ruby with more than an ounce of venom ever since she had lit up in the back of his cab. 'I'm paying over the odds for this ride as I told him I couldn't go longer than half an hour without reaching for one of my ciggies and he agreed that I could smoke, despite what his sneers might suggest right now. Fuck him, I say.'

As if to prove the point, Ruby took her cigarette packet from her bag again and lit another, retaining eye contact in the rear view with the driver as she did so. On her first drag, she deliberately blew the smoke in his direction and not towards the window. The billowing cloud that resulted before getting sucked out of the window in a long plume caused Lucie to cough.

'Sorry, dear, but really, his face could curdle milk. I'll leave him an extra couple of quid to buy a new air freshener for his rear view mirror.'

'I guess I can handle your smoking if *all this* means what I think it means.' Lucie indicated her mum's outfit and appearance as she said *all this*. 'I assume you've given up on all of the other bad stuff that I had to witness? You're looking pretty incredible.'

'Done and dusted.' Ruby shifted a little uncomfortably in her seat as she did so. Evidently, the prospect of talking about her drug habit with her daughter, the daughter she had lost for so long due to it, was not something she relished the thought of.

'Since when?' Lucie's words were direct and to the point, yet still contained an air of caring. Ruby would always be her mother, despite everything.

'I've been clean for a good few years now. Since before you went inside. Let's just say that losing you and some of the rather brutal meetings that followed your departure taught me the error of my ways.'

'Why didn't you let me know before? I could have been there for you?' Lucie said the words without true consideration.

'I'd let you down. I was ashamed. And besides, you were rather busy.' Ruby formed her lips into an O and blew a smoke-ring, rapidly demolished by the breeze as it shot out of the window, and winked to show her sarcasm. 'I'm not sure me turning up all drug-free and self-righteous at one of the hardest prisons in South America would have done either of us any good, do you? And believe it or not, I do try to stay away from any kind of temptation. And I bet it was rife inside, wasn't it?'

'I wouldn't know. I don't do drugs, remember. Not my thing. As I have tried to tell everyone unsuccessfully for the last six years.' It was now Lucie's turn to pile on the sarcasm. She smiled, albeit weakly, to stress her point. Her mother returned the smile. For a split second, all that had ever happened between them vanished as the bridge connecting them simply rebuilt itself with a smile. A union of happiness. Brief but definite.

Nothing more was said for a few moments, a mixed air of contentment and awkwardness wrapping itself around them like the summer sunlight that was finally making itself known through the window of the taxi. A once grey sky had now turned an electric blue, and the sinister clouds that had been present as Lucie landed had dispersed leaving a freshness. As the sun warmed her face through the window, Lucie felt a wave of trepidation cover her. Tinged with expectation. Maybe the sun was shining for a reason. Maybe there were sunny days ahead and perhaps, they would come from the most unlikely of places.

Ruby spoke. 'Take the next slip road, please.'

The driver, his face still a canvas of discontent at his passenger's behaviour, nodded abruptly and turned on his indicators to leave the motorway they were travelling on. It suddenly occurred to Lucie that she actually had no idea where she was going. It had been over a decade since she had last seen her mother and that had been at their council flat in Brighton. Her assumption had been that they would be heading back there. It struck her how silly the assumption was. Most people will have moved from a house after a decade and so much had happened to both her and Ruby that going back to the place where the rot that had destroyed their union had first taken seed was probably the worst idea possible.

'Where are we going? Back to the flat?'

'To that shithole. No. That's long gone. I think the block was condemned a few years back. I don't live in Brighton anymore. Don't need to. Not there anyway. I haven't done for a while. Too much temptation again if I went back there.'

Yet again, Lucie was struck by how much her mother had changed. The women in front of her was still physically the same one she had always known. The wiry body, the striking, if unconventional, beauty of her almond-shaped eyes, her wide mouth and fulsome lips, always slashed in her trademark bright red lipstick. But there was definitely a different air about her. The way she carried herself, the poise in her actions. The lines on her face, for a woman in her mid-forties, not appearing as the lines of age and decay, yet of experience and knowledge. For someone who had been through so much in her life, she had evidently come through the other side with a new found confidence. It pleased Lucie immensely.

It wasn't just the late-June sun that was finally shining. Ruby was too.

'So where are we going?'

It was less than fifteen minutes later that Lucie had her answer. The car had pulled up on a tiny street in a picturesque village. The place was pure chocolate box. They had passed a village green, complete with ducks. The pub on the corner of the street with chalkboard menu and nightly entertainment detailed outside. The tea room with red and white oil cloths spread across the tables within. It was light years away from their former life in the council high rise in Brighton. Lucie hadn't so much just landed back in the UK, it was like she had landed back in the 1950s. She couldn't help but smile at her surroundings.

Having paid the driver, Ruby and Lucie exited the car and watched as his car sped off down the street, a sharp screech of tyres sounding briefly as he made his happiness that the journey was over known to them. 'Silly fucker,' stated Ruby, her swearing the antithesis of their new surroundings.

'This is mine,' said Ruby, as she pushed open a small gate that lead to a path leading away from the street. Either side was green with grass, a lush green that only came from a well-tended garden. Flowers dotted the pathway which arced as it wound its way through the garden.

'When did you start having green fingers?' asked Lucie. 'From what I remember, you could kill a bunch of fake flowers just by looking at them. This garden is beautiful.' A flashback of her life inside the Peruvian jail coated her as she thought about her time locked away. Greenery and open spaces were one of the many things that she had missed dreadfully. The stark yard in the prison didn't even compare. The air there somehow polluted with vitriol.

'Lucie, I wouldn't know a violet from a Venus fly trap, but one of the many perks about living in a village that looks like it belongs on a postcard is that there is always a local handy man or a retired gardener ready to tend to your every need, including keeping this lot looking good. You'll meet ours no doubt. Nice lad.' She pointed to the flowers, although from her expression she may as well have been talking about little green men from outer space.

'So when did your life change so dramatically?'

Ruby didn't answer and if she had, Lucie wouldn't have heard her as the two women reached their destination. As the path curved once more, a large two storey cottage came into view. The sight of it took Lucie's breath away. The roof was thatched and an expanse

35

of pinkish wisteria looped its beautiful way across the front of the building. The front door was a bright shade of red. It immediately made Lucie think of her mother's lipstick.

'Wow. This place is beautiful. Just stunning.' Lucie could feel her eyes widening to take in the magnitude of its beauty. It was big without being colossal, sweet without being twee and grand without losing any of its homely charm.

'I like it,' remarked Ruby. 'Mind you, the wisteria is coming to an end now. You should have seen it when it was in full bloom as it literally covered the house. We're a touch late in the season apparently. A little something I learnt from the gardener.' Ruby grinned at Lucie, who had an air of disbelief written across her face. 'I know, listen to me, who would have thought it, eh?'

'So is this yours?' asked Lucie, unable to quite piece her mother and the cottage together in one sentence.

'Every last brick.'

'How?' The last time I saw, you could barely stand without the aid of drugs, let alone stand on your own two feet and own a place like this.'

'That was another me,' said Ruby. 'A forgotten me, one that is gone for good.'

'I'm pleased. Really I am.'

'So am I, Lucie, so am I. It cost me so much, and I don't mean financially. I'd lost so much in life. I thought it was time to try and put things right.'

'But how can you afford this?' It didn't seem like a rude question.

'I was lucky. The house was left to me and well, after everything I had been through, it came at the right time. The perfect time in fact.'

'Who by?'

'Let's just say I shall be eternally grateful to your Uncle Oscar.'

'Who?'

'My older brother, Oscar.'

'I've never heard of him,' said Lucie.

'I'm not surprised. He never really took any notice of me when he was alive. He was normally working his way through a bottle of Jack at nine in the morning. I guess addictive personalities run in the family. Well, breakfast boozing and doing 100mph on the motorway don't mix very well and one morning, he and his Aston Martin went out for a ride and neither came back. He left everything to me, his only sister.'

'He was minted then?'

'Successful artist. There's loads of his paintings in the loft if you want to look. I don't like them. All a bit weird and poncey for my liking. He sold them worldwide to all sorts of fancy people for ridiculous prices. But I didn't say no to his house. It's quite something, isn't it?'

'You never mentioned him.'

'He was more than a little distant to be honest. And we were like chalk and cheese. There was no love between us. I'm surprised he put me in his will, but I guess the stupid lush had no one else. Now, shall we go in and I can show you your room? You're happy to stay here I assume.'

Lucie looked around, turning her face to the sky above, the warmth on her skin from the sun's rays pleasing her. It was an utterly charming place and maybe just what she needed whilst she was trying to sort out the what-would-doubtless-be-horrible dealings with the death of her foster parents. And she had to admit that the new version of her mother was a pleasing one and much better company that she had ever imagined possible. Every girl needed her mother and maybe now was the perfect time for them to bond again. Maybe truly for the first time.

As Ruby inserted her key into the lock of the big red door and turned it, Lucie couldn't help but hope that maybe it was time for a new beginning. She'd had enough bad luck in her life and hopefully now, it was time for a fresh start. One much less cursed and studded with heartache.

Chapter 6

Now

'Did you sleep well?'

Ruby was sitting at a large wooden table in the kitchen of the cottage, an ever-present cigarette and swirl of smoke in her hand. A white dressing gown wrapped itself around her, a sharp contrast to the deep tanned colour of her skin. Whether it was out of a bottle or from Mother Nature herself, the end result was deeply golden, if not straying slightly into the realms of mahogany. A mug of coffee with a picture of Minnie Mouse on it steamed by her side.

'Like a log,' said Lucie. 'What time is it?' She scanned her eyes, still heavy with slumber to the large clock on the wall. It was just after nine.

Lucie was lying. She had not slept well at all. Even though she had been exhausted when she had laid down to sleep fairly early the previous evening, her sleep had been pitted with nightmares. When she had woken up, her body drenched in sweat from her mental visions, the hopeful return to sleep had evaded her.

'After nine. You want some coffee. I can make a fresh batch for you.'

'That would be great. What time did I crash out last night? I'm a bit all over the place with the time difference and my body actually feels like it's been smashed into.'

'That'll be the jet lag juggernaut. Gets you every time. I normally take a sleeping pill to knock me out if I go long haul.'

Lucie wasn't sure she could actually ever remember her mother boarding a plane to go anywhere let alone long haul. It was already clear that the woman before her was actually a mystery to her and that every day from now on would be a learning curve.

The kitchen window was open and Lucie could hear the sound of birds outside in the garden, their gentle tweeting a perfect symphony to start the day. The sky was cloudless and a deeper blue than it had been yesterday.

'It's going to be a scorcher,' said Ruby, somehow reading her daughter's mind. 'The fit looking weather bloke on the BBC said it could reach the early thirties today. I don't suppose you're used to the hot weather, are you? After having been cooped up for so long. I guess sunbathing isn't high on the list of things to do when you've been sent down for drug trafficking. Most people come back from South America with a tan, but I would imagine your circumstances were a bit different.' There was no hint of irony in Ruby's voice and yet again, Lucie could feel herself shrinking at her words. The glaring disappointment of her mother's tone loud and clear to Lucie herself even if Ruby seemed oblivious to the fact that it existed.

'Do you have plans for today?' asked Lucie, sitting herself at the table. She was wearing one of her mother's T-shirts, emblazoned on the front with some US football team slogan. Another thing she didn't know about her mother? Some kind of Superbowl fan? So many questions.

'I'll be off out in a bit. I've a few things to do. What about you? You should take it easy if you're knackered.'

'I'll be fine after a couple of these,' said Lucie, picking up the coffee that Ruby had placed in front of her.

'Sugar's on the table if you want it,' pointed Ruby.

'I'm fine.' She sipped at the hot drink, the heat of it burning her mouth slightly. 'I was thinking I had better go out and buy some clothes. I don't really have anything left and until I get up to Roger and Tanya's to sort some of my things out, I don't really have much to wear. Thanks for this by the way.' She pulled at the shirt.

'Welcome. Do you know when you'll head up there? Where is it exactly?' asked Ruby.

'Lancashire. Other end of the country so I'll go up there in a few days. I need to speak to solicitors and stuff. I'll try and sort the house out and do all of the legal stuff at the same time. I'm not sure if I'm ready to face mum and dad's house yet...' She stopped herself and altered her words. 'Tanya and Roger, I mean.'

'You can call them mum and dad if you like,' stated Ruby. Was there a trace of hurt in her voice? Lucie thought there might be. Her own imagination perhaps? 'They have been your parents for the last decade I guess. Even if the DNA doesn't say so.'

'I know.' It was all Lucie could think of to say.

'There's a retail park about thirty minutes from here. I can drop you there if you like and pick you up later, or give you the money for a cab. Either way. I may be out for a while so I'll give you a key for back here. The address of this place is on the pin board. Ruby pointed to a cork board on the far side of the kitchen. 'Will you be wanting a hairdresser too?' It seemed much more like a heavily suggested recommendation than a question. 'I can give you the address of mine. I tend to go into town for it. The hairdresser in the village is related to Edward Scissorhands if you ask me. She cut my hair once. I've seen sheep sheared better. Never again.'

Lucie ran her hands across her own hair, almost black in colour and tied in a ponytail which cascaded half way down her back. It was much longer than it used to be and she couldn't remember the last time she had treated herself to a pampering session on her hair. Maybe a cut and a treatment wasn't such a bad idea. *Perhaps a whole new look for a whole new me,* she mused to herself. The idea made her smile.

'Clothes and haircut it is then. That's my day sorted. And perhaps some shut eye at some point.'

'Sounds like a plan,' agreed Ruby. 'Right, I'm off to make myself look beautiful. Help yourself to my toiletries if you need and I'll bring you a mirror for your bedroom. So that you can see what you're doing. There's not one in there, is there?'

Lucie hadn't noticed. Ruby left the kitchen with a loud sniff and a raised hand of goodbye for now.

Lucie gravitated towards the window and looked out into the garden. It was such a pretty vista. It was little things like a beautiful view that she would never take for granted again. After six years staring at the delights of bare walls, hard beds and cold stainless steel toilets, every little drop of beauty would always be appreciated.

Lucie opened the large, wooden door on one side of the kitchen and walked outside into the garden. There was a small but appreciated breeze in the air and she yanked at the band gathering her ponytail together and pulled it loose, letting her hair fall free around her face and shoulders. Coffee in hand, she walked to a bench she could see a few metres away and sat herself down on it. The buzz of a bee sounded as it flew past no doubt seeking out pollen. All was calm and at complete extremes to her nightmares from a few hours earlier.

Images of Roger and Tanya had filled her dreams, the bloodied faces inside their car. Their bodies lying in their own coffins. The deep red of their cuts and the rich purplish hues of their bruises. Everything fused together in Lucie's mind with flashbacks to her time in prison. The sneering of a guard, the wandering hands of the other inmates searching for pleasure where none was to be found upon her body. The random searches and daily degradation of prison life. Even though it was still so recent in her life, it already seemed like another existence. A woman that she could never feel totally at ease with but yet she knew she would always be. Another Lucie. One that she could never escape, no matter where she ran.

The fatigue of a restless night gripped her and she tilted her head back to stare at the sky above. The same sky that she'd seen in prison. The same sky she had seen from her plane window flying back to the UK. The same sky that she saw in Peru during her happy times there. One sky the world over. An untouchable sky to symbolise her entrapment in the vicious world of the prison, an unknown sky to transport her to a new life in the UK, a welcoming sky that had warmed her skin so beautifully when she had first ventured to Peru.

As she took in the beauty of the cloudless British sky above the cottage garden, she allowed her eyes to shut and suddenly her thoughts returned to her time in Peru. Back to a place before her cursed life had all gone so horribly wrong.

Peru, summer 2012

The sand felt like powder beneath Lucie's feet. It was softer and finer and more beautiful than she had ever imagined. And she had imagined it to be as soft as silk and as fine as ground flour. To a nineteen-year-old Lucie Palmer it felt like heaven. Paradise. And that indeed was what it was. Paradise Cove, one of Peru's finest beaches and the place where Lucie knew she was to spend her summer. Paradise Cove was its nickname, the name given to it by the people who worked there, generally under 25s from around the world who wanted to lose themselves in a dreamscape of natural beauty, bottomless cocktails and the nightly parties under the stars. Its real name was something unpronounceable with far too many syllables and at least two xs. Locals, taxi drivers, tourists, workers in the nearby hotels and villages all referred to it as Paradise Cove. It was the perfect name.

Lucie closed her eyes for a second, enjoying the feel of the late morning air on her skin. She ran one of her hands thorough her hair, the base of it slightly damp with perspiration, unaccustomed to the heat. This was sheer bliss and something that Lucie Palmer had never imagined herself doing with her summer. Girls like her didn't seem to have this kind of opportunity in life. But sometimes, life hits the jackpot. She thought back to that morning at college just a few weeks earlier. If she hadn't been sat next to Jess Cleary at college, and she and Jess hadn't struck up a conversation about the retro Blondie T-shirt Lucie had been wearing, then they might not have spent the next college lunch break together discussing anything and everything. And if they hadn't done that, then they might never have realised they shared the same wanderlust for life and that Lucie was desperate to travel. When Jess had told her that she had spent the previous summer working in a trendy beachside bar in South America, Lucie's eyes had lit up with a mixture of both excitement and envy. This didn't go unspotted by Jess who said that she knew the bar was looking for a girl to work there for the forthcoming summer as they had already asked her if she could do it. She'd had to refuse due to family commitments. When Jess suggested that maybe she should put Lucie's name forward if the job was still available, the seed of temptation had been sown.

Lucie's mind had gone into overdrive. Peru. A land she'd only really heard of through Paddington Bear. Deepest darkest Peru. But the sound of the trendy beachside bar meant that the only thing that would be dark and deep would be her tan. Looking at her pasty skin in her bedroom back at home that night, she knew that she would do anything to try and secure the job and head to Peru. She asked her foster parents, Roger and Tanya, about the job and if they would be happy for her to accept it. It would be the chance of a lifetime. She may have been nineteen already and able to make her own decisions, but it still felt right to ask Roger and Tanya for their permission, especially as she would need help financially. They agreed straight away, happy for Lucie to spread her wings a little. When Lucie saw Jess the next day at college, she received the words she had been waiting to hear.

'I spoke to the guy who worked with me last year, Connor. He's a great guy. He's out there now gearing up for the summer and he says they still need someone. I could get him to ring you and if you fancy it, you could do it. You'd suit the place. Paradise Cove.'

The name, the thought, the prospect, the chance. Everything hot-wired Lucie's senses. She spoke to Connor that evening, who also spoke to Roger and Tanya to put their mind at ease, and before Lucie knew it, her ticket was booked and her dream summer working on the beach in Peru was as real as could be. She had still been pinching herself with disbelief even when she'd landed in Peru.

Lucie opened her eyes again and smiled. This was real. Paradise Cove was in front of her and so was a long, hot summer of exciting new adventures.

She opened a square of paper that was held tightly in her hand, along with her flip-flops. She tossed them onto the sand briefly to unfold the paper and read it. "Connor Perkins, Bar Dynasty, Paradise Cove". The instructions she had been given on the phone by Connor back in the UK. She slipped on her flip-flops and scanned her eyes down the beach. There was a variety of shacks scattered across the length of the beach, as far as the eye could see, but one appeared busier and somehow more lively and buzzing than the others. The heavy beat of music that seemed to hang in the air appeared to come from its direction. Something told Lucie that it would be Bar Dynasty. She walked towards it. As it became more visible, she could see from the large sign that decorated its straw roof that it was indeed the place she was looking for. Music burst forth from two large speakers either side of the bar. The building was like a beach hut, but on a much larger, more tropical scale. It was round and painted bright yellow and a row of brightly painted stools lined up 360 degrees around the bar. Beyond that, dotted across the surrounding sands were equally bright tables and chairs. Virtually, every one of them was filled with young people, laughing, chatting, smoking their choice of cigarette and apparently having the time of their lives. As Lucie walked towards the bar, a few of their heads turned to watch her approach. Her look of bikini top, tied sarong and dark hair hung loosely around her shoulders was obviously an eye-catching one. A thrill of happiness shot through her at their gaze.

She approached the bar. A girl, around the same age as Lucie, beavered away on the far side of it. She was blonde and petite and seemed to be expert in juggling the beer bottle she was de-topping for one customer whilst putting cash into the till from another. Her blonde hair, the same sunshiny yellow as the sand, was piled high upon her head. Lucie could tell, even from her position on the other side of the bar, that she seemed friendly. She immediately liked her. A second girl, her skin the enticing colour of liquorice, worked another area of the bar. She was equally busy and looked equally adept at balancing four jobs at once without breaking into a sweat.

The only man behind the bar area was currently on his mobile talking animatedly and was holding a bottle of beer in the other hand. Lucie couldn't tell what he was saying but it didn't seem overly happy. He had an air of annoyance in his mannerisms. He was bare-chested and wearing cut-off denims.

He finished his conversation and took a large swig of the beer. He appeared to need it. He walked over towards the bar and immediately caught sight of Lucie. In an instant, his flavour of grievance seemed to evaporate.

'Hello there gorgeous, what can I get you?'

Lucie took a moment to answer, automatically taking in the jet-black curls on his head and the finer ones on his chest. A chest that was naturally sculpted without the rigours of the gym she guessed and a stomach that was flat and toned and defined with muscle. His teeth, when he smiled, were as white as his hair was dark. Lucie may not have had that much experience with the opposite sex, but she immediately took a sharp intake of breath when he spoke to her. On a scale of one to ten, he was a double figure kind of man. Lucie's good looks had always gained her interest but she had always been what others called choosy when it came to more than mere flirtation. But right now, there was a heat on her skin that was not just caused by the overhead sunshine.

She composed herself. 'I'm looking for Connor Perkins.'

'You found him. What can I do for you?'

'I'm Lucie Palmer. We spoke back in the UK. I was speaking to you about the chance of…about…errr, working here for the summer.' She stumbled with her words a little, unable to keep eye contact with his rich green eyes as she spoke, her thoughts becoming lost in their depth. She gathered her thoughts and said, 'I'm here about a job. You said I could have it on the phone.'

'Well, you look the part. And I'm sure you've opened a beer bottle and stirred a cocktail before so if you want it, it's yours. Where are you staying?'

'Well that's the easiest interview I've ever had,' laughed Lucie, immediately relaxing in the knowledge that the job really was hers. Hearing it on the phone in the UK was one thing but the leap of faith of actually schlepping half way around the world for it was quite another. 'I'm staying in a hostel up the road. About ten minutes from the beach. It's not the best but it's cheap and well…that's about it really, it's cheap. There's not much more to say.'

'Well, if you fancy moving somewhere a little nicer, these two share a house not far from here and there's a room going spare there.' He motioned to the two girls working the far side of the bar. 'I'm sure Tina, she's the blonde, and Kara, will welcome you. As for the job, the pay isn't great and the hours can be long, but it's the happiest spot on earth and the summer will have gone before you know it. Paradise Cove is a fabulous place to be. If you like to party in paradise, then this is the place to be.'

'I've never really thought of myself as a party girl, but I guess this seems an amazing chance to learn. And yes, I'd love a job and any excuse to escape the hostel I'm at right now. When can I start? It is really mine, isn't it?' There was doubt in Lucie's voice. Not at her own decision but at the fact that she was the person being given such an amazing opportunity.

'Tomorrow at nine suit you? Tina can show you the ropes in the morning and we can sort everything out before we start getting busy with the midday rush. I'll be in by then for the afternoon shift.'

'Are you my boss then? You own Bar Dynasty?'

'Boss, kinda I guess. And sadly no, I don't own it. A local businessman does, but we never see him. He lets us get on with it, as this place is a goldmine. Busy all day long pretty much. Right through till closing.'

'Which is when?' asked Lucie.

'Whenever it feels right,' smiled Connor. 'Right then Lucie Palmer, what are you drinking, we need to salute your new job, don't we?'

'I'll drink to that,' said Lucie. She picked up a cocktails menu from the bar and began to look at it as Connor's words rang in her mind. *Whenever it feels right.* This felt right. Bar Dynasty. Paradise Cove. Her two new housemates. And her deeply attractive new boss. Kinda.

'Hello, you must be Lucie. Your mum said you were here.'

The voice, gruff and a little direct, startled Lucie and brought her back from her thoughts of Bar Dynasty. It came from a man stood behind where she was sitting on the bench in the garden. She turned to face the voice. The owner, an attractive man in his fifties, dark thick hair which was now almost completely shaded with grey and a full-figured face that seemed friendly and yet wary at the same time. It seemed somehow recognisable. The bottom half of his face sported a five o'clock shadow despite the early hour of the day.

'Errr, yeah, hi…and you are?' It was questioning without appearing rude.

He had answered before she had even had a chance to finish the sentence. 'Terrance Allen, I'm your mother's boyfriend. She must have mentioned me. I live here after all.' His tone was almost certainly rude and smothered in conceit.

Lucie wasn't really awake enough to react properly and merely muttered "okay" as if sufficient.

'I'm just popping in for something. Is Ruby here?'

This time Lucie didn't answer. She didn't have a chance. Terrance was already gone, his back all she could now see as he marched into the house through the kitchen door.

'Yeah, nice to meet you too?' said Lucie to no one.

Lucie wasn't sure she liked her mother's new boyfriend. She wasn't sure she liked him at all.

Chapter 7

Now

Lucie sat bewildered for a few minutes, a blanket of confusion coating her about her encounter with her mother's boyfriend. The early morning warmth of the elements on her face felt good. One of the few things in life that did right now. It was almost all that she could cope with – its radiance soothing and calming in a life that seemed so troubled, so extreme in its actions and at times so very cursed. Had she been a naughty child, an unappreciative youngster, not grateful for the things that her mother had been able to give her? Despite her faults and shortcomings, her weaknesses and her cracks, it must have been hard for Ruby and Lucie couldn't help but feel sorry for her mother. She had tried...hadn't she? She was trying now. Ruby appeared to have turned her life around. Turned it from the dangerously dark place that was their life in the fifth floor flat on the council estate and transformed it into a picture perfect portrait of wisteria-coated prettiness at the cottage. With a little help from Uncle Oscar and an unfortunate ride in an Aston Martin admittedly. But Ruby was on top. And if Ruby could steer her life back on track, then surely Lucie could as well. She owed that to her mother and to herself. Perhaps her actions as a child had been ungrateful. Maybe she had brought all of the misery that had possessed her in her life upon herself. Often, it felt that way. In her darker moments, guilt was a badge that Lucie wore easily. Perhaps a little too much so. The tendrils of self-blame wrapped themselves strongly around her.

It was another voice that disturbed her thoughts as she sat in the garden.

'You're a face that I've not seen around here before. Good morning.' It was questioning but layered in friendliness. Lucie snapped back to reality to be greeted by a young man, about her age, wearing a pair of cut off knee-length denim shorts and a white vest top, a colourful outline of Pegasus, the mythical winged horse in flight decorating its front. He was muscular, the vascularity in his arms evident and his hair, blonde and floppy, messed up in a designer aftershave advert kind of way, draped across his forehead. In one hand, he held a brick, slightly chipped and broken on one corner. He held out the other for Lucie to shake. He removed it before Lucie could take it in hers.

'Sorry, that's filthy, you don't want to shake that. I'm Drew, the gardener, I make sure this place looks like something out of magazine.'

As do you, thought Lucie to herself, allowing her eyes to scan him head to toe as surreptitiously as possible. Drew was definitely a thing of beauty.

'Hi, I'm Lucie, my mother owns the cottage. I've been…' She was going to say "away" but settled on "out of the country". 'You've done a great job as far as I can make out, although my fingers are far from green.'

Drew smiled, his expression as bright as the sun that was now heating up overhead.

'Thank you, I love it. It's a great space. I've always wanted to work here. I work at quite a few of the gardens in the village but I have always had my eyes on this one, ever since I was a young lad.'

'Have you lived here a long time then?' asked Lucie, it suddenly dawning on her how good it felt to be having a conversation with someone her own age about something so simple. And with someone who hadn't committed a heinous crime or wanted some kind of prison favours. Her life inside in Peru had been hard and brutal on many levels. Momentarily, a shiver passed through her as she attempted to banish a recollection that threatened to erupt.

'All my life. Born and bred here. I used to stare through the garden gate and try to sneak inside when the previous owner lived here.'

'My Uncle Oscar apparently,' said Lucie. 'I never knew him.'

'Neither did I, but I knew every inch of this garden and couldn't wait to be a part of it. I used to bug the old gardener that was here for years to let me help him. He was a right grumpy old bugger but he knew what he was doing and made the garden look wonderful. I guess I learnt most of what I was doing from him. The lady who lived here adored him. I think they were both about three hundred years old. Or at least they seemed to be to a young kid like me.'

There was a simple joy in his descriptions that made Lucie immediately feel herself liking Drew. His life had obviously been so much easier and straightforward than Lucie's could ever be. She envied him.

'An old lady? Who was she? Oscar's wife?'

'No idea, I just knew her as the old lady at the cottage. I never spoke to her. She used to shoo me away if she found me in the garden or hanging around at the gate trying to stare up the path to see what was going on.' Drew laughed at the thought.

'So how long have you worked here?' asked Lucie.

'Not long. Just shortly after your mum and her fella moved in. I knocked on the door and your mum answered. I asked if she needed a gardener and she said yes straight away. I don't think she is particularly green fingered either, is she?' There was a knowing smirk in Drew's words. Ruby Palmer could be described as many things but green fingered was definitely not one of them. Growing marijuana was probably as horticultural as she had ever been.

As if she had heard her name being spoken, Ruby appeared at the back door of the cottage and stared out into the garden at her daughter and Drew. As ever, cigarette in hand. She was dressed in a simple white blouse, loose fitting skirt combo and her hair tied neatly back upon her head. She shouted across to her daughter.

'Lucie, I'm off out. Terrance, you've met him I hear, is taking me. We can drop you at the retail park if you're quick or there's £50 and the address on the table if you want to go later. But I need to go soon.'

Ruby had made her mind up, that was clear to Lucie. 'I'll go later. Thank you. And yes, I met Terrance.' He too appeared alongside Ruby at the wooden door as Lucie spoke his name. Drew automatically raised his hand to wave to him. 'Morning,' he said both politely and dutifully. It was left unanswered.

Terrance seemed a little rushed, a state that Lucie suspected he possessed constantly and seemed to mutter something to Ruby. He wrapped his arm around her waist pulling Ruby towards him. Whatever he said, it was clear that Ruby understood.

'Look darling, we have to go. See you later. Have a good day. The mirror's in your room. I got it down from the loft. Love you.' Ruby had barely finished the words before Terrance had dragged her inside the cottage and out of sight.

'He seems such a charmer,' remarked Lucie. 'Is he always so brusque?'

'Oh that's just Mr Allen's way,' said Drew.

'Really?' Lucie was sure that Drew was just being loyal to his employers. Either that or he didn't understand the meaning of brusque. If first impressions were all, then Lucie would have to really see some kind of miracle to make her feel that Terrance Allen was anything other than a total pig-headed idiot. But it struck her that given her own past experiences, maybe she wasn't the best person at judging others.

'I suppose I had better get on,' said Drew. He held the brick in his hand aloft, closer to Lucie's face. She flinched a little, a habit that had come from her time inside. If someone held something close to your face in prison, then it would doubtless be spelling trouble and be a prelude to grief.

Drew didn't notice her flinch, the action slight and only really apparent to Lucie herself. 'I've got to fetch some more of these. There's a well in the far corner of the garden that is falling apart and not working properly and I reckon with a bit of TLC and some decent bricks, I could fix it. Build it back up really nicely. I'm sure I have some bricks in the back of my van. I'll see you later, Lucie. Nice to meet you. I hope to see more of you. You staying long?'

The million-dollar question. What to say. Was she? She could only answer with honesty. 'I have no idea, Drew. No idea at all. But yes, it's been nice to meet you. Let me know when you've finished the well and I'll come have a look.'

His broad smile showed that he liked the idea. He walked off, Lucie immediately noticing the size of his calf muscles as he moved away from her. He turned back to face her after a few steps, raised the brick in his hand once more and said "bye".

'Bye, Drew,' returned Lucie. Lucie was thinking about what Drew had said about the well. *A bit of TLC and some decent bricks I could fix it.* Never had a truer sentence been said about Lucie's own life.

It was what she needed. Some good solid bricks in her life to start rebuilding what there was. Bricks that could maybe disguise the rocky foundations of her life so far. Something solid to build on. To progress. So much had been taken from her. Years of her life. Her innocence. Her blood family and her foster one. Lucie really wasn't sure what she had left but whatever it was, maybe a bit of careful brick building would be able to bury the curses that she had felt blighted her life before for good. Yes, it was time for brick building.

Lucie stood up as she watched Drew disappear and, mug in hand, walked back to the cottage. Once inside, she placed the mug in the kitchen sink and went upstairs, back to her room.

There were four bedrooms in the cottage and Lucie had to admit that she had been struck straight away with the charm of the one that her mother had housed her in. A four poster bed dominated one half of the room. Lucie had no idea whether it was a genuine historical item, she'd only ever seen ones like it on school trips to Hever Castle when she was younger – one of the very few school trips she'd been able to go on – but it still looked the part and that was all that mattered to her. A young Lucie would never have dreamt that one day she could sleep in such imperial grandeur, and especially in a house owned by her blood mother. She had experienced affluence during her happy years with Roger and Tanya Grimes but this was on another scale of opulence.

The windows of the room were situated over a long dressing table that occupied one wall. There were two of them, both criss-crossed with leading and possessing metal swirl-shaped handles that felt good to turn and open. Being able to open a window was something that Lucie would never take for granted again after her years in prison. Such a simple action, but such an incredible privilege. Especially when the view beyond stretched out across the cottage garden and into the distance. A windmill sat proudly atop a hill on the horizon and a lush carpet of green was apparent as far as the eye could see.

The dressing table was vintage, the wood distressed with age. A flower-painted water jug sat on the table, alongside Lucie's backpack. A reminder of her life before that now sat slightly ill-at-ease in its new surroundings. Lucie had to admit that she herself felt somewhat at odds with the finery and unaccustomed frippery of the room, and indeed the entire cottage. But it definitely had a quintessential charm that she couldn't help but be seduced by.

The clothes she had worn for her journey home the day before lay on the floor in a heap where she had jettisoned them the previous night. A chest of drawers in one corner hinted that maybe she should have placed them there. Lucie opened the drawers. They were empty. Maybe after a trip to the retail park, they wouldn't be. Maybe new clothes and a fresh hairstyle could be the first bricks in her plan for a new life. One with less painful memories of days gone by. Memories that could never be erased but maybe their edges could be blurred and smudged into something less horrific and easier to bear.

Her mother had been good to her promise. The new addition to the room was a free-standing mirror, rectangular in shape and propped up against the wall at an angle so as to reflect her head-to-toe when she stared into it. The frame was wide and decorated in a rococo style, silver and eye-catching.

Lucie studied herself in the mirror. Wearing her mother's T-shirt, maybe Terrance's for all she knew. Long and covering the top part of her legs. It suddenly occurred to her it was how she had been dressed when she met both Terrance and Drew. The idea perplexed her a touch. New clothes were definitely needed. Her hair, longer than it had been in years, felt lifeless and outdated to her. She may have been locked away for six years but Lucie was fashion-conscious enough to know that it needed a makeover. One of the few luxuries in prison had been the magazines she had browsed. Anything to take her away from the greyness and the captivity of her surroundings. The celebrity magazines of Peru were full of actors and on-screen stars that she recognised even if the translation of the words escaped her. A haircut. Another brick. Small changes that could make such a difference.

Lucie knew that she was still fragile. Life inside may have toughened her up and made her experience things that she never wanted to see again. Evil atrocities. Hardship and hurt. Death both chosen and otherwise. But underneath, she would always be that timid little girl sitting on the end of her bed in the flat where she grew up, wanting to be loved and craving the affection that so many were lucky enough to have on tap. Her reflection in the mirror was showing merely the surface. The façade was that of a young woman, but her soul had been tainted and blackened by what she has endured and witnessed. A blackness that no mirror could ever reflect.

Lucie could feel the realities of her harsh life over the last six years flooding back into her thoughts. Like a dam breaking inside her mind allowing the badness to flow freely. She tried to stop it as she always did. Sometimes she could, but as she stared at her reflection in the mirror, her appearance something that she couldn't allow herself to like at that very minute, she could feel the callous stabs of a lifetime of hurt pricking at her eyes and threatening to detonate. Lucie breathed deeply to try and quell them. The curses that streamed within her.

She could have turned from the mirror. Removed her reflection, unable to see what appeared to cause her angst. But Lucie didn't. She continued to stare at herself, almost transfixed. Did she recognise herself anymore? She wasn't sure that she did. Instead of walking away, she chose to turn the mirror and make it face the wall. That way she wouldn't have to see her own reflection. There were moments when she couldn't face it. It would come from nowhere and possess her. It had started in prison. Her reflection in a bathroom mirror, in the window of her cell door. A stranger that she chose not to acknowledge. Ashamed of what she had become. Afraid of what would be. A feeling that the curse on her would never lift.

Tears needled her eyes, panic gripping Lucie as she went to turn the mirror. She grabbed the frame either side and made to shift it 180 degrees. As she edged it off the floor on one corner, a moment of horror took her as the mirror slipped away from the frame surrounding it and distorted until breaking point. With an ear-shattering crack and a subsequent splintering of glass, the entire mirror shattered into shards that fell useless and jagged to the floor. Each one a dagger of glass reflecting a little bit of her own sudden misery as they lay on the bedroom floor. A broken mirror. Seven years bad luck. A belief? An old wives' tale? It didn't matter what the truth was. Lucie's head rushed and span with a sense of what-could-be. To her, it was an omen. A sense that there would never be an escape from the evil that followed her. A mirror that had probably been in the cottage for the longest time, always useful, pristine and intact had shattered and become useless, defunct and foreboding in its destruction. And it had become so at the very moment that she had touched it. Spreading the misfortune that seemed to run in her veins. Like a toxic King Midas.

The tears erupted. Lucie sat on the edge of her four poster bed. The surroundings were different but suddenly in her mind, she was back in her bedroom at the council flat she grew up at in Brighton. Scared and lonely. Scared of what was around the next corner. Certain that it would be nothing good. She didn't deserve good things it seemed.

Chapter 8

Peru, summer 2012

'So, the rent can come out of your first pay packet and your room has a double bed. It's got a tiny balcony looking out onto the street and you don't have your own en suite but you can share the other bathroom with Kara. Does that sound okay?'

Tina, the blonde barmaid at Bar Dynasty, had a totally sing-song and bubbly style to her voice. She could have been telling Lucie that her potential room at the flat was covered in mould and infested by a million cockroaches and it would have still sounded like a totally wonderful proposition. She was one of life's happy people. But then, Lucie really couldn't see how anybody who spent their days at Paradise Cove serving drinks and bar snacks to life's lucky people partying on the super soft sands could be anything but ecstatic. Her new life in Peru seemed to be idyllic in the extreme and it was still only her first working day. Which so far was going incredibly well. A blessing after the shitty night's sleep that Lucie had suffered at the hostel she had booked into. She was in a dormitory of five other travellers and the girl in the bed next to her had obviously been entertaining in her own inimitable and distinctly loud manner all night long. None of the other three girls sharing the dorm seemed to mind and had slept right through every graphically verbally detailed moment of it. Judging by the smell of weed that hung in the air, all three of them were probably stoned. Lucie would have doubtless been permanently so too had she had to endure another night at the hostel. Thankfully, Connor's promise of her sharing a flat with Kara and Tina was not an empty one. It was an offer that she was more than happy to accept.

'That sounds way beyond okay; I'll bring my stuff around after my shift today. It's all here anyway.' Lucie motioned to her suitcase and backpack piled up under a clear area underneath the round bar of Bar Dynasty. 'I couldn't wait to get out of the other place.'

'Yep, that hostel has a bad rep for being a bit of a knocking shop,' smiled Tina. 'One girl nearly got raped there.' Again, her voice aired the horror in such a way that made even such an atrocity sound almost jolly.

'Bloody hell,' said Lucie. 'You're kidding me.'

'I know,' echoed Tina, 'rubbish, eh? Right, let me show you the ropes. It's you and me until mid-afternoon, and then Connor and Kara will be here in a few hours for the late shift. I normally stay for that anyway, even if I'm on opening up duty in the morning because it's always the best time. People are a little more relaxed, ready to party and much freer with their tips.' Tina patted a large glass jar on the bar, with a long strip of a hole in its lid. 'Which all go here and are shared out. We do well on tips. Last week's bought me these.' She wiggled the designer sunglasses she had perched on her nose. 'If you know how to work the customers, especially the lads, then that jar just keeps getting heavier and heavier. And that is always a good thing.'

The next half an hour was spent with the two young women circling the area behind the bar, Tina showing Lucie the positions of the bottles, alcopops, wines, spirits plus the cool boxes and fridges for the snacks. She also gave Lucie a crash course in how to make a special Bar Dynasty cocktail. 'To be honest, just shake whatever ingredients you like as long as vodka and rum are on the list and that the end result is pink. Most people are too wankered to notice what it tastes like after a while.' Tina laughed. Lucie didn't know whether she was joking or not. Sensing her confusion Tina said, 'I'm being deadly serious by the way. Most people drink with their eyes, not their taste buds, especially when they've been in the sun all day.'

Lucie told Tina all about herself and about her upbringing, even including her departure from her own mother and being placed with a foster family. Something told her she could. Tina in turn told her own story. Nineteen years of age from South Shields. First slept with a boy at the age of fourteen. Managed to fall pregnant at fifteen. Aborted before she hit sixteen. Needed to escape the UK and find some kind of excitement abroad to stop her going off the rails back home. 'I would have ended up stacking shelves in some crappy supermarket and scraping enough money together for bottles of prosecco and a wrap of coke once in a while.'

Tina, an open book with nothing to hide it seemed, could see a trench of semi-disapproval write itself across Lucie's features. 'Oh,

I assume you're a little whiter than me, then?' Tina wasn't talking about Lucie's lack of tan.

'No, it's not that, Tina,' stuttered Lucie, keen not to appear a prude. 'It's just that drugs are the reason I was taken away from my mother. She was addicted to them pretty much. I can't really say I've ever approved of what they did to her. They turned her into a pretty spiky person. There were times when she didn't even recognise me she was so off her face.' Lucie's smile fell from her face. 'But each to their own.' Lucie felt obliged to add the caveat for fear of not being accepted by her new friend.

'Shit, I'm sorry, me and my fucking massive gob. So big it would appear, I can get both my feet into it. You will see a lot of that shit over here though. South America is rife. I spent last summer working for a dune buggy driving company in Bolivia and I shit you not, I'd never seen so many drugs. Piles of coke so high you'd suffer vertigo climbing to the top of them.' Tina fell silent again. 'Sorry, probably not the best topic of conversation, eh? Drugs aren't obligatory around here, but you should be aware they happen. That way, nothing comes as a surprise.'

'Like I say,' uttered Lucie. 'I judge no one. It's just not my thing after seeing my mum become so dependent on it. But I'm not going to criticise anyone. Each to their own.' Lucie feared she was sounding preachy, the last thing she wanted. Tina's ear to ear smile suggested that thankfully, she wasn't.

Tina stared out across the golden sands. 'Okay then *Lucie newgirl*, it's time to prove you've been listening to me. These two lads approaching will be wanting a Bar Dynasty cocktail, I guarantee it. It's virtually all they ever ask for. That and beer, of course. They're called Logan and Billy, Australian, and they've been in Paradise Cove two weeks already. They'll be here all day, getting more and more pissed in the sunshine between cooling off in the waves. They also hold the prize for being the most persistent blokes I've ever met at trying to get their leg over with any female, including Kara and I. Not that I'd suspect they'd get anything up after a skin full of cocktails. But they'll try. Mark my words. You're fresh meat in town – they will use that phrase I bet you – and I suspect they'll zone in on you straight away. I'm guessing you can handle harmless pricks like these two stoners though.'

'Only one way to find out, I guess,' smiled Lucie as she watched the two lads, topless and tattooed, saunter towards Bar Dynasty. She wouldn't tell Tina just yet that she didn't exactly have a huge amount of skill at handling boys at all, and at 19, she was still one of those rare breeds in the modern world, a virgin. Sex for Lucie was not something she was keen to rush into with the first person to show an interest.

Logan and Billy spotted her straight away. 'Well, g'day, fresh meat in town...' Lucie smiled across at Tina. She'd been right. Lucie had heard smoother openers. 'Who's this rather gorgeous new addition to our favourite bar?'

'I'm Lucie. Now which one of you is Logan, and which is Billy? I've been waiting for you two. And I assume from the look of you that you are both Bar Dynasty cocktail kind of guys. Strong and potent. Just like you.'

'Our rep precedes us,' swaggered one of the lads. 'I'm Logan,' said the skinnier one, hardly an ounce of fat on his lightly tanned torso. One arm was completely covered in a sleeve of tattoos and a sprouty tuft of wannabe beard poked from his chin. His hair was mousey shoulder-length dreadlocks.

'And I'm Billy,' said the other with a smile. His skin was a shade darker than Logan and a bush of beard covered his lower face. A small triangle of matching hair adorned his chest. As he spoke, he automatically pointed straight ahead, his actions both quirky and unnecessary. Neither was particularly good looking but obviously believed in their own pulling power. 'And strong and potent we are, *Lucie-Loo*, so ten out of ten for your drinks skills. Cocktails it is.'

As Lucie set to making the cocktails, Tina loosely keeping an eye on her to make sure that she did the job correctly, the two Oz lads turned their attention to the bubbly blonde.

'Looks like we won't be bothering you any more, then Tina. Hope you won't be too disappointed if we move our attentions onto the new girl on the block. No hard feelings and all that,' laughed Logan.

Tina held up her arms and shrugged. 'Oh boys, I guess I'll live, but I dare say I'll be crying myself to sleep tonight in my lonely bed at the rejection.'

'You're not the first to say it and you won't be the last,' said Billy. 'It's a cross you'll have to bear.'

'Oh *Lucie-Loo*!' Tina emphasised the nickname the two lads had just christened Lucie with. 'How can you be so cruel to take two such beautiful specimens away from me?'

'Like the lads say, it's a cross you'll have to bear, Tina. How can I resist such a delightful duo?'

Lucie wasn't sure that Logan and Billy realised she was knee-deep in sarcasm.

Lucie finished mixing the drinks, poured the colourful pink liquid into two glasses and decorated it with a paper umbrella, feather-tailed parrot swizzle stick and a straw from under the bar. The two lads pushed the decoration to one side and sucked loudly at the straws. They both smiled and winked, showing their appreciation of a job well done.

Lucie winked back and pointed at the lads. 'Strong.' She pointed at Billy. 'And potent.' She moved her digit in Logan's direction. 'Just like you two, as I said.'

'You know it,' said Billy, unable to stop himself from pointing too. 'Keep them coming, Lucie-Loo. We have people to entertain.' They handed some cash over to Lucie for the drinks. 'Keep the change, darling.'

As the two lads moved away from the bar to another group of girls sat around one of the Bar Dynasty tables, Tina raised her hand to high-five the newest addition to the bar. 'Way to go, Lucie. You, baby girl, have got what it takes, even if you have stopped my chances of love with Tweedledum and Tweedledumber there. Woe. Is. Me.' If sarcasm were water, Lucie would have just been drowned there and then.

'So I pass…?' enquired Lucie.

'Flying colours, doll. *Strong and potent, just like you.*' Tina mimicked Lucie's words to the two lads.

'Just like the drinks,' said Lucie.

'Those boys are like the cocktails, but only in the fact that they may be kind of sweet but they do make you sick and become totally tasteless after a while. You just wait.'

Both girls collapsed into a fit of giggles. Lucie was enjoying her first day behind the bar and enjoying spending time with her new friend, Tina. As she placed the money in the till and subsequently potted the rather hefty tip into the jar on the bar top, she knew she was going to enjoy her new life in Peru. Right now, she couldn't see how things could get any better.

'Having a good time already then, Lucie?' She spun around to see a shirtless Connor Perkins standing in front of her. 'I thought I'd swing by early to see how you're doing.' He smiled straight at her.

Lucie hadn't expected things to become any better but with Connor's arrival, somehow they just automatically had.

Chapter 9

Now

Retail therapy and a new haircut may not have been able to eradicate the demons that Lucie felt about her own life, but she had to admit that as she made to leave the hair salon, that Ruby had recommended to her, and caught sight of her new look in the mirror by the front door she was loving her makeover. For once not repulsed and filled with hatred by her own reflection.

The sleek shoulder length bob she had opted for under the trained hands of Alvaro, one of the immaculately groomed stylists at the salon, and the streaks of soft blonde to contrast the darkness of her own natural hair colouring, made her feel that the girl she became when she was incarcerated under lock and key in Peru was a million miles away. Hidden for now, if not ever, to be forgotten.

It had been a busy day. But a good one once she'd left the cottage. For once, there was nothing more strenuous to think about than what to buy and where to buy it from. Despite the hideous start with the smashing of the mirror in her cottage bedroom and the feeling that her own life was doomed, the day had somehow turned out all right.

Lucie had asked Drew, the gardener, if he would help her clear up all of the broken glass. He readily agreed, seeming eager to please Lucie. At first, Lucie had felt cheeky even asking but her tears after watching the mirror shatter in her own hands had wiped all of her energy and had Drew not agreed to do it, she knew that she would have been defeated and gone back to bed, crying in misery into her pillow on the four poster. The day would have been lost. Drew's help was the reboot she required to function again. She wasn't being lazy. It just felt good to know that somebody was willing to help. For so long, no one had. Or couldn't. Or chose not to. She wasn't sure anymore.

Having taxied her way to the retail park and spent the morning buying a whole new wardrobe, Lucie had then ordered another cab to take her to the hairdressers for the booking she had made for early afternoon. For the second time in two days, she found herself staring out of a taxi window, once again marvelling at the fact that she was able to see scenery that actually moved past her. That she had the ability to travel from one place to another as and when she chose. A luxury that only a few short days ago was a light at the end of a never-ending tunnel. Unreachable.

For the first time in a long while, a sense of almost happiness descended upon Lucie. A change was what she needed and the bricks of rebuilding her life seemed to be a solid thing that was finally within reach. Having her mother back in her life had changed everything. On the flight back from Peru, she had assumed that life would mean going back to Lancashire, sorting the arrangements for the sale of Roger and Tanya's house, dealing with the solicitors and coping with the grief of having lost her foster parents. Having her own blood mother back in the picture had not been something that she had ever factored into the equation.

Lucie was keen to head back to Lancashire in the next few days. Above all else, she needed to visit the graves of her foster parents. She had not been allowed to go to their funerals for obvious reasons, both geographically and legally, and in some ways, Lucie wasn't even sure that she had fully accepted their deaths. She had not seen them for so long that not having them in her life seemed like the norm. But spending a few days at the cottage before even contemplating her next move was a welcome and seemingly necessary respite.

The salon was situated on the third floor of a shopping centre she was visiting and Lucie needed to descend to the car park underneath the mall in order to locate a taxi rank. She contemplated the escalators, but they were busy and with the half a dozen bags she was attempting to carry, she decided that the lift down to the sub-centre level was a better idea. She pressed the button and waited for the elevator to arrive. When it did, she stepped inside, she was alone in the lift, and chose the button for the lower level. The doors closed together and it whirred into action.

Her eyes focussed on a poster on the wall. A promotion for a local hotel. One of the budget ones where a wafer thin mattress for the night and a lukewarm breakfast somehow seemed to translate for the advert into a smiling happy couple looking like they'd spent the night sleeping at a five star fairy-tale palace. Not that Lucie would ever take any kind of comfort and semi-decent food for granted again. Life would always be seen through a much more grateful and appreciative pair of eyes post Peru.

The elevator stopped. The read-out on the display next to the door was flashing between zero and minus one. Something didn't feel right and immediately, the hairs on the back of Lucie's neck stood to attention as she pressed the button to try and open the elevator doors. At first, nothing happened. A nervous droplet of sweat formed underneath the hairline of her new crop.

Lucie dropped all of her shopping bags to the floor of the elevator and used both hands to press the button. The display continued to flash its oddity of numbers. After three more urgent pushes, the door finally opened. But instead of a clear exit to the car park, Lucie was greeted by a solid brick wall. It was clear that the lift had become stuck between the two floors. She immediately pressed the alarm button to activate it.

Lucie's brain automatically split itself into two halves. The sensible side began to rationalise about how these things happened from time to time and that she was just unlucky. Doubtless a team of engineers would arrive very shortly, shout a cheery "don't you worry, love, we'll soon get you out of here" and fiddle with a few buttons to re-activate the lift. Sadly, it was the other side of Lucie's brain that kicked in the moment she saw the solid brick wall blocking her exit. She stabbed at the alarm button again for no reason. It was already active. The droplet of sweat on her neck was joined by a gathering of them, forming a panicked rivulet that ran down below the collar line of her T-shirt. Identical droplets formed across her forehead too. Despite knowing that these things could happen to anyone and that technical failings were commonplace, Lucie couldn't help but feel a horrid and familiar sense of entrapment sweep through her. She banged both of her palms against the bricks, causing a tiny dust cloud to erupt from under each hand. Her palms stung as she did it. She shouted as loud as her lungs would allow but no voices returned.

Lucie could feel her breathing becoming heavier and more irregular. This couldn't be happening. Not to her. But she couldn't help but feel that if it was going to happen to anyone then it would always be her. Fate determined it. Her erratic breathing worsened. She continued to scream and shout; her breaths pitted with fear as she felt the walls close in around her. She circled her eyes around the lift looking for an escape. A feeling of weakness and helplessness washed over her, soaking her like the perspiration that now seemed to be free flowing from every pore. The smiley happy couple on the poster for the budget hotel seemed to swim in and out of focus, their features somehow mocking and maniacal as they appeared to drift towards Lucie. She shut her eyes and opened them hoping to find that the nightmare of her current entrapment was indeed just that, a nightmare. She opened them again, afraid of what she would see. Her vision was still watery and blurred. She realised that she was trapped.

She let out a scream and fell to the floor, her legs giving way underneath her, her knees arching up to her chest as she hit the floor, her shopping bags piled around her. In an instant, the four walls surrounding her were no longer the postered walls of a shopping centre lift; they were the scratched, dimly lit walls of her cell in Peru. The one where she was first banged up. The shared cell that smelt of human sweat and rang to the sound of pitiful cries from women who knew that life, for the moment, was over. As she had believed was hers. The feel of the cold steel bars and the hard concrete floor beneath her feet. The cloud of festering disease that seemed to hang in the air. The grunts of the guards as they walked past her cell, somehow flaunting their freedom. Lucie's tears would spring forth day after day, night after night until no more would come. Tears of innocence, of frustration, of resignation. Of a belief that she would never escape, never be freed. At the time, she genuinely believed that life was over. Thoughts of taking her own life had run through her head when she was first inside. Her short life so tainted and soiled. As she stared at the four walls of the cell, she wondered how she could do it. There was never an answer. In Lucie's life, it seemed there never was.

Lucie could feel the cold harsh roughness of the cell walls against her back, her body slumped in the corner, head leant against the metal sink positioned there. Her eyes were mere slits, heavy and puffy with tears. The woman sharing her cell, a Peruvian thirty-something, appeared in front of her of her face, close enough to touch. Her breath was dank and destructive as it hit Lucie's nostrils, her teeth black in places and many missing. Lucie had said no words to the woman but in prison, words were often useless, whatever the language. It was actions that counted.

Her body and mind both weak, Lucie could only watch helplessly and remain inert and unresponsive, her spirit crushed by her surroundings, as the woman reached to her, her bitten nails and twisted fingers wrapping themselves around one of Lucie's breasts and mauling it harshly. Lucie was unable to move, fear paralysing her as the woman moved her hand from one breast to another, roughly grabbing the flesh underneath Lucie's clothes. Lucie's body shook, the fright of her situation taking hold. An inability to react, to fight back. The struggle in her brain between what was right and what was wise.

The woman's lascivious eyes continued to stare directly at Lucie as she moved her hand down from one of Lucie's breasts where it had been roughly tugging at one of her nipples through her clothes and across her belly. As it continued to travel to the top of Lucie's trouser line, its destination clear, Lucie knew that she couldn't let this happen. What little strength and petrified fight she had inside her, bubbled as best it could and as the woman attempted to enter the confines of her trousers, Lucie's hand shot and grabbed her around the wrist. The shock and disgust on the woman's face was immediately clear. She used to other hand to try and remove Lucie's grip, but some inner strength from Lucie stopped her from doing so. The woman moved the hand and wrapped it around Lucie's throat, pushing the side of her face against the cold metal of the sink and the back against the rough surface of the wall. Lucie could feel the air escaping from her throat as the woman's grip tightened. She attempted to grab the hand away from her neck with both of her own. This freed the woman's other hand to continue on its chosen path. Lucie couldn't let this happen. She wouldn't. Finding a shred of remaining force within her, as the fingers around her neck seemed to tighten even more, Lucie began to claw and slap at the inmate's face with her hands, her nails scratching across the skin as she did so. The woman attempted to move her face away from Lucie's hands, her one hand remaining on Lucie's throat whilst the other roughly pressed against her groin. Lucie continued to slap and scratch and with what little breath she appeared to house within her throat, she began to scream. A scream of defiance that she would not be beaten. A volcanic burst of pain seemed to come from inside her throat. A burning heat.

She continued to slap and scratch at the woman's face. Her own eyes began to shut as she could feel the attacker's hands closing tighter on her throat again. The last thing Lucie remembered seeing before her eyes closed was a vague recollection of the cell door being flung open and a guard running towards them. She was still attempting to slap as her eyes closed.

'Hey, hey, hey, calm down, stop the slapping. You're okay. It was just a malfunction on the lift. It's sorted now, there's no need to panic.'

Lucie opened her eyes and in front of her, knelt a moustached man, mid 40s maybe. His hair was brown, his skin fair. Lucie had her hands raised to his face.

'I'm Adam Dawks, one of the security guards here at the shopping centre. You're safe. There's no need to worry. The lift got stuck between floors. I'll be honest it's not the first time it's done it, but you're okay. There's no need to…' The guard paused before completing the sentence, finishing with the word "panic". He had been about to use the phrase "flip out" but decided that given the state of the woman he had just found on the lift floor that perhaps it wasn't the most sensitive phrase to use.

Adam had been patrolling the lower level of the shopping centre when he had heard the alarm sounding from the lift. That had been followed by a set of screams that clearly stated that whoever was inside the lift was not dealing at all well with their sudden entombment. Adam had called for help and continued to push the lift button to try and reactivate it into movement again. Somehow, through more luck than any kind of technical expertise, it has started again after a few minutes. By the time the cavalry arrived, Adam was already inside the lift. He found Lucie on the floor, literally gibbering and screaming, eyes totally shut, and as he grabbed her to try and inform her of her safety, she had begun to slap his face and even scratch away at his skin. He'd have a red hairline scratch across his cheek to explain to his wife back at home tonight, but even though it stung a bit, it was all in the line of duty. The poor woman in the lift was quite literally freaking out.

As Lucie opened her eyes for a moment, everything stood still. Where was the prison guard and the evil bitch of an inmate trying to strangle her? Where was the putrid smell of her breath in her nostrils? Where were the hands mauling her body? Why was she surrounded by shopping bags and not the hard stone floor of a prison cell? Lucie suddenly understood that she had obviously been suffering a flashback. The brick wall had triggered it. It wasn't her first and it wouldn't be her last, she knew that.

As she realised that she was safe, she reached out and hugged the guard. She could smell her own sweat as she did so. It embarrassed her with its potency.

'I'm sorry,' said Lucie, letting go of Adam. 'I must have blacked out. I was suddenly back in…' She didn't finish the sentence, unaware how to carry on. She ran her hands through her hair. It was sopping wet.

Adam lifted Lucie off the floor and grabbing the bags the two of them vacated the lift.

'Are you okay?' he questioned. 'Do you need a hospital?'

'I am,' said Lucie, her voice timid and quiet. 'And no, errr...I don't. I just want to go. Grab a taxi and leave.'

'We need to file a report. As I said, it's not the first time the lift has broken. Thankfully, it was only for a few minutes.'

A few minutes? To Lucie it had seemed like an eternity. Long enough to transport her back to the hell of Peru. To a moment when she had feared for her life. It was one of many.

'No report. I just want to go,' she stammered.

Adam was insistent. 'But we do need to...'

Lucie wasn't listening. A line of taxis stood at the rank on the far side of the lower level. Lucie took hold of her shopping bags and ran towards them, leaving the guard mid-sentence behind her.

Thankfully, there was no queue. She ran to the front car, opened the back door and climbed inside. She gave her mother's address and reclined into the comfort of the seat as it pulled off. As the taxi exited the lower level and moved into daylight, she caught sight of her reflection in the rear view mirror. It repulsed her once more. She looked dishevelled, her clothes sticking to her and her new hairdo looked anything but salon-fresh. It was ratty and pressed against her head with sweat.

So much for starting afresh...

Chapter 10

Peru, summer 2012

Lucie's first day at Bar Dynasty had been a success. And she had enjoyed every minute of it. All eleven hours of it. The day had flown by and before she knew it, she and Kara were closing down the bar, piling stools on tables and wiping down surfaces at the end of a busy day.

Lucie hadn't even planned to be there all day. Her shift with Tina had finished hours ago and when Tina had left, she had been supposed to leave with her, taking her luggage to her new flat to move in with both of the Bar Dynasty girls. But something made her want to stay, to soak up more of the effervescent fizz and fun that working at the bar seemed to bring her. Something...or someone. And that someone was the beatific form of Connor Perkins. And when Tina offered to take Lucie's luggage for her so that she could "stay on to learn the ropes a bit more", Lucie had leapt at the offer. Especially when Tina leant over to whisper in her ear as she was departing "and by learn the ropes I mean spending more time falling endlessly into the green pools of joy that are Connor's eyes... I've seen you, Lucie...you can't get enough of them". Lucie could feel herself blush as Tina said it but she had to admit that she was right. There was something deeply hypnotising about the eyes of Connor Perkins, especially when teamed with a smile that had its own electricity and a body that was toned, tanned and very tempting. Even to a girl as pure of body and spirit as Lucie Palmer.

'So you've enjoyed your first day with us?' asked Connor, as he and Lucie piled the final set of stools behind the bar. It was mid-evening and the sun was lowering in the sky if yet still light years away from descending below the horizon. A soft breeze ran through the air, a cooling welcome against Lucie's skin. As she and Connor busied themselves with the stools, Kara stood at the till totting up the day's takings. It had been a good day and the tips jar was almost full of notes and loose change. Lucie's early winning streak of charm with Logan and Billy had continued throughout the day and even if she admitted to herself, it seemed that beach bar work and dealing with the young fun-loving clientele of Bar Dynasty suited Lucie down to the sandy ground. It was the most hilarity she had experienced in years and if this was just day one, then roll on one fabulously hot summer adventure.

'I can honestly say I have loved every minute,' beamed Lucie. 'And you have a great crowd in here.'

'Yeah, they're not all as daft as Logan and Billy, that's for sure. How those two survive day to day is beyond me.' Connor pointed to where Logan, still with drink in hand, and a comatose Billy lay on the sand about 100 yards from the bar. The Aussie duo had, as Tina said they would, spent the entire day propping up Bar Dynasty and attempting to get into Lucie's knickers. Despite their filthy talk and suggestive ways, Lucie already had a real fondness for them. Harmless and hapless.

'I like those two. Everyone seems really nice,' said Lucie.

'It's unusual for two tourists like those two to be in one place for such a long time. Most people spend a couple of days here before moving on. Peru's got some wicked places to visit. You should definitely try to check out a few whilst you're here.'

'I wouldn't know where to start,' exclaimed Lucie.

'You angling for a guide?' laughed Connor. 'Oh go on then, I'll see if we have a day off on the rota together at some point and I'll see what attractions spring to mind.'

Something told Lucie that Connor was flirting with her. The thought pleased her hugely.

'If you're my *kinda* boss...' Lucie stressed the word. 'Then surely you can fix the rota so that we are off together.' There was a cheeky tone of sarcasm in her voice.

Connor giggled. He let out a whistle through his teeth. 'Day one and she's making the demands already. The diva demands it. What will Kara and Tina have to say about that?'

Lucie felt a little flustered. 'No, I didn't mean to be a diva; I was just joking and would never put my own needs before...' She stopped as she realised Connor was laughing at her, obviously taking the mickey with his words. She grinned and picked up a beer mat from the bar to throw at him. It bounced off his arm and hit the sand.

'And she's violent too!' boomed Connor. 'Call for an ambulance.' He grabbed his arm in mock pain and let out a cry of anguish. He remained silent for a moment as they stared at each other, their eyes connecting. It was Lucie who broke the gaze first.

'You'll fit in here really well, you know,' said Connor.

'I hope so.'

'I know so.'

'What makes you stay?' asked Lucie. Given their surroundings, she didn't really need to ask.

'The jet-set lifestyle, the partying till dawn every night, the never ending supply of girls lining up to be with me and keep me satisfied.' Again his voice was soaked in sarcasm. Lucie did feel a pang of jealousy though at the thought of other girls. She made a mental note to try and keep a lid on her feelings. As yet, this was no more than an introductory crush. She had no reason to believe that Connor wasn't this flirtatious with every girl who worked at the bar, and indeed those who didn't.

'Same reasons as me then,' she replied with a smile.

'No, this is the reason… I love South America as a place.' Connor stopped what he was doing and looked out across to the beach to the waves crashing gently upon the fine sand. 'I have a real wanderlust for beautiful places and this one has to rank up there as one of the best. I remember the first time I saw Paradise Cove and it completely blew me away.'

Lucie knew exactly what he meant from her own experience of first impressions the day before.

'This place is magical,' he continued. 'It has a free spirit about it and I think that is reflected in the people who come here. I believe that everyone who is fortunate enough to lay eyes on this stretch of beauty will have a blueprint of it etched onto their mind for a lifetime. How could you not? It's not been called paradise for no good reason. I bet you've already been on the phone to your folks and friends back home telling them how beautiful it is. And I love the fact that it's a little off the beaten track. It's not like the bigger more popular resorts. It still has a charm and an edge that makes it the best. It's going to take something pretty extraordinary to make me leave here. Something or someone.'

Again, a frisson of delight passed over Lucie as she listened to Connor's choice of words. *Another deliberate flirtation?* She thought so. The tiny modicum of confidence that Lucie had inside her when it came to talking to the opposite sex, and it was tiny, swelled slightly as she took in his words. There were aimed at her, surely. Not even an inexperienced girl like her could fail to spot the meaning of what he was saying.

'I haven't. Phoned home that is. I must. I phoned my foster parents when I arrived to say I'd landed safely, but I haven't done so since yesterday. I should take some photos too.'

'No time like the present. You got your phone?' asked Connor.

'It's under the bar, my reception here is terrible so I left it there earlier.'

'Who needs Wi-Fi when you have the sun, surf and sand,' said Connor, reaching underneath the bar and finding her phone. 'Now come here.' He outstretched his arm and invited Lucie to join him. 'What's your code?'

'Like I'm telling you,' she said jokily, taking the phone from him and punching in her four digit number to free the locked screen.

'Spoilsport,' grinned Connor, 'I could have checked out your camera roll, seen if you have any dodgy photos. You and your boyfriend, exes, girlfriend?' He was clearly digging.

'None of those right now,' said Lucie. 'But if my next boyfriend takes any, I'll be sure to give you first showing.'

'Too kind.' Connor pulled Lucie towards him and lined up the phone with the two of then wrapped in a hug with the brightness of the golden sand and the drama of the surf highlighted behind them. He took the photo with a click. 'There you go, send that one to your folks.'

Lucie scanned the photo. They made a good couple, she could see that, even if it was still way too early to even work out what was going on. 'I will do.' Roger and Tanya would like that.

'Tell me to mind my own, but you said foster parents. Do you have a story to share?'

Normally, Lucie would clam up with the opposite sex but there was something about Connor that made her feel that she could tell him almost anything. As they finished closing up the bar, she relayed the story of her true mother and her subsequent removal to a foster family. She left out the details about Ruby's addiction. Something told her not to include it. She'd already perhaps overshared with Tina. She may not have had the most conventional of upbringings but Lucie was still proud of her roots. As she finished telling her tale to Connor, Kara approached them both.

'I'm done, all cashed up. Mind if I get out of here?' she asked.

'Sure thing. I'll count the tips later and divide them out for us tomorrow,' said Connor.

'See you later, roomie,' said Kara to Lucie. She puckered her lips, big and a focal point on her face, and blew a kiss at Lucie.

'See you later.' Kara may have not been as bubbly as Tina, but Lucie really liked them both. In fact, she hadn't met anyone in Peru as yet that she didn't like. Maybe the Peruvian air just made people much sweeter.

Kara left, leaving Lucie and Connor alone on the sand. The final panel of the bar was ready to be closed up, but before locking it into place, Connor reached through to one of the bar fridges and grabbed a couple of bottles of beer.

'One for the sandy road?' he suggested.

'Good with me,' said Lucie.

'I imagine it will be.' Connor smirked again. Another chink dented itself into Lucie's armour. She would soon be defenceless if Connor kept up with the compliments.

'So what about you?' she asked, as they walked towards the shoreline and seated themselves on the sand. 'You've heard my story, what's yours?'

'Mine? Not much to tell really. Thirty years of age, no real qualifications to my name, educated at the school of life. Mum sadly not around anymore. She died a few years back. Dad retired and living in rural England and doesn't really understand why I want to spend my life overseas travelling around. Thinks I'm the black sheep of the family, which is odd seeing I have no brothers and sisters which makes me the only sheep!' He let out a comedy "baaa" to make light of his story.

'No ties back home?' asked Lucie, hoping it didn't sound as "do you have a girlfriend?" in spoken words as it desperately sounded in her head.

'Not really, I go home as and when but the streets of my hometown are nowhere near as exciting as a million other places around the world.'

'No urge to settle down?' asked Lucie trying to steer the conversation in the direction she wanted.

'Who'd put up with me?' To Lucie, it was neither a yes nor a no.

'You said you had girls lining up,' remarked Lucie, taking a swig of her beer. As she pulled the bottle away from her lips, a slight dribble of it cascaded down her chin. Before she could wipe it away with her own hands, Connor reached across and used his own hand to wipe the wetness away. The act was friendly yet somehow intimate. His thumb brushed against her lips as he did so. For a split second, Lucie was lost in thought, thrilled by his touch.

'Yeah, I did, didn't I…' teased Connor, not even referencing what he had just done. 'Well Bar Dynasty is the party bar.'

'And you're the party man it would seem.' Lucie gave up on her probing. It was only her first day on the job and despite it taking every ounce of stamina not to try and kiss Connor's thumb as it touched her lips, she thought it best to quit with her questioning.

She downed the rest of her beer, cool against her throat. The sun, low in the sky overhead, was the perfect partner to it. 'Right, I had better move into my new home, hadn't I? I just hope I find it. Tina gave me the address.'

'It's literally around the corner,' said Connor, finishing his own beer. 'I can take you if you like.'

'No, you're good. I need to stand on my own two feet and find my way around. I am here all summer after all. That's if I'm allowed back for day two tomorrow. I hope I am?' She gave the words an intonation that required an answer.

'Oh yes, I think Bar Dynasty needs you all summer long. Welcome to paradise.'

Lucie waved her hand at Connor, said "goodbye" and started to walk off across the sand. She had taken about six or seven steps when Connor's voice sounded.

'Oh Lucie…' She turned around. 'I am single by the way. That was what you wanted to know, wasn't it?' He smiled.

Lucie didn't reply and merely smiled back, turning her head and walking off hopefully before Connor could see the flush of colouring to her cheeks.

She was still grinning from ear to ear when Tina opened the door to her new home ten minutes later and ushered her in.

Connor Perkins was single. Welcome to paradise indeed.

Chapter 11

Now

'It was hideous, mum. All of a sudden, I was back in the prison, feeling all of the horrible emotions that were poisoning me there. I honestly had no idea where I really was. That poor man in the lift could have had his face scratched off. It was being trapped again. It freaked me out. I had no control. There's nothing worse.'

Lucie was still shaking about her ordeal in the lift at the shopping centre. Something repulsive had automatically happened within the confines of the four hideously close walls of the lift. She had been transported straight back to one of the many abhorrent memories that she had been forced to endure during her time inside. As she spoke to Ruby and Terrance, both of whom were seated at the large wooden table in the cottage kitchen, Lucie lifted the sleeve of her fluffy white dressing gown, one of the day's new purchases, and ran her middle finger across a thin red scar on her wrist. She didn't know she was doing it, the action a subconscious one, but her mother noticed it, but chose not to say anything.

Ruby replied. 'You poor child. What a total freaking nightmare for you. You of all people. That was the last thing you needed. But you're safe now, back with us.' She reached her hand out across the table, a symbol of love and an offering of solace.

Lucie smiled weakly. Sanctuary may have been hers but she still couldn't stop thinking about what had happened in the lift. What would have occurred had she not come back to reality, if she'd been in there for ages? A panic attack like that could have induced a coronary. She had been terrified by her flashback.

'Thank God.' Lucie took her mother's hand. It felt chilled, at odds given the time of year, but somehow, it still felt comforting. 'So, how was your day? What did you two get up to?'

'Nothing much,' said Terrance, his words as direct and blunt as ever. 'Work stuff, nothing you need worry about.' Lucie had assumed that her mother's new boyfriend would have made more of an effort to get to know the new arrival in the house, especially one that meant so much to his partner, but Lucie was finding Terrance Allen a very hard nut to crack.

Ruby was more elaborate. 'He doesn't like to blow his own trumpet. I'll tell you though. We've been busy checking out a new property. Terrance is a developer and likes to find run down properties to do up, or land to construct new-builds on. We went to look at an old church house about forty miles from here. It's in a right state at the moment with trees coming through broken windows and floorboards ripped up to reveal the foundations but the place could be amazing. Put a cellar and a few walk-in wardrobes in there and maybe a pool house out the back and some rich bugger and his missus would snap it up. I'd be tempted myself if I didn't love this place so much.'

'It's going to take a shitload of work,' stated Terrance, scratching the stubble on his chin with his palm.

'And you will rise to the occasion,' snipped Ruby, lighting a cigarette and blowing the smoke in his direction. He coughed slightly, but still picked up her packet and lit one himself. As they both puffed, a cloud of smoke rose up into the air over the table. Lucie had never smoked and didn't particularly like the smell but after the fetid odours she had encountered in prison, somehow things like ciggie smoke didn't bother her anymore.

Terrance's phone sounded on the table, the vibration of it causing it to move a little. He picked it up and stared straight at Ruby. 'I need to take this.' He stood up and walked out of the open back door and out into the garden. His voice vanished into the distance as he answered the phone. Ruby and Lucie were left alone. They were still holding hands.

'The wheels of business never stop turning,' said Ruby. 'He's answering that phone of his all day long. Sometimes at night in bed too. It's a right pain.'

Lucie was keen to find out more about Terrance. 'So where did you two meet?'

'At a leisure centre. I'd gone in there for an exercise class and he was in there working out and we got chatting and that was that really. We went on a few dates and well…you can guess the rest.'

Lucie couldn't help but laugh. The last place she could ever imagine her mother was a leisure centre and certainly not doing an exercise class. Not unless every leotard came with a fitted ashtray.

'What's so funny? Terrance is a very fit man for his age. It's not everyone in their late fifties who can be so active. In all areas of life

I'll have you know, day and night.' Ruby grinned and blew another mass of smoke into the air. She somehow felt obliged to defend Terrance's age in front of her daughter. She wasn't sure why.

'Errr, too much information, thank you. I wasn't laughing at him. I just find the idea of you at an exercise class in a leisure centre rather amusing. It's not very, errr…*you*, is it?'

'I can be quite fit and active when I want to, I'll have you know.' Ruby now felt compelled to defend herself.

'When was this, anyway?'

'After all of my troubles, if that is what you're getting at,' snapped Ruby, a tad aggrieved at Lucie's mockery. 'Terrance is fully aware of it all.'

'I'm not getting at that at all,' barked Lucie, feeling herself backed into a corner. 'I'm very proud that you've turned your life around and that you've met somebody. You've been on your own for as long as I can remember. It's nice to have a father figure about the place, even if I haven't really gotten to know him yet.'

'He's nothing like your…' snapped Ruby, stubbing her cigarette butt forcibly into the ashtray. She stopped short of saying the word '…father.'

Lucie couldn't halt her reply. 'Well, I wouldn't know, would I?'

It was a subject that Ruby clearly didn't want to talk about. She never did. She stood up, scraping her chair across the floor as she did so and grabbed the ashtray. She took it to the breakfast bar near the window and threw it haphazardly onto the counter. A line of ash spilt out over the rim of the ashtray spreading a coating of fine powder across the surface.

'So what are you doing tonight?' Ruby was making a complete U-turn on the conversation. 'We were thinking of ordering in a takeaway. Chinese. Indian. Pizza. Take your pick. You'll be joining us, won't you?'

'Yeah. I'm not that hungry but I'll eat something. I need to get my energy together for tomorrow.'

Ruby span around from staring out of the kitchen window and stared directly at Lucie. 'Tomorrow? What's tomorrow?'

'I'm going to head up to Lancashire. Sort things out at Roger and Tanya's. And visit their graves. I'll be up there a couple of days. I want to start thinking about selling their house. I can't live there without them. I was going to put it off for a while, but I might as well bite the bullet and do it.'

'Do you want Terrance to look at it? You could think about renovating it and making an income out of it,' asked Ruby.

'No way. It was their house. I can't change it. Anyway, it's a beautiful house and doesn't need changing. It was a brilliant home.' It wasn't a dig at Ruby, but Roger and Tanya had cared for Lucie a lot more than Ruby had when she was younger. 'There's just too many memories there for me to keep it. I can use the money from a sale to get back on my own two feet.'

'So something good will come from it.' It was a throwaway comment from Ruby but it stabbed Lucie, irking her with its glibness. Roger and Tanya had been amazing parents to her and she would miss them until the day she died. Lucie chose to ignore the remark, putting it down to Ruby's sometimes less than tactful manner.

Lucie stood up and wrapped the dressing gown tighter around herself. She felt tired even though it was still only mid-evening. Jet-lag was still twisting her time clock into another world. She stretched her arms up and gave a yawn. 'I may go and lie down for a bit. Give me a shout when the…' she thought for a second, making her mind up. '…Indian arrives. Mine's a butter chicken and rice if that's okay.'

'Of course. But if you do want Terrance to look at the house for you, you should let him know.'

'Let him know what?' asked Terrance returning from the garden, phone in hand.

'If she wants you to take a look at her other parents' house in Lancashire. She's off up there tomorrow. It might help. What with you being a property developer and all.'

'If you like.' He stared at Lucie. 'You selling the place or renting it out. Or living there yourself? It'll be no use to them now they're dead.' Another tact void bombed the room.

'I'll let you know.' Lucie couldn't be bothered to explain what her plans were.

'Whatever.' His remark was more final than dismissive. He turned to Ruby. 'Drew has gone a good job on that well by the way, it's looking decent.'

Mention of the gardener jogged Lucie's memory. 'Oh I'm so sorry about the mirror by the way. Drew helped me tidy up. I'm such an idiot.'

'Seven years bad luck. No need to worry there, you've already had your fair share,' grinned Ruby. 'How on earth did you do it?'

'I just touched it, went to move it and it fell to pieces.'

'That takes some doing. I didn't even dent it moving it in there and you manage to break it straight away. That takes some doing indeed.'

'Anything I touch turns to shit, remember?' A mixture of sarcasm and belief.

Neither her mother nor Terrance replied. Lucie let out another yawn. She needed to sleep. She left the kitchen and climbed back upstairs to her bedroom. Tomorrow promised to be a hard day and she would need all of the strength she could muster.

Chapter 12

Now

It had been about six and a half years since Lucie had last stood on the driveway at Roger and Tanya Grimes' house. Her house. But it felt like an eternity. Another life. One that now seemed even harder to realise.

One of her first thoughts as she stood there staring towards the house was that she should have brought Drew, the gardener at the cottage, with her. Random, but the thought came sailing into her head as she scanned around the garden. The overgrown bushes and weed that had developed was an immediate eyesore, something that Tanya, the green-fingered one of her foster parents, would doubtless be spinning in her grave about. The house and the surrounding garden had always been immaculate. It needed a Drew. That was clear.

The journey to the house had been long, the best part of six hours on a series of trains and a taxi ride to the house itself. Lucie's emotions had been a bittersweet cocktail throughout. A rush of excitement at returning to the place that had bought her so much happiness and potentially saved her existence from a lifetime of misery with her mother as she was, fused with a shroud of heartache and hurt knowing that she was returning to a place that no longer housed the people who had shown her such love.

Tanya and Roger Grimes were good people. People who deserved the best in life. People who had hearts big enough to love the world. Their joy for others was unconditional. Both were in their late 30s when they had fostered Lucie. They had tried for their own family, but when Tanya, a primary school teacher, had suffered three miscarriages by the age of 35, it was clear that she and Roger, a doctor with his own practice, were not destined to be blessed the natural luxury of having the family that they always craved.

When they decided to foster, the seeds were sown that would eventually bring a teenage Lucie to them.

Lucie walked up the driveway and reached into her pocket for her house key. The keyring it was attached to showed a photo of her with Roger and Tanya on a day out at a theme park. Lucie must have been about sixteen at the time. It was one of her favourite photos, taken by a theme park photographer. Lucie and her foster parents had all just come off the log flume. They were all wet, but their radiant smiles could have lit up the brightest of skies. Roger, his ginger wave of hair and rich beard dripping from the ride, Tanya's blonde shoulder-length crop plastered against the smudged make-up on her face and Lucie herself with her own hair wrapped sideways across her face, virtually obscuring her eyes, nose and mouth. There was something so natural about the photo. A natural happiness that just shone through. When the photographer had offered copies on mugs, keyrings and in a souvenir brochure, Lucie had wanted them all. A fabulous reminder of a fabulous day.

Her life with Roger and Tanya had been fabulous. Right from the very start. Lucie turned the key in the door, opened it and thought back to her first visit.

2006

The door opened and a couple stood there. The man had his arm wrapped around the woman's waist, pulling her towards him. He seemed a little nervous and lifted one of his hands and ran it through the deep red hair on his head. A slight flush of colour came to the cheeks of the blonde lady stood alongside him. They were both smiling, a little more than people normally did, as if exaggerated, but Lucie couldn't help but smile back when she looked into their faces. Their smiles were infectious.

'Hello Mr and Mrs Grimes, I'm Georgina Waters,' said the nice lady who had accompanied Lucie on the long journey from the home she lived at with her mother. 'And this is Lucie.' She was holding one of Lucie's hands in hers and she raised it slightly as she spoke her name.

She turned to Lucie. 'Lucie, say hello to Mr and Mrs Grimes, they have kindly said that you can come and live with them and that they will look after you.'

Lucie knew this was going to happen but she still wasn't quite sure what she was supposed to say. They seemed really nice people though, she could see that. And their house seemed massive in comparison to the flat she and her mum had lived in. And there was a garden as well, not just a patch of discoloured grass five storeys down littered with fag butts and tin cans. She wished her friends could see it. The few friends she actually had.

Despite not knowing what to say, Lucie knew that it was polite to say something. 'Hello,' she grinned. 'I'm Lucie.' She knew they knew that but at least it proved she had a tongue in her head. And if she remained silent, maybe they would think that she didn't like them. And she did.

The woman spoke first and held out her hand to Lucie. 'Hello Lucie, welcome to our home. I'm Mrs Grimes, or Tanya if you like, and this is my husband, Roger. You must be very hungry after your long journey. Why don't you come in and have some food and a drink. Would you like that?'

Lucie was hungry, that was for sure. She'd eaten sandwiches and some chocolate on the train but whether it was nerves or excitement, she didn't know, but she seemed to be hungry again. She nodded and as Tanya and Roger Grimes opened the door to let her and the nice lady with her inside, Lucie couldn't help but stare in every direction at what was behind the front door. The colour of the walls, the photos in the frames, the smell of flowers in the air. Everything filled her senses. Back home, Lucie had been used to the pungent heavy smell of whatever her mother and her guests were doing in the flat. But here, with her new family, the air smelt floral and with the vitality and cleanliness of fresh air. It was totally new and almost alien to her.

She took her coat off and placed her bags in the hallway as instructed. She followed the couple through to the front room. It was there that Roger and Tanya offered her cake and orange juice and little packets of fruit. Bags of crisps, sandwiches, yoghurts and tiny sausages. Lucie gladly accepted them all. It was like being at a party. A party for her. She wallowed in its joy. She couldn't remember when she had last had a party. If ever.

After eating, Tanya and Roger had asked Lucie if she would like to be shown around her new home. Lucie was happy to. She had already been transfixed by the things that she had spotted in the front room whilst she was eating. A huge television sat in one corner. A table across the room had a large computer sitting proudly on it. And shelves of CDs lined up against one wall. If the rest of the house was exciting as the bits she'd seen so far, she would like staying here, even if it was without her mother.

As they wandered from room to room – a massive kitchen with a huge "island" in the centre where Roger said she could "sit and enjoy her breakfast every morning whilst looking out of the window into the garden". They passed through another room with a large dining room table and a cupboard in the corner. Tanya opened it to find it stacked full of board games and jigsaws. She recognised one of them as a jigsaw that she had herself back at the flat in Brighton. Ruby had bought it for her from a car boot sale down at Brighton Marina. The picture on it was a plate full of baked beans. Lucie could never finish it as the one in Brighton had loads of pieces missing which had always irked her. She doubted if the one at this new house did. Finally, she could complete it.

'Would you like to see upstairs?' asked Tanya, as the four of them reached the bottom of a large staircase, covered in carpet, which ran off the hallway. Stairs. Another luxury that she had never had back home, unless you counted the five floors of wee-smelling ones that you had to climb when the lift wasn't working. Finally, she would be able to go *up* to bed, a simple thing that had always evaded her. Lucie nodded her head and held out her hand for Tanya to take. Even though she had a million questions flooding through her head, a river of why's, when's and what's, taking Tanya's hand felt right. Tanya's face beamed as she wrapped her hand around Lucie's. Roger reached out to squeeze his wife's arm as she and Lucie began to climb the stairs, his smile also coating his face from beneath his ginger beard. Georgina, the social worker, nodded at them both as they made their way upwards. She already knew that Lucie would be happy here.

The tour upstairs started with two bedrooms, one that was where Roger and Tanya slept, a vision of white bedding, a pile of neatly stacked cushions and mirrored wardrobes which made Lucie immediately think of the rooms she had seen on television in programmes about princes and princesses. She liked those. They always had a happy ending. She hoped this would too. The second bedroom was more like an office, where Roger said that he often did some work at home. A computer sat on the desk there and a large bookshelf went floor-to-ceiling along one wall.

Lucie was shown a bathroom, a mixture of blues decorating its walls and big blue and white stripy towels, thick and fluffy, hung from a pair of radiators. A large jar of seashells sat on the window sill behind the bath and a separate shower cubicle dominated another area of the room. A selection of pretty coloured shower gels, rainbow-bright, lined up within its glass walls. 'Those are for you,' smiled Tanya. Lucie's eyes lit up. The bathroom transported her back to carefree days she had spent on the beach in Brighton with her mother. They had been few and far between, she struggled to remember when the last one was, but she knew that they had been happy times. She hoped there would be again.

The final room they went into was Lucie's very own bedroom. Nothing had prepared Lucie for how pretty it would be. Freshly decorated, not that she knew that, it was a girly swirl of pink and cream walls. The floor was varnished floorboards and a huge pink dotty rug sat proudly in the centre of the room. The bed, a double one, the first time she had ever had one so large, was an inviting cloud of comfort, cushions piled up against the pillows. A desk, a chest of drawers, a wardrobe and a dressing table were the other items of furniture that completed the room. A funky pink laptop sat on the desk and a large round mirror decorated the dressing table. Lucie's eyes widened as she took it all in.

'This is your bedroom, Lucie. Your special place. Do you like it, Lucie?' asked Tanya, her hand still in Lucie's. 'We can make it any colour you like and you can put posters on the wall or do whatever you like to make it your own. If you want to watch your favourite TV shows or watch some movies, you can. You have your own TV.' Lucie pointed to a bracketed television that hung from one of the walls. Lucie's eyes opened so wide she thought they might fall from their sockets. Her own television in her room. This was something that she had only ever dreamt of.

Lucie could feel a tingle of tears threatening to erupt but it wasn't through sadness. She was happy. Sensible enough to know that for now she was in the right place. And that it was a perfect place too. She clenched her fist into a ball to try and make the possibility of tears subside. She didn't want to cry in front of the nice people who had made this room so perfect.

'I love it,' she said, her own smile matching that of Tanya and Roger's. 'Thank you so much.'

'You're welcome. This is your new home and we want you to be happy here. To fill it with your favourite things. Now Roger will fetch your suitcase and how about you unpack your things and make this room even more special with your own bits and pieces. How does that sound? Fill the drawers and wardrobe with your clothes and do whatever you like. Then maybe after that, you'd like a shower after your long journey.'

'I'd like that.'

On cue, Roger left the room, only to return a few moments later with her suitcase and backpack in his hands. The three adults left Lucie alone to unpack.

For a while, Lucie did nothing. She merely placed the suitcase on the bed. She wanted to take it all in. It truly was a beautiful room. She couldn't have asked for better.

She walked to the window and looked outside, another view into the lush and fabulous garden. A large sycamore tree stood proud. From her vantage point in the window, Lucie could see a nest positioned in a crook of the tree, where a large branch collided with the main trunk. A baby bird sat proud in the tangled mass of twigs that made up the nest. Its beak was open wide but Lucie couldn't hear the noise that was coming from it. She guessed it was looking for food. As if on command, a larger bird, Lucie guessed the baby's mother, flew back to the nest, a small insect wiggling to its inevitable doom in the mother's beak. The baby bird opened its mouth even wider and Lucie could imagine it almost smiling as it chomped down the juicy offering, the hunger momentarily sated. A second later, the open-mouthed hunger seemed to return. The mother bird flew off again, obviously in search of another serving.

Lucie smiled, but something about the scene made her more than a little sad. It made her think of her own mother. Seeing Ruby's complete misery as her own daughter was taken from the flat that they had shared for so many years was a haunting and hurtful image that would be embossed on Lucie's senses for a lifetime. Lucie had no idea when, and indeed if, she would ever see her mother again. She knew that Ruby was in a bad place. A place from which maybe there was no return. A cul-de-sac of ruin. But she knew that her mother would never receive the true help she needed whilst Lucie was still under her roof. Ruby needed to be able to concentrate on herself without having the burden of Lucie to deal with. That was how Lucie felt about herself sometimes. A burden. She'd lost her mother as she had been unable to help her. Maybe somebody else could. Lucie hoped so. Ruby didn't need a hungry mouth to feed, to fly off and search for something to keep her baby happy. Ruby needed to look after number one. Lucie flying the nest was what had to happen as far as Lucie was concerned. It was only in her absence that hopefully, Ruby would be able to fly free and become well again.

Lucie turned away from the window and went to her suitcase on the bed. She opened it and pulled out a photo frame of her and Ruby together. It was taken on the beach in Brighton. Maybe the last time they had been actually. Lucie must have been about ten or eleven and she was holding up a small crab to the camera. Ruby, cigarette in hand, looked slightly repulsed by the clawed creature.

They had asked another lady on the pebbles alongside them to take the snap. Lucie loved it and had framed it straight away.

Lucie placed the photo frame on the window sill. An already perfect bedroom now seemed complete. Her mother was with her, despite everything.

She stared out of the window. As the bird returned to the nest again, another offering sandwiched in its beak, the excitement on the baby bird's feathered face was clear. Dinner was served again. Lucie hoped that one day her own mother would be able to fly back into her life and return to the family nest. One day.

Lucie had thought that that day would never come. All of those years that her mother was AWOL, missing in action as it were. No contact, no attempt to return to the nest, to gather her daughter back under her wing. Lucie had given up hope. She had given up on Ruby. But now, things had come full circle. Ruby was a different woman and back in her life. After everything they had gone through, perhaps the one good thing that could come from the whole sorry mess that Lucie called her own cursed life was that Ruby and Lucie could finally build bridges.

But as Lucie closed the door of her home with Roger and Tanya Grimes, the two people who had given her more love and welcome than she'd ever known, and gazed at the photo on the keyring again another crashing wave of sadness swept over her. They would never be able to see those bridges being built. She knew that they would have been happy for her to reunite with Ruby again. Her happiness was their happiness. Her love was their love. And to have as much love as possible in her life right now was something that Lucie desperately needed.

She placed the keys on the hall table and walked into the house.

Chapter 13

Now

The house was dusty. Why wouldn't it be? There was nobody to look after it anymore. Roger and Tanya didn't have any parents left alive, Lucie had never met any uncles or aunties, and she, of course, was their only child. Who would there be to pop around and make sure the house was clean? To water the plants and set the timer on the central heating. She'd arrange for someone to come around and do it. She'd arrange for somebody to come around and do everything. When the money from the will was released, which it would be now that she was back in the country and able to deal with everything, she could pay people to return it to its pristine state. Ready for selling. Lucie knew that she could never live here. It was too remote for her and it housed too many memories. All of them good, but memories that now splintered into her heart, each one a pinprick of pain.

Ruby had said to her before leaving, her words as ever a snowball of tactlessness, that Lucie should make sure she took anything worth keeping or of value when she cleared the house. But there was nothing that Lucie wanted. She would retrieve her own things, personal memories and photos, photo albums of fun times together, sentimental items, but everything else could be charity-bound. Even though Lucie had come back from Peru with pretty much nothing, she had no desire to store and stack up cutlery and crockery from her days with Roger and Tanya to keep for her own home when she eventually decided where her next chapter in life was going to take her. Settling down and making a home was not on the horizon as far as she could see right now, so bottom-drawing a whole host of her foster parents' items was not even a consideration. She would rather charity profit. She knew Roger and Tanya would have said the same.

Lucie went straight upstairs to her bedroom. It was where she always went first when she came "home". It was immaculate, apart from the dust, and unchanged from when she had last been there. Toiletries, bottle of creams and lotions, dotted the dressing table, and the photos on the window sill, the one of a young Lucie and her mother on the beach now alongside another copy of the keyring photo, framed in a sparkly mirrored frame, smiled back at her.

She opened a chest of drawers and looked at the neatly piled stacks of T-shirts, blouses, shorts and trousers inside. Some of the fashions were dated beyond belief, trends having moved on since her time out of the country, but there were some things that she could still wear. She picked up a T-shirt, one of her favourites with a gothic skull print on the front and placed it to her nose to sniff. She wasn't sure why she did it, but the scent, what there was of it, was somehow comforting. A mix of distant flowers and a million memories. She wondered why she hadn't taken it to Peru with her. Not that any of that mattered now.

Lucie had booked herself into a hotel for a couple of nights about twenty minutes from the house. She knew she wouldn't want to stay at the house as the hurt would be too great to bear. Today had been a long day and she felt tired from the journey. She would just check the rest of the house and then retire back to the hotel for the night. Tomorrow would be a fresh start and she could bag up what she wanted to keep and take it with her. She'd borrowed an empty suitcase from Ruby so that she would have enough space to take what she wanted. She made a mental note to contact the executor dealing with Roger and Tanya's wills whilst she was in the area. She'd been glad that a professional had been brought in to deal with everything. Given her location at the time of their unfortunate deaths, it was a good deal that neither of her foster parents had ever named her as executor. In Lucie's opinion, she was both too young and too weak, as well as, at the time, totally unavailable.

Lucie picked up the two photos on the window sill, leaving an oddly-coloured space with a moat of dust around it where the position of the frames had not allowed the particles to gather. She would take those with her now. They would bring some cheer to her evening in the hotel room. And she was sure Ruby would like a picture reminder of the happy days that they had spent together before everything that had come between them. The cottage may have been ridiculously picturesque but it was distinctly lacking a few home touches, and photos on display was definitely one of them. Lucie loved photos, although she has to admit that some of the snaps she had taken would always be beyond difficult to look at. But photos reminded her of when she had been able to really look at herself without feeling some hideous wave of overwhelming regret and dismay. Back in the days before prison. Before life had changed for good.

Lucie moved downstairs and was about to leave and call a cab to pick her up when she stopped herself. Maybe she should check the kitchen before she left. If there were any food that had been left in the fridge from before their deaths, it would now not just be beyond its sell by date but also beyond recognition. Lucie assumed that somebody might have come to the house after their deaths, a neighbour or somebody local, but she didn't have a clue who it would have been.

She walked into the kitchen and over to the large black fridge freezer. She opened the door, mentally clenching her nostrils together for fear of the smell that might hit them. Inside the fridge, there was no smell. There was no food. Somebody must have come in at some point. She would ask the executor.

As tiredness crept its way across Lucie's bones, she knew that she could face no more of the house today. It had not been as heart-breaking as she had expected, but being back in the place that was now no more than an empty shell of all the love and family activity that had gone before was never going to be easy. She shut the fridge door and turned to exit the kitchen. Before she could take a step, her eyes fixed on a photo pinned to the cork board on a pillar that rose out of the centre of the kitchen "island". The photo of her and Connor that he had first taken of them both on her initial day working at Bar Dynasty and that she had sent to Roger and Tanya saying what a good time she was having was there, pinned to the board. Why was it still there? Roger and Tanya had known that things had gone so hideously wrong and that Connor's name had been dragged into everything. Maybe they had left it there to try and delve deeper. To try and help with her release from prison, her protestations of innocence.

Whatever the reason, Lucie knew that she would never receive an answer. She stared at the photo, unable to take her eyes from it. Seeing them together, so happy. That was the hardest heartbreak of all.

Chapter 14

Peru, summer 2012

Living with Tina and Kara was proving to be a real experience. A really good one. Even though, between their time together at the flat and their work at Bar Dynasty, they seemed to spend virtually 24/7 together, the three girls instantly bonded. A bond tied together by common interests, the same sense of humour and a love for life. Lucie defied any young women living such a joyous and exotic experience not to have such a love. Lucie was the quieter and less partyish of the three but she loved the fact that the girls made her want to let her hair down more than ever before. To live a little.

Any downtime between shifts or after the bar had closed for the day was spent with the three women exploring the hot spots around Paradise Cove or shopping for clothes for themselves or souvenirs for people back home. Endless nights were spent moving their sun kissed bodies in some heaving nightclub, a mass of sensual, young bodies writhing on the dancefloor to the hypnotic rhythmic beats of the music. Pisco sours, a traditional Peruvian drink and beers would be downed with gleeful relish, hardly any of them paid for by the girls themselves. All three of the girls were magnets for men desperate to impress by flashing the cash. Between their varied looks, they seemed to suit every taste and attract guys of all types – from the chancing bravado of a hapless teenager through to the sickly sweet banter of a passing businessman gagging for a bunk up behind his wife's back. At first, a naïve Lucie was horrified by some of the chat up lines and offers coming their way but by her third week living and loving life with the girls, she was more than adept at handling the guys and giving them the brush off. But not until, as Tina always said "those losers have been to the bar and bought us all a round of drinks". A Musketeer spirit of "all for one and one for all" ran through the three housemates and their wellbeing as a collective always came before any one of their personal needs.

Many nights were spent back at the flat, drinks still flowing after club hours, as Tina and Kara invited people back to carry on the party. Lucie had already lost count of the number of times she had woken up for work the next day to find some random man sleeping on the couch or snoring spark out on the flat balcony floor. Often one of the guys they brought back would stumble blindly, smelling of cigarettes and beer, from either Kara or Tina's room, clothes, if worn, dishevelled from a night's revelry. Kara and Tina were unlike any girls that Lucie had ever met before. They were wild, rebellious, proud and upbeat and they made the best friends. They were everything that Lucie had never been. And Lucie loved being a part of their world. Not that she indulged to the same degree as them. Lucie wasn't ready to give herself quite so freely to any passing man. At the end of the nights where Tina and Kara would slink off to their rooms, an eager boy in tow, Lucie would often find herself happily fending of the advances of someone who was more than happy for Lucie to become another notch of their doubtless already heavily scratched bed post. Lucie didn't mind their advances, but giving in was not her style.

And besides, Lucie only had room in her head for one man and that man was definitely Connor Perkins.

She and Connor had definitely been growing closer at work. Or at least as close as working pretty much full on as the season became busier would allow. Furtive glances across the bar, a suggestive wink or a flirtatious raise of the eyebrows during their shifts were commonplace and many an evening shift ended with the two of them talking on the beach together until only the advancement of the rising morning sun would shine its radiance and suggestion that maybe it was time to go home. Staring into his eyes, Lucie had often longed for Connor to kiss her. To feel the sensation of his lips against hers, but it never came. And Lucie was far too coy to make the first move, despite being caught so joyously in his irresistible slipstream. He often questioned her about her nights out with the girls – what they did, where they went, how much fun they had and whilst Lucie was keen to state clearly that she had not ended up in the arms of another, feeling that for some strange reason, it needed to be said, she still couldn't work out whether Connor was romantically interested in her or not. He was a beautiful enigma that her inexperienced mind, when it came to dating, was unable to fathom out. Lucie may have been becoming a dab hand at being able to deal with the opposite sex when it came to binning off their lecherous and drunken advances but when it came to reading

Connor's mind, her own banks of experience appeared desert-dry and devoid of ideas.

It was one morning, almost midday, after another gloriously heartfelt yet heart-baffling "wee small hours" chat with Connor on the beach that Lucie lay in the bath at her flat. She was alone, both Kara and Tina already long gone off to work their shifts at Bar Dynasty. Her mood was one of reflection. Lucie had risen late and with the prospect of a day off ahead of her had decided that a bath, relaxed, leisurely and covered in soft, warm bubbles would be far more appetising than the quick in-and-out of the shower in a rush on her way to work. With nothing scheduled for the day ahead, she contemplated what to do. She could Skype Roger and Tanya at some point. They would be keen to know how her job was going and how her feelings for Connor were progressing. She hadn't spoken to them for a few weeks, the busy carousel of life in Peru somehow always seeming to offer up excuses to not contact home. Not that she was avoiding them, but something about the last few weeks had opened her mind to the possibilities in life and somehow phoning home and reminders of her life growing up there didn't always appeal. The problem really lay with her mother. She had been thinking about Ruby a lot, wondering just what had happened to her. Life with Roger and Tanya was phenomenal and she would always be grateful to them for giving her the life that she had never had, but she couldn't help but wonder what Ruby would make of her new life in Peru, what she would think of the opportunities that life had given her and what she would make of Connor. She longed to tell her. Didn't any daughter really want to share things with their mother? Why hadn't Ruby ever made the effort to stay in contact with her? Why wasn't she still a "mother" to her? Lucie had never understood why her own mother had simply vanished without a trace. If anything had happened to her, surely she would have been informed. She had discussed the situation with Connor the night before. He had hung on her every word and stroked her cheek as she talked about the pain that leaving her mother had caused her. She still never gave the true reason behind her necessary departure. It never seemed necessary. Maybe that was why she was feeling so reflective this morning as she lay in the bath. Maybe that was why she was slightly reluctant at contacting home. Even Roger and Tanya. By association, speaking to them would immediately make her think of her mother and what had been. And consequently about what had been lost. No, she'd phone them in a few days. They'd want to talk about Connor. Tanya had easily worked out that Lucie was smitten with him from their last Skype together and had joked about how good they looked together in the photo she had messaged them. Lucie's red cheeks and giggling were giveaways. But what could Lucie add to the conversation? As yet, there was nothing more to tell. Would there be? She wasn't sure. Reading men was not her best choice of subject. Maybe that was something she had inherited from her mother.

Lucie was enjoying the wafts of steam that were coming off the bath water, their rapturous odours of mango filling her nostrils as she lay there. She inhaled deeply and submerged her head under the water, enjoying the feeling as the smell of the mango fused with the warmth of the water wrapping itself around her face. For a moment, everything was still and almost dark as she let the water caress and undulate against her skin. A pocket of tranquillity. She loved the feeling. She always had. Submerging herself below the waterline was something she had always done. An escape. No matter what was going on in life, the ups and the downs, everything was evened out under the water. It was a place for her to lose herself. Just for a moment. To relax into a sea of nothingness, away from the world, away from reality.

Brighton, 2005

The bath water swirled around Lucie, covering her entire body. It was blanket soft against her skin, cocooning Lucie in its warm arms. A hug that wasn't reliant on another. Sometimes they were the best kind. The only kind you could rely on. One that you could sink into there and then. To take you away from what was happening above the surface in the real world.

She held her breath for as long as possible. Which was quite long it seemed. She'd looked up in a book just how long somebody could hold their breath under water. It was a long time. Lucie was nowhere near that, but her time under the water was lengthening from bath to bath and Lucie was still only twelve. It meant her escape from the world above was becoming more and more.

When her lungs could take it no more, a heat beginning to radiate from within them, Lucie knew that it was time to resurface. She opened her eyes as she did so and for a moment there was just silence as the water in her ears drained away from her body and back into the bath. It was only then that the noise returned.

The loud beat of music sounded in the air. It was accompanied by screams of pleasure and moments of laughter. To those it came from, it signified happiness and doubtless euphoria. To Lucie, it signified another night of being ignored, unwanted and seemingly unloved.

Her mother was having a party. Not a party like the other mums seemed to have. At least that's how to seemed to Lucie when other girls at school talked about parties. They always seemed to have parties where "aunty so and so and uncle whatnot came around and we all played Scrabble and danced to ABBA records" or "the food was amazing, we had the hugest cake and enough fizzy pop to make me burp for days". They sounded fun. Ruby's parties weren't like that at all. They were loud. Raucous. Full of people that Lucie had never seen before. A few familiar faces maybe but nobody that she could talk to. And certainly nobody of her own age. Lucie would never know that they were coming. They would begin to evolve with knocks on the door of the flat around mid-afternoon. People coming into their home, the noise of their conversation with Lucie's mum becoming louder and louder as the hours passed and more people arriving. Lucie was never introduced. Never even considered. The volume would ramp up to hysteria and more and more people descended as if by magic. It wasn't magic. Lucie had heard her mum on the phone, animated and jittery, telling people to come over and that it would be "worth their while". The air would become more and more matted with the smell of smoke and pendulous with their feverish delirium as afternoon turned to dark. Lucie forgotten again, a prisoner in her own room. She could have left the flat, ventured outside to escape the madness, but something always stopped her. The thought that maybe Ruby would knock on her door, ask if she was all right and if she wanted some food. It never happened. As ever, Lucie was left to fend for herself, raiding the bread bin and inserting two slices of bread into the toaster and then layering it with whatever she could find in the fridge. The ideal meal for a growing twelve-year-old girl. Lucie guessed not, but if she waited for Ruby on nights like this, she would be fed on a diet of thin air.

As the music grew louder and the night became longer, Lucie would take herself to the bathroom and run herself a bath. It symbolised comfort, cleanliness and an ultimate escape.

Lucie listened to the music. It was indecipherable. No more than mere noise. A beat and some female singers maybe? The soundtrack to her loneliness and rejection. She could feel that the bathwater was becoming less than warm. She needed to get out. To dry off and head for bed. To bury herself beneath the covers and hope that sleep would come. More often than not during the parties, it wouldn't. Their fun outweighing her own fatigue.

Lucie was about to reach for her towel and lift herself up from the water when the sound of the door opening stopped her. The action instantly shocked Lucie, as she was sure that she had locked it. Had she? It appeared not. In her haste to "escape", she had evidently forgotten. Lucie grabbed her towel as quickly as she could and wrapped it around herself, pulling it as tightly as it would go around her young body.

The man that entered into the bathroom was about her mother's age, maybe older, it was hard to tell and Lucie thought she recognised him as one of the men who often came to the house. She thought that she had seen him and her mother often laughing, joking and becoming louder and louder in the front room of the flat. He was skinny to look at and his skin was the colour of milk, except for the areas under his eyes that were darker, an unhealthy shade of grey. Lucie let out a scream as he entered into the bathroom to alert him to her presence. He turned fully to face her and grinned. One of surprise and not of particular friendliness. Lucie shivered a little and continued to try and wrap the towel even tighter around her. The man sniffed and rubbed his nose as he looked at her, his actions jittery and twitchy.

'Whoa. Hello little one. What you doing here? Don't mind me.' Without any hint of his interruption and no seeming awareness of the wrongness of his entry into the occupied bathroom, he turned to the toilet in the corner of the room, unzipped his trousers and began to urinate loudly into the bowl. Lucie didn't know where to look and was grateful that the man had his back to her. A rush of embarrassment swept over her, heating her body. After what felt like an age, the man finished what he was doing, zipped himself back up and turned back to Lucie.

'Better now,' he sniffed. He pulled at the toilet roll, took a couple of squares and blew his nose loudly. Lucie watched horrified as he stared into the paper after blowing to check the contents and then threw the scrunched ball into a wicker basket in the corner of the bathroom. Without saying another word, he pulled open the bathroom, the volume of the music beyond increasing as he did so, and left. Lucie stepped quickly from the bath, careful not to slip, and slid the lock on the door across to prevent further intruders. Harmless, though, he had been, Lucie couldn't help but feel dirty by his presence. Soiled in her own skin, despite the fact that she had just washed. She longed for her escape again. To be under the water. To block out the noise, the intruder, the ignorance. To block out her life.

The man had acted almost as if Lucie hadn't even been there. He'd seen her, even acknowledged her presence, but he hadn't respected her space. She may as well have been invisible to him. Just as she was to her mother most of the time.

As Lucie brought her head back above the water, she could hear a knock at the flat door. Her first reaction was to ignore it but the knocking persisted. Perhaps it was Kara or Tina. Maybe one of them had forgotten their keys. She knew they would need them later. Lucie decided that maybe it was best if she answered the door.

'Hold on, I'm coming,' she shouted, standing up in the water and reaching for a towel. Water still dripping down her body, she stepped from the bath and headed through the flat to the front door, leaving a trail of wet footprints behind her.

She grabbed the handle of the door, yanked it downwards and pulled it open. It wasn't Kara or Tina.

'Have I interrupted something?' asked Connor Perkins with a wink. He was dressed in a vest top and shorts, a pair of jade green Havaianas on his feet.

Lucie could immediately feel her flesh glow from an inner heat, a mixture of the bath water still warming her skin and the fact that she was stood wearing merely a towel in front of Connor.

She could feel herself grinning involuntarily as she replied, 'Just easing myself into the day.'

'Which will be gone if we don't crack on,' said Connor, raising his hand to jangle a set of car keys.

Lucie was confused. 'Sorry? Crack on? With what?'

'We spoke before about seeing some of the things Peru has to offer. We're both off work for the day as Tina and Kara are on shift today and I was thinking that a trip out in my friend's borrowed Jeep might be just what was required.'

'But I was going to…' Lucie let her words trail off. She was going to say "Skype back home" and make an excuse. The realisation that she had already rejected that idea and the idiocy of offering it up as a get-out-clause instead of a day with Connor slapped her hard in the face.

'I'm not taking no for an answer,' beamed Connor. He bit his bottom lip and raised his eyebrows staring straight at her. Even though she was only wearing a towel, Lucie suddenly felt naked under his gaze. It wasn't an uncomfortable feeling. She was powerless to say no. So she didn't.

'Then I had better wear something other than a towel, hadn't I?' countered Lucie.

'Might come in handy if we find a secluded beach,' volleyed back Connor. 'And if we go skinny-dipping then you won't be needing anything else, will you?'

Lucie turned away from him and headed to her bedroom. 'Help yourself to a drink and give me five minutes,' she yelled, as she disappeared into her room, pleased that Connor couldn't see the cloud of redness that was drifting across her face with embarrassed yet excited expectation.

Today would be a good day, she knew it.

Chapter 15

Now

Lucie had spent the entirety of the next day removing the things that she wanted from the house that she had shared with Roger and Tanya. It had not been a pleasurable task, every item stirring up a memory that could never be repeated. Often she'd cried, the tears flowing freely down her cheeks and onto the floor before she had time to catch them, their march unstoppable.

Items were bagged. Some in the empty suitcase she had bought with her, some in bin liners for charity and some in bags to disappear for good. Once the house was on the market, she would decide what to do with everything else but for now the bagging was all that she could manage.

It was mid-afternoon by the time that Lucie had finished. She had just been leaving the house to return to her hotel when her phone sounded. It had been the company dealing with her late foster parents' estate. They requested Lucie's company the next morning to discuss face-to-face what was to be done. Lucie agreed to meet them, a rendezvous she was keen to discuss with Ruby on the phone when she was back at the hotel an hour or so later.

'Do you think I'm doing the right thing, wanting to sell the house? It just felt so empty being there today without them in it,' asked Lucie. 'I can't help feeling that I'm taking the easy way out by just getting rid of it.' She still couldn't quite fathom why she was keen to discuss Roger and Tanya with Ruby as the muddying of those two areas still felt strange and at juxtaposition in her mind. But she needed to talk to someone and her mother seemed by far the best answer. The only one.

'Do you want my honest answer?' replied Ruby, a sharp intake of breath coming from the other end of the phone line as she took a heavy drag on her ciggie.

'Of course.'

'Get rid. Have a fresh start. You've been through so much that you deserve to move forwards, not backwards. And that means moving on from everything that has gone before.' There was an unusual softness in Ruby's voice despite the directness of what she was saying.

'So I'm not being callous by wanting to sell the house?'

'You've got to gather wood before you can build a fire, Lucie,' replied Ruby. 'Your life is a blank page and you can do whatever you want. Finally take control. If you were to stay living in that house or even rent it out, you would always be tied to it. There would always be constant reminders of your time there. The times were good, I know that, Roger and Tanya Grimes were loving parents to you, better than I ever was for sure.' She paused for a moment, as if in contemplation of her own failings as a mother before continuing. 'But those can never be repeated and you know that. A connection to that house would only ever be a connection to the past. See what the legal people say tomorrow and take it from there.'

Lucie knew that Ruby was right. Unexpectedly so. Turning to her blood mother for advice was not something that Lucie was used to. 'When did you become so bloody wise?' asked Lucie, humour peppering her words.

'When you've hit rock bottom, there is only one way to go and that is up, Lucie. I've been given a chance with the cottage and with Terrance and being able to shed all of the things that went before. I'm just lucky that you've come back to me too. I never assumed you would. I hoped and prayed, and well, even though the route everything has taken to bring you back to me has been a horrid one, I'd be lying if I said that I didn't love having you back in my life. I love having you here at the cottage and you're welcome to stay as long as you want, until you decide what you want to do with your life. Permanently, if you like.'

Lucie didn't know how to reply straight away, her mother's words causing her eyes to water over, tears near. Her pause let Ruby carry on.

'I need you in my life, Lucie. And I would love it if you needed me. I think every girl needs her mother, don't you? I just wish it hadn't taken me so bloody long to realise it. When I think of all those wasted years, when we could have been so much more of a family, it makes me so angry to realise what I've lost and the things I've thrown away.'

It was now Ruby's turn to pause, her own voice cracking as she confessed her feelings.

'Oh mum, I missed you so much.' The words tumbled from Lucie's lips, unleashed from behind a dam of emotions that had built up for years. 'I needed you so much.' The words were few but they said everything necessary.

'I missed you too, darling girl. But you're back now, we can make all of this right. If you let me.' Tears flowed. Mother and daughter momentarily united in their regrets.

Lucie listened, unable to speak, as a ribbon of tears streaked down her cheeks. It felt good to cry. In prison, she had learnt to stop herself from crying on those moments when her misery had threatened to show itself. It was a coping mechanism. Tears were signs of weakness, a wound that showed that you were vulnerable to others. Survivors didn't cry. Not if they wanted to stay that way.

But the tears she cried as she lay on her hotel bed talking to Ruby at the other end of the phone were tears of strength. Tears of a woman who was determined to do what was necessary to make sure that she never felt imprisoned again. Never felt scared again. Never felt vulnerable again. She knew that it would be hard for that strength to last, to always be her guiding force. Prison had left her weak, left her with a life unknown, but having Ruby back in her life was definitely giving Lucie a bonding of a strength that she hadn't counted on. For now, she was strong. For now, she could see herself as a survivor. Maybe it took a survivor like her mother, someone who had hit rock bottom too, to help her rebuild her own life.

As the two survivors talked, the family blood tie strengthened by tears, Lucie felt that she could face the future whatever it held. A life unknown was a blank canvas and that was the perfect canvas to paint whatever you liked on.

Their tears exhausted, Lucie wished her mother good night and hung up. She lay down on the bed and stared up at the drab colour of her hotel room ceiling. Tiredness took her and she closed her eyes. Tomorrow would be another day. Another day closer to knowing what her next step would be. A chance to start shading the colours of as yet her life unknown.

Chapter 16

Now

The legalities of the estate were as expected. Lucie's meeting, short and succinct, was just as she had been led to believe. No hidden surprises like the storyline from some huge Hollywood blockbuster. No, Lucie Palmer was the sole beneficiary from the wills of Roger and Tanya Grimes. Both of their individual wills had left their belongings to each other but in the event that they both die at the same time, all monies and possessions were bequeathed to Lucie.

Lucie felt strangely emotionless during the meeting. Maybe it was the austere surroundings of the office it took place in or simply that perfunctory manner in which it had to be done, but as she listened to the fact that she was now, in theory, a very rich woman, all she could think about was how death was a total leveller. Roger and Tanya had worked all of their lives, both been from wealthy backgrounds, been shrewd with their savings, invested wisely in their house and made a very financially comfortable life for themselves. But one journey in their car, a momentary lapse in concentration or a bend taken too fast and suddenly, all of that counted for nothing. Two bodies dead in their car at the bottom of a ditch. For richer, for poorer, till death do us part. It didn't matter about what had gone before. Death was an equaliser for everyone.

Lucie had instructed what was to be done. Some would say selfishly, but to Lucie, it was all that she could do. She instructed that dealing with the house herself would be too hard for her emotionally. This was the truth. Having removed all that she wanted from the house, she asked if what needed to be done could be arranged, to clear out the house of its belongings for charitable purposes and that the place be cleaned throughout and the garden tended to. The house was to be sold and that was that. If people thought that was harsh, then so be it. It was nobody's business but her own. She asked how much a house like that would sell for in the area. Half a million approx. The house was mortgage free. Lucie would find herself very wealthy. But none of that mattered. It was her feelings that came first, not her finances.

Lucie was ready to head back down south, back to the cottage. She had done what she needed to do. Well, almost. Only one thing remained and that was visiting the graves of Tanya and Roger. They had been buried in the same graveyard as Roger's mum and dad. Lucie knew where it was as she had often been there with her foster parents to lay flowers at the grave of the grandparents she had never been able to meet. They had died before the Grimes had fostered her.

Lucie stared at the two stretches of soil where Roger and Tanya lay. The overhead sun, strong and at its summer height, warmed her skin as she took in the makeshift headstones that had been erected at the end of the graves, the soil as not yet fully settled. She raised her hand to her lips, kissed it and then touched both stones, as if transferring the kiss. 'I love you,' she whispered, the quiet in her voice befitting the tranquillity of the surroundings. A gardener beavered away in the background tending to the shrubs and bushes that dotted themselves between the graves. He was the polar opposite to Drew back at the cottage. Whereas Drew was handsome, young and energetic, the gardener at the cemetery was easily seventy-plus, stooped a little, probably from years of bending over a garden tool, and wearing a grey cardigan despite the heat of the summer sun.

Lucie let her gaze wander to him, an action he spotted, and he nodded his head in her direction. Without invitation, he walked towards her.

'Hello, miss. You here to pay your respects?' He stared down at the graves of Roger and Tanya. 'Oh, these two. Such a nice couple. Such a shame about what happened. Car crash, wasn't it?' He tutted to himself and shook his head as he contemplated their fate.

'Yes, totally tragic.' Lucie was about to introduce herself when the gardener continued, lost in his recollections.

'There weren't many people here for their funerals. I was working here that day. Not surprised it was pretty sparse really. There's no real family left to speak of, is there? Plenty of friends came but his parents are dead as well. They're buried over there in fact.' He pointed to another row of gravestones. 'Hers too I believe. They have a daughter but she's not been seen for years. Bit of a bad lass from what I remember, caught up in some drugs scandal. A let-down I imagine. Didn't even come to the funeral from what I gather.

I used to see them all together up here years ago paying their respects.' He shook his head again before asking, 'Are you a friend of the family?'

Lucie suddenly felt herself compelled to lie. 'Yes, I knew them both. Our paths have crossed.' Why was she lying? Afraid to be *the let-down*? It seemed so. 'Such a lovely couple.' Why didn't the gardener recognise her? But then, she didn't recognise him and it was a long time ago. And what teenager would ever speak to the OAP gardener working in the local cemetery? In this day and age, not one.

'I still don't understand them dying, you know?' The gardener rambled on in his thoughts, his accent broad and strong. 'They shouldn't have been driving so fast along that road, you know. That's a twisty stretch and it's no wonder they ended up upside down in a ditch. Too dangerous. Kids I could understand doing it, they have no bloody sense when they climb behind the steering wheel of a fast car, but these two, it's such a pity. I know a lot of the families whose kids went to Mrs Grimes' school and were taught by her. They miss her a lot.'

'Who says they were driving too fast?' asked Lucie, keen to hear a little more about the accident. She had googled for information after she had been informed about their deaths, the prison authorities allowing her the chance to grieve. But the articles in the press amounted to little more than "local couple killed in accident" and an outline to their connection with "the young woman who had been imprisoned for major drug trafficking in South America a few years ago". Lucie had stopped reading after that.

'The car was fairly mangled. They must have been travelling a fair rate of knots. A policeman I know was one of the first on the scene and he said the car was in a right state. There was little chance of anyone getting out alive and, of course, we can see, they didn't.' He tutted again, not a critique, but one of pity.

'You know a lot,' said Lucie. There was a slight air of critique in her own words. She was sure he meant no harm, but the gardener was bordering on busybody and very judgemental.

'I should do, miss, I've lived around here all of my life and worked in this cemetery for many years. I should be retired now but I don't want to give it up. I care about it too much. If this is to be a person's final resting place, then I want to make sure that it looks neat and tidy for them. I'll want the same when I pop my clogs. Seems a crime to have seen so many young people losing their lives and being buried here when I'm still kicking around.'

Lucie felt a wave of sorrow for the man. It must be hard when you're surrounded by death all the time. Maybe that was where the judgement came from.

'I'm sure you've got plenty of years ahead of you,' said Lucie, placing her hand on the man's shoulder and smiling. The wool of his cardigan felt bobbled and rough to the touch.

'And then you have people like their daughter peddling such filth to the world. Doubtless causing death to lots of innocent people too.' Her empathy for him vanished again.

'Maybe she was innocent,' ventured Lucie.

'So then why did she get banged up, you tell me that?' replied the gardener. 'There's no smoke without fire, is there? Good riddance I say. Waste of space. These two must have been so disappointed. After all they gave her, to be repaid like that.'

Lucie could feel her anger rising, but the last thing she wanted was to have a row with a man in his seventies, even if what he was saying was scratching at her patience. She remained silent.

'Anyway, better get on. Nice to talk to you. It's nice that friends come and visit the graves, keeps their spirits alive. Funny, isn't it? Friends you can rely on. You can't always say that for family.' He tutted for a third time before wandering off.

Lucie could feel the doubt spreading like a plague throughout her body. Had she let them down? Did people really think that the Grimes' daughter was a waste of space? Her innocence had never been proved. She had been in prison for six years. She had served her time. People thought that she was guilty. She was the only one who knew that she was innocent. Well, Lucie and the person who planted the drugs in her suitcase in the first place. They knew how innocent she was. For a second, her mind drifted back to Peru, to thoughts of those involved. Where were they now? Certainly not standing alongside the graves of their dead parents being told they're a waste of space. That was her fate. One that the demons of her life had made happen.

All of the strengths that Lucie had been feeling the night before and the lack of emotions that she had been experiencing earlier that day in the legal office had been replaced with an anger. An anger at being misjudged, an anger at being the victim, an anger at being the one left to grieve. Had Roger and Tanya gone to their graves believing that deep down Lucie was guilty? That she had let them down. She wouldn't let herself believe it. They had paid for the most amazing lawyers to try and gain her freedom. They had done everything they could to prove her innocence. Hadn't they? They had never stopped doubting that she had been framed, had they? Lucie hated the fact that she was suddenly questioning everything. The old man with his stupid talk and rotten grey cardigan was suddenly making thoughts and doubts bubble to the surface like toxic bursts of lava.

'I never let you down, I promise,' said Lucie to the gravestones of Tanya and Roger. 'I was innocent, you know that, don't you?' But now, the seed of doubt had been poisonously planted in her own mind she couldn't be one hundred per cent with her certainty.

She touched both stones again, said "I love you" for a final time and turned away to walk back across the cemetery. One thought drenched her mind. She was determined to prove her innocence. To silence all of the doubters. She just wasn't at all sure how on earth she was going to do it.

'Goodbye, miss,' shouted the cemetery gardener, raising his hand as he spotted Lucie wandering off. She didn't reply.

Chapter 17

Peru, summer 2012

Connor flicked up the seawater with the edge of his hand and directed it towards Lucie. She squealed as the water hit her and attempted to run away from him, her passage hindered by the fact she was already knee-deep in the clearest sea waters she had ever imagined and her feet sinking into the soft wet sand beneath them.

'Didn't I tell you that this place was amazingly beautiful,' grinned Connor, his smile adding to the sunshine of an already idyllic surrounding.

'It's beyond stunning,' said Lucie, regaining her balance from where she had attempted to run. 'Have you been here before?'

'Not this specific one, but there are a million secluded little bays like this around here. All with clear blue waters, and sand as soft as a mattress.'

It was true, the sand was the most gorgeous colour of butterscotch and felt powder fine under their feet. Lucie had fallen in love with the place the moment they had parked the Jeep and wandered through a lush green woodland area to find it. A few other cars parked at the side of the road suggested that maybe there was something worth seeing for the crafty explorer who dared to venture a little off-track. The beach they had found was brochure-beautiful and unspoilt without a food hut, bar or souvenir seller to be seen. About a dozen or so people stippled the sands, their towels spread beneath them. A sprinkling of laughter filled the air. A presence of carefree floated blissfully across the entire vista.

'I thought Paradise Cove was beautiful but this is something else,' said Lucie, stretching her hands out in the air above her. She was wearing a bikini and her hair wrapped itself loosely around her face.

'That's because the likes of Logan and Billy aren't looning their way up and down it trying to down another cocktail and get into every girl's knickers,' said Connor, wading deeper into the clear blue waters, his board shorts disappearing below the surface. 'Paradise Cove is there for the tourists and for those passing through. I think places like this are undiscovered jewels that are only treasured by those who dare to explore a little.' He paused a second, turning directly to look at Lucie. 'And I knew you would appreciate it. Beauty deserves beauty.'

Lucie chose to ignore the much-appreciated compliment, putting it down to yet another of his flirtatious ways. 'I've never seen anywhere like it. I love the beach and always have done. I guess that comes from growing up in Brighton, but this is so far removed from the pebbles, pier and gluttonous seagulls that I am used to.'

'Well, if it's wildlife you want then come with me.' He held out his hand for her to take it. She noted the musculature of his arms, the thick hairs across his forearms and the corded bracelets that decorated his wrist as he did so. She took it gladly. 'I know there are stingray, blowfish and octopus in this area. I can't promise you those as we can't really dive deep enough without snorkels and masks but I can guarantee you some of the prettiest little fish you're ever likely to see. That beats a chip-hungry seagull, eh?'

'That sounds perfect, although I do have a bit of a soft spot for those gulls. Handsome birds. I used to love chucking bits of food to them down on the seafront. Mum and I used to do it all the time. My first mum, my real mum. Not that my foster mum isn't a real...' Lucie's words floundered like a fish out of water. Even after all this time, she still found it difficult to sometimes use what she felt to be the right words to describe the life she had led. Both women, Ruby and Tanya, had been mothers to her in their own unique ways. But Lucie would always house a vein of regret and upset about her life with Ruby. About what could have been. As she felt Connor's fingers wrap around hers and she marched her way deeper into the hypnotising sheet of the ocean alongside him, she couldn't help but feel a tinge of sadness about her birth mother and wonder just how it had all started to go so wrong.

Brighton, 2001

'So if I can get a babysitter, I'll see you down the Concorde 2 later then, yes?' Ruby leant across to the man sitting alongside her on the pebbled beach and wrapped her hand around the back of his neck, pulling his face towards her. Her lips parted and she allowed hers to find his, their tongues hungrily exploring each other's.

'Urgh,' said Lucie, sitting the other side of her mother from the man. 'That is horrible. Can you stop it? And I'm eight years old, I don't need a babysitter. I can look after myself thank you very much.' She returned her attention to the polystyrene tray of chips that she was wading into with her wooden chip fork.

The man and Ruby stopped kissing. The man reached around the back of Ruby and playfully slapped Lucie across the back of her head. Not enough to hurt but still sufficient to annoy. 'Oi, scamp, just shut it, will you? Eat your chips. We'll lock you in your room if you're not careful.'

Ruby turned to her daughter. 'Russell doesn't mean that, kid. I'll get one of the neighbours to look after you.'

Russell was her mother's newest boyfriend. If you could call him that. Lucie thought he looked like a scarecrow. His toast coloured hair was always sticking up everywhere, either in long curls piled on top of his head, a messy mop of a runway in the middle of a shaved head, or slicked down with so much gel that it was like a puddle of brown oil topping his features. His neck was tattooed, a large creepy skull and a flower decorating one side and his top lip housed a moustache that was pencil thin yet again slicked into place with the precision of a master craftsman. His overall look was that of an unkempt Dickensian villain. Not that a young Lucie saw that. She just saw someone who looked weird.

'You just watch me,' he teased, reaching across again to grab a chip. He succeeded before Lucie could grab them away.

'So what time are you going to pick me up?' asked Ruby. 'I'm looking forward to it. I've been wanting to go there since it opened.'

'Half seven. It's a fucking brilliant venue,' he swore, oblivious to Lucie's young presence. 'The turn there tonight is a young heavy rock band. I've heard their stuff. Fucking great tunes.'

The Concorde 2 had only opened the year before, right on the seafront in a building that had previously been an amusement arcade and before that a notorious bikers' café. A fact which Russell seemed to love. 'My old man used to go there when it was a café. The bikes would be lined up outside it like some fucking *Quadrophenia* poster. Cool as hell. Fucking crime when it became a slot machine joint. Thank Christ something good has been done with it again.'

'It was tea rooms back in the 1800s you know,' said Ruby. 'My friend Mandy told me.'

Russell neither knew nor cared. 'So are you up for some fun tonight then, Ruby. Me and the boys are getting a little something in.'

Ruby knew already from her two months with Russell that when he talked about his boys, a riotous evening was guaranteed if not always enjoyable. 'What do you mean, getting a little something in?'

'How naïve are you? A few bags of this.' He reached into the pocket of his denim jeans and pulled out a small bag of white powder. 'Coke.'

Ruby snapped and tried to grab the bag. 'Not in front of Lucie, Russ.'

Lucie looked across at the mention of her name. She saw the bag.

'She won't know what the fuck it is,' sneered Russ, his words cocksure.

He was right, she didn't. She watched though as Russell opened it, licked one of his fingers, dipped it inside and then rubbed some of the powder onto his gums. Ruby watched on, her face a weave of horror, intrigue and excitement.

'Try it,' said Russell. 'It's good stuff.'

'No, I can't, Russell, not here.' There was a hint of want despite her refusal.

'Come on.' He dipped his finger again and held it out for Ruby. Without even turning to see that Lucie was watching the entire thing, she grabbed his finger and put in in her mouth, rubbing the powder against her gums just as Russell had done seconds before.

'Is that sherbet?' asked Lucie.

Bad mothering gripped Ruby. 'No, it's…' A search for the right word. 'Medicine to make mummy's mouth feel better.'

Russell laughed, as did Ruby a little.

'Why, what's wrong with it?' asked Lucie. 'Have you got a bad tooth? Give it to the tooth fairy and she'll pay you.'

'Go and eat your chips and take a walk on the beach,' said Ruby, not sure how to reply. 'Go and see if you can find some nice pebbles for your room.'

'But I don't want to,' said Lucie.

'Do it now, Lucie. Don't argue with me. Now scram.'

Lucie stood up and wandered across the pebbles. She turned around to see Ruby and Russell kissing again, the bag of "sherbet" still in his hand. 'Gross,' said Lucie to herself as she watched the pair of them embrace. Kissing was horrible. Especially when one of the people looked like a scarecrow and the other one was her mother.

Lucie walked away from the pair of them towards the sea. The seagulls squawked as she made her way over the pebbles, her sandals slipping slightly on the surface. As she steadied herself, a chip tumbled from her tray and onto the beach. A hungry seagull spotted it immediately and swooped to devour it. Despite its fierce attack on the food, Lucie noticed how white its feathers were. As white as the powder in Russell's bag.

Lucie stared at her chip tray. About four or five chips remained. She had eaten enough. The seagulls could have the rest. She took hold of one of the chips and threw it into the air above her. A flurry of wings as the birds around her fought for the prize, the winner taking off before a mid-air feathery highwayman could come and steal it from him.

Every chip that she threw befell the same fate. Before she knew it, her tray was empty and yet a collection of hopeful birds marched around her, eyeing her next move. Their squawks increased; their displeasure on show. Lucie suddenly felt a little intimidated and watched as one of the birds flew towards her and tried to snatch the tray from her hands. She screamed and dropped it immediately onto the pebbles, turning to run back to Ruby and her boyfriend.

'Muuuuum, the birds are attacking me.'

But Ruby didn't seem to care. She had her own finger in the bag of powder and was busy locking lips with Russell again. She only stopped when Lucie sat down beside her and buried her head into Ruby's side. The gulls still circled and squawked around her.

It was the first time that Lucie had ever seen Ruby with drugs. That day on the beach on Brighton. Lucie had been scared and Ruby had been so "busy" with Russell that she hadn't seemed to care when her scared little daughter came running back to her. As if, she suddenly wasn't Ruby's priority anymore.

Russell may have only lasted another couple of months, Ruby's love of him cut down after having found him in bed with her friend, Mandy, but Ruby's love of the white powder in the little see-through bags seemed to grow and grow. With every boyfriend that she seemed to have after that, the ever present bag was like a third partner in the relationship. Lucie may not have understood exactly what it was, but she knew that it was bad and that it turned her mother into somebody who didn't seem to care about her any more. A rival for her mother's affections. And more and more often, the bag was the winner. Just like a chip in a gull's beak, Lucie started to feel her mother's love being snatched away.

Connor and Lucie were chest level in the water, their toes still scrunched into the sand beneath their feet. As they looked down into the beautifully translucent ripples, they could see a school of tiny blue fish darting around them. Jagged motions as they shot back and forth, causing a dance of colour and light beneath the surface. Small in size, but mighty in their glory. Connor still had his hand in Lucie's.

'They're gorgeous,' said Lucie, her eyes still looking downwards.

'As are you,' said Connor.

Lucie looked up, this time unable to shelf the compliment. Connor's green eyes stared deep into her and he brought his lips forward to find hers. There was a slight saltiness from the sea upon them. They felt good. Perfect in fact. Not all kisses between two people were as gross as a young Lucie had once felt.

Chapter 18

Now

Lucie was back at the cottage. She also felt that she was back at square one. If her life was a board game, then she was very much ready to throw the dice for the first time and see in what direction they took her. She'd had the snakes in abundance, the occasional ladder and now she was back at the beginning. Ready to make a fresh start and see where life took her. The board had been wiped clean and was now a fresh blank springboard to dive from.

Having journeyed back from Lancashire, the souvenirs of her life with Roger and Tanya packed away in her bags, she had dined with her mother and Terrance that evening before climbing into bed for an early night. She had been shattered and felt emotionally drained after heading to her former family home up north and also after the legal meeting. But as she lifted the ornate latch and opened the windows in her bedroom the next morning and stared down across the garden, she experienced a cocoon of contentment wrap around her. For a few short seconds, her seemingly cursed life seemed manageable and not so daunting.

She was alone at the cottage. Ruby had left a note on the kitchen table to say that she and Terrance were heading out for the day to look at more properties, that there was a fridge full of food she could raid for lunch and that her and Terrance would sort something out for tea. Lucie had to admit that it felt good to be looked after when she had read the handwritten note. Ruby had become a much more considerate person than Lucie had ever imagined possible. Who said worms couldn't turn?

Lucie could see Drew, the gardener, walking his way across the large expanse of green below her window. As if sensing her stare, he looked up, saw her and waved. A smile, bright and inviting, accompanied it. She waved back and watched as he disappeared down a narrow path on the other side of the garden. She guessed he was off to fix the well he had spoken to her about days before. As yet, she had not ventured to that side of the garden. Perhaps today was the day. She made a mental note to maybe head there later and see how the handsome Drew was getting on.

Lucie spent an hour or so unloading the clothes from her suitcase resting on the four poster bed and distributing the memories around her cottage room. The clothes would all need to be washed, having remained unworn for so long. She took them downstairs to the kitchen, located the washing machine and loaded them into it. Having started the machine, she made her way back upstairs. As she was heading up the stairs, the creek of the steps underneath her feet almost comforting in its vintage charm as she mounted each one, she spotted a square recess of wood on the ceiling. The loft hatch. A border of raised darker wooden, about an inch in width, encased it. The recessed hatch was held in place by a thick wooden peg, turned at ninety degrees to stop it from, Lucie assumed, falling. Temptation struck her. Within a few minutes, she had been back downstairs, collected a triangular metal ladder from the kitchen utility cupboard where her mother housed brooms, ironing board, a vacuum etc., and taken it back upstairs. A few seconds later, she was up it, turning the wooden peg and pushing against the flap. It arced open and rested at an angle against a beam in the darkness beyond the door.

Lucie placed her head through the hole and into the black. It was a while before her eyes became accustomed to the dark void she was staring into. She felt her way around the edge of the opening and located a light switch. A lightbulb in the middle of the attic space flickered into life and illuminated the area. It was busy in the extreme. Boxes piled high on top of each other stood at angles, Jenga-like as if the slightest movement could bring them crashing down, spilling whatever contents they held onto the boarded floor of the attic. Rolls of carpet formed a small pyramid in one of the far corners. Board games and jigsaws, playful remnants of days gone by, gathered dust in a heap and beyond them, a silver chest, old and battered, dominated the floor space. Alongside it, a tatty, faded blanket wrapped itself around objects as yet still hidden. Lucie found the entire scene one of invitation and climbed into the loft space, placing her feet gingerly on the floorboards to make sure that they were safe. They seemed to be as none of them creaked as she made her way across the attic.

A strand of cobweb swung, as if moved by an unknown breeze, in front of Lucie's face. She pushed it to one side, unafraid. Her mind was set on the chest, its silvery exterior cold to look at but yet hinting that it enveloped something that warranted investigation.

Reaching the chest, Lucie ran her fingers across the top of it. Black smudges of dust appeared on the tips of every finger. Whatever the chest contained, it evidently hadn't been opened for the longest time.

The chest wasn't locked, but the metal catch holding the lid to the base was scarred with age and peppered with dots of rust. Lucie tried to lift the catch upwards, giving her leverage to raise the lid. It wouldn't budge. She tried it again and a slight motion occurred, the catch stiff with lack of use. Lucie knew that her own strength would not be sufficient. Scanning around the attic space, she looked for something that might help the rusty catch burst into life. Alongside the board games and the jigsaws were a tower of books, both paperback and hardback. Without reason, she took in the titles on their spines. They ranged from historical information books through to classic novels from the likes of Daphne du Maurier and plays by Shakespeare. Lucie leant across and picked up a large hardback copy of one of the Shakespeare plays and blew the dust away from the cover, causing a cloud of dirty grey to roll its way into the air.

'I never did like Shakespeare,' she muttered to herself, as she raised the book and brought it down with a dull, yet hearty, thud onto the catch. It didn't budge. Lucie tried again, a succession of beats, as she attempted to release the catch using the book. After five or six attempts, the rusty catch sprang from its base, coming away from the chest. Lucie placed the book on the floor checking out the spine as she did so. 'Thank you, *Troilus and Cressida,*' she smiled. 'Good work.'

She opened the trunk. Whatever treasure she had been hoping to find inside, her sigh of disappointment expressed itself as she realised that hidden gold and gemstones or pirate pieces of eight were definitely not on the menu. The case contained bags and bags of papers, envelopes, receipts, books of scribbled notes and numbers. On an interest level, it was below zero, but Lucie found herself sifting through them nevertheless. A lot of them were handwritten, the numbers and letters faded with time, but she guessed they were business accounts. Rows of additions and multiplications immediately took her back to her maths lessons at school. It hadn't interested her then and it was faring little better now. Book after book she flicked through seemed to contain the same. Rows of numbers and dates and illegible scribbles of names. She guessed the names were companies. The numbers were large, running into tens of thousands suggesting that whatever the company was it had been a success dealing with many, many zeroes. For a moment, Lucie wondered if it was Terrance's company, but the fact that the trunk was covered in dust and the book keeping was not computerised suggested a company from days gone by. The only thing that was still clearly legible was the heading at the top of some of the handwritten sheets. "OPD Inc" alongside a telephone number and an address. There was no email or website listed again suggesting that the company was one from days gone by. The first thing that came into Lucie's head was that the O had to stand for *Oscar* and that the P would have been *Painting* perhaps. As for the D...*Decorating* maybe, or *Design*.

The thought of her mysterious Uncle Oscar made Lucie recall her mother's words that some of his paintings were still stored in the attic. She was surprised that Ruby hadn't already tried to sell them if they were worth what other people had already paid for them. Closing the lid of the trunk, she looked around to see where the paintings might be. She opened a few of the boxes, lifting the lids to peer inside. She found crockery, vinyl records, vases, light fittings, a cassette recorder and some old tapes, all sorts of ephemera, but none of the boxes seemed to contain any works of art.

Her eyes fell on the worn blanket wrapped around something that was lying alongside the case she had just delved into to find the business paperwork. Instinct told her that that was where her prize would be. Especially when she pulled the blanketed package out from alongside the trunk and lay it on the floor. Whatever was contained inside seemed to be tall and wide and thin. As she unwrapped the blanket, another roll of dust launched into the air and three pieces of artwork, wrapped back to back revealed themselves. Lucie felt a frisson of electricity and excitement run through her body. Oscar's paintings were a connection to her family. A talented branch that she never knew existed. To a life that had so far been unknown, a mystery, left to gather dust in the attic of a cottage that she had never been party to. Owned by a man who had drunk himself to death and cut short his own talent in a fatal joyride. A sadness clothed her at the thought of what could have been.

She laid the paintings side by side. The colours were still bright and blocky, not faded by years of secrecy. Lucie immediately sensed a connection to all three as she took in the colours. The slashes of blue reminding her of Brighton skies, the red, the pier lights that joyously twinkled in the night air, the yellow, the intense force of the warming sun overhead. Every shade a mental scrapbook of her years growing up. The three paintings didn't seem to be of anything in particular. There was no obvious subject matter but every stroke the artist had placed seemed to mean something. Squares ran into stripes, ran into dots, ran into swirls. There was a fluidity to the paintings that to Lucie showed a free spirit, a joy for the brush and a euphoria for the art. The colours danced across the canvas, their lack of choreography working to their own unique favour. The paint laid thick to create both texture and drama. Lucie ran her hands across the artwork, allowing the peaks and dips of paint to guide her fingers.

Lucie was smiling yet inwardly berating the fact that she had never been able to meet Uncle Oscar. She had a sneaking suspicion that she and him would have gotten on. If his artwork was a reflection of the man that he was, then she knew she would have loved him. If only he had given her the chance. Why was it that sometimes the most creative people were the most tortured?

Grabbing the blanket again, Lucie began to wrap the pieces of artwork back up. She placed two of them back to back and was about to add the third when her attention was drawn to the small signature in the bottom corner of one of the paintings. She narrowed her eyes to focus on it. As with most signatures, it was difficult to read, the letters forming little more than a scrawl. She checked back on the other two paintings and both contained the same signature. She tried to fathom the letters. An S was clearly visible, as was what looked like an A. What she couldn't see was an O. An O for Oscar. In fact, if she wasn't mistaken, the S appeared to be the largest of the letters, a capital. She tried to read it again. Whatever it said, Lucie couldn't define. But she knew that it didn't seem to say Oscar. And if he didn't paint them, then who did? Lucie longed to know, the inquisitive side of her nature rushing to the surface.

A creak sounded. Lucie turned her head to face the sound. Nothing. She shifted from foot to foot, her heart suddenly quickening. The air was silent, her own heartbeat the only sound apparent. She turned back to face the paintings and began to wrap the final one in the same blanket as the others. As she did so, a loud crack filled the air behind her as the loft door slammed back into place. At the same time, the lightbulb overhead flickered to nothingness plunging the space into pitch darkness. For a second, all was still. Another creak whispered in the air, from where Lucie wasn't sure.

The darkness wrapped its talons around her, rooting her to the spot. Her head told her to move. To find her way over to the light switch and turn it back on. But something stopped her. A fear. Of the darkness. Of the unknown. Of entrapment. Lucie's body began to shake as she closed her eyes, adding to the darkness. If she kept them closed, then she wouldn't have to face the darkness beyond. She called out, a solitary sound of appeal. Nothing came back. She called again, this time louder and soaked with panic.

The boards beneath her feet suddenly felt colder, as if from stone. She placed her hands to the floor and involuntarily let her nails scratch along the surface, the noise they made bringing no comfort but somehow necessary to try and stem the onslaught of panic that threatened to engulf her.

The musty attic air that filled her nostrils appeared stronger, ripping at her senses as it did so. Heat swallowed her. Lucie forced herself to move. To try and free herself from the nightmare that crept within her. As she stood up, another strand of cobweb brushed against her face. This time she was afraid. Very afraid. The feel of hands flitting across her face, pulling at her in the darkness. Invading towards her. The attic was no more. She was back in Peru. Back in the prison. Back in the dark.

Lucie let out a loud scream. The loudest she could.

Chapter 19

Peru, 2012

Lucie had never known a darkness like it. Not that it was any darker than any other. It was just what it signified. As the cell door closed and she lay on the hardness of her bed, praying that sleep would come but knowing that its journey to her would be as long and as fraught as ever, she let silence surround her, the sound of her own fear pounding deep within her, deafening to her and her alone. The darkness was her captor. The darkness was her enemy. The darkness was a noose that slowly looped itself around her neck and choked any last remnant of hope that dared to remain inside her. It also brought danger. A danger that she couldn't control. One that had to remain unspoken if she knew what was good for her.

The education of life in prison was one that Lucie had had to learn quickly. Cliques were formed, rules were set and it clear who was to be obeyed. For Lucie, this meant pretty much everybody. The new girl behind bars was easy prey at first, Lucie's innocence clear to see to her fellow inmates even if the law had thought otherwise. Her fair skin, tanned by the Peruvian sun but still lighter than most of her fellow inmates made her stand out. And as her sentence went from days to weeks and her tan disappeared, she became more of an anomaly. The women around her seemed to notice her more. Eyes would find hers across the tables as she tried to force down another plate of prison food or as she worked in the prison yard. The brush of an unwanted hand against her skin as she sat outside, minding her own business, trying to avoid eye contact with anyone around her. Trying to free her thoughts to take her to a place outside the prison walls. For a moment, there would be escape, which would then evaporate into her current hell as another inmate brought her back to reality. Lucie was different and that made her vulnerable. Showers were the worst. Communal and squalid. And often dangerous. As dangerous as the nights, but at least she could see her enemy then. When the darkness came, it was a different matter.

The sound of the cell doors slamming into place was the dreaded alarm that she hated. A signal that darkness was to come and that the hours before dawn were ready to play. As quiet descended upon the prison, the sound of her own panic and horror would rocket. She had no idea when it would come but often it did. In fact, fear allowed often to become many. The sound of her cellmate, a Peruvian woman that Lucie never cared to befriend, creeping out of her bed, the bunk above Lucie's, and the soft thud as her feet landed on the cell floor. The shadow in the dark, a shape creeping towards her like a demon in the night. Lucie knew what was about to happen. She always did, the horror of it playing in her mind every time, like a hateful tune that would never end, never be silenced. Her instinct to fight slowly being ripped away from her each and every time.

Prison education had taught her not to fight. Not to scream, not to complain. She had done that before. And what had it gained? Nothing but unpopularity. She'd seen her fellow inmates whispering in corners, staring at her. She didn't need to understand their language, she could tell what they were saying. She was someone who complained. Who did not play the game of prison life as they thought it should be played. And what started as defiance became chipped away with every menacing glance or threatening whisper.

So Lucie caved in...let it happen. And let it happen within her very own cell. A place from where, after the key was turned, there was no escape. That first time in the darkness was the worst. The soft thud of feet, the advance of shadow and then the hand across the mouth, holding her in place, silencing her scream. Lucie's automatic reaction to grab the hand to try and rip it away kicking in at first, her want for survival causing her to try and rip the fingers from around her face. But as the grip grew stronger and the fingers of her cellmate picked against her face, their frenzied moments like deadly cobwebs of fear against her face, Lucie could feel her fight disappearing.

A knee either side of her body as she lay there, knowing that fight was futile, that there was no point if she wished to survive life inside. The hand crawling down her body, over her breasts and down to her trousers, tugging at the fabric and pulling it down to expose the desired destination. The roughness of the fingers as they found their treasure. Lucie's tears would come, the evidence of her failure to battle, running down her face to meet the hand placed across her mouth. As her cellmate continued to use Lucie's body for her own uninvited pleasure, Lucie would try and think of anything she could to remove herself from the situation. With time, it became easier, but that first night of failure in the darkness of her cell was a horrific experience that Lucie would never forget. She would always bear the mental scar. Not just from the roughness of the action, but from the fact that she gave up, let another person win. Something she felt she had been doing all of her life.

As her cellmate moved back to her own bed, Lucie refused to make a sound. She wanted to scream, she wanted to shout, to tell the world of the injustice and hurt that had been caused, but she didn't. That wasn't wise. Silence was king. She simply turned over in bed and lay on her side, letting one of her arms dangle over the side of the bed. Her skin came into contact with the cold, rough metal of the bed frame. She could feel her scream mounting. Despair needing to escape. She had to halt it.

Lucie rubbed her wrist against the frame. Faster and faster until the action burned, the heat taking her away from her want to scream. She must have rubbed it for minutes, the searing heat from her wrist burning. She clenched her teeth and let more tears run down her face. But no noise came. Sleep eventually took her. She didn't see it advancing. You saw nothing in the darkness.

The next morning was when she saw the bloody welt, the streak of red, sore, exposed flesh that decorated her wrist. Like a badge of dishonour. In time, it would fade, but a scar would always remain. Another one to sit alongside the mental one of her own failure.

A scar from life in the darkness.

Chapter 20

Now

The light coming in from the attic hatch as the door swung open softly illuminating the interior of the loft was as welcome as the most beautiful sunrise. And the face that appeared through the hatch space and stared into the darkness was Messiah-like in its coming as far as Lucie was concerned. The dark took away some of the evil, the feeling of being trapped and the curse of being entombed in a place that Lucie didn't want to be. The light. The friendly smile. They signified freedom.

'Jesus, are you okay, Lucie? I heard you screaming from downstairs and thought I had better see what was going on. I'd only come in for a glass of water. What are you doing up here?' It was Drew. His face innocent and caring. 'Do you need a hand?'

He switched on the light in the attic and raised himself up onto the boards lining the space. Lucie was still rooted to the spot, tears running down her face, a look of sheer panic still etched upon her face. It faded a touch with Drew's approach. 'God, you look awful,' he said. 'What happened?'

He reached out to hug her before allowing her to answer. His touch felt comforting, the strength of his body against hers and his arms around her transporting Lucie away from her fears.

'I don't know. I was up here rooting around looking at things, seeing what was up here and then all of a sudden, the light went out and the hatch slammed shut leaving me in darkness. I felt so trapped. It was horrible. I guess that's when I screamed. And kept on screaming.'

'It's an old cottage. The electrics probably aren't what they used to be and all sorts of gusts can run through a place like this. It may have blown shut. The force of it shutting must have caused the catch to turn back on itself. Good job I heard you as you could have been up here for hours on end.'

'That's what I was afraid of,' said Lucie, her words shivering with what could have been.

'Let's get you down from here. Come on...' Drew took her hand and led her towards the hatch and down the ladder. She wobbled slightly as she descended, causing Drew to steady her with his hands. His touch was appreciated. 'I'll make you a cup of tea and you can tell me what you found up there.' He reached up, locked the hatch into place and pushed the ladder back together, taking it back downstairs alongside Lucie.

The two of them sat together at the kitchen table, tea in hand. The warmth of the drink was welcome despite the heat of the sunshine outside. Lucie still felt chilled from her experience in the loft.

'So what did you find?' asked Drew. 'Any skeletons or dead bodies like they do in the movies?'

Maybe not the most tactful of things to say given Lucie's fear but Drew's childlike and charming nature could see him forgiven for anything. 'No, just a load of business papers, some household stuff and what might or might not be a few of my Uncle Oscar's paintings. They were really cool. I should bring them down really,' said Lucie.

'I don't think you should be going back up there for a while. If you want anything, I can fetch it for you. I'm not as scared of the dark as you are.' Drew's words were totally caring and not at all bragging.

'They can stay there for now, but if I do want to take a look at them again then, I'll let you know. Apparently, his work sold for a lot of money. At least that's what mum told me.'

'So he was a famous artist then?' enquired Drew. 'Cool.'

'Didn't you know?' asked Lucie, assuming that Oscar would have been somewhat of a local celebrity.

'No, not a clue. But then, it's not the kind of thing that would have interested a young lad like me. I would have been more interested watching him paint his shed or a fence panel than some kind of fancy art thing. I've always been more of the outdoorsy type. I hated art at school. I got bored easily and painting was way too dull. I was happier doing the sporty stuff or messing around in the school garden. I've always loved it.'

'That reminds me,' remarked Lucie, 'when you have a free few days from here, if you like, I may have a job for you. It's at the other end of the country but it's one that's close to my heart. It's at my foster parents' house. They died recently and their garden needs an overhaul as I'm selling their house. I'd rather trust you with it than somebody anonymous.' Lucie could see Drew's face swing from delight to dismay as she went from garden design to recent death.

'I'm so sorry to hear that,' he said, his words a little unsure given the subject matter. 'But I'd love to help.' He paused for a moment, again uncertain if he should go on. He chose to continue. 'Foster parents? I thought Mrs Palmer was your mum.'

It felt odd to hear Ruby referred to as Mrs Palmer, the name causing a curling of Lucie's lips as she considered it. 'Ruby is my real mum, but things haven't always been so easy. This is the first time in a long while that the two of us have actually been able to talk to each other or even be in the same house. Ruby has had the most complicated life and as a result, so have I.'

'I didn't mean to pry,' replied Drew, placing his now-empty mug on the table and shuffling his feet as if impatient to move away, worried he'd overstepped the mark.

'Oh, you're not. Not at all. In fact, it feels good to talk to someone my own age about it all. It's been a strange few days. In fact Drew, I've had the strangest few years.' She hesitated. 'Maybe even the strangest of lives.'

Lucie started her story and Drew listened intently as she unravelled her tale so far. Once she started, her story was a snowball that kept gathering momentum. She told him about having to leave her life with Ruby and the flat in Brighton to go and live with Roger and Tanya in Lancashire and then about her trip to Peru and the subsequent consequences of her hideous life in prison. Drew sat agog, taking in her words as they unravelled. It was only when it was clear that she had finished that he dared to speak.

'Bloody hell. You've had a life and a half, haven't you? You look so innocent.'

'I am innocent.' Her words were a little harsher than need be, a fact that she was quick to try and rectify. 'I'm sorry Drew; I know exactly what you mean.'

'I didn't mean that you were guilty. I can't imagine someone as nice as you being involved in anything horrible like that. Not looking at you right now.' Drew stuttered his words, floundering a little at having to watch his every syllable for fear of misinterpretation.

Lucie reiterated her belief in him. 'No, I know that. I know what you meant. It's just that I am determined to prove to people that I was innocent. That I am. I need to bring the person or people who were behind it to justice. How I do that though, I don't know.'

Drew stared blankly at her.

'Wouldn't that mean going back to Peru? Having to face all of that again? Are you sure you want to? Or that you're strong enough. You didn't seem very strong when I found you upstairs. You were so spooked out in the loft. You were crying your eyes out.'

Drew reached across the table and touched Lucie's cheek. 'It was horrible to see you so upset.' The action and his words were caring and immediately reminded her of that moment when Connor had first touched her face back at Paradise Cove. But with Drew, it seemed different. He was simply looking out for her as a friend, as someone who had confided in him even though it was only their second meeting.

'I was crying because the darkness took me back to being inside the prison in Peru. Back to the fears that I had to face. Back to the horrors of being trapped with no escape.'

Drew didn't know what to say and merely smiled. The action was enough for Lucie. 'Thanks, Drew,' she said.

'For what?' he asked.

'For listening. I haven't really talked about my experiences with anybody for the longest time, and it's really good to speak to someone who doesn't have any connection with anybody in the story really. To talk to someone who doesn't really have to care.'

'But I do care, Lucie.' He kept smiling.

'I know you do.' Lucie drained her own mug and placed it on the table. 'Right, I'll tell you what, if you wouldn't mind, I've changed my mind. Would you mind fetching those paintings out of the loft for me? They're wrapped in a blanket. And they're only gathering dust up there. I'd like to find out a little more about Uncle Oscar and see if they were his. If he did paint them, I'd like to see if they've been documented at all. Such a shame he's dead. I would have loved to have talked to him. I think we would have been good pals.'

'Well, you could always ask the old woman who lived here with him,' said Drew, as he opened the cupboard door to collect the ladder.

'What?' Lucie raised her eyebrows with shock. 'You mean she's still alive?'

'Yes, I'm sure she is. She's knocking on a bit but I'm sure she lives in a care home just outside the village. She's been there for a while, long before your Uncle Oscar died. I've not heard anyone say that she's died and word gets around in a small village like this. I'm sure I would have heard somebody mention the old lady from the cottage dying.' Lucie watched, her mind ablaze, as Drew grabbed the ladder and disappeared upstairs. 'I'll bring you the paintings. Be right back.'

'Thanks,' said Lucie absently, her mind deep in thought. She was wondering if the old lady from the cottage would be up for a visit. Because Lucie loved the idea of paying her one.

Chapter 21

Now

Finding the care home was easy. There weren't many near to the village and a Google search and a few phone calls meant that Lucie was able to narrow it down to one in particular, Robson Lodge, about thirty minutes in a cab from the cottage.

The woman behind the reception counter greeted her with a smile as she approached.

'Hello, can I help you?'

'Hi there, my name is Lucie Palmer, I phoned about an hour ago and spoke to someone about one of your residents, a lady called Sarah Powell. I understand she used to live in a cottage with my Uncle Oscar. She may have been his wife, so she may have been my aunty.' It was more information than the lady behind the counter either needed or wanted.

She was quick to interrupt. 'Oh yes, you spoke to Debbie, one of the other receptionists here. She said you were coming. Sarah doesn't get a lot of visitors, in fact I can't remember the last time she had one. She seems to have been here the longest time. Poor woman. Life can be so cruel. But she is in the best place, given her condition.'

'Can I see her?' Lucie's request was simple.

'Yes, of course. But have you visited somebody in a home like this before?'

'No, I haven't.'

'Sarah is a very old lady, in her late eighties now and she is away with the fairies most of the time. She is what you would refer to as quirky and eccentric and very dotty. She's adorable but if you are expecting her to make sense, then I would say brace yourself.'

'She has dementia?' asked Lucie.

'Dementia takes many forms and Sarah is lucky in the fact that she is still able to converse and talk and make conversation. It's just that the conversation doesn't always make sense. You'll see what I mean. And she can get agitated sometimes. She's in room 29, one flight up, the stairs are over there.' She pointed to a flight of carpeted steps in the far corner of the reception. 'There's a buzzer in the room if you need help with anything. Just press it and somebody will come as quickly as possible.'

'Thank you.' Lucie experienced an air of trepidation as she mounted the steps, located room 29 and knocked on the door. No answer came. It occurred to her that there wouldn't be. She pushed the door open and went inside.

A grey haired lady sat in an armchair staring out of the room's main window. The room was large and well decorated, a bed, bedside table and two large armchairs dominating the space, an open door off one wall revealed a bathroom on the other side. The lady's hair was pulled back into a bun on the back of her head, a neatness about it that gave her a class and elegance. Her cardigan, neatly buttoned into place over a white blouse across her tiny frame and a string of pearls around her neck added to the elegance. Both hands were decorated with rings, a selection of impressive gemstones on view.

The woman's eyes were closed, despite her seemingly taking in the vista outside the window. Lucie sat down opposite her on the other armchair and wondered if she should wake her. Her decision was made when the woman opened her eyes, a fluttering of eyeshadow decorating them, and stared directly at her.

'Hello, you're a new nurse. Who are you? What do you want?'

Lucie immediately liked Sarah. She was direct and was still able to hold court despite her advancing years and condition. It seemed that she was immediately in charge. Lucie was struck by the fact that if she had indeed been Uncle Oscar's wife, then she imagined that he must have strayed well into the category of toy boy by a good twenty years.

'Hello Sarah, my name is Lucie Palmer. It's nice to meet you.' Lucie could feel the gaze of the old woman roaming across her as Sarah obviously tried to work out her opinions on the stranger in the room. 'I think you lived at the cottage that my mother, Ruby Palmer, now lives at. I thought I would come and introduce myself as I am staying there too. It's a beautiful place.'

Sarah remained silent, her eyes still travelling across Lucie. It was only when she had decided that she thought the visitor was worth talking to that she answered back.

'Many years at the cottage. Happy times. Who are you?' The old lady's hands shook as she spoke, the light from outside catching in her jewellery causing them to sparkle. Lucie guessed they were no costume pieces.

Lucie repeated who she was. 'You lived there with my Uncle Oscar.'

'Uncle Oliver? What a good boy, what a nice man.'

'No, Uncle Oscar,' said Lucie, correcting her mistake. 'You were related to him I assume?'

'He was my son, mother's pride and joy. Always such a happy child.' Her voice was singsong and playful in its notes. She smiled, revealing a set of teeth, dullish white in colour but clearly still her own.

That would explain the age gap, mused Lucie. So much for the toy boy theory.

'Oscar left the house to my mum, Ruby, when he sadly died. I found some artwork in the attic which I think he might have painted. He was very good.'

'Loved to paint. Loved so much. We were happy. He was a happy boy. He was a silly boy.' Sarah shook her head as she reflected on her son. 'Loved his garden. Pretty flowers. Pretty ladies. Horrid ladies. Lovely garden.' She stared away from Sarah and back out at the garden through the window of her care home room.

The lady on the reception was right. Sarah liked to talk, it appeared, but it was clear that not a lot of it, if any, made sense. Her words were rambling at best.

Lucie tried to continue the conversation. 'It's a lovely garden at the cottage. The gardener there is a new one, a young man called Drew who has been taught by your gardener back in the day. It looks so beautiful. I can take some photos for you if you like and bring them in.'

Sarah remained silent, her eyes alert and taking in what lay beyond the window. For a moment, nothing was said between the two women, both deep in contemplation. Lucie not knowing quite what to say, Sarah in a world of her own. A place that only she could visit.

It was Sarah who ended the silence. 'Such a wonderful garden. The well. The flowers. The trees. Such a joy. I'd like to see it again. See what I built. What we built up. What Oliver did with it?'

Lucie guessed she was talking about the garden at the cottage and that Oliver was the gardener that Drew had spoken so highly of. Sarah's words were for once strung together in a sentence that was far from random and almost incomprehensible. 'Maybe I can take you there?' she offered. 'Are you allowed release from here?'

'It's not a prison,' snapped Sarah. 'I don't need to be released.' Lucie realised her mistake. Some words would always trespass into her vocabulary.

She continued to stare across at Lucie. 'Do you like my diamonds?' she flashed her rings, fluttering her fingers like the wings of a hummingbird, as fast as old bones would allow. 'All mine, all mine, never for anyone else. Never for the likes of the others. Not for you, dear. I see you looking at them. Not for you. I like you. You seem nice.' Sarah's lucidity seemed to have disappeared as quickly as it came. 'Time to go now, time to go.'

Sarah snapped her head away from Lucie as if to prove her point. If she wasn't looking at Lucie, then she obviously had no interest in speaking to her any longer.

'Thank you for seeing me, Sarah. It was nice to meet you,' offered Lucie, standing up from the comfort of the armchair. It was clear that her audience with Sarah, for now, was at an end.

As she moved to the door of the room, Sarah's voice burst forth. 'I like you, Lucie Palmer. Come again. And we can talk about Oliver.'

A surge of warmth burst within Lucie's core. Sarah being Oscar's mother, if that was the case, meant that she was her grandmother and just the fact that she had said her name and admitted that she liked her, hit a place in her heart that had never been touched before. She liked Sarah too. A lot. Even if she did want to talk about Oliver, the gardener. Next time, she would bring some photos of Uncle Oscar's paintings and they could discuss him. Lucie was keen to learn as much about her talented uncle as possible.

'See you again, Sarah.' She stood by the door waiting for an answer. None came as the old lady continued to stare out of the window, having returned into her private existence. 'Bye,' whispered Lucie and vacated the room.

She was walking towards the stairs when a woman came towards her. She was in her late forties Lucie guessed and of a short, squat figure. Rotund yet not fat. Her hair was tied back behind her head and her cheeks housed a ruddiness that suggested a constant breathlessness. Cosy, homely and immediately friendly. She held out her hand for Lucie to take.

'Hello, you must be Lucie. I'm Debbie, we spoke on the phone. I said it would be okay for you to visit as you're living at the cottage. How was Sarah? She doesn't talk a lot of sense I'm afraid. Was she okay with you? She can sometimes be a bit off and bloody-minded.'

Lucie's smile said it all. 'It was wonderful to meet her. And I think she made a lot of sense. Not offish at all. We had a terrific conversation. She's quite a woman.'

As Lucie departed Robson Lodge and phoned a cab, she said to herself, 'Quite a woman indeed, why wouldn't she be, she's my grandmother after all.' She was finally gaining another piece of the jigsaw to make the family that a young lonely Lucie had so often craved.

Chapter 22

Peru, summer 2012

The iciness of the drink as it slipped down her throat plus the potency of the alcohol it contained was a heady and dazzling mix to Lucie. And a much needed one too.

'What did you say was in this, again?' asked Lucie, running her hand through her hair. It was moist from the sweat of being twirled around to the beats of the traditional Peruvian sounds scoring the air.

'No idea,' said Connor, downing his own similar drink at the same time. 'I just thought you'd like the colour as it reminded me of the cocktails at Bar Dynasty.' It was a vibrant pink, more pink than any cocktail Lucie had ever served, and looked like something that would be dished out at a five-year-old girl's birthday party. But this was no children's party. Connor and Lucie were enjoying the excitement and colourful delights of the annual Paradise Cove street festival. Held at the height of summer, it was a riot of celebration as every road, avenue and alleyway around Paradise Cove was cordoned off to hold a 24-hour street party. And Connor had made sure that he and Lucie were off the Bar Dynasty rota for the day allowing them both to fully immerse themselves in the fiesta.

'It's bloody glorious,' said Lucie, waving her hands in the air as she finished her drink and holding the empty glass aloft. 'More maestro, please!' she cried out to no one in particular.

It was past midnight and Connor and Lucie had been dancing in the streets ever since the air had become saturated with music a good few hours earlier. The day had started mid-afternoon with a parade, a succession of flower-covered floats and people wearing tiny flesh-flashing outfits or an oversized papier-mâché head of various animals or cartoon-like morochucos, the cowboys of the plains of the Peruvian Andes. The effect was sparkling with ticker tape raining down on the revellers – both those partaking and those who merely chose to watch the parade. The parade finished at Paradise

Cove itself, on the beach where every corner seemed to be filled with DJs playing hypnotic Latin beats, pop-up bars offering a variety of rainbow concoctions and at least half a dozen specially erected dancefloors where couples were demonstrating Marinera, a traditional Peruvian dance. It showcased the courtship of two would-be lovers and was full of romance and grace, the couple using handkerchiefs as props to accentuate their loving intentions. Clarinets, drums, bugles and guitars accompanied the dancers.

Lucie had never seen anything like it in her life and was entranced by their movements from the moment she saw it. The moving of the two bodies together, almost becoming one, was a truly magnificent spectacle. One that she loved watching and she attempted to soak up every move. It was her attempt to replicate the romance of the Marinera, waving a napkin in the air as a pretend handkerchief whilst flinging her sarong around and gyrating her body against Connor's that had caused her body to heat up and require yet another icy burst of drink.

'This is an amazing festival. I love it. Can we do this every day?' asked Lucie, her voice a little slurred from the endless hours of drinking.

'I don't think my poor feet could take it,' laughed Connor. 'You've had me dancing for hours. And yet somehow, I can't seem to stop. You must be the perfect partner.'

'I think the drinks have had something to do with it,' said Lucie. 'Thank you a million times over for not making me work today. I wouldn't have missed this for the world. I hope Kara and Tina don't mind.'

'They'll be having a ball too. The bar is situated right in the heart of the celebration. They won't have stopped all day but it's an amazing vibe. But I wanted you to be a real part of it and not just see it from behind the bar. You can guarantee that Billy and Logan will be giving them a blow by blow account of what's been going on, including what we've been up to.'

'Which is what, exactly?' questioned Lucie, again her words running together as one.

'Dancing, laughing, drinking, having the best time together. And this of course...' He pulled Lucie towards him and kissed her fully on the lips. She allowed her mouth to explore his. As they pushed together, she could feel his excitement pressing against her. Since their first kiss together when they had visited the secluded beach, the two of them had often let their lips find each other, but it had never gone beyond that. Connor had never pushed it and Lucie had never sought it out. The timing had never been right. But something about today, the heat of the carnival, the drama of the air and the celebration on everybody's face made Lucie feel that perhaps the time was right. She moved her hand down his body and placed it on his erection. Connor moved his head back from hers, their lips parting, and stared her directly in the eyes. His eyes, wide and inviting, looked deep into her soul, as if reading her mind. She smiled in confirmation.

Connor took Lucie by the hand and led her into one of the small alleyways leading off the main streets of Paradise Cove. It was dark but enough light still came from overhead, the fireworks sporadically lighting up the sky and the light from nearby bars and restaurants in neighbouring streets to allow the couple to see where they were going.

Within moments, they were both wrapped in each other's arms, mouths together, in a secluded doorway towards the back of the alleyway. As the sound of the music from the carnival spread itself across the air and across Lucie's heightened senses, Connor ripped the sarong from Lucie's body in a fit of passion and the couple made love. It was Lucie's first time and despite the pain that inevitably occurred with her passage into womanhood, Connor was gentle and loving and took her to places she had never been before. When it was over, there was no regret, just a feeling of celebration. For Lucie, the timing was right. And from the smile on Connor's face, it appeared that for him it was too.

'Are you okay?' he asked, as they walked back towards the beach and the main carnival, her sarong wrapped back around her. 'I didn't intend that to happen in a backstreet but the timing just seemed…'

'…to be perfect.' She completed his sentence. 'It was amazing. I hope I was okay for you.'

'You were incredible,' he said, pulling her towards him again and wrapping his grip around her. For a moment, they just held each other in silence, not even moving.

'I love you,' whispered Lucie, her head buried in his chest. It didn't matter if he had heard or not. That wasn't the purpose. Connor squeezed her tighter in his arms.

'Shall we go get a drink?' said Connor. 'Now we have another thing to toast…'

As he unwrapped himself from her, Lucie felt her legs buckle under her and she stumbled downwards. Connor caught her. 'Whoa, somebody is a little drunk I think.' Lucie didn't know if it was the post-sexual euphoria fatiguing her or indeed the cocktails she'd been drinking, but either way, a feeling of fragility took over.

'I guess I'm tired,' she said, not meaning for the words to vocalise.

'Then I have an idea,' said Connor. 'Why don't you try some of this?' He reached into his pocket and pulled out a small clear bag filled with white powder. 'This is the only thing keeping me going tonight,' he laughed. 'Especially with your dancing skills. I'm not sure I'd keep up with you without the odd line. As if to demonstrate, he pulled out a key, dipped it into the bag and then snorted a mound of the powder off the end of it.

'C'mon you should try it. Everyone does.'

She knew that. Better than anyone.

'I'm all right,' she smiled, trying to ignore what Connor had just done. 'Let's go get a drink instead. Maybe some water will sober me up.'

She watched as Connor placed the bag back into his pocket, sniffed loudly, running his fingers across his nose and then took her hand in his. She wouldn't let the little bag of white ruin the moment. Not this one. Not such a special one. Hadn't it ruined enough in her life, already?

Chapter 23

Now

'It's not possible. The woman is quite clearly barking mad, Lucie,' said Ruby, stubbing her cigarette out into the ashtray. 'I think I'd know if my own mother was shacked up in a looney bin just down the road.' She lit up another cigarette whilst the one in the ashtray still gave off a curl of smoke. Terrance, who was sitting alongside her, did the same.

Lucie had come out with her mother and Terrance to a pub in the village near the cottage. She had been keen to tell her about her meeting with Sarah and what she had discovered. She had not expected Ruby to pooh-pooh it quite so brutally.

'Lucie, do you not think that if my mother, your grandmother, was living nearby that I would have told you. My mother is dead and has been for years. You know that. Like most of my family, she disowned me. You also know that the woman that you spoke to at the care home was a few sandwiches short of a picnic hamper and that means that she doesn't know her own name half the time let alone what relation she is to you. She was probably telling her next visitor that she's related to the President of the United States.'

'But a lot of what she said made sense. She knew about Uncle Oscar. Even if she did keep getting his name wrong. But she's eighty odd. And she remembered about the gardener that used to work at the cottage before Drew. The staff at Robson Lodge said that she has moments of lucidity when she is fully aware of what she is talking about.'

'There, you've said it yourself, child,' said Terrance, his tone rich with sneer, 'she couldn't even get her own son's name right, if that's what he was.'

'So what was she doing living with your brother, then?' Lucie aimed her question at Ruby.

'I haven't got a bloody clue. Maybe illusive brother Oscar had a thing for older women. Some men do, you know? Some women like younger men and some men like women a third of their own age.' Her tone was jovial and unnecessarily dismissive. 'My mother is dead, okay? All I know is that if I knew where my mother was buried or cremated or whatever she decided to have done in the end, then I would take you there right now and show you. But I don't, so I can't. Now will you kindly drop this nonsense?'

Lucie knew when there was no point in continuing.

'Terrance, will you run inside and get us both a drink please. I'll have a vodka tonic and Lucie will have...' Ruby left the sentence hanging.

'The same,' said Lucie, as she watched Terrance flick his unfinished cigarette into the air and march into the pub.

'There's an ashtray there,' said Lucie, already longing to be back at the cottage and alone in her room on her bed. For the first time since her return to the UK, her mother was annoying her, and the fact annoyed her even more.

'Just leave him be. Terrance is a good man, I've told you. He looks after me, makes me happy.'

Lucie nodded with a shrug, displaying her happiness layered with a lack of care.

'So what else have you been up to lately?' asked Ruby, 'apart from discovering long lost relatives that don't exist that is.'

'I was trapped in the loft space. That freaked me out.' A chill crept over her at the recollection.

'How the hell did you manage that, silly girl.' Was it Lucie's imagination or was everything that was coming out of her mother's mouth a touch derisory tonight?' Lucie decided that maybe she was just being a little too overly touchy.

'The winds in the house must have blown the door back on itself and the catch managed to turn somehow. If it hadn't have been for Drew, I'd still be there now. It was just horrible being plunged into darkness.'

'There is a light up there you know.'

'That went off too. I swear I'm cursed. The mirror, then the lift, then the roof space. It just took me back to being inside in Peru. Feeling so helpless and not being able to fight back.'

'If you were cursed, then we wouldn't have been able to find each other again, would we? The cottage is old, it has draughts. It was just unfortunate that the catch took hold. I should get it changed and get one of those swanky ladders put in. The retractable ones that glide effortlessly down. I'll get Terrance to sort one out. I'll need to get back up there to clear out all the tut at some point. I saw there was a whole heap of crap up there when I went up there to fetch the mirror. Not that I needed to have bothered in the end, eh? Maybe when it's clear, we could think about converting the loft space into something a little more usable. A games room or a separate room with en suite. I'd say a granny annex but seeing as there isn't one, a grandma that is, that would be useless.' Ruby smiled, pleased with her wordplay. 'Anyway, what were you up there for?'

'I was curious about the paintings you said were up there. Uncle Oscar's. I've bought them down now. I thought they were fabulous.'

'We should sell them, pocket the cash. If people want to pay good money for that shit then let them. How on earth can you like them? It was like a toddler had painted them.'

'I thought they showed a really creative edge. I loved them, whoever painted them. We can't all have the same taste, can we?' Just to prove her point, Terrance returned to the table, three drinks in his hands. Ruby moved a menu on the table in front of them and he placed them down. Lucie was grateful that she hadn't been passed down the family genes that made you fall for the same type of men as her mother. Terrance had *thug* written through him.

'I suppose not.'

'There were loads of business things up there as well, invoices and stuff for a company called, if I remember correctly, OPD Inc. I tried googling it but nothing came up. I was wondering if it had something to do with Oscar Palmer. I googled him too, but nothing. There was a lot of money going back and forth with the company and that could have definitely been for sales of his paintings.'

'Well, they're no use to us now, are they? They'll make for a cracking set of kindling for the living room fire come winter time.'

'Isn't kindling wood?' corrected Lucie. 'Not paper.'

'Who cares as long as it starts the fire and keeps us warm in the depths of winter.'

'But all of that paperwork is somebody's history. Uncle Oscar's. Maybe we shouldn't burn it.'

'Who cares about that? It's his history, not mine,' said Ruby. She picked the menu back up off the table and perused it accordingly. 'Now, who fancies a dessert?'

History. Or lack of it. That was rapidly becoming apparent to Lucie in her reconnection with her mother. No parents, no grandparents. Ruby didn't seem to have any history of her own, which meant that Lucie didn't either. But whereas her mother seemed to thrive on it, she herself hated the fact.

Chapter 24

Now

Lucie was sitting in the garden at the cottage. Her mood had been one of distinct confusion ever since her visit the day before to see Sarah at Robson Lodge. She had been convinced that the elderly woman was her grandmother and that finally she was able to piece a part of her family history together. Another family member that she had always longed to have.

She had slept badly and was still smarting about the fact that whilst she was intent on planting a family tree and seeing what grew, her mother was determined to act as human Dutch Elm disease and kill the tree off before it had even had a chance to grow any roots. What irked her most is that she knew Ruby could be right. What was she basing her knowledge on? Merely, the ramblings of an adorable old lady who didn't really seem to know which way was up most of the time. Lucie was hardly learning from the best.

It was mid-morning and Lucie had come into the garden to try and clear her head, to try and grasp at some semblance of sense from everything that had been going on. The sky overhead was heavy with cloud, the air a little darker and cooler than it should have been for the time of year. She shivered slightly, dressed merely in a new pair of jeans and a T-shirt from her shopping trip a few days earlier.

As if sensing her chill, Ruby appeared from the cottage and walked towards her. Both of her hands were full.

'From the look of those clouds we're not going to see any sun today. If you're going to sit outside, I thought you might like this. I got it from your room.' She held up a sweatshirt in her hands, another of Lucie's new purchases. 'Here you go.' She passed it to Lucie who gratefully slipped it over her head with a "thank you".

Ruby herself was dressed in a similar attire. Skin tight jeans and a cashmere jumper. The look was a little over the top and glam for the early hour of the day but it somehow suited Ruby. She sat herself down on the bench next to her daughter, placed what she held in her other hand on the bench too and reached into her back pocket to pull out a slim cigarette case. She took one out and lit it.

'Don't you think you ought to consider giving that up?' asked Lucie. It was less a critique and more of a branch to move away from her annoying feelings towards Ruby after the pub meal the night before.

'Probably,' smiled Ruby. 'But I have no intention of doing so.'

'It's bad for your health, you know that.'

'And so is being told to give up everything that you enjoy. I think I have done pretty well to give certain things up, don't you? At least let me hang onto this one for a while.' There was no annoyance in her voice.

'I'm only saying it for you, mum. I care about you, that's all.'

'And I care about you, dear Lucie.' Ruby took Lucie's hand in hers and squeezed it lovingly. 'Which is why I wanted to speak to you.'

Lucie turned to face her mother full-on, swivelling her position on the bench to do so. 'Really? What about?'

'You're hurting about what I said last night. About the lady at the care home potentially being a mad woman and everything she said not being true. I could see that you were upset...and that you still are now.'

'Her name is Sarah and she's not a mad woman. She's an old lady who becomes confused about things sometimes. It just felt that you were being totally heartless and dismissive about her. You should come to see her, she used to live here after all. She genuinely said that Oscar was her son, and as he's your brother that automatically makes her your mother too, doesn't it? I just don't understand.'

'Lucie, there is nothing to understand. I am sure Sarah is an adorable if somewhat quirky individual. I am sure that a lot of what she says is all true and factual, but she is not my mother. And if I was being glib about it last night, then that's only because I'm totally certain of that.'

'There's just so little I know about my family that sometimes it really gets to me,' said Lucie. 'I feel like I want to go on one of those TV programmes and find out about my ancestors because I don't seem to have any roots. No brothers, sisters, grandparents. I know more about Roger and Tanya's family background and they weren't even my real...' She stopped herself from completing the sentence, suddenly hating herself for the sense of betrayal that washed over her. Roger and Tanya had been a true family to her, no matter what their bloodline said.

'They were beautiful people for looking after you and keeping you safe. And maybe their family background was a little easier than ours.' Ruby paused a moment, and picked up the object that she had placed beside her on the bench. 'Look, I want to show you something.'

Lucie's mother placed a large square album, twelve inches across and about an inch deep on her lap. The cover, a candyfloss shade of pink, a little faded and worn in places, stared up at her.

'What is it?' asked Lucie, her curiosity piqued.

'It's my scrapbook. I may not be the most sentimental of people when it comes to family life, but I don't always have a heart of ice, you know. I know I can be a complete cow at times and God knows I haven't been the best mother to you, but I do care about family. Despite what you may be feeling right now.'

Lucie could feel her annoyance towards her mother abating. 'A scrapbook? How long have you had that?' It was not something that she would ever have associated with her mother.

'It's something I've been collating over the years. It helped me get through everything, especially when you...' There was a moment's hesitation before she added, '...weren't there.'

Ruby opened the scrapbook and the two women stared down at the first page. A black and white photo dominated it. It featured two people, one a babe in arms and the other a young girl. The young girl was in bed. Lucie guessed it was a hospital bed as it had that old-school starched sheets, austere look about it.

'Is that you as a young girl?' asked Lucie. The girl was very pretty, a mass of dark hair falling about her face. The expression was of someone who had been told to smile for the photo but the features were somehow not quite willing. There was an awkwardness about her.

'No, that's me as a baby. Just a few hours old. Before I'd discovered the joy of men and bad living.' Ruby laughed, coughing a little as a mass of smoke hit her throat.

'So that is...' Lucie knew the answer.

'My mother, sixteen years of age and suddenly a single mother to me, little Ruby Jane.'

'I never knew Jane was your middle name,' smiled Lucie.

'There is a lot you don't know about me, Lucie, which is why I thought this trip down memory lane might help.'

'Why have you never shown me this before?' asked Lucie, her finger subconsciously stroking the photo of her mother as a baby.

'You were taken away from me at the age of thirteen. I'd never found the right moment. And there's also the fact that memory lane is not a particularly nice place for me to revisit if I'm being honest. It never has been in many ways.'

'Your mum looks confused,' remarked Lucie, taking in her expression once again.

'My mother never wanted a child at sixteen. She was still at school, or supposed to be, I was told she used to bunk off and go missing quite a lot. On one of those absences, she hooked up with one of the local boys in town and well, you can guess the rest, and boom…nine months later, along comes me.'

'So you were an accident?'

'If the dictionary definition of accident is a bloody great big unwanted mistake then yes, I was an accident.' Ruby's voice was an attempt at humour but there was a deep sadness in her tone.

'But your mother loved you. How could she not? You were a beautiful baby.'

Ruby turned the page. A double page spread of photos stared up from the pages. A young Ruby at Christmas, playing in the garden, holding onto an adult's hand. The normal photos of a young girl's first steps into the world. But one thing was missing. The girl with the mass of black hair was nowhere to be seen.

'That will always be the million dollar question, Lucie, and one that I will doubtless never get answered. Let me explain. The woman at the care home can't be my mother as she would have to be sixteen years older than me and that would put her in her early sixties. You said she was eighty odd. So it's a physical impossibility as far as her age is concerned, unless I'm really in my late sixties and somebody forgot to tell me. I don't think I look *that* old, do I?' Ruby smiled and squeezed Lucie's hand again.

Lucie said "no" and left it there, not wanting to interrupt her mother's flow.

'My mother never wanted a child. Not at such a young age. From what I understand, the father, and it could have been one of a few apparently, wanted nothing to do with my mother and if it had been down to her alone, then I think she would have pulled the plug and had me aborted. Naturally, I am pleased she didn't. The lady in the photo here, the one holding my hand, she was my grandmother, Alice. She was the woman who looked after me growing up. My grandad had died long before I was born and Alice was alone and ready to take the reins when my mother couldn't.'

'Why couldn't she?' Lucie was finding it hard to understand how anybody could turn their back on the cute bundle of joy in the photos.

'She disappeared. Did a runner. Vanished without a trace. Totally missing in action. Nobody knew where to, not even Alice. She couldn't cope with having a child, whether it was the burden or the stigma or the shame I don't know, but she packed her bags not long after I was born and just disappeared.'

'You said she was dead.' Lucie stated the fact but not in an accusatory manner.

'To me, she is. That's what I feel in my heart, so that's what I believe. My grandmother tried to find her until the day that she herself died, just before my nineteenth birthday. My mother had always been a free spirit and invariably managed to get herself into trouble. Maybe that's where I get it from. I'm from bad stock. But every avenue that Alice tried to explore was a dead end. My mother had simply vanished off the face of the earth. Saying she's dead made more sense as it gave a full stop to the story. In my heart, I believe she is. I just hope she was happy when she died and could forgive herself for abandoning me.'

A ripple of chill ran across Lucie's body, not just from the freshness of the day but also from the melancholy of the story.

'Can you forgive her?' It was a simple question.

'I've tried. She failed me as a mother, that's clear. But then, I failed you too. Maybe I can't forgive her as I blame her for my own failings. I reckon this apple didn't fall very far from the tree, don't you?'

It was the first time that Lucie had ever heard Ruby speaking like this and even though many would have deemed it far too late, she was still pleased to hear it. It helped her understand. Just a little, but a little nevertheless.

The two women sat and stared at the photos for a few moments. 'What was Alice like? My great-grandmother.' Lucie liked the sound of the words.

'A wonderful woman. She looked after me. She gave me the life that my own mother never could. We didn't have a lot but she did everything she could to make us happy.' Again, the similarity between Ruby's story and her own struck Lucie. Alice was Ruby's saviour in the same way that Roger and Tanya had become hers

139

when Ruby couldn't cope. 'You would have liked her, and she would have loved you. It's a shame you never knew her.'

'I wish I had.'

For the next twenty minutes or so, Lucie and her mum flicked through the pages of the scrapbook. Photos of Ruby as she grew up dotted the pages, dates scribbled alongside the pictures, the occasional sentence scrawled in handwriting detailing what was being shown. The album featured Ruby with many of her men friends, a fact that Ruby giggled about. 'Do you remember Russell, the tattooed fella? That went badly wrong. I don't know why I still have a photo of us in here seeing as he cheated on me. Bloody scumbag.'

'I do remember him. He tried to nick my chips on the beach. I always remember that. He was a bad man. Very.' The last reference was about the drugs, not the food. Lucie was pretty sure that it was Russell that had started her mum's decline into drug abuse.

'Then there was Haydn. And Johnny. Another two losers when it came to finding a good man. I told you memory lane wasn't exactly my preferred destination. But at least there are lots of photos of you and me together. I used to look at these day after day when you were with Roger and Tanya. I really believe they helped me realise what I'd lost exactly.'

There were loads of mother and daughter photos. Lucie felt herself pulled in to the images, the memories suddenly bursting back into her psyche, returning from a hidden place she had somehow long forgotten. They were beautiful snapshots, moments in time hiding the struggles and strife that lay behind virtually every one. Trips to the pier, Lucie's face peering through a hole as if she were a fat lady in a bathing suit or the head of a cartoon muscly lifeguard. Ruby's smiling face alongside her. Rides on the carousel or carefree seconds, hands waving, as Lucie descended the swirls of a helter-skelter. If only life could have been one long piece of bunting, connecting those idyllic moments and nothing else, then maybe things would have been so different. A fiesta of fun and laughter, instead of the sinking of her mother into a life addicted to drugs. Before the curse of it all.

A thought rushed into Lucie's brain. A question she had ventured to ask many times, but not for the longest one. It seemed right to approach it now.

'Are there any photos of my father?'

Ruby sighed outwardly, not from exasperation but from expectancy. Lucie had the right to ask. She knew that.

'No, there aren't. Your father and I weren't really together long enough to consider capturing every sweet and tender moment.' The tone of her voice suggested that sweet and tender were two words she would never associate with her feelings for Lucie's dad. That she had chosen their lack of suitability deliberately.

'You never talk about him. Why is that?' said Lucie, her voice quietening, almost afraid to ask.

'Simple answer. There's nothing to tell. I could make something up about him being killed in a war, or running off with another woman or joining the circus if you wish, but it would all be a lie. Your dad was merely there at your conception and after that, well, he didn't want to know.'

'I would have liked to have known him.'

'Well, he never gave you the fucking chance, did he?' Ruby spat the words, her venom clear.

Lucie's face dropped, causing Ruby to apologise. 'I'm sorry, I shouldn't swear. That wasn't aimed at you, you know that.' She placed her hand on Lucie's face as she spoke. The action felt tender and sweet. 'That was aimed at him. Your dad and I were good friends, and then we became lovers and then...' Ruby's voice wobbled, as if shaken by the ground beneath her feet.

'And then you fell pregnant?' It wasn't really a question. Lucie knew the answer.

'Yes, and that was that.'

'Did he want to know me?' That was a question. One that Lucie had never aired before.

'He didn't want to know any of us, Lucie. Not a single one.'

'Where did he go?'

'Why, are you thinking of trying to contact him? If you are, you had better try one of the mediums on Brighton Pier. He's long gone. Dead to us all, Lucie. You know that.'

Again, Ruby's words were overly harsh, but Lucie knew that they had come from the heart and not from any place of malicious, spiteful intent. She didn't take any offence.

Ruby continued. 'I was left to bring you up on my own, after everything that I'd been through. I know I didn't do the best job ever, but Christ knows I tried. I really did. I just hope you believe that, Lucie. It's all that matters now.'

Lucie did. It may not have been parenting one-oh-one but Ruby had tried. Unsuccessfully, but she had always tried. Hadn't she?

Silence fell across them both for a while, the breeze in the air still blowing across them. It was Ruby who broke the calm. 'I should go,' she said, shutting the scrapbook. 'Terrance has some more properties to visit and well, I should be accompanying him to keep him out of trouble I suppose. He'd buy Buckingham Palace and try to convert it if he had his way.'

'You like him, don't you?' asked Lucie.

'Of course, I do. Why wouldn't I? He's a little older than my normal type but, yes, I do. He's promised to buy me some jewellery today. I said I wanted a diamond. A huge one. If it's good enough for all of those telly stars you read about in the magazines, then I want one too. That makes him worth liking in my book!' Ruby winked as she went to move away.

Lucie had one more question ask. Something that suddenly made no sense.

'Mum?' Where are the photos of Oscar? If he was your older brother, where was he in the scrapbook? He would have been there with you and Alice, surely?'

Ruby hesitated a little before giving her answer, working out how to best unravel the tangled knots of her family history. 'Oscar was my step-brother really. He came into the frame later when Alice remarried. He was older than me and didn't seem to have any time for me. He was my step-grandad's son but seeing as we were such a weird family set-up, he wasn't around for long before running off to do his own thing.'

'The painting?'

'I guess so. I really didn't have that much to do with him. Especially after Alice died, the connection was kind of lost. Not that there was any real connection to begin with. Which is why him leaving me all of this,' she pointed to the cottage, 'was such a surprise. But there were no other step-siblings so I guess I was lucky on that front. Some conclusions do come together nicely in the end even if you're not quite sure about the journey you had to take to get there. Good old Oscar.'

'Good old Oscar indeed,' repeated Lucie, as Ruby disappeared to continue her day.

The breeze was becoming stronger, but Lucie, warmed by the sweatshirt Ruby had given her decided to stay outside. The air was helping to clear her mind and she had to admit that her talk with Ruby had made her realise that there were always two sides to every story. People could criticise her mother all they like, but Lucie felt more of a tie to her knowing what Ruby had just disclosed.

Lucie stood and walked across the garden to the narrow pathway that she had seen Drew walking up a few times as she stared down through the leading of her bedroom window. The path was more overgrown than the rest of the garden, weeds and a few thistles dotting the edges of it, but it held a random, forgotten charm that Lucie was instantly drawn to. The path, an angular mass of slabs forming a concrete mosaic of bricks seemed to lure her in as she followed it around to the hidden depths beyond. An area she had never visited before.

As she approached, she could hear the sound of a song playing, one of the tunes that she had listened to many times on the beach in Paradise Cove. The rhythm of the song immediately took her back, for once her memories of her time there totally happy ones, enjoyed before they had the chance to expand. The path opened into a sizable clearing and the source of the melody became apparent. A radio, small and compact, sat on the grass and singing along to it fairly tunelessly, quite oblivious to Lucie's arrival, was Drew. He was wearing combat trouser shorts and a sports vest. Both were dirty with mud. It was clear that he didn't feel the cold as Lucie did. His back was turned to her and he was sorting through a pile of bricks.

Lucie coughed softly to announce her presence. Drew immediately turned towards her. A smile spread across his features. 'Hey.' He made the word much longer than it needed to be. 'How are you?'

'Obviously much more of a softie than you,' grinned Lucie, waggling her finger at his outfit. 'Are you not cold wearing just a vest?'

'I spend my entire life outside so I think I am hardened to all weathers,' laughed Drew. 'I could be out here in a hurricane and I'd still be warm wearing next to nothing. Working on this keeps me warm.' It was now his turn to point. He gestured to the well that was semi-collapsed behind the pile of bricks.

'Ah, the famous well you were telling me about. I can see what you meant about it needing some TLC. It's a pity it's so dilapidated. This is a beautiful little clearing.' She let her eyes scan around. The circular well was surrounded on all sides by a copse of shrubs and bushes. A grouping of trees stood proud, their branches swooping down into the clearing.

'I know, it's like a fairy glade, isn't it? The way the light comes through the trees when it's sunny is just gorgeous. I love it here.'

'What happened to the well?' asked Lucie. The main triangular roof of it was still intact but the round base had collapsed on one side, causing a spillage of bricks, a lot of them broken, to sprawl their way across the lawn. The two posts that connected the base to roof were still in place but had escaped collapsing by the merest fraction.

'General wear and tear. The well did manage to function back in the day. I remember the old gardener telling me all about it. Apparently, it was stunning to look at and the water in it was said to be drinkable it was that clear.'

Lucie wasn't sure she believed the drinkability story but her head suddenly flooded with scenes of Sarah, beautiful and serene, raising the pale that still hung from the roof of the well, and ladling fresh clean water from it, the sun dappling her skin as she did. It was a magical image. It made her smile.

It was not unnoticed by Drew. 'See, you've fallen in love with this place already, haven't you? It's amazing, isn't it? That why I wanted to bring the well back to its former glory. Give your mother and Mr Terrance the chance to see it like it was in its glory days.'

'So the water isn't so clear now, then?' said Lucie. 'Not from the look of your clothes, anyway. They're filthy.'

'Oh yes…' A half-embarrassed Drew wiped his hands against his trousers as if trying to remove the mud, suddenly self-conscious of his appearance given the person he was talking to. 'Sorry about that.'

'I'd expect a gardener to have a fair few stains on their clothes,' grinned Lucie. 'Otherwise they're not doing their job properly.'

'It's from going down the well this morning. I grabbed a rope and climbed down there. The water has dried up long ago sadly but there were loads of things blocking the well down at the bottom. If it is ever to be restored, it will need cleaning out which is what I did. I found all sorts down there.'

'Like what?'

There was a small pile of things gathered just behind the radio on the lawn. They were all dirty in the extreme, obviously stained by the drama of being outside.

'Coat hangers, plastic bags, all sorts.' He knelt to sift through some of the collection. 'And these.' He picked up a big bundle, about the size and shape of a small rugby ball. Lucie couldn't quite make out what it was, the outside covered in a soft brown sludge.

'This is all wet, so most of the bits here are stuck together but I tried to prize it apart. It's all held together with elastic bands,' stated Drew. He yanked at one of the bands and it snapped in his hand as he did so.

Lucie joined him, kneeling alongside the gardener to look at what he held in his hands. 'May I?'

Drew passed her the bundle. It was still cold and fairly damp, especially around the edges, from where it had braved the elements hidden down the well. It looked like a bundle of photos. Lucie attempted to peel one of them away from the others, there must have been about thirty or so in all, but it ripped between her fingers and disintegrated slightly.

'These need drying out,' said Lucie.

'You reckon?' asked Drew.

'May I take them?' asked Lucie. 'Unless you need them.'

'Sure. I was just going to throw them out. They're just rubbish. Do you want the coat hangers too?' Drew was being serious.

'Errr, no, you can throw those.' Lucie curled her lips into a smile. 'But I'd like to dry these out.'

As Lucie walked back to the house, the bundle of photos in her hand, she couldn't help but wonder what they had been doing down the well. It appeared that there were some photos you were meant to see, like the ones in the scrapbook, and others that you were most definitely not.

Chapter 25

Peru, summer 2012

It was one of those ridiculously hot nights where sleep would never visit. Even with the air con beating at full blast in her bedroom, Lucie could still feel her body glazed with sweat, the sheets sticking to her body as she tossed restlessly from side to side attempting to deal with the heat that hung heavy and smothering in the air.

Connor, lying on his back beside her, his chest rising up and down and a satisfying noise of his unconscious state emanating from his lips, was obviously having no trouble dealing with the heat. He had managed to sleep as soon as they had turned off the lights. Lucie stared at the body next to her, the dark stubble of his chin and the slight shudder of his lips as he breathed. It was a beautiful sight and one that she was becoming more and more used to sharing her bed.

It had been nearly three weeks since they had first made love at the street carnival and even though neither of them had ventured to actually admit that they were in a relationship, the pair had spent virtually all of their time together since. If they weren't working alongside each other at Bar Dynasty, then invariably Connor would be stopping over with Lucie at the flat she shared with Tina and Kara.

Lucie knew she loved him. Again, it hadn't been properly mentioned but she felt it didn't have to be. Their actions together showed that. The way he stared into her eyes as they made love, the green of his own penetrating into places that had never been touched before. The delicacy of his caress as he held her body against his, as they spooned in bed, drifting off to sleep, his hands moving up and down her skin, every inch a thrill that she would never tire of. The legitimacy of his smile as he shared a joke, a tender glance from behind the bar or a knowing nod as he saw her expertly dealing with another bout of idiocy from customers like Billy and Logan. Little actions that to her said so much. Lucie had come to Peru to discover herself but she was rapidly realising that she was discovering something so much more. A man that she had fallen head over heels for. And it was a treasure that she was doting on.

Lucie ran her fingers across Connor's chest hair, his thick black curls luxurious to her touch. He stirred a little but not enough to wake up. He licked his lips, let them slap together gently and turned onto his side with a hint of a murmur, his back turned to Lucie. Even that, broad and muscular, seemed a beautiful thing to her. She lay and stared at it, taking in the selection of moles and freckles that scatted across his tanned flesh. A darkening of hair dotted the lower reaches of his back. Lucie felt the urge to run one of her fingers down his spine and guide it into the hair that lay there, but she resisted, fearful of waking him up.

She herself was now wide awake. Sleep would not be taking her tonight, she knew that. She turned and stared at the clock on the bedside table. Just before half two. They had only been in bed for just over two hours. As she moved, the sheet beneath her followed her, stuck to her skin with its wetness. It was not a pleasant sensation. Peeling herself away from it, she rose out of bed and left Connor to his slumber. Maybe a drink of tea would help her sleep? She didn't know but was keen to find out. If she was to be able to undertake a full shift at Bar Dynasty the following day, then sleep would be essential.

She slipped on Connor's T-shirt and wandered into the kitchen. Kara and Tina were both away, one staying at a friend's and one camping for a few days at a resort not far from Paradise Cove. It was lovely to have the place to herself, even if all of her time "alone" had been with Connor. That was her kind of solitude.

Lucie boiled the kettle and poured the water into a mug, the water changing colour as the tea bag within diffused its contents into the liquid. She added milk, stirred it vigorously and took her mug into the front room. Without turning the light on, she slumped onto the sofa, picked up a remote control and flicked the TV on, decreasing the volume as she did so not wanting to wake up Connor. A baseball match filled the screen. It held no interest for Lucie and she quickly flicked it over, replacing it with an old black and white movie, spoken in English with Spanish subtitles. That was much more her kind of viewing. It must have been Connor who had been watching the sports channel before climbing into bed. She never watched it. He had been in the front room whilst Lucie had been in the bathroom preparing for bedtime.

Sipping on her tea, Lucie became engrossed in the movie. Two kooky old women cooped up in a house together. She recognised the actresses but couldn't place their names. She'd seen the film before a long time ago though and remembered enjoying it. Scary and maniacal if she remembered rightly. She'd watched it one night at Roger and Tanya's. The flickering black and white images of the two women on the screen, a volley of words flying between them, caring from one, venom from the other, filled the room of the flat, illuminating Lucie's surroundings. Lucie pulled her knees up under Connor's T-shirt and watched as the two old matrons bickered, her heart skipping a beat as she found herself drawn into their squabbles. Before she knew it, her tea was drained and an hour had passed, the credits rolling on the film. She felt more awake than ever.

She flicked the TV off, the room plunging into darkness again. She moved to a lamp in the corner and pressed the switch. A cone of light filled the corner, Lucie's eyes immediately finding what she wanted on the table underneath the lamp. Her book, a Martina Cole, rested there. Lucie reached for it and was about to pick it up when she noticed Connor's credit card laying across it. The edge was dusted with white. She knew exactly what it was. She'd seen it too many times in her life. She bent down to stare closely at the book. It was dotted with white specks too. It was clear what Connor had been doing before he came to bed. It didn't surprise her. She'd seen him do it a lot since his first admission of it at the carnival. Despite her love for him, she couldn't help but hate it. What it represented. What it could do. How it could destroy.

It was the first time he had done it, or she had caught him doing it, inside her flat. Maybe with Kara and Tina being away, he felt he could. Maybe he did it with them too. Tina had told her that she used to enjoy it. Lucie knew that she would have to confront him. Whatever Connor chose to do on his own patch was his own choice, but bringing it into her home was something else. She hadn't explained the full story of her mother's narcotic downfall to Connor and part of her didn't want to but if he was to carry on using, then another part of her felt obliged to air her disgust for the drug. She just wasn't sure how to do it. They had only been together a matter of a few weeks and it seemed way too early to be laying down the law, no matter how strongly she felt.

Lucie picked up the book and carried it into the kitchen. Grabbing some kitchen towel, she wiped the back of the book and along the edge of Connor's credit card. Screwing up the paper, she moved to the bin, pressed the lid and went to throw the scrunched up ball of white inside. She gazed inside the bin. A cigarette packet and a mound of cigarette butts lay there.

Suddenly, she was back in Brighton, half a decade or so earlier. She was staring down into the pedal bin in the kitchen at the fifth floor flat. A mound of cigarette butts and a few empty packets stared back at her. A teenage Lucie had put them there, having swept through the flat in an attempt to tidy another of her mother's impromptu gatherings. Another day had begun with Lucie waking up to find her mother still asleep, no surprise as it was barely three hours since she had heard Ruby stumbling her drunken way into bed in the first place. No breakfast. No ironed school clothes. No welcome to the day. Instead, the flat had stunk of her mother's fun from the night before. Ashtrays overflowed, a molehill of cigarette butts decorating every surface in the front room. The air flavoured heavy with the dry, stale odour of smoke. Rizla papers lay torn and redundant, their work done. Tell-tale smudges of white dotted the room.

Lucie could have walked out. Left it and just washed, dressed and headed to school. But she couldn't. She knew that Ruby would be in a foul mood when she eventually awoke and that tidying the devastation of the night before would be the last thing on her wish list. Despite her hatred of having to touch the toxic offerings of her mother's previous night, Lucie wanted to help. Wanted to make sure her mother wasn't in the worst mood possible. Not that she was ever thanked for it, but to Lucie, it was almost an obligation, a want and a daughterly desire that made her clear up after her mother. She did it because she wanted to, not because she had to. As if removing the evidence would almost signify removing the fact that it happened in the first place.

The bin would be full. Almost to the top with bottles, empty cigarette packets and a variety of butts, some showcasing a band of lipstick around them, others not, but all nestled amongst the scrunched up kitchen roll that Lucie has used in an attempt to clean. It was an image that she would never be able to unsee.

The bin at her flat in Peru had transported her back there immediately. One pile of rubbish reminding her of another. Both dirty in more ways than one.

'What are you doing up?'

Lucie span around from the bin to find a naked Connor standing in the kitchen door, rubbing his chin with one of his hands. He was only half awake.

'I couldn't sleep. It was too hot. I didn't mean to wake you.' Why was she apologising? She knew she hadn't done anything wrong.

'You didn't. But I thought I had better see where you are when I didn't find you in bed. You okay?'

'Not really,' said Lucie. It was the truth. She held up the credit card in her hand and waggled it towards him. 'We need to talk.'

'What about?' Connor seemed genuinely clueless.

'What you have been using this for,' she said. 'There's a reason I hate this stuff and I think you need to know why that is.'

'Oh.' It was all he could say.

Before he could say anymore, Lucie told him all about why she had been moved to her foster parents and all about Ruby's addiction to drugs. Connor, still naked, just stared and listened.

Chapter 26

Now

The heat was stifling. But Lucie knew that it had to be. Despite it still being late summer and the weather outside not being exactly as warm as the season would dictate, her bedroom at the cottage was unbearably warm. But she had chosen it to be. Ever since she had moved back inside the cottage from her well-side rendezvous with Drew, Lucie had been determined to find out what was contained in the pack of photographs that the gardener had given her. But whilst they were still damp and virtually destroyed with the moisture from the well, Lucie had little chance of seeing what lay beneath the elastic bands. She needed to dry them out which was why she had put the radiator in her room onto full heat and placed the photos on the top. She could have let them dry at room temperature but her impatience wouldn't allow it. She wanted to see what images had been bound together and discarded and she wanted to see them as soon as possible.

In an effort to dry them out as quickly as possible, Lucie had closed all of the windows too. And even though she knew she didn't have to sit and watch them dry out, something about the mystery of what the package could contain saw her spend the next few hours literally perched over the radiator watching the package dry out. A moth drawn to the lure of the potential flame within. Temptation beckoned her to try and prize the photos apart from each other as soon as she could, but Lucie managed to sit diligently in the overbearing heat waiting for the right moment to arrive. Only once did she attempt to slide one of her fingers between the bundle of thin mysteries, resulting in a cut across the soft flesh of her index finger. A small dribble of blood leaked across the edge of the photos leaving a rusty smear on the border as she pulled her finger away.

It was approaching early evening when Lucie finally felt the moment might be right to try and unravel the mound of photos. She took the package downstairs to the kitchen table and opened all of the doors and windows, the coolness of the air outside a welcome mat of comfort after the enforced heat of the afternoon.

Gingerly, she removed the elastic bands wrapped around the photos and brushed off as much of the excess dirt as she could. Crumbs of brown spread themselves across the wooden surface of the table. One by one, she tried to peel away each of the photos from the one beneath it. Time after time, they seemed to just disintegrate in her hands, decaying into nothing but a pile of dust, whatever image they held destroyed into oblivion. As photo after photo ripped, shredded or broke up into obscurity, Lucie could feel her frustration rising.

She was reaching the middle of the bundle, the photos there still a little damp from their time down the well but yet seemingly better protected against the elements from the others around them. There must have been about half a dozen photos left. As she carefully peeled the next layer away, for once the photo seemed to hold, the image revealing itself. The photos were colour so must have been taken within the not so distant past. They certainly weren't relics from historical times. The background was green. The photo had been taken outside. As Lucie continued to peel, she saw the well from which Drew had recovered the photos coming into view. So the photos had been taken at the house. An explosion of success voluntarily rippled within her. Even if the photos were no more than mere innocent snapshots of days gone back at the place her mother now called home, she couldn't help but feel the photographs would give her more of a true understanding of what had once passed at the house. Of perhaps life when the old lady, Sarah, and Uncle Oscar had lived there.

She peeled further, every millimetre causing her to hold her breath. A leg started to appear. It was female. A sudden burst of excitement from Lucie at the thought of a discovery at long last caused her to yank a little too hard at the photo, keen to reveal its secret. Like a pinprick to her balloon of hope, the photo began to tear and the rest of the image was destroyed as a rough bolt of torn white appeared across it.

'Fuck it,' said Lucie, her words coming without consideration.

The next three photos destroyed themselves in a similar fashion until Lucie was left with just two photos. The images on both of them were stuck face to face. If there were any memories of days forgotten on the photos, then this was her final chance to find them out.

She stopped herself as she began to try and peel them apart, aware that failure would mean game over. A chill passed over her, a breeze from the open door and windows. She shivered, her teeth clattering a little not just from the temperature but also from exasperation.

After a few moments, Lucie picked the two photos back up and began to peel. As if by magic, luck finally on her side, the two photos separated perfectly, two colour photos revealing themselves to her in their full glory. The first showed the well again and featured Sarah, her arm linked with a man. He was model-handsome and a good deal younger than Sarah. He wore a suit, tight fitting that highlighted his strong frame to its most beneficial. Lucie guessed that he was Uncle Oscar.

'Aren't you a looker, Uncle Oscar...if that's who you are,' murmured Lucie to herself. He was one of those men who just epitomised cool without having to try at all.

The other photo also featured two people, one was Uncle Oscar again, wearing the same outfit. Doubtless, the two photos were taken at the same time. This time, though, his arm was not linked with Sarah's, it was linked into the arm of a woman much more his own age, maybe a few years younger. It was a woman that Lucie knew only too well. She'd seen the same woman, at the same age, starring out from the pages of the scrapbook earlier in the day. It was Ruby.

Questions flooded Lucie's mind. Why was Ruby with Uncle Oscar? How come she was next to the well? Why hadn't she mentioned that she'd been here before? Or that she must have met Sarah?

A shriek of loud laughter sounded from outside the back door and across the garden path leading to it. It belonged to Ruby. For a moment, Lucie knew the she was mere seconds away from gaining answers to her questions. She moved to the door, photos in hand and watched as Ruby and Terrance approached.

She made a snap decision. Pulling open a kitchen drawer, she placed the two photos quickly inside and pushed it shut again. Now was not the time. A flush of worry shot across her face as Terrance and Ruby reached the back door. Ruby was still animated and laughing merrily. Lucie grabbed the mess of the other useless photos from the table and deposited them into the kitchen bin in lightning speed. The door opened just as she completed the task.

'Oh Lucie, look at this,' squealed Ruby as she held her hand aloft and wiggled her fingers in front of Lucie's face. 'Terrance has bought me the most incredible diamond. Isn't it huge? I feel like I should be walking on a red carpet and hanging out with the A-List.'

The rock on Ruby's finger was indeed huge. Vulgarly so. Lucie attempted to smile, but her features didn't quite manage to appear genuine given the hurricane of thoughts that were whirling through her mind. Ruby noticed.

'Well *I* love it!' she said. 'I'm going to shower and change and Terrance is taking me off to London for a night out so that I can show it off. I'd ask you to come but you're looking a little peaky. Are you okay? It's fucking hot in here.' Ruby's voice was more indignation than it was compassion.

'I'm fine now,' fudged Lucie. 'I've just been running around all day and I felt a bit odd, so I had the heating on for a while. You go and enjoy yourself and show that bad boy off. It is pretty colossal.'

'We'll be stopping out until tomorrow. I'll be booking us into a hotel so that we can…' It was Terrance talking, and he left a gap in his sentence to slap Ruby's backside before finishing. '…make a night of it.'

Ruby giggled and let out another high-pitched shriek, both the thought and Terrance's suggestion pleasing her. 'Fabulous. Well, in that case, I had better pack an overnight bag as well. Right, I'm off to beautify myself. Enjoy your evening, Lucie, whatever you do. And keep that heating off, it's roasting in here. You'll bloody melt.'

Lucie looked on as her mother disappeared up the stairs. She wouldn't be doing anything tonight she knew that, but her mind was already made up. First thing in the morning, she would be heading back to Robson Lodge to see Sarah. And she'd be taking the two photos with her.

Chapter 27

Now

Lucie stared at the number 29 on the door. It was silver in colour yet a little tarnished around the edges. She raised her finger up to it and ran it around the outline of the digits. She paused before knocking. Why was she hesitating? She'd been stood outside the door for the best part of five minutes as it was. Hadn't she come to Robson Lodge seeking answers? She knew she had. So why was there a heavy bolus of angst weighing itself down at the bottom of her stomach? What was she afraid of? Was it the thought of answers that Sarah could give her about the photos? But surely, whatever was said would only add to potential clarification. Could Sarah tell her anything, and if she did could she believe it? Last time, she had left Robson Lodge thinking that she had discovered more about her own family history in a few moments than she had in a long time, but that had been smashed into place, and with great authenticity, by Ruby's protests and her subsequent scrapbook. All Lucie wanted was a family; it was all she had ever wanted since dreaming of having a brother when she was small. Was that too much to ask?

Courage steeling her, she knocked on the door. No sound came from within. A reply was not always to be expected. Lucie had already learnt that. She knocked again out of courtesy and pushed the door open.

Sarah was sitting in her armchair as usual staring out of the window. Her hair was neatly tied back into a bun, as it had been on their first meeting and the outfit, almost identical, only seemed to differ in the fact that the white blouse was now one of a buttermilk colour. Her lavish jewellery, a gemstone decorating virtually every finger, again seemed to catch the light as Lucie moved across the room to sit down.

Sarah's eyes were open and she immediately scanned them across her visitor.

'Lucie Palmer. Back again. I said you could. I'm glad you have. Are you all right?'

Lucie was astounded that the old lady had remembered her but inwardly thrilled at the thought.

'Yes, it's me. Hello again, Sarah. It's nice to see you. I'm so pleased you remembered me.'

'Why wouldn't I?' snapped Sarah without malice. Lucie didn't know quite how to reply.

'It's a beautiful day,' said Lucie. It was indeed bright outside. The sky blue, yet a crispness pecked at the air, not that she suspected Sarah would know that from her vantage point inside.

'The garden looks beautiful. They look after it. I would do it better but it is as good as can be expected, given the situation.'

Lucie wasn't sure what the situation in question was and chose to ignore it. Sarah offered her elucidation nevertheless.

'They don't have a gardener like we did. Back at the cottage. You should see it. It's a wonderful place,' said the old lady, obviously forgetting that that was where Lucie was indeed living right now.

'Oliver looked after it for you, didn't he?' replied Lucie. 'I have seen the garden, Sarah. I was there yesterday exploring. I was near the well. Do you remember the well?'

'The well. The well. The well.' Sarah repeated the phrase somehow enjoying its sound. She semi-circled her fingers into a smile in the air, as if finding extra melody in the words. 'Yes, of course I do, Lucie Palmer, of course I do. So pretty to paint.'

The use of her full name made Lucie smile again. And mention of painting spurred her into reaching into her bag and pulling out her phone. 'May I show you something, Sarah? I have some photos of Oscar's paintings that I'd like to show you. I think they're fabulous and thought you might like to see them again.'

Lucie scrolled through her camera roll on her phone and stopped on the photos she had taken of Oscar's paintings. She clicked on one of them and opened it, a firework of colours bursting forth from the canvas as she did so.

Sarah said nothing as Lucie moved towards her and knelt down to show the old lady the photo. 'Do you remember Oscar painting this?'

Sarah stared directly at the phone and remained silent. She reached out to touch the screen as if expecting to feel the texture of the painting itself. Lucie watched her as she stared at the screen, the lady's eyes becoming misty as she took in the colours. She seemed lost and a little overwhelmed.

'There are more photos too,' offered Lucie. 'Of the other paintings I found in the loft at the cottage.' She passed her finger across the screen, flicking through the photos of the artwork. Sarah's smile seemed to grow wider and wider with each one. If Lucie wasn't mistaken, there were tears forming in the corners of Sarah's eyes.

'Do you remember Oscar painting them?' asked Lucie again. 'They obviously mean a lot to you.'

'That's because I painted them. They're all my very own.'

A wash of confusion gripped Lucie. The kilter of her expectations becoming warped yet again. 'Your very own? I thought Oscar painted these? I didn't realise painting ran in the family. If he was related to you.' Lucie realised that she still hadn't quite grasped just how blurred the lines between fiction and fact really were.

'I painted them. They're my paintings. My paintings. Nobody else's.' Sarah's voice was raised and slightly agitated, as if vexed that somebody would even dare to suggest that the artwork on show wasn't hers. Lucie knew that she had to continue her line of questioning though if she was ever to discover the truth. If that was indeed what she was uncovering?

'I'm sorry,' stuttered Lucie. 'I thought they were done by my Uncle Oscar. I didn't realise they were yours.'

'I've signed them. Can't you see?' questioned Sarah, her voice still swathed in indignation.

Lucie touched the screen of her phone and enlarged the area where the signature was. Of course. The S. It had never occurred to her that it could be for Sarah.

'So, you liked to paint too? Did you sell them like Oscar? They're amazing.'

Sarah's frustration showed no signs of abating. It became bordered on anger as she replied. Frustration seeping into every word. 'I painted them. Not anybody else. Who is Oscar? Uncle Oscar. I don't know Uncle Oscar. Why are you saying this? Why do you want to hurt me?' The anger increased as Sarah pushed the phone away, shoving it with her hand. Lucie flinched as the hand came towards her, a natural reaction from her days inside. Unable to keep hold of the phone, Lucie dropped it to the floor and losing her own balance, fell from her knelt position onto the carpet. She reached out her hand to try and raise herself back up.

'I don't want to hurt you, Sarah. Oscar lived at the house with you. I can show you.'

Tears began to flow down Sarah's face, her frustration mounting. Lucie knew that she should leave, she'd been told not to upset Sarah by the Robson Lodge staff, but she had come there to show Sarah the photos and it was a task that she needed to complete. A destination that needed to be reached no matter how miserable the journey.

'Please don't cry, Sarah. Please.' Lucie reached into her bag and pulled out the two photos. She placed the first one, the one containing Sarah herself, in front of the old lady's face. 'Look, I've found a photo of you with Oscar in the beautiful garden.'

At first, Sarah wouldn't look at the photo, her head hanging down, staring to the floor as tears streaked down her cheeks. Her hands twisted together as she moved them in her lap, writhing like two fighting snakes, their agitation and distress clear.

'Please, Sarah. It's a beautiful photo of you and Oscar...' Lucie's voice was pleading, soft in tone yet streaked with desperation. She needed Sarah to engage with her, to supply her with some answers even if it was causing upset.

Sarah moved her gaze in the direction of the photo. Immediately, her hands stopped writhing and she took hold of the image, her gemstones dancing in the light again as she did so. Her emotion changed from black to white almost instantaneously as she took in the two people on the photo.

'You look gorgeous,' said Lucie. 'You still do.' It was true, the image of Sarah in the photo was resplendent, her face regal in its beauty, a lady of wealth and style, her elegance shining through. Even in her eighties, Sarah was clearly a beautiful woman, but it was clear that in her heyday Sarah Powell was a woman who could turn heads at any juncture.

Sarah ran one of her fingers across the photo. Lucie was suddenly struck by how fragile they looked. Moments passed in silence as Sarah continued to stroke the image, seemingly lost in her thoughts. Moving her hand from the photo she placed it on Lucie's cheek and cupped her face, a smile spreading across the old lady's features. Sarah's cheeks were still damp with tears but the smile spread a rapturous happiness across her features. Whatever thoughts were now preoccupying her mind, they were definitely euphoric ones.

'Do you remember when this was taken?' asked Lucie, praying inwardly that Sarah's current state of joy and lucidity would remain for as long as possible.

'Many years ago. Many years ago indeed,' said Sarah. 'Oliver and I together in the garden. Poor Oliver, I miss him dearly.'

Confusion gripped Lucie. 'Oliver, isn't this Uncle Oscar?'

Sarah, who still had her hand cupped around Lucie's face, immediately withdrew and her smile vanished, replaced once more by annoyance.

'Who is Uncle Oscar? This is Oliver, my son. My only son. I recognise him. Why are you saying that I don't? He left me alone. I miss him so much. Miss him every day. Why did he have to go? Why did he put me in here?' Her words increased in both speed and volume as she spoke.

Was Sarah telling the truth? Was the man in the photo her son Oliver and not Uncle Oscar? If so, where was Oscar? Sarah may sadly not have been the most reliable of sources, but she had spoken of Oliver during both of Lucie's meetings with her. In that, she was consistent. Lucie had been the one who had assumed that Oliver was the previous gardener. Sarah had never talked of an "Oscar".

Sarah was becoming visibly distressed again. 'My poor Oliver. I never see him now. He never visits. Never comes to see his mother.'

Lucie knew that she had to show Sarah the other photo. 'I have another one of Oliver too. He's with another lady in your beautiful garden.' She forced it under Sarah's nose, her actions necessary but shaded by the regret of knowing the upset it would potentially cause.

Sarah stared at the photo. She began to rock back and forth in her chair, her actions almost demonic, like a caged bird, as she stared at the photo of Oliver and the woman linking arms with him.

'Why are you showing me her? She wanted to take Oliver away from me. She wanted him. I would never have allowed that. He was better than her. Why do you have this? My poor Oliver. Oliver, Oliver. Oliver.'

She continued to repeat the name as she rocked in the chair, her actions stronger as her lucidity became blatantly weaker. Lucie tried to rationalise what was being said in her head, taking in all of Sarah's words yet aware just how much distress she was causing. Sarah was an old lady and despite her outward appearance of elegance and beauty, who knew how frail and fragile her insides were. Lucie had visions of Sarah's heart giving up with the distress she was causing. She'd seen enough death in her time in Peru and she didn't want to add the old lady's name to the list. Especially when Lucie herself would be the only person to blame.

Sarah pushed the photo away from her like a disgruntled toddler, bored with the sight of it, with no further need. She placed her hands back in her lap and squeezed them together as she rocked. Lucie could see that her nails, strong and long for a lady of her age, were digging into the frail skin of the palms. Sarah began to bang them together, one hand clawed so that the nails pounded against the flesh of the other. As she did so, her incantation of "Oliver, Oliver, Oliver" continued, the soundtrack to her upset and madness. Lucie couldn't let it continue any more. She needed to fetch help. She looked quickly around the room for a panic button. Is that what they had in care homes? She wasn't sure. Hadn't the woman on reception said that there was a buzzer somewhere in the room? Lucie was sure she had but in her haze and panic to help Sarah, she was blind as to where it was. Perhaps she should run down to reception. She decided that would be the best option. She needed to act now or Sarah would be drawing blood with her nails. Lucie couldn't have that on her conscience.

'Sarah, I'll be right back.' She spoke but Sarah didn't hear her as she was still busy repeating the name.

Sarah ran from the room, down the corridor and down the stairs, taking them two by two in her urgency. Debbie, the woman she had spoken to and bumped into on her last visit, was sitting there.

'Can you come and help Sarah. She's flipping out. I don't know what to do. I'm scared she might hurt herself.'

Debbie leapt from her chair, as did another woman sitting beside her. 'You should have pressed the buzzer. We'd have come straight away.'

'I couldn't find it,' said Lucie, ashamed of her own stupidity as she said it. 'I was confused.'

Back in the room, the woman who had been sitting alongside Debbie on reception, knelt down alongside Sarah in an attempt to calm her down. The word "Oliver" was still coming from Sarah's lips, but as the nurse holding her worked her magic, the regularity of it seemed to slow down as did the rocking actions of the old lady.

'She can get like this from time to time. It's all part of her condition,' said Debbie. 'If it happens again, then press the button over there.' Debbie pointed to a small yet very clearly indicated button alongside Sarah's bed. Why had she not seen it before? Why had she been so blind? She'd been shown it on her first visit.

'I'm so sorry,' said Lucie, tears pricking at her own eyes.

'These things happen,' smiled Debbie. 'You can normally see these episodes coming so we try to nip them in the bud before they become out of hand and dangerous. What caused it do you think?'

'I was showing her a photo of her son, Oliver, and she became upset.'

'Oh. That makes sense. He was the one who had to put her in here because of her condition and on those moments when she remembers that Sarah can become very angry. She didn't forgive him, I think. He had no choice though. He couldn't look after her at the cottage. She was becoming a danger to herself.'

'Is this him?' Lucie showed Debbie the photo of Oliver with Ruby.

'Yes, that's him. Look...' She pointed at a framed photo of Oliver that sat on a shelf on the far side of the room. Why had Lucie not seen that before either? Had she been so focussed on the old lady herself and trying to obtain answers that she hadn't even properly taken in the old lady's surroundings? It would appear so.

'And that woman with him is the woman that was going to marry Oliver I would imagine,' whispered Debbie. 'Sarah's talked about it before in her clear moments. She wasn't a very nice person according to Sarah and she didn't think she would be a fitting match for her son. I'd say there was a lot of dislike between those two. Bordering on hate judging from some of the things Sarah has said. It'll be seeing that photo that has caused her to lose her rag. I wouldn't show her that again if I was you.'

Lucie felt like she'd just been punched in the stomach. Ruby and Oliver, Sarah's son, had been an item. She had been engaged to him. Why hadn't Ruby ever said? And what about the illusive Uncle Oscar?

Lucie knew she had to ask. As Sarah seemed to calm down in the corner, her rocking becoming gentler and less frenzied, Lucie lowered her voice to almost a whisper as she asked the question.

'The cottage I live in at the moment with my mother, Ruby. Did that belong to a painter called Oscar who lived with Sarah?'

Debbie smiled, unaware that her answer was about to shatter Lucie's existence into a million shards of untruth. 'Oscar? No. I've been living around these parts for a long time and that cottage was always owned by the Powell family. Sarah owned it for as long as I can remember and then when her son had to admit her into here to be looked after, I think it became his. There were some legal dealings to let him take control given the condition of his mum.

Sarah has been here a long time. The Powells were a very rich family, they ran a very successful business.'

Another blow landed squarely in Lucie's ribs. There was no Uncle Oscar. There was no painter, other than Sarah it appeared. Lucie could feel her brain clouding over, a fog of hurt and confusion taking her.

'Sarah said that Oliver never visits her here. Why is that?' Lucie knew the answer but she needed to hear it.

'Did she say that? Oh bless her. She forgets. He can't visit as sadly he's dead. He died of cancer, I think. It was only a couple of years ago. Sarah understands. She was at his funeral, but she forgets every now and again and expects him to turn up. It's so tragic.'

A third punch crashed into Lucie. She had one final question to ask.

'The woman in the photo, the one who Sarah didn't like. Did Sarah ever say why she didn't want her to marry her son?'

Debbie again replied, her arrows of her truth landing directly in Lucie's heart.

'Well, I don't know the full story as it was a long time ago. Nearly three decades ago probably. Give or take. I may be old but I'm not that old. But there was talk that the woman wasn't from a particularly good background. A bit rough I guess you'd say. Sarah has her rather particular standards and I guess the woman didn't measure up. It's a bit harsh really, isn't it? Especially if her son was in love. But the story goes that he was engaged to her because he'd gotten her in the family way. That he was doing the right thing because she was...' Debbie left the sentence floating in mid-air.

Lucie completed it. 'Pregnant. With child.'

The final blow had landed. Lucie could take no more. She made her excuses and moved from the room, down the corridor and stairs and out into the grounds of Robson Lodge. She kept walking as fast as she could, almost running, until she found a bench. She sat down on it and began to sob, her emotions finally catching up with what she had learnt. If Ruby was pregnant almost three decades ago...give or take, then unless she had fallen pregnant once before, then it had to be with her. Which meant that Oliver was her father, and sadly now a dead one, and that Sarah was indeed her grandmother after all. In a matter of seconds, she had gained a family member and lost one as well.

Tears began to pour. Plus all of those lies from her mother for years. Protection or deception? She needed to know.

Chapter 28

Now

Lucie scrubbed her flesh with the sponge. The soap in her hands almost worn away to nothing. The force of the water on her head felt like needles on her skin. She moved the sponge up and down her arms, speed gaining momentum with every stroke, determined to cleanse herself of every dirty, charred, soiled fibre that was spreading like a disease within her body.

Lucie hadn't returned to the cottage straight after she had been to Robson Lodge. She couldn't. She needed to try and clear her head. An impossible task. So much had been flung her way in such a short space of time. A thousand questions boomeranged inside her brain and every last one without real solution. Had she ever felt so confused? She wasn't sure and heaven knows her life had been filled with varied moments that had slammed into her from a force way beyond her own control.

She'd found herself walking around a park on the outskirts of the village. She had no idea how she had gotten there. It didn't matter. Nothing in life seemed to have direction at the moment. The curse of her own existence striking again, like an anaconda plunging its toxic fangs deep into her once more. She stood on the side lines of a play area, a wooden climbing frame, shaped like a galleon, and a set of swings dominating the grassland within it. A mother and child played together, the toddler joyful and jubilant in his elation as his mother pushed him backwards and forwards. Lucie watched as he ran excitedly from the swings and over to the galleon, climbing the mesh of thick rope that weaved its way up to the main body of the ship, an area where the toddler could swivel and turn, duck and dive between the wooden poles and knotted ropes pretending that he was a pirate on the high seas, riding the crashing waves and stealing hidden treasures. Lucie couldn't help but feel that it was her own life that had yet again been stolen from her.

A pang of jealousy pierced her as she watched the mother and child play, their innocence and unity so evident. Had she ever had that with Ruby? Even if she had, those moments were suddenly shaded with clouds that she feared would never disperse. Lucie must have been there for nearly half an hour, not that she was at all aware of time passing, when a man came to join the mother and child. A kiss from the woman and an excited cry of "daddy" sliced through the air as the toddler ran towards him and up into his arms. It was too much for Lucie. She turned her back on the scene and walked away, tears again dressing her cheeks as she left the park and walked back towards the cottage. It was a scene to which she had never been able to relate. Never been allowed to. Ruby had seemingly mugged her of that.

When she returned to the cottage, she had gone directly to the bathroom, removed all of her clothes and entered the shower. Her phone sounded as she was about to step in. A message from Ruby. She and Terrance would not be back until tomorrow. He was "treating her to another night in a London hotel". Lucie didn't reply. She couldn't. She had nothing to say, her thoughts about her mother too dark to contemplate right now. The love was there but for the moment, it had been dropped and shattered into pieces that were irrevocably ill-fitting.

The heat of the shower was intense. She had turned the dial almost to boiling. The water burnt against her flesh but anything less didn't feel capable of cleansing, of doing the job required. The soap, which had started as a sizable block of marble-white in her hands was now manhandled into nothing more than a sliver as it had worked its way across her skin, a lather forming sticky and rich across her body. A sponge then used to scrub the lather. Her scrubbing continuing needlessly in purpose yet necessary for her own mentality long after the white lather had left her body and spiralled its way hypnotically down the plughole.

Lucie felt incapable of stopping, even if she'd wanted to. She worked the sliver of soap some more, up and down her arm, halting only for a brief moment as she stared at the scar on her wrist. The scar she herself had caused as she rubbed her flesh angrily against the metal frame of her prison cell bed. Flesh that had been infected in her mind from the attack of her cellmate.

Lucie dropped the soap, raised her hands above her head and pushed her face into the direct stream of hot jets that rained down upon her. She let out a scream. Not of pain, but of recollection...

Peru, 2013

The water poured down onto Lucie's face. If she shut her eyes for a moment, she could be anywhere in the world. Under the running water of an idyllic waterfall in a remote beauty spot. Under the sand-cleansing jets of a beachside shower, like the ones she had enjoyed at Paradise Cove. Under the shower in the bathroom back at the sanctuary of Tanya and Roger's in Lancashire at home in the UK. But she wasn't. When she opened them, she knew exactly where she was. In the stark, green-tiled captivity of the prison showers at her jail in Lima. The shower was one of the few moments in her imprisoned life where she could metaphorically escape.

Water felt the same everywhere. In a world where sleep would never be the same, a satisfaction to her slumber always missing and pitted with fitful, fearful slashes of nightmare, and where day to day living, if you could call it that, would be threaded with dread about what lay around the next corner, Lucie's time in the shower was an escape. A chance to pretend. To pretend that she was living somebody else's life and not her own. One outside the four walls of her own trapping. One where the sun shone and the horizon could be seen. Her time in the prison shower was her own. Despite the communality of the actual bathroom itself.

It had been a long day. No longer physically than any other but somehow, the day behind her had dragged. After over a year inside, already Lucie wasn't sure if days were supposed to go quicker or more slowly. There were no rules. But today had been a hard one for Lucie – one of working in the prison laundry, of witnessing a fight between two of the inmates, a brutality that had led to one of them being taken to the prison medical department, and watching some of her other inmates excitedly hurrying off to speak to visiting family and friends. No one visited her. Why would they? Tanya and Roger had done all that they could and would doubtless be there for her when she finally secured release, but they were still time zones away. Her mother? Who knew where she would be? And those who had let her down? She would never see them again. Lucie was a lone spirit in the prison and one that would never be fully understood.

Lucie was just finishing her shower and was about to turn the water off when the door of the bathroom opened. It hit the tiled wall with a loud bang, causing her to turn in its direction. Three women entered the bathroom. Two of them were Peruvian; she recognised them as women who had been in the prison for much longer than she had. Lifers maybe. She wasn't sure. She didn't care. But she knew they were dangerous. The other one was a woman she hadn't seen before. Thick set, tattooed, shaven head. A look that would have to be deemed fashionable given its popularity within the prison. Lucie slightly pulled back the thin plastic shower curtain she was washing behind and peered across at the women. The three of them moved towards her cubicle, their quest obvious. Alarm bells immediately sounded within Lucie.

The only other woman showering in the bathroom watched as the three women moved towards Lucie. She knew better than to stay and grabbed her towel and ran naked from the bathroom as quickly as she could. Lucie attempted to do the same but knew that she stood no chance of escape as the first of the women yanked the towel from her and threw it across the room, landing in a pile on the floor. She sandwiched her other hand around Lucie's neck and pushed her against the back of the shower, the water still pouring down onto her body.

Words were spoken between the three women but Lucie was unable to hear them, the water hitting her ears and the pain of the fingers around her throat increasing somehow silencing their words. One of the two women, who didn't have hold of her, turned off the shower and both of them each grabbed one of her arms and forced them harshly against the wall either side of her. The first woman released her grip on her neck and as Lucie unsuccessfully lashed out with her legs in an attempt to kick the women away, she bunched her fist and crushed it forcefully into Lucie's stomach. Lucie coughed in pain and would have doubled up had it not been for the two women holding her arms aloft. An agony radiated across her core as pain replaced energy.

The actions that followed were mercilessly quick. The fingers inside her, the biting of her breasts, the mauling of her flesh. Lucie was helpless as the three women took it in turns to do what they wished with her. Any energy and fight she could muster was punched away from her. The ordeal became mercifully blurred as her vision glazed. She tried to disconnect with what was happening to her. Aspiring for a mental victory even if a physical one was impossible. To somehow cope.

When it was over, the seeming ringleader of the three women punched her again and left her slumped inside the cubicle. She turned the water back on and Lucie felt the spikes of water hitting her tender flesh once again as she watched the three women walk out of the room, their outlines blurred by Lucie's own fragility.

She didn't know who found her. She'd blacked out after that. When she awoke, she was being treated in the medical unit. When questioned who had done such damage to her, she remained silent. Maybe that would save her the same ordeal again.

It didn't. The same thing had happened once again during her time inside. Different women, but the same unspeakable actions. Lucie was able to remove herself from it, a taught numbness of experience somehow protecting her. But the memory would always fester within her.

Lucie doubted if she would ever feel clean again now. She couldn't. Uncertainty and dishonesty was staining her. Staining her a colour she feared she could never rid herself of. Lucie exited the shower at the cottage, feeling no cleaner than she had when she first stepped in. She knew she never would.

Chapter 29

Now

The message had arrived in the night. A voice message around 4:15 a.m. Lucie hadn't heard it as her phone was switched to silent. It was just past eight when she listened to it, having awoken from a fitful night's sleep, her brain too active to switch off with any degree of relaxation. It was from Ruby. She sounded pissed, her words slurring from one into another, but peppered with an excitement that would have been infectious had it not been for the inner demons Lucie couldn't help but feel towards her mother after Sarah's revelations.

'Darling, we're going to be away for a few more days. Southern Europe somewhere. I'll be back Friday. If you need anything, then just shout. I'll be on the mobile. If it works there. Not really sure where we're going, to be honest.' Ruby's words were rushed and pitted with laughter, but the meaning was there. She and Terrance would be out of the picture for a few days. She said Friday. That was three days away.

Lucie wasn't sure how she felt about the news. There was a definite feeling of relief that maybe she would have the chance to douse the flames of her anger somewhat before confronting her mother about her father, but the very same flames were being fanned by her annoyance that her mother was leaving her alone so soon after all of their years apart. Obviously, some things took priority and Terrance, whose voice could be heard, albeit fairly muffled, in the background of the message as Ruby hung up the phone, was one of them. He sounded just as giddy as she did, his voice a definite octave higher or two than his normal gruff self.

Loneliness wrapped itself around Lucie as she hung up her phone. The last thing she needed to do was brood. She had done enough of that inside the prison in Peru. Every day of her six years inside had been a carousel of solitude, alone with the thoughts in her head, every second a moment of despair, heartache and betrayal from those around her. If she were going to be alone at the cottage for the next few days, then she would use the time wisely. And that meant trying to sift the grains of truth from the mass of information that was currently pulling her every thought into a quicksand of uncertainty.

As she lay in bed, staring at the decorated canopy of the four poster bed above her, Lucie made a decision. She would try to find out as much as she could about the man that she believed to be her biological father. Her eyes took her beyond the canopy and into the loft, and to the paperwork that still sat there. Within minutes, she was out of bed, into the attic space and had retrieved the pile of papers that she hoped would be able to potentially cast a ray of light onto the darkness of who her father really was. If she were ever to fully know about the man who had deserted her and her mother, then she had to start her journey somewhere and that seemed as good a place as any.

As she sat down at the kitchen table, a freshly brewed mug of coffee in hand, and began to flick through the paperwork, her thoughts considered the fact that maybe it wasn't Ruby that she should be angry with. Not totally. Yes, she may have lied about "Uncle Oscar" but surely, she was only trying to protect her only child from the man who had indeed walked away from them. Abandonment was not exactly top of anyone's list of excellent paternal skills.

Lucie considered the paperwork and was immediately drawn yet again to the company name, barely legible but still strong enough to read at the top of some of the old sheets. "OPD Inc". The lack of website and email irked her. A website would be much easier to Google in the hope of information.

Lucie reached for her phone and searched for the words "OPD Inc" on the internet again. Nothing showed. Why would it? It hadn't the first time she'd tried so why would it now? Her attempt was nothing but frustration. As if another search would provide another result. Her brain whirled with the possibilities of how she could explore further. A thought struck her. The man in the photo had been Oliver Powell, not Oscar as she had originally thought, so it made sense to think that the O and the P stood for Oliver Powell. She googled the name.

A plethora or results appeared across her telephone screen. Actors, barristers, sportsmen. There seemed to be a lot of Oliver Powell's in existence. Lucie touched on "images" and scanned across the photos that appeared. None of them even vaguely resembled the man in the photos retrieved from the well.

Lucie tried again, this time using both the name of the man and of the company. A list of results appeared. Lucie scrolled through until her attention was caught by a listing that mentioned Oliver Powell Diamonds Inc. She clicked on it and a newspaper article appeared on her screen. She let her eyes roam around the screen looking for a publication date. She found one at the bottom of the article. June 2011. She began to read the copy. It was an article about a variety of gemstone companies that had secured business deals abroad. Lucie guessed it was from an industry magazine or website. Oliver Powell Diamonds Inc was listed as one of the companies. The information was a little sketchy but it said that the company had gone from strength to strength under the guidance of company CEO Oliver Powell and that deals were being sought in various foreign territories. There were no photos within the copy so Lucie again pressed her fingers on the images tab. Under this more concentrated search a series of photos, nearly all of them black and white, appeared. She flicked on one of them and then kept swiping to look at the images. Having flicked across a dozen or so, she stopped on one that grabbed her attention. It was of a group of people, mixed in gender, standing in an office. Something picked at her brain as Lucie looked at the photo. Was it recognition? They were stood in a line and glasses of what appeared to be champagne were being raised in salutation towards the camera. Lucie enlarged the photos on her screen with a swish of her fingers, making one of the women in the group much more visible to her. Her instincts had been right. The woman in the photo was undoubtedly Sarah Powell. A good couple of decades younger, but the air of class and elegance was undeniable. Her hair was tied back from her face, her cheekbones evident, just as they were in Robson Lodge. Lucie clicked on the website address given with the photo and the image filled her screen. A caption underneath it read "The staff of Oliver Powell Diamonds celebrate another sparkling business success. Board members including CEO Oliver Powell toast another deal".

Lucie diligently scrolled across the faces, enlarging each of them to study fuller. None of them matched the face in the photo she had shown Sarah. Which meant that he couldn't possible have been Oliver Powell.

A cloak of disappointment enveloped Lucie. Suddenly, she was doubting every word that Sarah had said to her. In a heartbeat, any tower of hope and truth seemed to crumble. Could the old lady's word be trusted?

She knew she had no choice but to make another visit. At no matter what cost. She drained her coffee mug and left the table.

Chapter 30

Peru, summer 2012

'So, is he your boyfriend, then?' Logan reached his tattooed arm across the bar to pick up his beer as he asked the question. His Australian twang emphasised the BF word making the question sound even more teasing than it already was.

'That is none of your business,' smirked Lucie, swiping the back of the young man's hand with a beermat as she replied.

'You're sleeping with the boss and everyone knows it. Is he giving you the best shifts and making sure that you always clock off early?'

'No. Just shut the fuck up.' She mouthed the F word, lowering her voice to a whisper. Connor was serving another tourist on the other side of the bar and Lucie didn't want him to hear her swearing at a paying customer. Not that it mattered. Between her, Connor, Kara and Tina, the pesky yet somehow lovable likes of Logan and his constant sidekick Billy had been called all of the names under the sun. To their faces. To them, it was almost like acceptance.

'So, where's *your* boyfriend today?' grinned Lucie, thinking of Billy. 'He's not still lying in his pit and cutting into your valuable drinking time, is he? It's getting late for you two to just be getting started.' She checked her watch. It was two in the afternoon.

'Actually, he is. He met some bird last night and she stopped over at ours. I suspect he'll be balls deep as we speak. Either that or spark out dreaming of Miranda Kerr. He'll be heading here as soon as he can, I dare say. You can always count on dear Billy Boy to want a beer or two for breakfast.'

'So he's left you to fly solo? Are you boys not over Paradise Cove yet? You've been here pretty much since the beginning of the season, haven't you? Are you not thinking of moving on?'

'Why, are you finding it hard to look at me every day knowing that you're still to taste the delights of all this?' he laughed, moving his hand across his chest and down his skinny frame until it rested on his board shorts. Any time you like, doll, it's yours.'

'I think I can resist, but thanks for the offer.' Logan had a charm but looks-wise, he was everything that failed to push Lucie's buttons. The wiry body, three chest hairs attempting to gain root against a somehow permanently never-more-than-lightly-tanned skin, an achievement that she still failed to understand given the constant sunshine, and a sleeve of machismo tattoos combo were never going to float Lucie's boat. And his dreads looked in dire need of a good wash.

'You don't know what you're missing,' pointed Logan, swigging his beer. A dribble of it curved down his chin and soaked into the bum fluff there.

'I guess that is a mystery that I'll just have to leave unsolved.'

For a moment, there was silence between them, Logan fiddling with the beermat Lucie had placed in front of him. Lucie scanned the bar. Connor was talking to a man on the far side of the bar. A new body to the beach. No surprise there. There were new visitors to Bar Dynasty every day. It was one of the many things that kept the job so fresh and so easy to get up for every morning. The clientele was incredibly transitory, faces hanging around for a couple of days, a week at most, before moving on to equally tropical climes. It was only the likes of Logan and Billy who seemed to stay any longer. Laziness or loyalty. Lucie wasn't sure.

Logan appeared to read her thoughts. 'I think we will move on at some point. Your man was telling us about this new gig in Ibiza. The bar there sounds awesome. And if ever there was a banging place to visit, then Ibiza is it. The clubs, the bars, the women, the *fun* times.' He made the word fun about four times longer than it needed to be to emphasise his delight at the thought of heading there. 'As much as the ladies of South America will mourn our leaving them behind, I think a trip to Ibiza to finish off the travels would be good move. Get down Pacha and Amnesia and lose my way. Go out on a high so to speak. Plus it's kind of on the way home if I think about it that way. I guess I'll need to head back to Australia at some point and dropping off in Europe sounds like a plan.'

'Your geography stinks. You'd be quicker getting back home from here.'

'But then, we wouldn't get to go to the party isle, would we? I'm telling myself it makes sense to do that so that we can justify the cost. I'd have to get the folks to send me the money anyway. I'm almost out of cash. Must be the price of your pink cocktails.'

173

'Logan's logic.' Lucie raised her eyebrows and smiled. 'Anyway, when did Connor speak to you about Ibiza?' It was news to Lucie and a little piece of her heart skipped a beat at the thought of Connor maybe contemplating leaving Peru behind. Even though they hadn't officially called themselves a couple, the notion that he had been speaking to the likes of Logan about somewhere on the other side of the world irked her somewhat.

'Couple of days back. A friend of his is opening a bar over there. Really good spot too, right by the beach, not far from the main clubs and the action and he was talking about heading there at some point. I guess he'd like to see some familiar faces there and that's why he mentioned it to us. He knows he can rely on Billy and I to drink that bar dry and get the ladies buzzing!'

Right on cue, Billy shuffled up the bar. His dark hair was dishevelled and his eyes looked like mere slits cut into his face.

'Yo, bro,' grinned Logan, raising his hand to high-five his friend. 'Someone looks like they could have done with more sleep.'

'What can I say,' smirked Billy, rubbing his chin and leaving Logan hanging. 'A man's got to do what a man's got to do. I was up all night satisfying that little number from the bar. Now give us a chug of your beer.'

'Get your own,' snapped Logan. 'It's thirsty work chatting this one up.' He pointed at Lucie, who was already taking the lid of a bottle of beer ready to pass to Billy.

'Not as thirst making as being nuts deep all night long, mate. Sweet.' Billy raised his hand and Logan received the high-five he had wanted a few minutes earlier. 'Boom!'

'You two are just charming,' said Lucie with a smile as she passed Billy the beer. 'Now, if you'll excuse me, I've got work to do.'

'Off to see your boyfriend, eh? Planning date night?' teased Logan. 'I'm up for a threesome if you are.'

Lucie didn't answer and walked across to Connor.

'Those two up to no good again?' he asked.

'Not really,' replied Lucie. 'Logan was just telling me about his intentions of maybe heading off to...now, where was it?' She left the sentence levitating, expecting Connor to finish it for her. When he didn't, she herself did.

'...Ibiza...where you might be going as well?' Lucie tried to mask any sticky mess of nagging disappointment that caramelised her thoughts as she enquired.

'Oh.' The one word said it all. Connor obviously knew that Lucie was a little miffed at not knowing.

'Well, something exciting has possibly come my way and that little shit shouldn't have said anything. Not until I'd spoken to you.'

'So are you thinking of quitting Peru and heading to Ibiza?'

'There's an option but I wanted you to hear it from me.' Connor flashed a smile, dazzling as ever, but for once, Lucie's core didn't melt at the sight of it.

'Why? It's not like we're joined at the hip. You can do whatever you want. I'm not your keeper. Why would I care?' The defensive harshness in her words was clear, Lucie unable to stop it before the words fell from her lips.

'Because I wanted to talk to you about it all tonight. I was going to take us out at the end of the shift for a bite to eat and a talk about the future. I wanted to show you the place in Ibiza.'

'You can do what you like. I don't need to see it to give you permission to run off. What's your future got to do with me?' Were those tears stinging Lucie's eyes? She feared they were.

'Because I wanted you to come with me. Because I don't want to do it without you.'

The potential tears moved from misery to merry.

A customer approached the bar. Connor moved to serve him.

'So can we talk tonight?' he asked Lucie before taking the man's order.

Lucie nodded. She was already counting the minutes.

Chapter 31

Now

'Sarah's had no visitors for the longest time and now you're popping up virtually every day. She must have made quite an impression on you. She calmed down after you left yesterday. In fact, she said she was looking forward to seeing you again. Talking happily about days gone by with her son, Oliver, and everything. She was pointing to the photo in her room and talking very fondly about him.'

Debbie on reception at Robson Lodge was in an effervescent mood. 'If she does start playing up again though, we may have to ask you to leave her be for a while. Even though it's good for her to have visitors, she is in her eighties and potentially in a very fragile state of health, so we have to be careful of course.'

Lucie nodded, her mind still not really able to concentrate as thoughts of the man in the photo with her mother, and the photo of Oliver in the magazine article crashed into each other in her mind. The wreckage left was one of confusion and frustration. Lucie was keener than ever to try and get her life back in order and to move on. To do that, she needed to know which signs were leading her forwards, onwards and hopefully upwards, and which were leading down a dark alley of more misery, rejection and despair. Onto another chapter of her own cursed unknown life.

'I just need to show Sarah something, if that's okay. Another photo. She's actually in this one. I found it on the internet and it might help me piece a few things together about...' She paused for a second to contemplate what to say, then added '...Uncle Oscar.'

'Head on up. Sarah's just had her lunch so she should be all happy and content as it was one of her favourites.'

Lucie smiled and walked away from the reception and up the stairs. The colours and patterns of the carpet were already becoming familiar to her. The areas that had faded and those a little stained with general wear and tear. She approached room 29 and habitually knocked before entering.

Sarah turned to face her as she walked into the room. 'Back again, Lucie? How lovely. I had a tuna salad for my lunch and it was splendid. What can I do for you?'

Debbie on reception evidently knew Sarah very well. If a simple plate of greens and fish could put Sarah in such a good and seemingly focused mood, then Lucie wondered why the home would ever consider serving anything else.

Lucie approached and kissed Sarah on the cheeks. It was the first time she had done so but somehow, it felt right. She was becoming fonder and fonder of the old lady and even if their blood relationship was still a little muddied, she was warming to her more and more with each visit.

She sat herself down on the floor alongside Sarah, her eye line level with Sarah's gemstones. A prize from the success of OPD Inc no doubt.

'Do you not like the chair?' The old lady's words were a little caustic as if suggesting her furniture was below par.

'Of course I do,' smiled Lucie. 'I just want to be close to you to show you something.'

'Another photo of Oliver?'

'Maybe.' Lucie was unsure what to say, not really knowing what was being shown anymore.

She took out her phone and showed the photo from the magazine article to Sarah. She enlarged on the face of the woman she guessed was Sarah. She knew it was.

Sarah's face lit up immediately when she looked at the screen. She touched it tenderly, as if wanting to physically connect with the reflection of her own past. 'Oh my, that's a long time ago. Look at me there. That's me, you know. I've not always been like this.'

Lucie smiled, a river of warmth flowing through her at the woman's reaction. She was obviously pleased to look at the photo.

'Do you remember when this was?' asked Lucie.

'In the good old days. When the company was going so well. I've seen you looking at my diamonds. You like them, don't you?' The old lady flashed the gemstones on her fingers under Lucie's nose. 'Oliver always kept the best for me you know. Such a good man.'

'Is Oliver in the photo with you, Sarah?' She moved her own fingers across the screen to take in the other people in the photo.

Sarah sat staring out of the window for a few seconds. Lucie was worried that she had lost her, her concentration dissipated in a mere second. Without saying a word, she looked back at the photo and scanned her eyes across it. Once more, her face lit up as she looked at the faces of those featured but she remained silent.

'Is Oliver there?' asked Lucie.

'Of course he is. It was business and he needed to be there. Of course he's there, silly girl.' Her tone was one of naughtiness and not annoyance.

'Which one, I don't recognise him from the photo over there.' Lucie pointed to the image across the room.

Sarah tapped her nail, tough and still beautifully manicured, against the screen. 'There he is. My Oliver.'

'This man here?' Lucie enlarged the photo again to show a dark haired man, matinee idol handsome with a leading man masculinity that could have seen him on the silver screen back in the 1950s. He possessed an air of cool about him that made him stand out from the other males around him.

Sarah kept stroking the screen, her actions tender and steeped in thought, as if looking at a reflection of another life, one sadly now beyond her reach.

'Yes, my Oliver. How I miss him.' Sarah brought her hand up to her neckline and touched the skin there. To Lucie, it seemed as if she was trying to transfer a piece of the love she obviously inwardly felt for the man on the screen back to her own physical being. Trying to build that connection between the past and the present. Worlds apart, coming together just for a moment.

'But that man on the screen is not the same man you have in your photo frame over there,' said Lucie. 'They can't both be Oliver.' Lucie's confusion was choking her.

'Of course they can,' quashed Sarah. 'That photo on your telephone is my late husband Oliver, may he rest in peace. The most amazing man I have ever known. Everybody loved him. But he loved me. He'd hate to see me like this. Stuck in here.'

'And the man in the other photo?' Lucie knew that she needed to get answers as quickly as she could. Sarah was lucid but previous experience had shown Lucie that she could flip into a lost grasp on reality at any time. Luck was mercifully on her side today.

'Our son, Oliver. Named after his father. Oliver Junior. Peas from the same pod. So proud of his father, he was so respectful. I guess they're together now in heaven. I wish I was there with them too.' Sarah's voice began to crack as she considered those lost. 'Anything would be better than this. I wish I were dead too.'

Sarah pushed the phone away from her and began to rock in her chair as she reflected upon her solitude. 'They've all left me.

They've all gone now. I'm on my own. With nobody to care for me. Both of them gone. My family destroyed. I have no family to speak of now. Nothing. Nobody cares. Nobody cares. Nobody cares.' She repeated her thoughts, the speed becoming quicker and more frenzied with every word. Sarah began to dig her nails into the palm of her hands again. As it had done the day before, the action terrified Lucie. She had to try and stop her.

'You do have family. There are people who care for you. Like me.' Lucie spat the words, hoping they would take effect and anesthetise Sarah's pain. She grabbed Sarah's hands and shook them in desperation. Again she spoke. 'I care for you. You have me. I'm your family.'

Sarah stopped and looked directly at Lucie. Whether the words had been understood or not, in Lucie's mind, there was no going back. She knew the truth, she knew that what the old lady had said was correct. She knew that Ruby had lied to her. It all made sense.

She knew she had to tell Sarah.

'I care for you. I'm your family. I'm your granddaughter. Oliver Junior was my father. I know it.'

In her heart, she did. For the first time in a life unknown, Lucie Palmer was certain who her father was.

As the two women stared into each other's eyes, they both cried. Tears from the same gene pool.

Chapter 32

Peru, summer 2012

The photos of the bar looked incredible. Right on the sea front, a golden sand stretching away to land in one of the bluest seas that Lucie had ever seen. The area surrounding it still somehow unspoilt by the concrete brashness of tourism. An oasis of beauty that promised to be an epicentre of hedonism, relaxation and good, chilled-out vibes to anyone who enjoyed its appeal. It made Bar Dynasty look almost pedestrian in comparison. Lucie could see why Connor was keen to sample it in the flesh.

The two of them were seated outside a restaurant looking onto the now-somehow-not-so-glorious sands of Paradise Cove. 'Are you sure that's not an artist's impression?' asked Lucie. 'How can something look so damned magical and manage to make this slice of paradise look drab in comparison?'

Connor stubbed out the cigarette he had been smoking in an ashtray and leant across the table at Lucie. 'It's an incredible spot, isn't it? And that is a photo, taken last week by my friend, Ashton, who lives in Ibiza. He's the guy who's going to be running the bar. And he's the guy who wants me to head over there to help out. And I'm the guy that wants you to come with me.'

The thought made Lucie smile. 'I thought you loved it here.'

'Lucie, don't get me wrong. I do. This place is incredible, but now and again, I get itchy feet and there's only so many days I can get excited about serving the likes of Logan and Billy and organising another rota for Kara and Tina. I think I might have already been packing my bags if it hadn't been for you. You've made this season worth sticking around for. I'll always love it here, but this offer does seem a little too good to refuse.'

'What if your friend, Ashton, doesn't want me to work there?'

'It's a condition. If he wants me, he has to want you. We're a party pack. And who wouldn't want your beautiful face persuading clubbers to part with their euros for a cocktail or two?'

'What about Kara and Tina here?' Lucie could hear that she was asking questions that didn't really need to be asked.

'What about them? If you weren't about, then maybe I would have asked one of them if they wanted to come with me, but you are about. You're my first choice. You're the one I want to be there with me. Their work here is still safe. The owner of Bar Dynasty will get somebody else in to sort out rotas and shit. People like me are ten a penny.'

Lucie wasn't sure that was true. Certainly not from the way that she felt about Connor anyway. He seemed pretty unique to her.

'Have you said anything to them as yet?'

'No, why should I. Nothing's certain until you say yes.'

'When would we have to go?'

'A few weeks. Maybe sooner. Whatever suits us really? We don't want to leave it too late as the season will be coming towards an end. Although give or take a few months, Ibiza is pretty banging all year around.'

'I'm not sure what my parents would say.'

'After all you've been through in life, I would imagine that they'd be happy that you could sample another golden opportunity and surely the fact that you're going to do it with a strong, handsome man on your arm would please them hugely.' Connor smiled, his charm poster-boy bright.

Lucie could feel her resolve and any doubts being beaten out of her with the answer to every question. But she still had one more.

'What if I say no and decide I don't want to do it?'

'That's your decision, but to be honest, if you don't, then I don't think I will. I'd miss you too much. But if we're having a lot of fun here, just imagine how much fun we could be having in Ibiza. And the pay will be better too. And you could nip home to the UK whenever you fancied really easily. It's only a few hours away whereas here you're literally light years away.'

'You've thought of everything, haven't you?'

'If I want something, then I will try and make it happen. I need to build my empire. It's how I roll. Listen, why don't you sleep on it, take a few days if you want and then let me know. I said I'd try and let Ashton know by the end of the week. It's up to you.'

Lucie said she'd sleep on it. But she didn't need to, she already knew her answer. She just hoped that Roger and Tanya would agree with her.

Chapter 33

Now

There were still two days to go until Friday. Friday marked Ruby and Terrance's return. Lucie hadn't heard from them at all during their absence. She had considered ringing her mother, keen to discuss the revelations of her family tree with Ruby. But something stopped her. This was a conversation that needed to be done in the flesh. So that every nuance of reaction could be analysed and critiqued first hand.

Lucie still didn't feel in control of her own emotions, her inner thoughts a grey area that seemed disconnected from her own being. A tangle of turmoil. Did she blame Ruby for hiding her father's identity from her, or did she blame Oliver for not being the one who was there for her? A pendulum of thought processes traversed her mind.

For once, Lucie found herself at a loss. With endless hours to fill and a restless heart, she wasn't sure how to occupy her time.

Drew was not working at the cottage for a few days so there was no conversation time to be had with the handsome gardener. Lucie was craving conversation from people of her own age. Any friends she had made before leaving for Peru had long gone, none of them wanting to be associated with a notorious drug mule who had served time.

Lucie tried reading a book, but nothing gripped her. For a while, she simply stared at the television, trying to connect with the faces and stories that she found there. Long lost families, relationship disputes, couples fresh from some reality TV show that made no sense to her. Nothing gelled. She flicked the remote control to off and threw it across the sofa, not knowing what to do next.

The cottage felt lonely without anybody else there. It felt wrong to Lucie that after six years of imprisonment of the cruellest and strictest order, she should feel trapped in the solitude of the cottage.

Abandonment and loneliness kicking in where it had no rightful place.

She decided to go out. Explore the surrounding area. She phoned a cab company and told the driver when he arrived at the cottage to take her "somewhere pretty with lots of people". She needed to be surrounded with laughter and happiness. She needed to hear life as it should be. Vibrant and joyous. Exciting and animated.

The cab driver took her to a village about half an hour away from the cottage. It must have been on the coast as a harbour dominated the central area of the village, row upon row of boats lined up, bobbing up and down gently in the rich blue waters beneath them.

Alongside the harbour itself, people of all ages seemed to be happily going about their day. It was just what Lucie needed. Young couples with babies in pushchairs, tourists snapping away with their cameras and phones at the picturesque aquatic scene, baseball-capped teenagers riding their skateboards along the harbour front. All life was there.

Lucie paid the cab driver and began to walk along the harbour side. The cobbled walkway under her feet felt knobbly and oddly strange under the flimsy sole of her sandals. Seagulls sounded overhead. The sound took her back to her days in Brighton once more.

The sky above was bright blue, barely a cloud visible. The heat of the day was growing and Lucie could feel a bead of sweat forming at the back of her neck and running down underneath her T-shirt. A young child walked past with an ice cream in his hand. The pink dome of it was decorated with sauce and nuts. A simple pleasure yet one that had been missing from Lucie's life for so long.

She scanned across the harbour and saw an ice cream shack on the far side. Heading towards it, she began to read the list of flavours written out on the sign at the front of the shack. Each one of them was a forgotten delight.

She placed her order – salted caramel with sauce and nuts – after years of being told what to eat, any offered extras would always be a positive and hard to say no to – and returned to sit on a bench to savour the treat and watch the world go by. As the heat started to melt the ice cream, a spritz of cold liquid ran gloopily down her ice cream cone and onto her hand. The feel was cold, yet not unpleasant against her skin. Lucie stared down and watched as more of the melted ice cream made its way down her palm and onto her wrist, looping around the scar that would always be there.

Triggered by the feel and appearance of the ice cream on her wrist, Lucie suddenly found herself remembering back to a similar moment on a day out with Roger and Tanya. Life with her foster parents. Life before the scar. Happier and easier times.

Blackpool, 2007

'You'll need a cloth to wipe that up,' smiled Roger Grimes. 'Tanya, Lucie's getting that ice cream everywhere. Have you got a wipe in your bag?'

Tanya smiled back at her husband. 'I'm a teacher of primary school kids. Of course, I have a wipe in my bag. I've probably got an entire medicine cabinet and at least three boxes of plasters in there. It's what we do.'

Lucie grinned across at her foster mum and dad and held out her arm. A messy swirl of chocolate ice cream was running merrily down her arm. As she held her arm aloft, a few drips of the liquid plummeted from her skin and fell with a rewarding splash against the wooden panels of pier floor beneath her feet.

Tanya handed her a wipe and Lucie mopped away at the disarray of ice cream on her arm.

Life with her foster parents was as sweet as the ice cream she had just removed from her arm. Lucie knew that she was lucky to have such amazing people in her life. People who, in just over a year, since she had been sent to them the previous summer, had given her the true sense of family that she had never been allowed to achieve in her life with Ruby back at the flat in Brighton.

But Lucie missed her mother. No amount of love and warmth and happiness from Roger and Tanya would ever change that. She was especially missing her today. There was something about a trip to the seaside that automatically brought her back to days gone by with her mother. The smell of fish 'n' chips in the air, the sound of the waves crashing against the sand, the musical cheeriness of the colourful fairground rides as they rotated. There was a feel of Ruby about all of it. Whatever her mother had done, however good or bad a mother she had proven to be, Lucie would always feel that her mother had done her best. Days out to the beach back in Brighton growing up may have been an excuse to spend a day with her latest squeeze but Ruby always took Lucie with her. And that made Lucie feel special. In a mother-daughter relationship, where a helpless feeling of remoteness had often been pushed upon her, those moments when Ruby and Lucie were together seemed even more precious and diamond-dipped.

Ruby had tried her best. Even if it had been decided that her best hadn't been good enough.

Today's venture to Blackpool was the first seaside visit that Lucie had gone on with Roger and Tanya. In the space of a year, they had visited everything from theme parks and museums through to Christmas markets and wildlife parks, but today's trip to the bright lights of Blackpool was a special one for Lucie. The kerching of the slot machines and the cries of people riding the ghost train would always remind her of where she had come from. And that was something that she never wanted to forget.

'Shall we go and play in the arcade?' asked Tanya. 'I want to see if I can try and win a toy on one of those grabby machines. Not that I have ever seen anybody win on those. But who knows, maybe we'll be the first. Miracles can happen.' Tanya, her blonde hair bright in the sunshine, looked at Lucie with added tenderness as she said the last sentence, her meaning clear. There wasn't a day that neither Roger nor Tanya didn't bless the fact that Lucie had come into their lives.

'Sounds good to me,' said Lucie. She was about to tell the Grimes that she hadn't gotten to the age of 14 growing up in Brighton without mastering the art of those grabby machines. Her bedroom growing up had been full of toys that she had won on the pier. She made a mental note to try and win one just for Tanya.

'And I fancy a game of air hockey if you're up for it,' said Roger, stroking the hairs of his beard. 'Though I've got to warn you, Lucie, I'm a demon at it.'

Lucie grinned as the three of them walked down the pier and towards the covered area of the arcade. She loved the fact that both of her foster parents had a *joie de vivre* that never seemed to diminish with age. Not that she actually knew how old they were. It didn't matter.

Lucie continued to lap at her ice cream as they walked into the arcade. The shade of the area was a welcome relief, the coolness hitting her skin with gratifying mollification. The air filled with the sound of the arcade, almost deafening in its volume, but delightful in its melody and rhythm.

Lucie was just about to walk towards one of the grabby machines, stuffed from edge to edge with multi-coloured Care Bears when her attention was caught by a peel of laughter from one of the nearby machines. There was something about the tone and bravado of it that reminded her straight away of a distant moment. It came from a woman who had her back turned to her. She and a male companion were laughing at one of those machines where little creatures pop up out of lit-up holes and you have to whack them on the head with a plastic covered hammer before they disappear again. Judging from the shrieks coming from the woman, who was the one holding the hammer, she wasn't doing a very good job but was finding the entire experience hilarious.

The woman was dressed in a tight fitting lime green T-shirt, a little too tight for her frame given the two dunes of back fat that showed across her garment, and a pair of knee length neon pink shorts. The clashing of the two colours showed a devil-may-care attitude about what she looked like. Her hair was bobbed into a shoulder length style, messy yet evidently teased into place. A plume of cigarette smoke rose from the hand not carrying the hammer. The entire look was instantly recognisable.

Something swept across Lucie. If the woman was who she thought she was, then why hadn't she been in touch? Why had she abandoned Lucie? Why had she simply disappeared from her own daughter's life? Lucie needed to know.

'Mum,' she screamed, dropping her ice cream to the floor and running towards the woman. Roger and Tanya both looked on aghast as they watched Lucie in motion. Neither was sure what was happening or what to do.

Before either of them could do anything, Lucie had reached the woman. She grabbed her by the arm and yelled "mum" again. The woman span around, startled by the interruption and dropped the hammer to the floor. It bounced slightly on the rope attaching it to the machine. The man with her spontaneously tried to grab it as it fell.

A look of confusion spread across the woman's face as she stared down at Lucie. 'I'm not your mother, dear. You've got the wrong person,' she said, her voice shaky from the intrusion and more than a little angry.

It wasn't Ruby. Lucie had been certain it was. Something about the outfit, the hair, the cigarette. All the clues were there. All of the pieces. But none of them now fitted together.

Tanya and Roger rushed towards the group.

'Lucie, what on earth are you doing?' asked Roger.

'I thought… I thought she was my mother,' stammered Lucie, her voice on the edge of tears. 'It looked like her. It did.'

'We're so sorry,' said Tanya, directing her apology at the woman and her male friend. 'Lucie must have been confused.'

'Well, pity she didn't work that out before scaring the crap out of me and spoiling my T-shirt,' snapped the woman. She gazed down at the material which was covered in sticky ice cream from where Lucie had grabbed her. Lucie stared at her own hand and saw that it was equally messy. She hadn't noticed it running down her arm again as she had been staring at the woman.

Roger took an instant dislike to the woman's petty tone but did his best to diffuse the situation. Reaching into his pocket, he pulled out a ten pound note and offered it to the woman. 'Here, take this for dry cleaning or whatever and please accept our apologies. Lucie didn't mean to scare you, did you Lucie? Now apologise to the lady, Lucie please.'

'I'm sorry.' Lucie's tears began.

'Well, I should think so,' said the woman grabbing the money from Roger's hand. She dragged on her cigarette and blowing a cloud of smoke into the air, turned and walked away, leaving a tearful Lucie with Roger and Tanya.

Tanya reached into her bag and wrapping her arm around Lucie's shoulder, gave her another wipe. 'You're going to need another wipe to clean that up, Lucie. Here you go…'

Lucie took the wipe and cried.

'Excuse me, would you like a tissue to wipe that up, dear? It's going everywhere.'

Lucie was brought back from her thoughts by the sound of an old lady leaning over her, standing in front of the bench she was sitting on and blocking the sun. She was holding out a packet of tissues. 'Your ice cream is running all down your arm.'

Lucie looked down at her arm. The cone of her ice cream was virtually empty, the ice cream having melted down the ridges of the cone in the sunshine and weaving down onto her flesh. Nearly all of her hand and the bottom part of her arm were covered in stickiness. Only a small patch remained untouched. The area with the scar, as if the ice cream was scared to go there.

Lucie thanked the lady, took the tissues and cleaned herself up. Despite the warmth of the summer sun, a chill passed through her. Thoughts of days gone by.

Chapter 34

Peru, summer 2012

Tina chinked her glass with Lucie's. 'Well, bon voyage, sweetie. I have to say that we didn't expect to be looking for a new housemate so soon. So, when are you going exactly?'

'Probably next week,' said Lucie, bringing her pink cocktail to her lips to taste the fruity goodness. The two girls were sitting at Bar Dynasty, having closed up for the day after their shift. They had been joined at the bar by Kara and Connor and also by Logan and Billy for an after-hours beach "party" to celebrate Connor and Lucie's news. Connor and Kara were swaying drunkenly on the beach, dancing to the latest from Rihanna, and Logan and Billy were pretending to light sabre fight with beer bottles. The dimming sunlight was accented by the lights of the bar reflecting in the still waters of the ocean.

'So, tell me you're going to miss us,' smirked Tina, running her hand through her blonde curls.

'I really will. I thought I would be here a lot longer than a few weeks but when something comes up that's worth following, you just have to do it I guess.' Lucie unconsciously stared across at Connor as she spoke. He was oblivious, lost in the music, beer bottle in hand.

'You've fallen for him big time, haven't you?' asked Tina. 'I don't blame you, he's a hot guy. Not my type of course, but you two look good together.' She winked, expressing her cheekiness.

'I have I guess. Not that we've really discussed it. But I know that going with him to Ibiza is the right thing to do. I'd only be here regretting it if I didn't go and I would be missing him.' Lucie giggled at her confession.

'And girl, I do not need a sulky faced misery like that around me so it's a good job you're going.' Tina paused for a second, draining some more of her cocktail before asking 'do you love him?'

Lucie felt her cheeks redden. It could have been from the drink but she knew it was from embarrassment at being asked. Especially as she knew the answer.

'I think I do, yes.' She clenched her teeth as she spoke, almost afraid to hear her thoughts out load. 'He's such an open person, carefree and happy with the world. He never seems to get angry and he has the patience of a saint. He must do to put up with customers like the dynamic duo over there.' She pointed at Logan and Billy, now both play ninja fighting on the beach.

'And it helps that he's gorgeous too, right?' added Tina.

'Hell yeah!' replied Lucie. 'He's the first man I've ever been with, you know. There was nobody before him.'

'You're telling me that you'd never...' Tina's voice petered out in disbelief.

'That's what I'm telling you,' laughed Lucie. 'I was waiting for the right one and he was it.'

'OMG. Was it romantic? Tell me all.' Tina poured them both another cocktail from the jug sitting between them on the bar, draining the last drops from it, and raised her glass. 'I'm all ears.'

Lucie cast her mind back to their first encounter in the back alley at the carnival. 'Well, I wouldn't say it was a romantic location exactly...' She explained to Tina what had happened.

Mercifully, she had finished the story by the time Connor and Kara, having danced themselves into a golden glow over the latest summer tunes, came to join the girls at the bar. Connor instantly slipped his arm around Lucie's shoulder, his skin slicked with a little moisture from his dancing.

'Is that a jug of cocktails screaming to be made I hear behind the bar, Tina?' teased Connor, staring at the empty jug.

Tina took the hint and picked it up, waggling it at Connor as she did so. 'I am off duty, you know,' she smiled, jumping down from her chair. 'Same again, folks? I'll make a couple.'

The group nodded.

'I'll give you a hand,' said Kara, following her friend behind the bar. Connor and Lucie were left alone.

Connor leant in and kissed Lucie gently on her neck, his teeth nibbling slightly against her skin. Lucie curved her neck in appreciation.

'So this time next week, we'll be staring out at the Mediterranean and basking in the rays of the sunset at Café del Mar. That sound good?' Connor continued to nuzzle as he spoke.

'It sounds divine. Have you found out all of the flight details yet?' Despite the romance of the situation, Lucie was still keen to know the whys and wherefores and the practicalities of how their adventure to Ibiza was going to happen. Life had taught her to never make assumptions about things always going smoothly and to plan.

'Ashton's booked the tickets for us. He's paying. He can't wait for us to arrive. I was Skyping him earlier. Telling me all about you again. He's booked us both on flights. You go on the Wednesday and I head out the next day. He couldn't get us on the same flight as they were so busy. It's the time of year. He's arranging to meet you when you arrive in Ibiza. Take you to where we're going to be staying, let you settle in and get ready for my arrival twenty four hours later. I literally can't wait.'

A moment of disappointment passed through Lucie. For once, it was an alien feeling. 'So, we're not travelling together? That's a bit shitty.' Her words sounded harsher than she meant them to be.

'And Ashton paying for us to fly off to paradise is in what way at all…ahem…shitty?' Connor teased, knowing that there was no real upset in Lucie's outburst.

'Sorry, it's not shitty. I just meant that I'll miss you if we're not flying together.'

'I get that,' sniffed Connor. 'But at least you'll be able to help me straight away with my jet-lag when I land in Ibiza. If you know what I mean.'

There was no doubting his intention as he moved his hand up Lucie's leg, where it had been resting, and tried to ease it underneath the hem of the loose-fitting shorts she was wearing.

She slapped it away gently. 'Easy. Not here. Kara and Tina will see. And Logan and Billy's eyes will be popping out on stalks.'

'Not just their eyes!' laughed Connor, moving his hand away.

'I'll actually miss them a little bit, you know?' said Lucie, looking over in the direction of the two Aussies.

'Well, they may turn up in Ibiza. And if they don't, well I'm sure there are a million equally daft ravers like those two who will.'

'I've had such an amazing time here. It's been pretty special. It's nice that for once in life everything is working out so well. I'm so used to things going wrong and never being the one who gets what she wants that I guess I find it hard to believe sometimes.'

'Not getting cold feet, are you?' There was a trace of worry in Connor's voice.

'In this heat? Are you kidding? Not possible, mister,' laughed Lucie, allaying his fears.

'You had better believe it. In just a few days, you'll be getting just what you deserve. The sun on your back, breeze in your hair and chilling at one of the most magical places on earth. And if you don't mind, I'll be there by your side. Being here in Paradise Cove is special, but I feel that there's something extra special about where you're going. About where we're going. I can't wait to prove it to you.'

'There was just such a long time in my life where things were always so wrong, that everything seemed so hard to deal with, that I guess I find it strange when things go my way.' Lucie became a little lost in her thoughts as she spoke. 'Life wasn't easy until my foster parents came along and even then, I was always thinking back to days with my mum and I guess I didn't always know how to really enjoy myself. I guess I feared that everything would eventually go wrong and be spoiled, so I couldn't let loose. I was always so worried about what might be around the corner that I couldn't enjoy the moment. Does that make sense?'

'Yes. But look around you. Things are good. How many people can say that their view right now is as glorious as this?' Connor placed his hand under Lucie's chin and lifted it towards his face. 'And that includes me being in your eye line, Lucie,' he added cockily. His eyes, as green as centre court at Wimbledon, reached into her soul, melting any doubts. 'All of the old Lucie that you've told me about with your mother and the feeling of being abandoned is over. You're here, things are good…very good…and we're about to embark on another incredible adventure.'

Connor let his lips find Lucie's, the connection needed and welcome to her.

'So how did you manage to persuade Roger and Tanya to let you run off to Ibiza with a man they've never met?'

'I said it was what I wanted to do and they thought it was a good idea and said that if I was certain about staying away a bit longer, then it was up to me. They've always been there for me. The only ones who really have. I know I'm lucky to have them.'

Tina and Kara arrived with the two jugs of cocktails, this time a swirly mass of yellow and red liquid filling both, slices of fruit bobbing up and down within them.

'We've created something special just for you two,' smiled Kara, the black curls on her head bouncing with delight as she spoke.

'What's in it?' asked Connor. 'No gin I hope, as this one is getting all maudlin and woe-is-me.'

Lucie could see in his eyes that he was only joking and not trivialising what she had said at all. She smiled back at him.

'I think we've used pretty much every alcohol we serve at the bar,' said Tina. 'Looks good, doesn't it?' She poured the liquid into four glasses and handed one each to the group.

'Cheers. To your new adventures in Ibiza and thank you Lucie for sharing this one. It's been a blast.' Tina lifted her glass into the air and the four of them followed suit. A little splash of the liquid slopped over the side of Lucie's glass as she did so. 'All for one, and one for all,' said Tina.

Lucie nodded at both Tina and Kara and took Connor's hand in hers, as the four of them tasted the cocktails. It tasted strong and not particularly pleasant. But Lucie didn't mind. At that moment, any thoughts of the upset that she'd been served in life disappeared into thin air. Any melancholy woes vanished. All she felt was happiness. And excitement for what was to come. For the next chapter in her life. A life that certainly seemed to be going her way. For once.

Chapter 35

Now

Lucie and Drew were sharing an evening together at an Italian restaurant not far from the cottage. She had offered to take the gardener out as there was still a day before Ruby and Terrance were due back from their trip and Lucie was craving company and conversation. She liked Drew a lot. He was close to her age and fun to be around. On top of that, she wanted to thank him for clearing up the broken mirror in her bedroom a few days earlier and also for rescuing her when she became trapped in the attic. And she could discuss Roger and Tanya's garden too. Plus there was also the issue of sharing her latest news. The reasons to see him seemed plentiful.

She had already shared her latest family news as they began to tuck into the two oversized bowls of pasta that had just been placed on their table.

'So Uncle Oscar is really a man called Oliver and he was your real dad. That's pretty cool...' Drew took a spoonful of food, before adding with his mouth full, '...isn't it?' unsure whether he should actually be pleased or not. His words, as ever, possessed a playful, innocent nature. He could describe some of the worst atrocities in history and still make them sound fairy-tale.

'I think it is. Finally, I can say who my dad was. I can put a name to him. That was something that I'd never been able to do before, so that's a good change. But there are two things that I can never change and one is the fact that he's dead, so I will never know him, and the second is that he did choose to abandon me and my mum. He didn't want to know us. That really sucks. Why would he do that?'

'Yeah, I don't get that. If I were ever going to have a child, then I would never abandon them. You don't do that. It's so wrong.'

'In your world, Drew, yes. But sadly, he did. Maybe he wasn't a very nice person. I have to contend with that idea. In my head, the idea of my dad had always been this picture perfect image of a caring, loving, strong, handsome, "everybody-loved-him" kind of guy. How I wanted my perfect family to be in my dreams. Maybe he wasn't that loved by others. I know his mother loved him, and obviously my mother loved him at some point but maybe that's where it ended. Perhaps love wasn't something he was that capable of either. Everybody wants a hearts and flowers kind of family, don't they? It's not just me. But that's something I will never have.'

Drew listened on as Lucie spoke. He could see a sadness in her eyes. One that he wanted to try and quash.

'But you've gained a grandmother and at least now you can talk about your dad and know who he was. He was a big businessman. Dealing in diamonds. That's fancy. Like something out of one of those posh American series you see on TV. Mine was a dustman, not that there's anything wrong with that, but it's hardly diamonds, is it?'

'At least you knew yours though,' said Lucie, chasing a piece of pasta around the edge of her bowl. 'There's a normality there that I've always craved for. I don't mean to sound heartless as I know I'm not the only girl in the world who has been raised by a single mother who wasn't always able to cope, but I just feel as if there's always been this huge gap in my life, a massive space where my dad should have been, where my family should have been. As if there was a connection that I never knew about. And now I know that the space will be never be filled.'

'But you've found Sarah.'

'And that is fabulous. Having a grandmother and one who seems genuinely happy to have me in her life. Or at least I think she is. I can't help feeling that I've found her too late as well. Her dementia can be crippling. As much as she has been able to give me information and fill in some of the gaps, she's a very old woman who sometimes doesn't even seem to know what day it is. I wish I could have spent more time with her when I was growing up. When she wasn't trapped in the care home. When we could have had that normal life.'

'She sounds like a nice lady. Even though she used to scare me when I stared through the fence looking into the garden. Like one of the wicked witches in *The Wizard of Oz*.' Drew laughed at his comment, remembering days gone by.

'There is nothing scary about her. She's an old lady who loved her son and obviously didn't like my mum for some reason.'

'What does Mrs Palmer say about it all?'

'I've not spoken to her yet. She and Terrance don't get back until tomorrow and I really don't want to have a conversation about my dad over the phone. I need to ask mum what happened and why it happened. There's a little bit of me that really blames her for not telling me about my dad when he was alive and I hate the fact. She must have kept it hidden because she felt so abandoned by him. I can understand that. I just wish I could have talked to him.'

'I did. I talked to him.'

'When?'

'When I was little. He caught me looking over the fence once and into the garden and he was out there for some reason or another and he came and chatted to me. Asked what I was doing?'

'What did he sound like? What did he say?' Lucie was desperate for any scrap of information she could find about her dad. It was easy enough to try and Google business details about Oliver Powell, but the human side was what she really wanted to know.

'He seemed really nice. I think he knew I was scared of the old lady as he said he'd seen me there before and he'd once watched me run off when the lady came out of the cottage. He asked me why I was staring into the garden, staring up the path, but not in a horrible way as if to say keep out, he was genuinely interested in what I was doing there.'

'What was his voice like?' asked Lucie, the words falling from her lips in rapid succession, keen to soak up any titbit of information like a sponge.

'Oh gosh, I just remember it being deep and that he was a really handsome man. I was only young, probably about eleven or twelve and even though I was growing up, I remember that he was a lot taller than me and towered over me as he spoke. But he didn't seem menacing or anything like that. Not like a giant. He just seemed…' Drew searched for the word. 'Cool.' He paused for another second. 'Yeah, cool. That's how I would describe him. He seemed like he actually liked speaking to me. Normally, if the old lady was about, I would scarper, but when he spoke to me, I didn't seem to mind. I didn't really speak to him again as the old lady seemed to spend a lot more time in the garden than he did. I guess he was busy. But I liked him.'

It wasn't much in reality, but to Lucie it felt like an opus of information. Her father was kind, caring, strong and cool. For a while, as she juggled the four words in her head, a contentment spread across her being, a happiness that her dad was a good man. Then an ink spot of doubt and torment began to escalate from within. If he had been that kind, then why had to tossed Ruby and her unborn child aside? Why had he not wanted to know her? Why had he been missing in action throughout her entire life? And why, if he didn't care at all, had he left the cottage to Ruby in his will?

The unanswered stain of confusion and doubt took hold of Lucie.

She finished her plate of food and reached across the table. She took hold of one of Drew's hands and squeezed it gently. He too had finished eating. The action surprised him but he didn't move his hand away. It was more of a personal action than an intimate one.

'Thanks, Drew. At least I have something. I think I would have liked him too. I think.'

Lucie couldn't be sure. Not until she'd spoken to Ruby the next day.

Chapter 36

Peru, summer 2012

The effect of the cocktails was definitely shading the edges of Lucie's thoughts with a fogginess that was definitely making the sand beneath her feet a little more unsteady than normal. Perhaps that second jug that Kara and Tina had made hadn't been such a good idea after all.

Lucie sat herself on the sand in an attempt to stop her wobbling. The short walk she had made from Bar Dynasty to the edge of the sea had only proven to her how much the constant drinking at her and Connor's leaving "party" had taken hold of her ability to balance.

The evening felt like it was coming to an end and Lucie had to admit that she had loved it. All of her life she had struggled to sometimes let herself go and give in to enjoyment just in case it was snatched from her. Getting drunk was not something that had ever sat comfortably with her. Memories of her mother she guessed. The mess it made. The heartache it caused. Even at college, when her fellow classmates were heading off night after night to the student union to drink themselves into a blurred pit of hedonistic pleasure, Lucie always seemed to hold back. The sensible one some said. The foolish one said others. The boring one said Lucie about herself.

But they hadn't seen what she had seen. Her mother hungover after another night of drink and drugs, unable to even send her own daughter to school with a decent packed lunch or an ironed blouse for her school uniform. That was bound to blur a person's perception of what joys could be found inside a bottle or a bag or powder.

Lucie leant forward and placed her finger in the soft sand by the water's edge. It was damp to the touch but not soaking. She moved her finger and made the shape of a heart in the sand. She looked around to see if any of her friends from Bar Dynasty were watching her. She couldn't see any of them. No surprise as the bar was easily a few hundred yards from where she was sitting. Lucie had wanted to be alone with her thoughts for a few seconds, weighing up just how lucky she really was to be facing such an idyllic future with such a good man by her side. Leaving a smiley Connor to dance again with Kara and the daft Logan and Billy sharing their tried and tested tips on "how to please women in the bedroom" with a totally non-convinced Tina, Lucie had excused herself and said that she was going to walk along the water's edge. The gentle waves that lapped the sands were illuminated by the moon overhead and Lucie felt drawn to spending a few minutes alone with them.

Smiling to herself, she moved her fingers and wrote her initials in the heart. Underneath it, she wrote the number four and below that "CP" for Connor Perkins. It was a childish action but one that made her woozy brain smile. A smile that automatically spread itself to her face. She reached into the pocket of her shorts, pulled out her phone and took a photo of it. The tide would have taken it away by the morning and somehow, it seemed the perfect simple reminder of what a good time she had experienced in Peru. Perhaps one day, she'd even show it to Connor. Who knew what the future held?

The sound of the water was hypnotic to Lucie's mind. The lapping back and forth, its beat regular and somehow calming. As she listened to its rhythm, the world immediately around her seemed to blur, not from the alcohol but from the feeling of being sucked into the sound, lost in its tonality. There was something safe about it. It reminded her of the many times she had sought sanctuary in the bath at the flat back in Brighton when she was younger. The language of the waters around her as she moved her hand across its soapy surface, causing a small splash and a soft sound. Delicate enough to be subtle and flowing yet somehow monumental enough to mentally drown out the sounds of her mother and her friends enjoying themselves on the other side of the bathroom door. An action so small yet for her sufficient enough to, albeit temporarily, block out the mayhem and the madness. The shrieks of laughter, the thud of the music, the constant arrivals through the open front door. Lucie would immerse herself below the surface as ever, the splashing of the surface a prelude to her own immersion. A baptism of peace and sanity. Away from her mother's pleasures.

Sitting on the beach, the sound of the water filling her head, Lucie thought of her mother and of the times when a young Lucie would sit on the toilet or the edge of the bath and cry her eyes out, afraid that she was not good enough to gain her mother's affection. Or her attention. Not realising that it wasn't her own fault. The drugs made Ruby unable to love, unable to comfort. If only a young Lucie had been able to realise that.

As Lucie came back from her thoughts, she realised that she had frenziedly scratched her fingers across the heart and the letters within in. The heart was now unreadable. Lucie was unaware of doing it, her destructive actions coming to her unannounced when deep in her thoughts.

The look of the heart now saddened her. Thank goodness she had taken the photo or the moment would have been lost.

She took a few deep breaths and tried to work out just how her head felt. It seemed somehow clearer than when she had sat down. The real test came when she stood back up, her feet not as wobbly as they had seemed before. She walked back in the direction of the bar and her friends.

The night had obviously taken its toll on Logan and Billy. The two lads were both flat on their backs on the sand, eyes shut, a gentle hum of snoring coming from one of them. Lucie couldn't tell who. The sound of the music, David Guetta's *Titanium*, filled the air, the volume softer than it had been earlier but still loud enough to know that some kind of good time was still in swing. Tina came running towards Lucie as soon as she saw her, her blonde mop of hair jiggling about her face as she did so. An air of excitement and relief flowed from her.

'There you are. I thought you'd bottled it and gone back to the flat. I want to dance to this. It's the tune of summer and will always remind me of you, me, us and this. The good times. Come on!' Tina grabbed Lucie by the hand and pulled her, almost dragging her to nearer the source of the music.

The two girls danced; Lucie's drunkenness a little easier to deal with as she moved her body to the beat. Tina's face was pure euphoria. As the song ended, she automatically hugged Lucie in her arms. The grip was limpet tight.

'I'm so going to miss you.' A tear started to stain the corner of Tina's eye. She scrunched her eyes in an attempt to stem any flow. 'No, I promised myself you'd never see me cry!'

'I'll miss you too,' echoed Lucie. 'Now, don't you make *me* cry.' She pointed to Tina's face as a tear began to tumble down her cheek.

Tina wiped away the tear and smiled. 'Damn. I'm sorry. It's just that it's been fun having you around and it won't be the same when you go. Kara and I have loved having you at the bar and as a roomie. The Three Musketeers! I'm really happy for you though.'

Mention of Kara picked at Lucie's brain. 'Where is Kara? She's not gone home, has she?'

'Party girl Kara! No way! She was dancing with Connor and then they disappeared about ten minutes ago. Not sure where.' Tina could tell just how odd the situation sounded, not to mention a little suspect, as she spoke each word. Lucie too felt a streak of worry flood through her. She wasn't sure why. Perhaps it was her own self-doubt?

'I'll go and find him and demand he shift his sorry ass back on this sandy dance floor with us right now,' said Lucie, her words jovial but desperate to try and camouflage the knot of worry that was definitely tightening inside her.

'I'll fix another set of drinks,' said Tina, heading towards the bar.

'Not like the last ones, eh? Maybe go a bit lighter on the…well, on the everything!' Lucie laughed. Again, it was to hide her own worry.

Lucie walked around the back of the bar. There was no sign of either Kara or Connor. The moon shone overhead and lit up a large expanse of the beach. A few late night revellers still dotted the sands but Connor and Kara were not amongst them.

He wouldn't have gone home. She knew that. He would have said goodbye. They were about to travel half way across the world together, so she couldn't let herself believe that he would disappear without so much as a goodbye. Especially when it was essentially their night of celebration. Lucie kept trying to extinguish any worries but something niggled the back of her mind and kept fanning the flames.

It was as Lucie was passing a series of huge rocks that stuck out of the sand that she heard laughter. The rocks were often used during the day by sunbathers, their presence, wide and flat-topped, made them perfect for sun worshippers who preferred not to rest their oiled bodies on the golden sands.

The laughter was female and was coming from behind one of the rocks. Lucie stopped to try and concentrate on the sound. It came again, this time accompanied by the laughter of a man too. She instantly recognised it as Connor.

A million hazard lights went off in her mind. What were the two of them doing behind a rock, secluded and hidden from the others? Surely, Connor wasn't being unfaithful to her. And not with Kara. She was supposed to be Lucie's friend. Neither of them would be that heartless or indeed that stupid would they? Something in her mind told her that it could be true, that her own failings had caused it.

Lucie took a deep breath and walked behind the rock to the place where the laughter was coming from.

Both Connor and Kara were fully clothed. That was the first thing Lucie noticed. If they were getting down and dirty, then either the moment had passed or they were not yet at the clothes-shedding stage.

Kara spotted Lucie first. She beamed a huge smile and stumbled towards her. 'Lucie…we were just…just…' Kara didn't finish the sentence.

Lucie stared across at Connor, who was also now looking in her direction and smiling. He was bent over a flat area on the rock with a rolled up note shoved up his nostril. Two fat lines of white powder decorated the rock in front of him. Without saying a thing, he turned back to the coke, snorted it and wiped his nose. He was smiling throughout.

He handed the note to Kara who took her place over the second line and vacuumed it up.

'Hello babe, I know you don't like this so we didn't want to do this under your nose.' His words were slurred a little. 'No pun intended.' He laughed at his choice of words. He sidled up alongside her and linked his hands around her waist. Lucie didn't stop him. Again, she wasn't sure why. 'Unless you want some of course. There's plenty more to go around.'

Flashes of anger popped inside Lucie's head. After all she had said to him about life with her mother, Connor was still flaunting his drug use. As much as she was relieved that she hadn't caught the two of them cheating, she still felt cheated by his actions. How could he? She'd opened up to him and it felt like a betrayal.

Yet when his lips found hers, she couldn't help but respond. When he ran his hands down the side of her body, she still got thrills. When he explained that taking the drug out of her sight was a kind and thoughtful thing to do, she felt herself believe him.

She was still holding his hand when the three of them walked back towards Bar Dynasty.

She hated that Connor took drugs. Especially after her confession. Why did he have to do it? Almost flaunt it. But something made her forgive him, even if she couldn't forget he'd done it too. She guessed she did love him after all. More than she had realised. A strong and painful kind of love. Strong enough for

her to forgive him for the very thing that had snatched her own
mother from her.

Chapter 37

Now

'Spain really was bloody marvellous, Lucie. We should go. Isn't that where you were kind of going when you got stopped in Peru? Marvellous for topping up my tan even more. Terrance is staying there for a bit longer, doing some more work or something. He has friends there so I left him to it. Him and his mates can play big boys or whatever it is that they do but I wanted to come home and see you.'

Ruby was in an excitable mood and, as ever, not an overly tactful one. She had been ever since she had walked back into the cottage.

'He wanted me to stay on, but I thought *screw that* and got one of those cheap airlines home. You can get anywhere for the price of a bean. It's nice to have money, but sometimes you do think why pay £500 when you can do the same for £50. I guess you can take the girl out of the council estate, but you can't always take the council estate out of the girl.'

Lucie sat and listened. As she had done since her mother's arrival nearly an hour earlier. She'd heard detailed accounts of hotel room décor, minuscule facts about what was eaten during restaurant business meetings, and been given a fashion-mag-worthy rundown of every scarf, hat, pair of boots, belt and dress that Ruby had bought. She'd even sat and smiled as her mother presented her with a bottle of perfume and a box of milk chocolates that she had bought back for her. The perfume was one that she didn't like at all and the chocolate was milk. Lucie preferred dark and always had. But Lucie was polite and accepted the gifts with the gratitude that they deserved. Even if they weren't to her taste.

Inside, her mind was bubbling. Ready to ask every one of the questions that had been beaming around her brain for the last few days. Her heart felt like it was beating out of her chest too. But Lucie needed to wait for the right moment. If she started to unravel everything that was whirl pooling around inside her, then there would be no stopping her and Lucie was determined that the moment be right.

The right moment came when the two of them had finished dinner at the kitchen table that evening. Steeled by a shared bottle of wine, the two women were just finishing a risotto made by Lucie when she began her questioning. Lucie fiddled nervously, one of her fingers subconsciously running along the length of the scar on her wrist as she started.

'I went to see Sarah again, mum. You know, the lady at Robson Lodge, the one who lived here with…'

'Your uncle Oscar, I know, Lucie. I know who you are talking about, Lucie, the mad woman who lives down the lane. Has she become your best friend or something?' Any jollity that decorated her voice as she had been speaking about her time in Spain suddenly seemed to be replaced with a barbed wire of defensiveness and annoyance.

'She told me about Uncle Oscar. Your step-brother.'

'What did she say? More nonsense?' Ruby lifted her wine glass and took a large swig from it. A nervous action? It appeared so. The diamond on her finger danced in the light that shone from the bulb hung above the kitchen table, the stone's oversized facets looking almost fake in their enormity.

'Why don't you tell me?'

'What is there to say about him?'

'That's for you to say, isn't it?'

Ruby placed her wine glass back down on the table a little too quickly as if misjudging the distance. The red liquid within moved angrily from side to side as she did so.

Lucie continued her interrogation. God knows she had been on the other side of one too often over the last few years. For once, it felt almost good to be the person asking the questions as opposed to being the person sweating under the spotlight.

Ruby sat in silence, her fingers fiddling nervously with the bottom of the wine glass. Lucie could see her mother's cheeks starting to turn in colour, their shade almost matching that of the wine. It was clear that she was not enjoying the conversation.

Lucie spoke. 'There is no Uncle Oscar, is there? You've haven't got a step-brother, have you?'

'What do you want me to say?' Ruby's voice was uncharacteristically frail in its delivery. A sign of defeat?

'The truth. It's all I've ever wanted. Don't I deserve that?'

'I didn't mean to lie to you. It just seemed like the easiest thing to do. The least harmful. I don't know what to say.' There was genuine sadness in Ruby's eyes and a confusion as to how to continue.

Lucie attempted to coax her mother's words. 'Too many people have lied to me in my life, mum. I'm only 25 and I know hardly anything about my own existence. I've been hurt too many times but finally, after everything I've gone through, I might be getting somewhere at long last. Finally discovering who I really am. You weren't there for me for so long but I have never stopped loving you, despite everything. We've always been connected. It's so special to have you back in my life. That's something that I never expected so come on, do the right thing.' Lucie reached across the table and took her mother's hand in hers, hoping the connection would jump-start conversation. 'Just tell me the truth, that's all. Tell me about Oliver Powell. Tell me about my father.'

Ruby hung her head down, unable to look at Lucie in the eye, as if a visual connection would break her own inner frailty, rendering her unable to explain her actions.

'Maybe this will help.' Lucie stood and moved to the kitchen drawer, opening it and locating the photo of her father and mother together. A realisation of the fact that she was staring at the only photo of her two parents together that she had ever seen hit her and for a second, she needed to steady herself against the kitchen counter as her mind blurred at the thought. Still a little dizzy on her feet, she returned to the table and placed the photo in front of Ruby.

Ruby picked it up, her hands shaking a little, the edges of the photos moving slightly and revealing her nerves. 'Where did you find this?'

'Where do you think?' Lucie was answering questions with questions. It had been done to her so many times in Peru, a technique that had always broken down any walls of avoidance she had attempted to build. She hoped it would do the same to her mother.

'That bloody gardener give it to you, did he?' Ruby knew exactly where the photo had come from.

'Don't blame Drew. He was going to throw away all of the crap he found down the well. But luckily, I was with him when he'd uncovered the stash of photos. He thought they were just junk. I'm guessing you did too?'

'I thought it was best they were gone. Nobody needed to see them.'

'I did. They're not rubbish to me. That photo has helped me discover what I needed to know. Why did you do it?'

Ruby looked Lucie directly in the eyes. Her own were a little bloodshot from the threat of tears. 'I wanted to protect you.'

'From what? From the truth? That's not fair.'

Ruby crumbled, any unwillingness to explain finally evaporated. 'There was no Oscar, you know that now. It was your father, Oliver, who lived here with his mother, Sarah.' She considered her words. 'Your grandmother.'

Lucie nodded without saying a word.

'Everything I said to you about your father when I showed you the scrapbook was true. He did walk away from me. And from you.' She touched her belly without thinking, as if recalling her days of pregnancy. 'I was happy with Oliver, your father, we were going to get married. We weren't together for very long but I thought everything was good. Huh, I thought. He was so much more than I had ever imagined I would have in life. Everybody seemed to think I was punching above my weight when we were together. I did lie to you when I said that he was just there at your conception. He was much more to me than that. But sadly, it appeared he didn't feel the same. Not in the end.'

The family bond within Lucie couldn't help but feel some sympathy for her mother. Had she really wanted for a happy family with Oliver Powell? Wanted the same thing that Lucie had always dreamt of. It seemed so. She needed to know how.

'Tell me about him. You owe me that.'

Ruby poured herself another glass of wine, removed a cigarette from her packet, lit it and dragged heavily on it with her deep red lips. As she released a thick mist of smoke into the air, she stared into Lucie's eyes. To Lucie, it felt like her stare was reaching right in to the deepest recesses of her soul. Perhaps for the first time ever.

'Yes I do. I do owe you…'

Chapter 38

London, winter 1991

'So Miss Palmer, my name is Cassandra Wilkes, the head of this department. This will be your desk and you will be working in a team of secretaries for the board of directors themselves. You'll be taking letters, filing invoices and generally dealing with all of the admin that comes with a company like OPD Inc. If you need any help, then I am here if need be, although obviously I am very busy being Mr Powell's *personal* secretary. There are jobs that only I can do as his chosen PA. But Katherine and Samantha are secretaries too so they can help you with day-to-day tasks if need be. You'll have an hour for lunch, not a minute more, and that will be taken from half past twelve. You'll be back at your desk for half past one of course. And we finish at six o'clock although sometimes there may be some late-in-the-day emergencies that need to be dealt with before leaving. I trust that sounds perfectly okay.'

Ruby had already decided that she would happily punch Cassandra Wilkes squarely in her badly-made-up face from the moment that the 40-something stick-thin wasp of a woman had met her at the lift of her new office job. When Ruby had nodded her hellos to Katherine and Samantha, the two secretaries sharing the room with her at the OPD Inc diamond company, she suspected that they felt exactly the same. Both of them carried an air of knowing that their immediate boss was so far wedged up her own backside that she had a perfect view of each and every one of her internal organs.

It was nineteen-year-old Ruby's first day on the job. A job she had found through an agency in Brighton. She hadn't ideally wanted to work in London, but money was tighter than ever, especially since the death of her grandmother, Alice, a few months earlier, the woman who had raised her singlehandedly since her own biological mother had done a runner shortly after Ruby's birth.

Ruby needed a job and albeit temporary, the one at OPD Inc, a diamonds company no less, seemed swanky, sophisticated and ultimately posh, a definite step up from her friends that were flipping burgers or washing dishes in one of Brighton's eateries. Her secretarial skills were not brilliant but they were definitely passable and if any of her bosses needed competent words per minute and a good grasp of shorthand, then she was definitely their girl. So despite not enjoying the prospect of the daily commute from Brighton to London, Ruby took the temp position. If it meant being surrounded by diamonds every day, then perhaps it would be like something out of *Knot's Landing* or *Falcon Crest*, her favourite US TV escapism. There was always some kind of rags to riches going on in them. One day out on the streets, next day dripping in jewellery and shopping for fur coats. A girl could dream.

By the end of the first day, Ruby was already realising that a life dripping in diamonds was unlikely to occur in an office that sat in silence for hours on end. She had suggested they put the radio on, a notion which both Katherine and Samantha seemed to love but had been speedily vetoed by Cassandra. Cassandra had even stopped Ruby from smoking at her desk as she said that "I do not want to leave the office and return home at night to my husband smelling as if I've spent the day bathing in forty B&H". Yet somehow, the stuffy Cassandra was more than happy to take dictation for Oliver Powell, head honcho at OPD Inc, in his office as he puffed on a cigar fatter than Cassandra's emaciated waist. Double standards at its best. Katherine and Samantha seemed okay, having a bit of a spark inside them – they had discussed Cassandra and her lack of make-up skills at great length every time their boss was absent. The general decision was that Cassandra obviously did her make-up in the dark. How else could they explain the poorly blended foundation and the overly applied mascara? No, the two young women who shared secretarial duties with Ruby were pleasant, but Ruby couldn't see her adding them to her Christmas card list.

As Ruby finished her day and took the lift down from the 27th floor of the office building in London's SE1 that housed OPD Inc, she reached into her bag and took out her cigarettes. She took one from the packet, already contemplating maybe taking another so that she could chain smoke as soon as she hit the air outside. Who the hell worked in an office where smoking wasn't allowed? Cassandra Wilkes it seemed. And as a result, so now did Ruby.

Ruby was no less than half a second through the revolving doors at the front of the building than her cigarette was lit. She let out a sigh of audible relief as she blew a cloud of smoke into the cold evening air and stood still in appreciation of its welcome, savouring every moment.

She was about to take a second drag when a man coming through the revolving doors behind her slammed directly into her, unable to stop himself from moving onwards due to people behind him in the doors but unable to walk freely because of Ruby blocking his way.

'Excuse me, we need to move.' His voice was deep and direct without being authoritative. He grabbed Ruby around the waist and pushed her to one side freeing the way for those behind him. Ruby stumbled slightly on her heels and dropped her cigarette. It rolled away from her into the gutter, fizzling out as it met with the dampness of the ground.

'Oh for Christ's sake, I've been waiting hours for that. What the hell do you think you're doing, you…' She was about to add a few choice words of description when she turned to face the man who had grabbed her. He was about her own age, perhaps a couple of years older, and every lustrous dark hair on his head was coiffed into position. His eyes were bright and the smile that beamed out at her somehow took all of her fire away, extinguishing the heat of her own anger the same way that the damp pavement had done to her cigarette seconds earlier. He possessed an air of class that was only added to when he spoke, his voice rich in tone yet tender in delivery.

'I am so sorry but you were blocking the exit. I thought I was going to have to take another lap of the doors instead of getting out. Here, let me give you another cigarette.' He reached inside the breast pocket of the suit he was wearing and pulled out a cigarette case. He flicked it open and offered Ruby the contents. She gladly took one, happy to accept a free replacement for the one she had lost. He too took one from the case for himself.

He reached into another pocket and pulled out a lighter. He flicked it open and lit both of their cigarettes. Neither of them spoke until they had both exhaled a billow of mist into the air.

'Nothing like it, eh? Always feels fabulous.' It was the man who spoke.

'Yes.' It was all Ruby could say, still transfixed by the handsome stranger.

'I'm Oliver, nice to meet you.' He held out his hand to shake hers.

She did so, returning the compliment. 'Ruby, you too.'

'Do you work here?' he asked. 'Silly question, I suppose. Why else would you be heading out of the door just after six in the evening? Which floor are you on?'

'Up near the top. It's my first day. Some jewellery company. I thought it was going to be like some glamorous soap opera but to be honest, I was stuck with a bitch of a boss who looked down on me like shit on her shoe and two other secretaries who, nice though they are, were a little too meek and mild for my liking. What about you?'

Oliver smiled. 'I'm up near the top too. Dealing with figures and tedious stuff all day. I won't bore you with it. I'm always glad when I can walk away.'

Ruby smiled, unsure what to say. She took another drag on her cigarette, checked her watch and threw the butt into the kerb. 'I suppose I had better get going; I have to catch a train back to Brighton. That's where I live.' Despite her words, she made no immediate attempt to depart.

Oliver finished his cigarette too. He stubbed it out on an ashtray mounted to the brick wall at the side of the building. Ruby suddenly felt a little foolish that she hadn't seen it and had thrown hers away so carelessly. 'So, you thought your first day at a diamond company would be all beautiful gemstones, fancy lunches and champagne by the magnum full, did you?'

Ruby had no real idea what a magnum was, other than the hairy-chested detective she'd watched on TV growing up and merely nodded again.

'Look,' said Oliver. 'If you don't have to shoot off too quickly, why not let me take you out for a drink. Just to say sorry for nearly knocking you over. Maybe a little champagne to make your first day better.'

Ruby considered the invitation. What did she have to go home for? There was no one there? A council flat and a TV dinner for the night or a glass of fizz with a handsome man? Even if it were just the one glass it would surely make the train journey home and a night in front of the television much more palatable. Before she could reconsider, she accepted Oliver's offer.

It hadn't just been one glass. The wine bar they had gone to had served champagne by the bottle. A bottle later and they had both indulged in buoyant conversations about everything from their tastes in music through to how much of a snotty cow Ruby thought Cassandra was as she relayed the events of her first day to Oliver. Reluctant to leave, but knowing she must, after what had been a most pleasurable evening, she decided that it was time to be on her way. A kiss on the cheek from Oliver as she left was the cherry on the icing on the cake and it definitely sparked something in Ruby. A heart-fluttering interest in the man who had literally run into her. When he asked if they could swap telephone numbers, it was clear that he was interested too. There was a definite rosy glow to Ruby's cheeks and a spring in her step as she made her way back to the train station after leaving the wine bar.

It was the next day at work, just before half past twelve, that the office door opened and in walked the same handsome man. Ruby felt her skin darken in colour as he stared over at her. She looked straight down at her desk unable to retain eye contact for fear of laughing nervously and making an idiot of herself. Unsure what to do and realising how odd she must have looked, she then stared across at Katherine and Samantha. Both women were staring directly at Oliver, a definite glaze of admiration across their faces.

Cassandra leapt up from her desk, as if on springs, and almost skipped towards Oliver. 'Oh Mr Powell, are you here to see your father? Would you like me to see if he's free for you, although I'm sure that he's never too busy to see his son and heir? I don't seem to recall there was anything too important in his diary today that I've scheduled in. I do know all of his movements after all.'

'No, thanks. I'm not here for dad. I'm here to see if this one will join me for lunch?'

Oliver sauntered over to Ruby's desk, sat on the edge of it and smiled as Ruby stared up at him. Both Katherine and Samantha sat catching flies across the office, their mouths hanging open. 'So, are you up for lunch, Ruby? I'll try to have you back for half past one, as requested.' He looked over at Cassandra as he spoke. She smiled, totally unsure what to say.

'I'm sure we can spare Ruby for a few minutes longer if she happens to be a little tardy coming back,' said Cassandra, not wanting to appear officious with her timekeeping.

'Oh good, because there's a place around the corner I'd like to try and I have no idea how quick the service is. So, get your coat on Ruby, it's…' He stared at his watch. '…half twelve on the dot.' As she stood up, he reached over the desk and kissed her on the cheek. Cassandra's eyes widened in disbelief and an almost audible gasp came from Katherine and Samantha.

As Ruby wrapped her coat around her, Oliver reached into his own coat pocket and pulled out his cigarettes. This time there was no cigarette case, just an ordinary packet of Benson & Hedges. He lit one, offered the packet to Ruby and then linked his arm into hers to escort her to lunch. As they passed Cassandra, Oliver blew the smoke in her direction, subtly enough to not appear deliberate but unsubtly enough for Ruby to know that he had indeed done it on purpose.

Ruby's cheeks reddened even further and she held her breath until they were safely in the lift together and heading down from the 27th floor. It was only then that she started to laugh hysterically.

Chapter 39

Now

A warmth ran through Lucie as she listened to her mum's story of how she had met her father.

'So you had no idea that he was heir to the company that you'd started working for until that moment?'

'No, I'd only met him for a few hours and we'd shared no more than a peck on the cheek. I thought he was charming and very handsome and looking back, I know that I fell for him pretty much straight away and I loved the fact that we shared the same sense of humour. Buying B&H cigarettes because I had told him what my boss had said just so that he could blow smoke at her was genius. So romantic in a totally evil and ridiculous kind of way.'

It seemed to Lucie that the telling of the story had somehow placated Ruby's nerves about the confrontation with her daughter. As if explaining it at long last had somehow washed her of any regret she harboured about lying to her own flesh and blood.

'Why have you never told me about this before?' asked Lucie. 'It's a great story of two people embarking on their romantic journey together. The first chapter of their love story.'

'Because it turned so sour. Became something that I wanted to forget. Wanted to leave behind me. As much as was possible.'

Lucie listened as Ruby continued with her story.

'Being with Oliver opened up a whole different world for me. I was not even twenty years of age and I was going to swanky parties and glamorous occasions and being treated like a princess. It was the total opposite to anything that I had ever experienced before. Our relationship took off pretty quickly. After the first few weeks of dating, Oliver made it clear that he wanted to take things further and that we should become an item. You know, boyfriend and girlfriend.'

Lucie nodded as she listened, afraid to interrupt by uttering a single word. Not now that she was finally hearing the truth. Gaining some family history.

Ruby continued. 'I was blown away by him. Believe it or not, I'd not had a huge amount of experience when it came to boyfriends by the time I was with Oliver. There had been a couple along the way. Nothing serious. I wasn't innocent, I'd played around, but I certainly wasn't used to being spoilt and treated so wonderfully like Oliver was doing to me. It felt a little alien, but completely incredible. For a while, I continued to work at the office. It was fun to see how much Cassandra's attitude towards me changed once she realised that the boss's son was into me. Plus, I needed the money. I still had rent to pay even if Oliver was rolling in it. I didn't want him to own me. I'm stronger than that. But then, it became a bit too awkward. I would feel strange every time he would come into the office and also, by that point, I had met his mum and dad. Oliver Senior, who owned the company and his wife, Sarah. The woman who you now know from the care home. It was becoming stupid for me to be sitting taking dictation and filing letters and invoices for someone whose Michelin-starred restaurant table I had been sharing the night before. There was too much of a clash between talking all sorts of fancy things at parties and gatherings with them as their son's girlfriend and then being their employee the next day.'

'So what did you do?' Lucie couldn't help but ask.

'I gave up the job. It was only going to be temporary anyway as I was covering some girl on maternity leave but it made sense for me to walk away from it whilst I was with Oliver. Every day, the other girls in the office would question me about my love life and it was becoming unprofessional. Oliver agreed to pay the rent on the flat in Brighton, although I was hardly ever there as I used to stay at his place in London a lot. I think that's when it started to become a bit tricky. Especially with his mum and dad. I think they thought I was sponging off Oliver, which looking back maybe I was, but we were in love. We wanted to be together.'

For a second, Ruby's eyes glazed over as she immersed herself in her own recollections, a mixture of joy and regret coating over her.

'It became clear that Oliver's dad and Sarah really didn't like me. There were times at parties and family gatherings, some of them in this very cottage which they referred to as their "country residence". How ridiculous is that? They would almost ignore me, act as if I wasn't even there. There would be snide comments about me not understanding things and how someone with my education – because I hadn't been born with a silver spoon in my mouth or didn't speak like one of their friends or business colleagues – couldn't possibly have an interest in the multi-million goings on of a jewellery empire. I didn't care about the company and its dealings. Why would I? I was in love with Oliver. But I did care that Sarah and Oliver Senior were being so crappy to me. It felt like I was being abandoned again by people who were supposed to care for me. I suppose it took me back to when my own mother had run off after giving birth to me. Of having that feeling that I wasn't good enough. It's a horrible feeling. I guess you know that.'

Again, Lucie just nodded, not wanting to stem the flow.

'Oliver and I had been together a little while when I knew something was wrong. Well, I say wrong. It wasn't wrong, it was just unexpected. I was late for my period and at first, I just thought that it was my body playing up. Even though I knew it didn't make sense, I kind of convinced myself that I was late because I was upset about being treated so badly by Oliver's mum and dad. That the balance of my body was being upset by my own dislike of the situation. It wasn't of course. I was pregnant. With you.'

A smile involuntarily spread itself across Lucie's face. A knowing that she was conceived from a bed of love, even if she already knew that it was not to last. 'How did dad react? Was he pleased?' Lucie prayed that the answer would be what she wanted to hear.

'At first he was, yes. I remember when I told him, he just picked me up in his arms and span me around. Spin after spin. I was so giddy that I threw up. I told him it was from morning sickness but actually it was because he'd spun me around too much. But he was genuinely excited about the thought of a family. I was just twenty and he was just a few years older. You were unplanned but we knew that it made sense. The future seemed mapped out and a bright place to consider. A family giving a proper home to a baby. One with a mum and a dad. As it should be. I was going to give up the flat in Brighton, move in with Oliver and we would start a new life together, as a family. But then, it all went wrong.'

'But weren't you engaged to be married?' asked Lucie, unable to contain the information she'd learnt at Robson Lodge. 'You and Oliver were due to be married, weren't you? Why did he leave you? What did you do?'

'You automatically blame me, don't you?' replied Ruby. Lucie realised what she had said, indeed assuming that it was Ruby who had screwed up any game of happy families. But she didn't apologise. She couldn't. Not until she had heard what had happened.

'We did become engaged. Oliver presented me with the most amazing ring. Diamond of course. It's where my love of them comes from.' Ruby waggled the one that she was wearing, the action unnecessary but giving her time to consider her next words. 'It was very romantic. We were away for the weekend at a hotel in the countryside. I had told him I was pregnant about two weeks before and he planned it as a way of celebrating. He hadn't said anything to his parents at that point, though, as he said he was waiting for the right moment. He told me after getting down on bended knee that it seemed right to tell them that we were engaged at the same time. I was elated. Everything was falling into place. Suddenly, I had gone from missing your grandmother Alice and being alone and miserable and not seeing a good future at the flat in Brighton to being engaged to a beautiful, rich man and heir to a successful business and having a family all ready to go. It was all I had ever dreamt of.'

Once again, Lucie was suddenly hit by the realisation that she and her mother were not dissimilar. Maybe Ruby had considered her own life as cursed and lacking as she herself had always thought about her own.

'But things changed?' asked Lucie.

'Yeah, they did. We came here, to the cottage, to tell them. I was genuinely excited and I thought they would be too. Who wouldn't be excited to hear that they're going to be grandparents? It was a beautiful summer's day. It was when this was taken.' She held the photo of her and Oliver aloft. 'I actually had butterflies in my stomach as we told them. I felt them punched out of me as I watched for their reaction. The butterflies just flew away never to be seen again. Gone on the wings of their own unhappiness. Both Sarah and Oliver Senior looked horrified. I thought having a family with Oliver would make his parents accept me, realise that I was here for the distance, not just some passing floozy who wanted their son's cash. Believe it or not, I didn't really give a shit about all of the money. I loved him. I really did. But as we told them there was just this frosting over of their eyes, as if they automatically put up some kind of barrier that disabled them from actually feeling happy about the news. Oliver saw it too, I know he did. He tried to pretend that they had been happy when I spoke to him about it in the days after, but I knew he was just trying to placate me, to not let me become upset given my condition. It was in those weeks after telling his parents about the pregnancy that I could feel Oliver slipping away from me. He became distant. Stayed late at work or found excuses not to spend time with me. It was as if he too had suddenly became ashamed of me. For no good reason that I could see. It was almost as if he was afraid to speak to me when we were together. I would ask him questions and try to fathom out why his mum and dad were being so bloody awful about us being together but he would say I was imagining it and that I shouldn't get all upset. It wouldn't be good for the pregnancy. I cried myself to sleep night after night, mostly alone as he was working somewhere, or so he said.'

'Do you mean he was having an affair? Did you doubt he was working?' Lucie didn't want to hear the story become even more tragic than it already was but she knew it had to. She could see Ruby's tears, glistening on her face. Something stopped her from reaching out, again scared of shattering the moment by connecting physically with her mother.

'Oh no, he wasn't having an affair. But there was another woman in his life, all right. His mother. She was the one who wore the trousers in that relationship. She was the head of that family. She was the one who destroyed the relationship.'

'What, Sarah?' Lucie found the words hard to equate with the old lady at the care home.

'Oh yes, it was that bitch that stole everything from me. It was her that destroyed any future family happiness that you could have had, Lucie. She was the bitch that did it.'

Chapter 40

The Cottage, late summer 1992

The phone call had been curt. Sarah Powell summoning Ruby to the cottage at a certain time. It may not have been barked down the phone but the request was definitely more of an order and not at all decorated in niceties.

Ruby was feeling at an all-time low. Her hormones weren't helping, neither was morning sickness, water retention, sore breasts and a permanent lethargy. Plus the fact that she had tried, not always successfully, to knock the cigarettes on the head ever since discovering she was pregnant. She was still craving a nicotine hit. But all of that would have felt so much better if she'd been experiencing the medicinal qualities of undying adulation from a man who loved her. But as her waistline became bigger, the divide between her and Oliver seemed to be becoming bigger and bigger too. And she still had no idea why. The once carefree, loving Oliver had seemingly become stuck in a quagmire of his own uptight ways. When he and Ruby were indeed in the same room, which was becoming less and less frequent, their conversation was staccato to say the least. Any attempt from Ruby at finding solutions as to why the two of them were seemingly drifting apart at what should have been such a happy moment in their lives was met with a dead end of silence or diversion tactics. She would find herself snapping angrily at him in frustration at his inability to communicate, followed by a slamming of the front door as he fled and a prolonged absence.

Ruby took a taxi to the cottage. The country residence. It was a place she adored. The picture postcard nature of it had appealed to her from her first visit. So cosy and welcoming despite the owners. The garden with its twisty paths and hidden dells was enchanting and mysterious and a million miles away from what she had been used to living on the fifth floor of the council estate in Brighton with Grandma Alice. At the cottage, every green area offered up multihued flowers and mysterious leaves, smells that drifted in the air and contended insects marching their way through their very own jungle. At the flat, all the green areas offered up were dog excrement and broken glass.

Ruby knew that this was not to be a pleasant visit from the moment she saw Sarah striding from the cottage and marching down the looping path towards her even before she had vacated the taxi. She was on a mission. Some deadly obsession brewed within her. That was clear.

By the time Ruby had paid the driver, Sarah was already holding the door open for her to exit. She manoeuvred herself as best she could, given her burgeoning size, her back already damp with sweat from the heat as she pulled herself up and out of the back seat, using a hand from Sarah to steady herself. Sarah merely said hello. Before shutting the door, Sarah pushed her head back inside the car and barked something that Ruby didn't quite catch at the driver. She closed the door with a bang, Ruby only just moving her fingers away from harm near the door frame before she did so.

'You need help?' Sarah linked her arm through Ruby's and walked her towards the cottage.

Ruby didn't but didn't have either the energy or the desire to say so. 'This is a pleasant surprise,' said Ruby. 'Is Oliver not home? Is it just us girls together?'

'Save your breath for when you're sitting down,' said Sarah, not a trace of compassion on show.

Neither of them uttered another word until they were both sat down on a bench in the cottage garden. Ruby couldn't help but wonder why they weren't going inside. Especially as the heat was causing a puddle of sweat to form across her neckline. Somehow, Sarah managed to look as cool and as collected, Ruby would say icy, as ever. Sarah broke the void that filled the air.

'You'd care for a drink?' It was more of a statement than a question. 'I'll fetch you one.' Without waiting for an answer, Sarah stood up and walked to the house, returning a few moments later with a glass of water.

Ruby sipped at the water. Despite its coolness, she felt far from refreshed. She suspected she wouldn't until her meeting with her mother-in-law-to-be was over.

'I'll not beat about the bush, Ruby. I don't want you marrying my son. Neither does Oliver's father. We won't let this happen.' Sarah's words were as direct as she intended. They slapped against

Ruby's face, each one stinging with its venom. Harsh, if not unexpected.

'But that is not your choice. Oliver asked me to marry him and that's what we will do. We'll be a family together.' Ruby cradled the bump of her belly as she spoke with one of her arms.

'Actually this is Oliver's choice. He has decided that he has made a mistake and he wanted me to tell you that he won't be marrying you. The engagement is off.'

A coward and a prick, thought Ruby as she took in the words. Hiding behind his mother's apron strings. *Now that's cheap.* Ruby still didn't believe it.

'And just why would that happen?' asked Ruby. She could feel her anger mounting but desperately tried to keep a lid on it. Her doctor had said that any kind of distress would not be good for a pregnant woman.

It was clear that Sarah was not thinking along medical lines as she carried on.

'Because both Oliver's dad and I believe that you're not suitable enough to be his wife. You're not exactly what he needs in a wife, even if you have managed to get yourself pregnant by him. How very cunning of you. Securing your future. It is definitely his, isn't it?'

'Now that's fucking low,' snapped Ruby, desperately trying to keep control. 'It's his and you know it is. So does he. Has he ever told you that he doubts that?'

'Not in so many words, no,' said Sarah, rising to her feet. She wasn't going anywhere but maybe it made her feel stronger to be towering over Ruby as she sat on the bench. Ruby was not to be intimidated. 'But he has been made aware that marrying you would not be a beneficial thing for him to do. Not for his future.'

The penny was dropping. 'His future? A future totally shaped by you and your husband I'm guessing. One in which you bully him to do exactly what you want him to do. Well, I'm not bloody having it. Until I hear it from Oliver himself, then I'm afraid this conversation is over.' Ruby went to raise herself off the bench too, but a forceful hand on her shoulder pushed her down and back onto the bench. Ruby's eyes couldn't help but notice the amount of gemstones gathered on Sarah's fingers. To a point where they all seemed to be fighting for a space to shine.

'You won't hear from Oliver. You won't be seeing him again. You're out of his life.'

'Over your dead body, lady. FYI, I think Oliver will want to be there at the birth. There's a little family matter to be considering.'

'Oliver is happy to contribute to make sure that he pays for what he's done.' Sarah made it sound as if her son was responsible for a hit and run as opposed to becoming a father.

'He's going to be a dad. We're going to be married. Man and wife. It's what he wants.'

'What he doesn't want is to be throwing his life away on a tramp like you at such a young age. He has learnt his lesson and it has cost us all, but the decision is made.'

Ruby felt as if her life was being talked about as if it were a business acquisition. Sarah wasn't discussing flesh and blood, she was discussing facts and scenarios. Solutions to problems. And the problem was Ruby.

Ruby reached into her pocket and pulled out a slip of paper. She unfolded it and handed it to Ruby. It was a cheque made out to her from OPD Inc. It was for £50,000. Ruby stared at it but for a moment failed to take in its meaning. That she was being bought off. Settlement money.

'I think you'll find that this is an adequate amount to keep you in nappies and baby blankets for a while. We'll arrange to pay the rent on your flat in Brighton too. I understand it's a nominal monthly amount. A small price to pay for Oliver's redemption.'

'But you'll be a grandmother? Won't you want to be there?' Ruby cradled her belly again, suddenly pondering what the future held for her precious cargo.

'I can live without this.' Sarah pointed at Ruby's belly. 'Oliver is young, rich and attractive. He will have the chance to father many more children. He just needs to be a little more selective about who's having them.'

Ruby was at boiling point. 'Screw you. Your son and I live together, we're going to be parents together and our future will be together with or without you and your hen-pecked husband as grandparents. Does he even know about this? Or is this all your own fucking idea?'

'Is there any need for that kind of language?' stated Sarah, oblivious to the fact that obviously there was. 'Oliver's father was quite clear as to what would happen if he were to marry you and put you before his own future. His real family. There's the small matter of him being heir to a rather successful company. One day all of that will be his, but the last thing any of us want is a woman alongside him who doesn't really…how shall I put this…fit the brand.'

'So you've told Oliver that if he marries me, he's cut out of the company? Just because he's chosen a woman that you don't particularly like. What kind of mother are you?'

'One who cares for her child and wants to make sure that he comes to no harm. Isn't that what any mother should do?'

'You're unbelievable. But this isn't happening.' Ruby shoved the cheque into the remaining inches of water that she still had in her glass and watched as the paper soaked up the liquid, the writing on it becoming illegible. 'You can't buy me.'

'I thought you'd try something like that which is why I'm glad we have your bank details at the office. You did temp there after all. We'll transfer the money to your account instead. We need it to pay your rent anyway.'

'Don't bother. I'm living with Oliver at the flat in London.'

'Actually, you're not. Your stuff is being cleared out as we speak. About now, it should be heading down the motorway to Brighton.' Sarah checked the time on her watch. 'Oliver had a set of keys cut so the van drivers can dump it there when they arrive. Fifth floor, wasn't it?'

'You fucking bitch.' Ruby couldn't help but feel defeated. 'I'll go to the papers. Say how this family tried to ruin me.'

'Try it. Half of the newspaper editors out there are friends of ours and the other half can be bought with a diamond or two. I don't think that would be a good move on your behalf, do you?'

'You can't do this?' stammered Ruby.

'I think you'll find it's already done.'

'You won't get away with this. It's wrong. Completely wrong.' Ruby could feel her heart beating wildly inside her chest. She took a couple of deep breaths to try and calm herself down. 'I'm engaged to your son. This proves it.'

Ruby held out her hand and flashed the diamond on her engagement finger.

'Ah yes, one final thing,' said Sarah, swooping eagle-like onto Ruby's finger. 'I think we should have that back. I'd rather it go to a better home. It belongs in the family and you'll never be part of that.' Before Ruby could pull her hand away, Sarah had grabbed her wrist with one hand and yanked at the ring forcefully with the other. The ring slid a little painfully down Ruby's finger and was gone before she could fight back.

This final action was more than Ruby could bear. A final death-knell in the brutal battlefield between them. Her tears began to flow at the realisation that she was beaten.

'Save your tears for the car. The taxi is still waiting. I've paid him enough money to take you to Brighton. And don't think about heading back to the flat in London. Oliver won't be there and I think you'll find the locks have been changed so your key will be useless. We're done here.'

The sound of her own sobs seemed deafening as Ruby watched Sarah walk away back into the cottage. She shut the door behind her leaving Ruby alone with her tears.

The taxi was still there as instructed. As a shell-shocked Ruby walked down the path towards it, she knew that she needed to speak to Oliver. He wouldn't be in agreement with this surely. He wouldn't choose the family business and his own destiny before that of his own future family, would he? She couldn't believe that. She turned to look at the cottage before it disappeared out of view as she walked to the taxi. Her eyes were watery with tears but something caught her attention. There in one of the leaded windows on the second floor stood Oliver. The man she thought she was going to marry. As soon as he noticed that she had spotted him, he disappeared behind the curtain out of view. For a second, Ruby doubted her own vision, but she knew that she hadn't been mistaken. Suddenly, she did believe. Oliver was just as bad and as pathetic as the rest of his family. Without thinking, Ruby walked back towards the cottage, picked up a large stone from one of the garden rockeries and hurtled it as best she could towards the window. Her aim, fuelled by rage, hit its target and smashed through the pane of glass.

She walked back to the taxi. A small boy, no more than four or five years of age at the most, stood by the garden fence, peering through as she climbed into the taxi. Before she shut the door, he spoke. 'I was watching you. Great shot. You're like She-Ra, Princess of Power. That was awesome.' His smile illuminated even Ruby's dark misery.

'Thanks, kiddo. What's your name?'

'Andrew. But everyone calls me Drew.'

'You have a good day, Drew, okay.' Ruby attempted a smile.

'You too,' he smiled back.

He was still smiling as the car sped off, destination Brighton and to a future that was destination unknown.

Chapter 41

Peru, summer 2012

Lucie bolted upright in her bed, fear gripping her like an outstretched hand. For a second, she panicked, the clasp of her bed sheets twisting around her, soaked from her own sweat, causing her to strike out, keen to push them away as if they were the sides of an enclosing coffin.

She reached across to a glass of water on her bedside table and gulped the contents, its coolness momentarily quenching the dry heat that spikily lined her throat. She flicked the switch on her bedside lamp and her flat bedroom illuminated. A huge pile of clothes sat atop an open suitcase that lay on the floor at the end of the bed. How she would fit them all back into the case that appeared resigned to its fate beneath the skyscraper of a pile was beyond her. But she had managed to squeeze them in for the trip to Peru in the first place so she would somehow wedge them back into the case, alongside the things she had bought since arriving in the country, for her forthcoming trip to Ibiza. It was now less than sixteen hours until she would be up, up and away to a new life alongside Connor.

She was scared about it. Petrified, if she really thought about it. It was a big move. A leap into the unknown. Her brain could think of nothing else. But she knew it was the right thing to do, an exciting thing to do, but still the ever-sensible side of her brain was telling her that life didn't always go to plan and she shouldn't get too excited. Count her chickens. Maybe that was why she had just suffered a somewhat colourful nightmare. Images of herself being pulled into the sand by some invisible force, sinking to her doom like in some cheap horror flick had filled her thoughts. Crawling cockroaches and hissing lengths of slithering snakes had surrounded her as she made the descent to her finality, the sand encasing her like a dusty sarcophagus. It had been full on. She had just been at the point of her lips being pulled below the surface, the first trickles of sand tumbling into her mouth when she had been ripped from the nightmare by her own terror.

Lucie's breathing slowed a little, back to a normal rhythm as she attempted to push the nightmare away. A smile attempted to cross her cheeks as she considered the fact that in just a couple of days, she would be in Ibiza, and that shortly after that Connor, the man that she loved, would be by her side. If that wasn't enough of a prize to banish any thoughts of cockroaches and snakes, then she didn't know what was.

Where was Connor? The thought struck her that he had been alongside her in bed when she had drifted into sleep. He'd offered to help her pack. Insisted on it. They hadn't exactly got very far, no further than literally emptying Lucie's wardrobe into the pile she now stared at, but the fact that they were in this together and that he was by her side made her feel good. She'd offered to help with his but he'd told her that a pile of T-shirts and umpteen board shorts would not take much packing. And besides, he would be on a later flight so he had more time.

For a second, a needle of worry pierced her. What if Connor was in the flat doing drugs. Maybe clearing his stash before departure. But even she knew that, it was unlikely he'd be taking a hit of cocaine on his own in the middle of the night in a silent flat. It was hardly party central. They had talked about his taking drugs with Kara at their leaving celebration. He was apologetic but only in a "don't shoot me, I was having fun" kind of way. What could she say? She was nineteen, not ninety.

Kara and Tina had left the lovebirds alone at the flat for their last night together before departing. It had been Connor's request and both girls had agreed readily.

Lucie pulled the damp sheets away from her and wandered into the front room. The room was dark apart from the dim light being thrown out by a solitary lamp by the sofa. Connor was laying on his back on the sofa, mobile phone in hand. He turned to face Lucie as she caught his eye.

'You couldn't sleep either, eh? I've been sat scrolling through social media for the last half an hour.' He was wearing just a pair of loose fitting PJ bottoms.

Lucie sat down alongside him on the sofa. She ran her hand across his chest, playing with the dark curls of hair that rested there. A happiness that he wasn't snorting another white line of heartbreak cleansed her as she stared at him. He was a beautiful man and the thought that they were leaving together thrilled her more than anything else she could remember for the longest time. She'd forgive him anything at moments like this.

'I had a nightmare, all creepy-crawlies and burials. It was pretty gross, but I'm okay now. Now I'm with you.'

'Oh, baby.' Connor elongated the words as he spoke to show his sympathy. He placed his phone on the table and raised himself up, taking Lucie in his arms. 'I wish I had been there for you when you woke up. Are you sure you're okay?'

'Yeah, I'm fine. I guess I'm just a bit stressed about the journey and what lies ahead.' Afraid that she sounded like she was backtracking, she added quickly before Connor could interject. 'I can't wait though. It's going to be amazing. I guess I'm just a little stressed as I haven't packed yet and I'll be travelling alone. We should have finished it last night really. But we were kind of busy, eh?'

Connor smiled as he cast his mind back to the sex they had been having the night before. 'Now that was a rather fabulous bon voyage,' he smirked. 'If it was always a choice between packing your underwear and removing your underwear, I know what I would pick every single time.'

Lucie smiled too. It had been quite an experience, her body tingling head to toe as it had shuddered into orgasm.

'I'm just worried I won't get it all done before I have to leave to go to the airport. I really wish you were coming with me.'

Connor raised his eyebrows at her and grinned.

'I need to stop worrying. Is that what your oh-so-cute face is trying to say?' Lucie put her hand under Connor's chin and brushed the stubble that darkened his face.

'Yes, you do. I'm sorry I can't come to the airport but I need to sort out some of the bar stuff before I head off to Ibiza too. If I'm leaving it in the hands of Kara and Tina, then I need to make sure that the big boss man is happy. I'll be seeing him most of the day and be pretty uncontactable. But it needs to be done.'

'I know.' There was a glum resignation in Lucie's tone.

'What time is it?' asked Connor.

Lucie picked up her own phone which was also laying on the table and stared at the screen. '4:05 a.m.'

'I don't know about you, but I'm wide awake,' said Connor. 'So how about we crack on with your packing now? We could have it done by sunrise. Let me help, please. It's the least I can do seeing as I won't be there at the airport.'

Lucie considered the request. She did feel wide awake. As much as the thought of going back to bed made sense given the hour, she was sure she would do no more than just lie there until it was time to get up. And it made sense to pack the case together. A problem shared and all that.

'You're on.'

'And maybe when we're done, we could have a repeat performance of last night.'

'If your packing skills are up to scratch, then maybe…' teased Lucie.

For the next two hours, the pair of them folded all of Lucie's clothes neatly into piles and placed them inside the suitcase. For some unknown and welcome reason, the clothes didn't fill out the case completely as she had imagined, although the addition of a few souvenirs of her time in Peru and her toiletries did.

It was just after six o'clock that Lucie attempted to shut the lid of her case, squashing her belongings into place. It refused to shut.

'Oh crap,' stated Lucie, a little exasperated at the thought of having to either repack or leave things behind.

Connor laughed at her annoyance. 'I'll tell you what. You go and put the kettle on and I'll get your case closed. Is there anything else you need in it?'

Lucie pondered the question. 'No, I have my travelling clothes sorted. I can borrow Tina's toiletries before I leave and everything I need for the flight can go into my hand luggage. So do your thing.'

Lucie bounced from the room, leaving Connor to sit on the lid of the case to try and close the contents within. When she returned five minutes later, two steaming mugs of tea in hand, Connor was sitting on the bed, still in only his PJ bottoms, and the case was securely closed into position.

'Well aren't you the good boy?' she said, handing him one of the teas. 'It all went in?'

'It was a tight squeeze and I did consider binning about a dozen of your outfits but seeing as I remembered just how good you look in every one of them, I decided that I'd persevere. It's a heavy case, but it's packed, locked and ready to travel.'

'A heavy load, eh? Well, I guess a girl has to always be prepared for choices so perhaps travelling light would not be a good idea anyway.'

Connor placed his tea down on the bedside table and pulled Lucie towards him. Her own cup of tea spilled a little onto the white sheets of the bed as he did so.

'Hold it, soldier,' cried Lucie as she guessed Connor's intentions. 'Mind you, the sheets will need to go into the laundry when I'm gone anyway.' She placed her mug alongside Connor's and allowed herself to be pulled down onto the bed.

'So, are you prepared for my heavy load then, Lucie Palmer?' asked Connor.

Lucie didn't have to give an answer.

It was about an hour later and Lucie was in the shower. Despite the shower gel, the scent of her love making to Connor was still detectable on her skin. Part of her hoped that it would never wash away. She sang a tune at high volume as she washed, another sound of her summer in Peru, the horrors of her nightmare just a few hours earlier disappeared as if they were suds vanishing down the plughole below her. Happiness filled every note. Her case was ready and so was her mind. In just a few short hours, she would be heading to the airport and to her new adventure in Ibiza. With Connor ready to join her. Peru had been wonderful but it was time for the turning of the next page.

Connor stood listening to Lucie's singing from the front room. It was just before seven thirty. Keeping one ear on Lucie's rendition at all time, he moved to the table and picked up Lucie's phone. He scrolled through to Camera Roll and selected every photo of them together. Plus the one of the heart on the sandy beach at Paradise Cove. It made him smile momentarily, seeing it for the first time. The moment passed. He pressed the delete button and watched the screen rearrange. He then headed to the deleted files section and again selected the photos to permanently delete them. He also removed his name and number from her contacts list and any exchanged messages between them.

He moved to the kitchen and grabbed a plastic bag from the cupboard underneath the sink. He walked back to the bedroom, reached under the bed, found what he needed and stuffed it into the carrier bag. The vocals of Lucie continued from the shower.

Connor took one last look down at the suitcase before leaving the bedroom. He smiled. Taking a sheet of paper from a pad on the dressing table in Lucie's room, he scrawled the words "see you in paradise" and left it on top of the case. Lucie was still singing in the shower as he closed the door behind himself and left the flat.

In the already warm air of the early Peruvian day, Connor knew that he had to act fast. He took his own phone, dialled a number and waited for the other end to pick up. A click followed by the word 'so?'

'It's done. All packed. Just as we'd discussed.' He gave the flight details and hung up.

By the time Lucie had come out of the shower and read the note, a tear springing to her eye at the thought that she wouldn't see Connor again until Ibiza, her first love had binned the carrier bag full of Lucie's clothes in a skip at the bottom of her road, thrown his phone, a cheap pay-as-you-go one, into a canal just a few blocks away and hailed a taxi to take him to his own flat where his own suitcase was also fully packed and then onwards to the airport. He needed to make sure that he was completely out of the country and totally out of reach by the time that Lucie hailed her own taxi to head to the airport and to her new life. His work was done.

Chapter 42

Now

Confusion suffocated Lucie. Her mother's story had floored her. Suddenly, the pendulum of her love had once more swung away from her lifetime of thoughts for a father she had never known and from the new-found affection for her new grandmother back to the woman who had raised her for the first thirteen years of her life. Ruby.

She had taken in every word of her mother's story. Watched as the tears of obvious woe curled down her mother's cheeks as she unravelled the story of both her husband and mother-in-law to be turning their backs on her and abandoning her and her unborn child. Abandoning Lucie even before she had taken her first breath.

Lucie felt more cursed than ever. Crushed by the rejection. That even before she had made an appearance into the rich colours of the world that her life had been blackened, turned to ash and charred by the neglect of her own father and grandparents. She had always believed that deep down, it was Ruby who was to blame but after hearing her mother's story of how the class difference between Ruby and the man she had fallen in love with had driven a stake between them, one that could never be removed, she knew that Ruby was not to be blamed. She too had been abandoned. Left to cope alone. Told that she was not worthy to be part of the Powell family.

What was Lucie to do? A part of her wanted to head back to Robson Lodge with Ruby by her side to confront Sarah. To face her front on with the neglect and the hurt she had caused. To hear her admit that she was the woman who had written the very first word in the book of misery that had become Lucie's life for so long. But what would that gain? Ruby had no wish to spend another moment in the company of the woman who had so viciously ripped the ring from her finger and simultaneously ripped her heart from her very core. And as for Sarah. Despite the moments of clarity, what was she now but a frail, old woman with a brain that had become as unwanted as her wish to keep Ruby and Lucie in her life. Lucie could shout and scream as much as she liked but the only one who would be hurting afresh would be her.

For a while after her revelation, Lucie watched as Ruby sat in silence, seeming scared of what to say next, the effort of telling her daughter the true tale of what had happened with her father and his family leaving her little more than a husk of emotion.

Lucie sat in stillness too, watching. Happy to be there for her mother, somebody that she could rely on after all of the rejection she had faced over the years. She felt a closeness that had been absent before. One ingrained in a sudden realisation of the inherent connection between them. A linking of their feelings of abandonment and inner shame. Of self-loathing and worthlessness. For all of their faults and shortcomings, Lucie could feel a love that had always shone inside herself suddenly becoming neon-bright. The demolished bridge between them being rebuilt. Stone by stone.

The silence between them must have lasted for over five minutes, an eye-contact and the curled lip of a smile between them sufficient to count as the necessary communication. The sounds of summer still hung in the air, birdsong from outside, the distant sound of a lawnmower, a bee in flight, but neither of them added to the maelstrom of noises. It was only when Ruby's phone sounded that the connection of silence between them was splintered and broken.

Ruby looked at the screen and pressed a button to answer it. 'Hello Terrance, how's your end? Where are you?' There was no jollity in Ruby's voice despite the question, a lack of interest in her boyfriend's geography apparent. A fact he obviously noticed judging from her next comment.

'I'm just in a shitty mood.' She paused before adding. 'Missing you I guess.'

'Oh, you're coming home. I thought you were staying away for business for an extra couple of days. It fell through? Oh well, see you later I guess? What time will you be back? Okay, bye.'

Lucie listened to the one-sided conversation and spoke as her mother hung up.

'Terrance is coming home? Is everything okay?' She was merely feigning interest for her mother.

'Oh yeah, he's fine,' said Ruby. 'Just a little earlier than planned. He'll be back later today.'

'Does he know about my father and everything that happened?' Lucie had been pondering about what Terrance would have made of all of Ruby's baggage. She suspected that he didn't really house an opinion, the past being exactly that. Something that didn't affect him so why should it clog up the arteries of his thoughts?

'Let's not tell Terrance we've had this chat, okay. He's a proud man and looks after me very well. I don't want him feeling that he's second best. That he was second choice. He knows this house was left to me and that's enough really. He knows who left it to me but sometimes I think he would rather live somewhere else. Somewhere of our own as opposed to somewhere from my past. In fact I know he would.'

'What did he say when you were first left it? Did you tell him it was from *Uncle Oscar* too?'

'No, you were the only one I lied to, Lucie. Or tried to protect. He knew it was from your father. He knew of Oliver because I had told him. But he doesn't like the fact. It somehow dents his machismo. You know what men are like, such tragically frail little creatures at times.'

'Why didn't you sell it? Why do you keep on living here if he doesn't like it?'

'Because I felt I was owed it. After having the engagement ring snatched from me and being banished back to Brighton, I felt like utter shit. Oliver was paying me money to look after you but I never saw him again. For years, I just accepted his money and imagined him sitting in this place and at the other Powell family houses and enjoying his life, whilst I suffered and struggled to raise you. That cash was my pay-off. It was that money I first used to buy drugs at the flat. It was his money. I guess I was reacting to being tossed aside. I wanted to show myself and indirectly him that I could still have a good time. That I hadn't lost every semblance of my own life by having a baby and that his rejection couldn't crush me. He paid for me to become the mess I turned into. The bad mother you knew. Not that he knew of course.'

'Why do you think he left you the cottage?' asked Lucie.

'Guilt. That's an easy one. It was the guilt of abandoning us all. He was ashamed. He chose his family business over you. I'd like to think he lived with the regret of chucking you and me onto the scrapheap until his dying breath. Useless sod. He left me a lot of money too. More than I've ever had. That must have been against his mother's wishes. But he turned on the old cow. It serves her right. I've wished her dead for years.'

'But why keep the cottage? Surely, you and Terrance would be better suited living in some swanky London pad or in a gated property with stone lions on the driveway. That would be much more you. You can certainly afford it with your money and Terrance's property business. If he buys you diamonds, he's obviously loaded. This place is quaint, rustic and smells gorgeous, but it definitely isn't you. You're never going to be a country girl, mum.'

'You mean why did I keep it? To be honest, that's just because of you. Because I wanted you to see it. Wanted you to know a little piece of your dad. Even though I had no real intention of telling you about your father, the thought of you breathing the same air as him filled me with some kind of satisfaction. An atonement for all of my worries. Does that sound strange?'

Lucie thought about it. 'Not really, no. I'm glad that I have managed to see it, even if the backstory of it now horrifies me. You would never have told me, would you? Not if I hadn't found out from Sarah.'

'Probably not. I didn't think things through. I was ashamed of the fact that he left me. That he chose *them* over me. But I am very proud that out of that little rendezvous came something so precious, namely you, and that eventually I got my hands on this. We will sell it soon enough. Unless you want it of course.'

Lucie didn't know if she was supposed to answer, or indeed what she would say if she did. She left the question unanswered. For now. How could she answer? She wasn't certain of anything. What the future held. What she wanted. Or deep down what she actually deserved. Despite its beauty and wisteria-covered charm, could she ever be happy in the place where her father had turned his back on her? The beauty would fade, but she suspected that the ruined burnt edges of her family history never would.

Chapter 43

Now

It was hours later and well into mid-evening when Terrance returned home. Lucie watched him walk across the garden towards the cottage and disappear from view as she looked down from her bedroom window. From downstairs, the heavy tone of music and a constant thud of backbeat filled the air. Ruby was playing Motown tunes, ones Lucie recognised from the days of partying she'd witnessed back in Brighton all of those years before. After their conversation earlier, Lucie and Ruby had separated, without saying so both making the unconscious decision to give each other space. After the sharing of their memories, it seemed only right that they should both gather their thoughts and rationalise what had been said. Lucie retired to her room and lay on her bed for a long while, her mind a typhoon of images. Faces of so many people filled her thoughts, all of them jostling for space and understanding. Ruby, Sarah, Oliver, Connor, Roger, Tanya…the people who had shared her life, some enhancing it and others so intent on stamping it underfoot and breaking it beyond repair. For a while, she had dozed, but again the images remained, somehow finding their way into her dreams. Distorting and merging, a collage of recollections. When she awoke, Lucie felt far from rested.

Lucie opened the window and breathed in the freshness of the evening air, tinged with a slight chill yet somehow still heavy and drab. The light outside the cottage had dimmed into a murky grey, all semblance of the summer day that had been there earlier smothered for good. Heavy, drab and grey. Symbolic of her own thoughts? Lucie couldn't help but feel that it was. She cocked her head further upwards towards the sky and opened her eyes as wide as they could go. In her mind, it was as if she was looking for sympathy. None came.

The music thudded against her brain. The beat loud enough to be recognisable yet somehow blanketed enough so that no tune was apparent. A party in another room. One that she wasn't invited to. Another symbol of her own existence. Lucie guessed so.

Despite its lack of clarity, the soft thud transported her back to years earlier, to sitting alone on her room, her knees hunched up against her body as she sought sanctuary on her own bed. Her arms wrapped tightly around her legs pulling them close as she rocked back and forth, her bedroom door closed tight, the hallway beyond, and then beyond that the closed door for the front room of their Brighton flat. The room where the music came from, the laughter, the screams, the dramas. And for Lucie, the rejection. The place into which her mother disappeared with her friends and as a consequence automatically pushed her own daughter to the back of the line when it came to affection, love and caring. Lucie would fight to acknowledge the feeling that her mother truly loved her. How could she not? They were flesh and blood but as she sat on her bed, eventually pulling up the duvet around her and burying her body beneath it, hoping to silence the music and the misery from beyond, she couldn't help but question the love between them. As the darkness wrapped itself around her, she became a girl in solitude. A girl unknown to her mother. One who didn't exist. Those moments were the worst. The ones where she was unable to escape her own thoughts. Helpless to run away.

Years later and still listening to the heavy ominous thud of a tune played from another room. Chosen by someone else. Hers for the listening but not the choosing. It still took her back to those melancholy moments in her childhood bedroom. It had happened in Peru when Kara and Tina played music from their bedrooms at the flat. It had happened at Roger and Tanya's on the nights when they were entertaining friends downstairs as Lucie lay in her room, the music carried on the air bringing with it a host of recollections. Lucie knew that it would be like that for a lifetime. No particular recognisable tune having to be the soundtrack to her own memories, but the dull generic beat always taking her there without consideration.

Lucie listened to the muffled music as she turned her eyes back down towards the garden. The tunes were recognisable if she concentrated even if they were a little deadened by the walls in between. Diana Ross and The Supremes. One of Ruby's favourites. Always had been. The CD had been on constant rotation back in Brighton. Lucie knew every song. *Baby Love, The Happening, I'm Livin' in Shame.* Yet their joyous poppiness was lost on her. It always would be. There would never be a choice. Their beat connecting her with a dark emotion that she would never escape. Solitude by association.

Her attention was taken away from the music by the sight of a fox moving its way across the garden. It wasn't the first she had seen one there since her arrival. Drew had told her that the garden was often frequented by the creatures. She watched as it slinked its way across the lawn, its movements rapid and beautifully fluid.

Suddenly, it stopped, its paws seemingly rooted to the spot. Statue still. Even in the dimness of the evening light, she could see its back arch upwards and it was clear that something had spooked it. The answer became apparent as another fox moved into view from its hiding place in the bushes on the far side of the garden. The second fox took a few steps towards the first and then he too remained motionless, his back also arched as he stared at his rival. One lawn, one territory, two foxes. The maths was off. Within seconds, the first fox leapt, the high-pitched shriek of his attack piercing the air. They pushed against each other, testing their strength, both of them determined that they would not be the one to back down. A discord of noise from both animals sounded, harsh and brutal, a spiking of hatred evident. For about thirty seconds, the bodies of the two creatures became entwined, mouths open, teeth bared, ferocity displayed. It was only when the intruding fox submitted into a tight ball on the floor and then limped off back into the bushes from where he'd come that the fight came to an end. His territory claimed, the first fox, his movements a mixture of pride tinged with an expectation of potential revenge, scurried across the lawn and out of sight.

Recollections gripped Lucie once again. The fight for territory. The display of ferocity. The quest to be top dog. She had seen that first hand. Witnessed the anger. The hate.

Suddenly, Lucie was back in Peru at the place that had been her nightmare, her own personal fight for survival, for so long…

2016

The food never looked any better. Or tasted any better either. Lucie didn't class herself as a gastronomic snob by any stretch of the imagination but even she could see when food was at its blandest and most colour-free. She was used to it by now. The surprise and contempt she had first encountered a few years earlier now just another miserable layer of her daily existence inside. The white lump of potato landing with a slap on her plastic plate. The bullet-hard vegetables somehow devoid of both any kind of flavour and natural goodness. As if only the runts of the food world were force-fed to those banged up for crimes committed, or in Lucie's case, not. The puddle-like gravy, weak and insipid, drizzling its way across a piece of gristle masquerading as meat. Cordon bleu it was not.

Her tray full, Lucie took her place at a table. Any one that happened to be free. Unlike many of the women inside the prison, Lucie was not part of a tribe. She didn't belong to a group, a bonding of personalities and egos that looked after each other. Sometimes she felt that she should be, that maybe what little strength she had inside her would be bolstered somehow by having a team around her. But that was not how Lucie had ever worked inside the prison walls. She was a loner, an outsider, someone who didn't belong there. And the fellow inmates, mostly south Americans, seemed to know that. She wasn't feared, she wasn't beyond hurt and violence, but after years inside, she had become someone who was respected more than most. Purely by the length of her stay. Prison may have hardened Lucie to what life dealt out, how could it not, but she would never be part of their world. The world of dog eat dog, of top dog, of fighting for supremacy. She had taken the beatings, the horror of the sexual violence, but she would never be the one to hand it out. Not even the squalor of her festering surroundings would reduce her to that.

The fight happened quickly. It always did. Bursting from nowhere with a violence that managed to accelerate from zero to a hundred in a matter of seconds. Lucie's grasp of the local language was still just a little more than passable. She never really understood what was said and what the reasons were for the fight in the first place but that didn't matter. After years inside, she was now able to watch proceedings without any kind of fear or inner turmoil. Nothing shocked her anymore. She suspected nothing ever would. Prison toughened your shell. You had no choice. Not if you wanted to survive. And she did. That was one fight that would never leave her. One that she was always prepared to battle for.

One woman stood up. She was small, wiry and tattooed. Lucie had seen her a few times. They'd never spoken. Why would they? In a split second, the tray the woman had in her hand swung around and smashed across the head of a woman sitting alongside her. The second woman was round and squat, defined from the prison gym yet still weak enough to crumble forward onto the table under the attack of the tray. The women on the tables either side of the attack stood up, their cheers erupting at the explosion of the violent cabaret.

Finding her strength, the second woman stood up, pushed the table away from her, sending plates crashing to the floor and swung around, landing a punch on the tattooed woman's jaw. Her head jolted to one side on impact. Another punch followed before she could retaliate, the power of it sending her head reeling back the other way. Realising her opponent was off-guard, the second prisoner grabbed her head and forced her face down with a sickening thud onto the table. Even through the excited cries of those watching, the sound of the woman's nose crunching onto the surface could be heard. As she raised her head back up, a bloodied mass hid the middle of her face, causing a whoop of respect from those obviously belonging to the tribe of the aggressor.

The wiry woman, despite being dazed by the beating, seemed to find a miraculous strength from somewhere. It often happened. The choreography of a fight was always strangely similar. Lucie, chewing on the meat on her plate, found herself almost able to second guess what was going to happen next. The only thing that was certain in a prison fight was that nothing was certain until one of the parties involved was out cold. The fights were feral and ferocious and even though Lucie would never openly admit it, sometimes she found herself almost ashamedly enjoying the display of violence. She continued to eat as she watched.

The wiry woman reached out her hands and grabbed the other one by the throat. Her thumbs pressed against the jugular. Despite her smaller size, her strength seemed to poleaxe her opponent. Her hands raced to her own throat to try and remove the squeezing digits. They were unable to do so. Her eyes appeared to bulge, the force of the fingers on her throat becoming deeper. She stumbled slightly, her vision no doubt stained at the edges. The smaller woman, sensing victory, spat into the other's face. Again, a cheer rose up. Lucie watched on, chewing on another mouthful of food. She looked down at her tray and pushed a collection of vegetables onto her fork. When she looked back up, the woman with the bloodied nose had her opponent on her knees. Her hands were still around her opposition's throat. Her foot kicked out and landed in the fallen woman's crotch. She repeated the action, the pain on the woman's face clear to see as her foot found its destination.

Doors at the corner of the room opened and two guards walked into view. Lucie swallowed the last of her meat. She'd not even registered any taste as yet but somehow, it was already gone. She suspected that the guards had been watching the fight from the other side of the doors. They seemed to find it as entertaining as the other inmates did. Something to break up the monotony of yet another day. An extra moment of something different and exciting.

Within seconds, the two women were being carted off, their hands held roughly behind their backs. The woman with the bloodied nose left a trail of blood dots as she was forced smiling from the room. Lucie guessed that she would be off to solitary. The other woman, barely able to walk on her own two feet, stumbled out of the room too, the red pressure marks around her neck clear for all to see. She was not smiling. Knowledgeable to the fact that even though the fight hadn't been allowed to reach a proper end that she had lost out. She was finishing second of two and in this world, that wasn't good enough.

Lucie watched as the spectators animatedly spoke to each other, a verbal post mortem of the fight obviously in full swing. She took another final mouthful of potato and then placed her cutlery back on the plate. She moved it onto her tray and stood up, taking it to a unit on the far side of the room where trays were piled for collection. As she did so, she stood in one of the drops of blood, the redness staining the bottom of her shoe. She didn't notice. The fights didn't faze her anymore. Neither did the violence. As long as she wasn't involved. She'd suffered her share.

Lucie subconsciously rubbed her finger across the scar on her wrist as she left the canteen. She wondered if either of the two women who had been fighting would be left with scars. Probably. How could anybody in this place not be left with a permanent scar? It went with the territory.

The cackle of laughter from downstairs pulled Lucie back to the here and now. Ruby was obviously enjoying herself. How she could be laughing after everything she had said earlier was beyond Lucie but different strokes for different folks. People reacted in different ways. Lucie craved solitude and reflection but Ruby was obviously happy that Terrance was back home and that for her, a sense of normality had returned. It seemed to Lucie that maybe her mother had the right idea.

Bored with her own recollections, Lucie decided that the present needed her attention. She would go downstairs and join the others. Maybe a drink and a laugh was the tonic that was needed. There hadn't been much to laugh at lately. If Ruby could show her how, then she would be silly to resist.

Lucie opened the door to her bedroom and the sound of the music became clearer. No longer muffled. *You Can't Hurry Love*. It struck her as somewhat apt. She'd always loved her mother but maybe all of the tribulations of their life together and their time apart and Lucie's time inside had all been brewing up to this. A clean slate where their love for each other could finally blossom into something that wasn't infested and ready to rot. Despite the intention of others.

Downstairs, Lucie went into the kitchen. It was empty. The music came from a speaker in the corner of the room. Two bottles of red wine sat on the table alongside an ashtray piled high with cigarette butts. One bottle was already finished, the other half empty. Through the window, Lucie could see Terrance out in the garden pacing around on his mobile. His face was agitated and whatever he was talking about, he was obviously not happy. It occurred to Lucie that he hardly ever was.

Ruby was absent. Maybe she was in the living room. Lucie went to find her. As she did, her attention was drawn to the door of the cloakroom that adjoined the hallway connecting the kitchen to the living room. It was ajar. A noise came from within. Without thinking, Lucie moved towards it and pushed opened the door. The cloakroom housed a large dressing table and a toilet.

Ruby had her back to Lucie. There was a mirror on the wall but Ruby didn't see her. Lucie could see everything though. She could see as Ruby continued to rack out a fat line of white powder and bend over it with a rolled up £10 note. It one swift action, she sucked the powder up through the note and into her nostril.

Any love within Lucie immediately seemed to rot, so close yet immediately oh so far, festering away into nothing but disappointment, betrayal and hurt. She moved away from the door and headed back upstairs to her room before Ruby could see her. She wasn't sure why.

In an instant, her brutal recollections about the past seemed so much more palatable than the here and now.

Chapter 44

Now

Lucie lay on her bed and stared through her tears. Tears that never seemed to end lately. A stream from each eye coursed down her cheeks and onto the sheets below her, soaking into the cotton. Thoughts of her mother downstairs filled her brain. She could hear the laughter of Ruby and Terrance. Well, Ruby's laughter and his raised voice. Was he angry? Maybe he had discovered Ruby snorting the coke too. She wasn't sure. She didn't care. Lucie didn't know what to think anymore. How could her mother be doing what she was? After everything that she had said. After everything she had been through. Losing her daughter, becoming clean, finding happiness with Terrance and the cottage. After all of the shit she'd suffered at the hands of Oliver and Sarah. Why had she let herself slip back into her old ways? Was it a one-off? Lucie knew enough about the dreaded drug to know that it was highly unlikely. Once was never enough. The mere nature of it was that the user craved more. Ask any fat cat drug dealer around the world. Ask Connor Perkins. He had never been able to settle at just one line. He was never able to stop, despite his protestations at the innocence of it all.

Connor Perkins. The last time she had been betrayed by someone because of drugs. The last time she had felt betrayal like she was feeling now about Ruby. The last time she had felt so cursed. So alone. And so stupid.

Peru, 2012

'You say that Connor Perkins must have put the drugs in your suitcase?'

Lucie was being questioned by a swarthy officer at a police station in Lima. According to the clock on the wall, it was the time that her flight should have been taking off to speed her to

Amsterdam and then onto Spain. To a future happiness. How quickly life could throw a destroying curveball.

'They weren't there earlier. I don't do drugs. He must have put them in there. He's the only person who could have done it. He was the only person there when I was packing my case.' Lucie's words were breathy as she spoke, catering for the dryness of her throat and the intermittent sobs that needed to come.

'And Mr Perkins was going to meet you in Ibiza in a few days' time? Do you know his flight details?'

Lucie didn't. She hadn't bothered to ask. She just knew that it wasn't her flight and that was the only fact she had needed to know.

'We've tried to contact Mr Perkins at Bar Dynasty, the place where you said you worked at Paradise Cove, but he is not there.'

'But Kara and Tina will vouch for me. Connor was their boss too.' She was going to add the word *kinda* before *boss* but decided not to. It hurt to say it. It made her realise that maybe she only *kinda* knew a little about Connor, even after all of their time together.

'The bar has a sign on it saying "closed until further notice" and as for the address you gave us that you were staying at, there is nobody there. In fact, it appears to be empty.'

'That's not possible. Kara and Tina live there too. They work at the bar. Their stuff was at the flat when I left there this morning.'

'A neighbour said that two girls were seen leaving earlier in the day but we have no idea whether it is the two girls you are talking about. Although their descriptions do match.'

'Well who else would it fucking be?' spat Lucie, her venom and worry mounting in equal measures.

'No need to swear.' Even smothered in accent, his words were condescending and full of sneer.

'I've been used by Connor Perkins to traffic drugs and the two girls that I've been living with for weeks suddenly do a runner as well. Don't you think it looks a bit fuck…' She stopped herself from completing the expletive. 'That it looks more than a little suspicious.'

He didn't answer the question. 'You don't have an address for Connor Perkins, do you?'

'No, I'd never stayed at his.' The futility of her situation was beginning to fall into place. How had she been so stupid?

'Well, he seems to have disappeared into thin air? Very convenient for him if not at all for you.'

'Have you phoned him? His number is on my mobile. And so are photos of me with him, and with Tina and Kara. I can show you.

You can track them down from their photos. Stick up wanted posters or whatever it is you do.' Lucie's words were again steeped in futility.

'This is not a cowboy movie. This is a very serious accusation. But their photos would be helpful.'

'You've taken my phone away. I can show you. Please. I'm not making this up. I don't take drugs, I don't smuggle drugs and I don't know how the drugs got into my suitcase unless it was Connor. I didn't put them there.'

'You don't know your own boyfriend's number? You did say he was your boyfriend, didn't you?'

'Yes, he was. He is.' The word *kinda* lingered on her tongue again but she ignored its haunting of her.

Lucie began to cry. As she wept, the police officer picked up a phone in the room and spoke Spanish hurriedly. Lucie was unable to understand a word.

'I don't know his number. He put it in my phone and it's in there. Do you know everybody's number off by heart? I bet you don't.' Lucie was still crying, her tears unstoppable as she questioned the officer.

She was still crying when a further officer came into the room. He carried Lucie's phone in a clear plastic bag. The two officers spoke in Spanish again.

The main officer spoke to Lucie. 'My colleague says there is nobody on your phone by the name of Connor Perkins. Did you have him listed under another name?'

'No.' Lucie's voice was raised. 'His name was Connor Perkins.'

'Can you show us a photo?' He removed the phone from the bag and handed it to Lucie.

Wiping her face with the back of her hand in an attempt to dry her cheeks, she clicked on her camera roll and scrolled through the photos. All photos of Connor and any of her with Kara and Tina had gone. Even the photo of the heart on the sands of Paradise Cove. She checked her deleted folder. It was empty. A search for Connor's name in her contacts was fruitless too, as was a number she had for Tina. She had never taken one for Kara.'

'I don't understand. I've been working with them all summer. Three people can't just disappear. Especially when one of them is…'

Lucie couldn't bring herself to say "the man I love". The words felt toxic on her tongue. Even though she didn't want to believe it, she knew that the past few weeks of her life had been little more than a lie. Another few paragraphs in the latest cursed chapter of her life. Connor, Kara and Tina had gone and it was clear why. There was obviously much more to the three friends than just random people who worked at a bar. Were the three of them all in a plot together to make Lucie suffer? Through her tear-stained eyes in the police station, it certainly seemed so.

The questioning had lasted for hours, days, weeks. Lucie had one photo of Connor that she had sent back to the UK for Roger and Tanya. They had produced it as evidence to prove that Lucie's story of innocence was true. But even though police forces across the land tried to find Connor, Tina and Kara, they had simply disappeared from trace.

The police believed that they had all disappeared as a result of Lucie getting caught red handed. That the fourth corner of their drugs-smuggling square risked bringing them all down so they had vanished. Into thin air and into obscurity to keep them out of prison. Lucie was the perfect scapegoat and as long as someone took the blame, it didn't matter who it was. Even if she did protest her innocence. Illegal drugs were found and all that concerned the police was that the law breakers received their just desserts. Results were achieved and what did it matter if they were dished out to the wrong person? To them, and to the world, Lucie Palmer looked guilty. And needed to pay.

There were moments when it felt as if Connor Perkins and the two girls from Bar Dynasty had never existed. Had Lucie dreamt it all? Had it been some kind of tropical nightmare? How had something that was so good at the time rotted so quickly? Even up until the moment she was sentenced, Lucie had imagined that Connor would come into view like a knight in shining armour and save the day. Tell the world that there had been some hideous mistake and that really the two of them could live happily ever after at the bar in Ibiza. But he never did. Word reached her before her trail that Bar Dynasty never opened again, the owner choosing to sell it. When questioned about his employing of Connor Perkins as a boss, he merely said that Connor had been highly convincing in his interview and that he had let him govern over things. He had no documentation as everything was cash in hand and as laidback as beach life in Peru in general.

Lucie would never forget Connor's face until the day she died. Or his electrifying touch. If she closed her eyes, she could still revisit the feeling of when they had first made love. Recall that moment when she had lost her virginity to the man who had gone on to betray her so badly. In a world of perfect harmony, it wasn't supposed to be that way. But Lucie's life was far from perfect and always a million miles away from harmonious.

Lying on her bed, Lucie heard another shriek of laughter and various loud noises from downstairs at the cottage. The notion that Ruby was enjoying herself whilst she was immersed so deep in such misery irked her. In fact, it made her see red. A deep dangerous shade. She moved off the bed and went downstairs to face Ruby.

Something told her – a niggling scratch at the back of her senses – that it might be for the last time. There was only so much betrayal one life could take. Especially from her own flesh and blood.

Chapter 45

Now

Every step Lucie took as she headed downstairs felt like it was one step closer to a destiny she really didn't want to experience. As if another horrible chapter in her life was about to open afresh, like a wound that had suddenly become infected. This time to a critical state. One with no cure.

She walked into the kitchen. The music was still playing and Ruby was stood with her back to the kitchen table staring out of the window into the garden. A cigarette was held in her right hand, a twist of smoke ascending into the air from its tip as always. She was drumming her nails on the work surface in front of her in time to the beat of the music.

Lucie moved to the table and poured herself a hefty glug of wine from one of the bottles standing there into a dirty glass alongside it. Ruby's, she assumed, but she didn't care. She wanted a drink and the glass was empty so it was now hers. She downed the red liquid in one, savouring the taste as it passed down her throat. She placed the glass back on the table, the slight noise it made causing Ruby to spin around. A few scatterings of ash fell from her cigarette as she did so.

'Oh, I was wondering when you were going to come down. I kind of figured that the noise Terrance and I have been making down here might get you out of your bedroom eventually. What have you been doing up there?' There was no smile or any sense of friendliness in either her voice or across her features as she spoke. It seemed at odds with her mood before.

'I was thinking. And dozing a little. Today's been quite a day.' Lucie's words were equally devoid of emotion.

'And it's not over yet, is it?' smiled Ruby. A smile that seemed to be far from carefree or loving. Lucie knew it must be the coke.

'Apparently not,' deadpanned Lucie looking at the table. 'Somebody's having a party, aren't they?'

'People are allowed to enjoy themselves, Lucie. We don't always have to wallow in our own misery, do we? Like you say, today had been a rather emotional day and I felt like letting my hair down a little. And besides, Terrance is home and that's always a reason to celebrate, isn't it?'

'If you say so, mother. Where is he, anyway? I saw him arriving across the lawn. Or is this a party-for-one?'

'He's in the front room making a business call. The entrepreneurial wheels of industry need to keep on turning, don't they?'

There was something odd about hearing her mother say things like that. Words of six syllables were not normally on the radar of Ruby's vocabulary. She spoke the word as if it was something she had heard Terrance say and then attempted to copy.

'Does he know you're on drugs?' The question was direct and to the point. If Lucie harboured any sympathy for her mother, then it was truly buried fifty fathoms deep.

Ruby let out a large sniff. Due to the drug or a derisory sense of non-caring? Lucie wasn't sure.

'I'm on drugs, am I?' It wasn't a denial.

'I saw you, mum. How could you? I thought you were clean.' Lucie could feel the tears of her own sorrow pricking at her eyes. It had only been a few short hours before that she had felt closer to Ruby than ever before, the connections and similarities between them bringing them together in a way that Lucie had only ever dreamt of. What she hadn't ever dreamt of was having to confront her mother about drugs again. She assumed that it was something that was firmly in the past. For a second, her own mind attempted to wander to every conversation that she had engaged in with her mother since arriving back in the UK. At the airport, in the cab, at the pub, here at the cottage. Had she been on drugs for all of those conversations too? Had Lucie just been too blind and too naïve to notice? How could somebody like Lucie, who had been through so much in such a short life still be so naïve? Sometimes the hardest person to understand was her own self.

'Oh Lucie, do you really think it's that easy to just give it all up. I had to for a while, when they took you away from me, but that inner demon was always there. Always waiting to be reignited. And reunited with what it really wanted. And that was drugs.'

'How can you be so calm and collected about it all?' Lucie spat. 'You're talking about something that has ruined my life. And it has ruined yours. I remember being taken away from you like it was yesterday. You were crying as they took me away. Those were genuine tears of misery. Not even somebody like you could have painted those on and done such a convincing job.'

Ruby dragged on her cigarette and walked to the table to stub out the butt in the ashtray. Her face was still as cold and as emotionless as it could be. Lucie couldn't help but feel that her mother was more than ready to be confronted about the drugs, as if finally talking about something that she'd hidden for so long might actually make the secret she'd kept a little more understandable. A little less problematic. Either that or she genuinely didn't see it as a problem.

'You really think I was crying because they were taking *you* away? Is that what you've thought all of these years? Then you're wrong.'

Ruby's words punched Lucie like a clenched fist. Finally, she had been feeling that a person close to her was actually somebody who cared and loved her. After all of the trauma she'd been through, the image of her mother's tears as she had been taken away from the Brighton flat proved to her that despite everything – the drugs, the partying, the drink, the lack of self-control – that underneath it all, Ruby had always loved her deep down. That lying underneath all of that bravado and indulgence, despite everything, was the loving heart of a mother who idolised her daughter. The thought that it might not be true seemed like it could be the most crippling blow of all.

'What? How can you say that? I saw you in floods of tears...'

'For my friend, Joan. I'd just learnt that she'd been killed in an accident at her work a few days earlier. We were good mates. We shared a lot together. You can ask Terrance if you like. He was there.'

Lucie held her hand out to steady herself on the table. It was as if a barrage of blows were being rained down upon her again. Her brain span in an attempt to try and work out just what was happening. Why Ruby was suddenly being so cruel. Why she was admitting to this without a scrap of compassion or regret. She thought of what Ruby had just said.

'Terrance was there? What, at her place of work?'

'No, at the flat. You don't recognise him, do you? I didn't really meet him after you were taken away. We go back much further than that. He's a little fatter and a lot greyer I guess but he's one of the gang that used to come around to the flat to party in Brighton. In fact, he was the one who supplied the best gear. So in answer to your previous question, yes he does know I take drugs. He's known and loved it for years.' There was almost an air of blasé with her answers.

Lucie remembered that she had found Terrance somewhat recognisable on their first meeting. Just not enough to pinpoint him as one of the men who used to frequent their flat in Brighton. Doubtless she had answered the door to him on many occasions, let him into the sanctuary of the home she'd shared with her mother. Allowed him to bring the evil intruder that had cursed her very existence for so long. Perhaps for an eternity.'

'I thought you were crying for me. I always have done. This is why you shouldn't take drugs, mum. They make you a different person. They make you forget about your feelings. They make you hurt me.'

'I've spent my life being hurt, Lucie. You saw to that the moment you came into my life. It's your fault. You're to blame.'

Lucie's world had always been one that had been built on the most unsteady of family foundations but as she stared into Ruby's eyes and saw the hatred that seemed to dwell there – something she had never imagined and after their conversation earlier today certainly never expected – her world seemed to crumble into a ravine of despair from which there would never be any turning back. Even though she wasn't able to understand what was happening to her at that very moment, she could feel any flicker of love that attempted to burn inside her being extinguished for good. A light that could never be relit. One that would darken her soul for a lifetime. At that precise moment, she hated her mother too.

'Why is it *my* fault? Why am *I* to blame?' It was something she had always felt deep down. That she herself was to blame. She now needed to know why.

Lucie never managed to hear an answer.

The door of the kitchen swung open and Terrance walked into the room. For a second, time seemed to stop, the moment hanging ominously in the room. Terrance looked on as the two women stared at each other. Hatred in the eyes of one, heartache and loathing in the eyes of the other. Impossible to comprehend.

'What's going on?' he asked.

'She knows,' said Ruby.

'Knows what?' replied Terrance.

'It doesn't matter anymore. You don't need to worry.'

Ruby turned to a drawer by the kitchen door, opened it and pulled something out from within.

Lucie watched on in horror as her mother raised her arm and pointed it at Terrance. A single shot sounded and he fell to the floor. It wasn't the first time Lucie had seen death close up, but this was different. Out of context. Her eyes blurred and she felt darkness envelop her as she too slumped to the floor.

Chapter 46

Peru, 2013

Death. The battle was bloody. They always were. Lucie thought it was over supplies. Cigarettes or drugs within the prison. Guards thought it didn't happen. At least the naïve ones did. It was the others who made it happen. Corruption both sides of every cell door. Profitable for all.

It had started in the open-air yard at the centre of the prison. The place where maybe two or three times a day the women were herded out to wallow in each other's company. Some for physical recreation, some to work, some to just enjoy a moment of fresh air. Well as fresh as prison air could be with the pollution of expletives, cigarette smoke and fear stitched into every fibre of it.

A makeshift gym had been built in one corner of the yard. Nothing fancy, but it housed a basic bench press, a set of ropes for cardio work and a variety of pull up bars. Free weights littered the floor of the area, none remaining there for long as the women inmates hustled over their use. In a prison like this, the size of your muscles would often equate to the size of your importance in the prison hierarchy and the women would find themselves puffing out their chests, hard and beyond unfeminine from their constant workouts, to gain control of the weights. Lucie had tried on many occasions to use them but had found herself under the watchful and hate-filled eyes of women twice her size and tattooed with menace. She would stop, not through intimidation, but through a knowledge that a refusal to share and give up your place was an open invitation to war. To Lucie, it wasn't bulging biceps and rock solid abs that achieved survival, it was knowledge and common sense. The gym was a place for the women to display their strength in more ways than just the physical.

The fight had started as it so often did. One woman working out on a bench press, raising a barbell above her face as another of her crew spotted her, her legs either side of the head of the woman with the weights. Grunts would echo from the woman as she pumped iron, a sign of both the stress of lifting the weights and a display of bravado to those within earshot. From out of nowhere, another of the inmates would appear and storm over to the woman, a bedlam of anger and urgency. A push would come, contact made as the barbell was tossed to the floor. The arms of the woman on her back would buckle and fold, and then in an instant, she would be on her feet ready to fight back. Punches would fly and flesh bruised as the battle took hold. Lucie would often watch, a curiosity gripping her as to their technique and to the frenzy of the violence. The fights were like a spectator sport to her, the violence somehow becoming almost gladiatorial and Romanesque in its flamboyant entertainment.

Often the fights would be stopped within a matter of minutes before real damage could be done. But today's was different. The catcalls of the surrounding women egging on as the two sides progressed without interruption, prison authority failing to appear.

Knuckles hit cheek bones, a spray of blood arcing across the air and landing with a dull splat on the concrete. Headlocks and punches to stomachs followed, hair pulled from its roots and clothes torn at the seams. Fights could end in three ways. Both sides pulled apart by the guards in uniform who were there to stop such altercations. Or one of the women would give up the ghost and skulk off, beaten into defeat, to lick her own wounds and contemplate her loss locked away in solitude in her own cell, her embarrassment at losing her only company. Or as would occur today, it would be a fight to the death.

As yet, Lucie had never witnessed the latter. She'd seen suicide but never a death served cold to another. The final prize. Today was the day.

The woman who had been pushing the weights was physically stronger and a good few inches taller than the attacker who had come screaming out of nowhere. The circumference of her arms was way bigger too, doubtless the result of regular workouts. It was clear to Lucie that she was winning the battle, having regained control from the out-of-the-blue attack. After a barrage of punches had stormed down from both parties, the stronger of the women was able to push the other to the floor. Kicks followed to the face and core, a symphony of Bronx cheers gaining momentum from the crowd.

Spurred on by their jeers, the woman in control decided to take matters further. As the body on the floor writhed in agony, her will to fight slowly leaving her, the other woman raised her arms aloft in victory. A slick of red ran down her skin, viscous and vile from her mouth to her chin where it pooled before dripping down onto her clothes. She spat, attempting to rid herself of any blood that kept flowing. As the cheers increased, the woman's own sense of self-importance seemed to increase, smothering any semblance of sense. She was enjoying being the centre of attention, the cat who gained the cream, the dog who would come out on top.

Smiling through the mass of blood that decorated her chin, she reached down to pick up one of the free weights that littered the floor. She wrapped her knuckles around it and just as a prison guard finally arrived to stop the fracas, she brought it smashing down upon the attacker's face. Lucie watched as the skull of the woman on the floor caved in on itself, a matted knot of flesh and bone exploding from her features. The woman's body convulsed a little, like an animal hit on the roadside, and then became still, death taking hold. A detonation of noise hit the air. Lucie was watching someone die. It didn't shock her. She had known she would see it sooner or later. Prison life taught you to realise that at some time it would be there, in your face. That finality was to be expected.

The guard had witnessed the final blow. The woman's victory was short-lived. Within minutes, she had been removed and taken away. Her brawn had gained the victory but her brain had let her down. With that fatal blow, she would doubtless gain another sentence which meant that it was unlikely that she would ever leave the prison. That freedom would never be hers.

Lucie watched as the crowd dispersed and the dead body of the victim taken away. She had seen death. Witnessed it first-hand. Something that a young Lucie sitting in her bedroom in Brighton would never have imagined. Something that only happened in films and to nasty people.

Was she a nasty person? No, she knew she wasn't. But she knew that she wasn't the same person who had entered the prison all that time before. She was harder. Stronger. Tougher. Wiser. Perhaps damaged. Yes, definitely damaged.

She knew that one day, freedom would be hers. Surely, good things had to happen eventually to the innocent. Even to those who felt their damaged lives were cursed.

She walked back inside. She stared down at the blot of blood that still stained the floor of the yard. She felt nothing.

Chapter 47

Now

Her eyes attempted to open as she felt a searing burst of pain splash across her face. For a second, Lucie couldn't remember where she was and how she had gotten there. It was only when she saw her mother standing in front of her, a cigarette burning in one hand and a piece of black gaffer tape in the other that the horror of her own thoughts came flooding back. It had been the tape being ripped from her face that had caused the pain. Obviously placed over her mouth by her own mother. An attempt to silence her once again.

Lucie went to raise one of her hands to her face to rub the sore flesh. She couldn't. They were both tied behind her back. She was sitting on a wooden chair in the front room of the cottage. Her feet were also tied together. Movement from the neck down was impossible. How had it come to this?

A cloud of smoke blew into her face as her mother spoke to her, Ruby's face just mere inches from hers. It had never smelt more horrid. And Ruby's smoking was a habit, a stench that Lucie had become more than used to decades earlier.

A maniacal look possessed Ruby's expression. Her eyes seemed jittery and housed a madness that suggested both complacency, pride, hatred and a woman tipped over the edge. Into the abyss of lunacy. A stranger to Lucie, yet with a face so well known. Once so loved. Still loved by Lucie? How could it be?

The sight of Terrance's dead body falling to the floor suddenly filled Lucie's mind. Until then, it had been inexplicably shelved in the moment. Ruby had shot her own boyfriend. Shot by Ruby in cold blood at virtually point blank range. Terror gripped Lucie. Terror at the realisation of what her own mother was capable of. How had this come to be?

It was Ruby who broke the silence.

'It's finally all coming together. The end is in sight. At long last you can see what you've done to me. Why you're to blame.'

There it was. That word again. Blame. Ruby had used it before. Just before she'd shot Terrance. Saying that Lucie was to blame. For what? For loving a mother who had sometimes made it an impossible task?

Lucie attempted to speak. Her voice felt dry and raspy, the words hurting as they came. 'Why am I to blame? What have I done?'

'You've ruined my life. You always have. Right from the very first day. Actually from even before then.'

'What do you mean?' Even before then? I wasn't born. What are you talking about? At least I'm not a killer like you.'

'Actually you are, Lucie.' The words were blunt and brutal to hear. Coated in confusion for Lucie. She watched, unable to speak as Ruby placed the cigarette to her mouth again and took a heavy drag. 'You are a killer. That's why I blame you. You killed your brother, Lucie. You killed your brother.'

Even if she had been able to move, Lucie would have remained totally still as she took in what her mother was saying. How could that be? She didn't have a brother. God knows she'd often longed for one in the solitude of her bedroom in Brighton. Felt that she deserved one. In some ways, almost that she had one. How nice it would have been to have been able to share the nightmares of having a mum like Ruby with somebody who could understand exactly what being the offspring of Ruby Palmer entailed.

'But I don't have a...' Lucie began to speak. She didn't finish the sentence as Ruby placed her hand over Lucie's mouth. It too smelt of cigarettes.

'Hush, Lucie. Don't say a word. Just listen. I've been waiting a long time to tell you this. To eventually make you understand.'

Lucie took in every word as Ruby removed her hand from her mouth and began to speak. Horror gripping her with every cursed syllable.

'You were a twin. A fraternal one. Dizygotic was the word they used at the hospital. I'll always remember it. Twins run in our family so it was no surprise to me at first. Although I was told at the time that people in the family had sometimes struggled during the pregnancy with complications. I thought how bloody typical. If something can go wrong or be arse about face then it will be. I'm cursed like that, always have been.'

Lucie couldn't help but feel her own feelings of insecurity and inadequacy rise to the surface as she heard Ruby speak. Maybe it wasn't just twins that ran in the family, perhaps it was a feeling of being cursed too.

'I was happy about it though when I managed to get my head around the idea. I really wanted two boys when I first found out I was pregnant. I thought boys would be what Oliver would want. But as it happened, he was thrilled when he found out that I was having a boy and a girl. I've always wanted a son. I think I'd have been a much better mother if I'd have had a boy to be honest. I'm more suited to boys. Females don't like me.'

Ruby was lost in her thoughts for a moment as she unravelled her story. Lucie could feel her throat tightening as she listened on.

'Everything was fine until about 24 weeks into the pregnancy. I'd actually managed to come to terms with the fact that your father didn't want me. That he didn't want to be a father. That he had decided to side with that evil bitch of a mother of his and turn his back on us. I thought I could handle it. I really did. I didn't think I'd need a man. I'd have my own little boy to play with soon, wouldn't I? And you, of course.' The last sentence came across as an afterthought. Lucie knew that it truly was.

Ruby continued. 'But then I had to be admitted to the hospital and the doctors there told me that I was suffering from some kind of internal complication. I was having all sorts of pains and knew that something wasn't right. A lack of blood supply apparently. Fucking typical again, eh. As if I hadn't been punished enough already. One of you wasn't getting the blood you needed and the organs were struggling so I had to do something about it in order for the twin to try and survive. It was the boy, your brother, my precious dear boy, who was struggling the most so refusing the surgery wasn't an option. I knew what I had to do.'

Lucie wanted to ask if the surgery would have been doubted, if it had been she herself who had been mostly lacking in blood supply. If the female twin had been at risk. Scared of the answer, she refused to let the question escape her lips.

'The condition was becoming worse and worse. I was told that the situation was so serious that it wasn't necessarily expected that either of the twins would survive.

After losing the chance of happiness with your father and being made to feel so fucking worthless from Sarah, I was not going to risk losing my babies too. It was too devastating a thought.'

Ruby's bottom lip began to quiver as she spoke and the long curve of ash that dangled from her cigarette broke off and fell down onto Lucie's trousers. Ruby didn't see it, her thoughts understandably elsewhere.

'A termination was considered. I could have gotten rid of you. But I refused of course. Your brother deserved a chance. I had some kind of laser surgery which I was told might help with the blood supply. I was awake for some of it. I could see you both on the screen. Your brother looked incredibly small but so very beautiful. Just like the boys I had always imagined I would have. I had the operation and miraculously I was told that it was a success. You were both going to be okay.'

Lucie could feel the tears running down her own cheeks at the thought of having a brother. Hadn't she always felt it? That she wasn't meant to be alone. But she knew that there was not to be a happy ending though. That was clear. She heard herself asking "so what happened?" before she could contain the words.

'The next morning I knew something had happened. Call it a mother's intuition. Something just didn't feel right. Something was telling me that something awful had happened. I knew it. It was confirmed that your brother had died. I had to carry his body inside me until you were born a few weeks later. You were premature and small and for a while the doctors were worried about you too, but you somehow survived. You were able to get the blood supply that you needed. Not like your brother, he couldn't do anything because you had it all. You killed him. You made sure that he didn't survive.'

'But that's not true. It was an accident. A freak of nature. It wasn't my fault.' Lucie could tell that her pleas were falling on deaf ears. Ears that didn't want to hear. To a person who had made her own mind up many years before. Lucie was to blame for the death of her own brother. For the death of the son that Ruby had always wanted.

'I couldn't even look at you at first when you came into this world. I blamed you for killing him. I still do. It was like you were possessed to me. Like a devil that had done something so evil. Can you ever imagine what it's like to give birth to your own dead son? To have to buy a cot for one baby and a coffin for another. After all of that rejection from your father's family to then watch your son be rejected by your own body. I couldn't cope. Not in the long run. It was all too much. It always has been. I tried to forgive you. Tried so hard to forgive you, but I couldn't. I never could. Every time I looked at you, even till this day, I can see your dead brother's body lying in my arms. That's an image, a vile horrible memory that I just wanted to make go away, to take away and never see again, but I can't. It's here.' Ruby pointed to her head, banging her fingers against the side of her skull. 'It never leaves me. The drugs make it better. They block it out for a while. But then, it returns. That's why I started taking them. I'd had it at the beach one time and then I tried it properly at a party. With Russell, you remember him? And for a while, all of that hurt and despair and hatred that I felt about losing my baby boy went away. It was camouflaged by the drugs. That was it. I was suddenly hooked. Whether I liked it or not.'

'But you had me. I was there. I was your baby girl. Why couldn't you love me?'

'I tried. I did. But I couldn't. You remind me of too much heartache. Of too much hurt. You're the reason my life has been as it has. You're the reason I could never contemplate kids with anybody else. I was too scared of things going wrong again. I couldn't risk that happening. Losing another baby boy. You're the reason my life has been controlled by drugs. You're the reason I have felt trapped in my own existence for so long. You took all my love away from me when you killed your brother. You made me never able to love again. I can't love myself, so how can I love someone who caused so much pain?'

A moment of sympathy passed over Lucie as she stared at the bitter and twisted hatred in Ruby's face, but it passed as soon as it had arrived.

'You loved Terrance, didn't you?' asked Lucie.

'No. I loved the fact that he had money and drugs. It's very easy to fall for your supplier when you're desperate for your next hit.' Ruby reflected for a second. 'I was clean for a while you know. After they took you away. It was as if not having you there anymore made me feel that I could achieve things. Give up the gear. The catalyst was gone. That not having to see your face meant that I couldn't possibly be reminded every waking moment about what you'd done. About what I'd lost. I did want things to get better. But Terrance came to see me, offered me drugs again and that was that. I crept back into my old ways. I never loved him. I just loved being with him. Being with someone. Not feeling rejected.'

'But you killed him?' The words came with a strength that had been missing in Lucie's voice since she had first came around in the living room of the cottage. Since she had witnessed Terrance's death. 'Why did you kill him?'

'Oh. Yes. I killed him. I did that for love. Finally, I found the love I'd been incapable of finding for such a long time. For a lifetime. *Your* lifetime.'

258

'But why?'

'Because I fell in love with *him*.'

Using all of her might, a strength which seemed to come from within, at odds with her wiry frame, Ruby manoeuvred Lucie's chair to swivel it around so that it was facing the other side of the living room. Sitting on another wooden chair, his feet and hands tied just as hers were, a large inking of blood on his forehead, was a man.

Lucie felt herself unable to breathe as she looked at him. Misery and confusion intertwined their fingers around her again. It was Connor Perkins.

Chapter 48

Now

As Lucie sat staring at Connor, Ruby marched over to where the man was sitting unconscious and slapped him as hard as she could around the face. A burst of sympathy popped within Lucie at the point of contact. Connor Perkins was there, in the same room as her, for the first time in over six years. The last time she had seen him had been that morning after they had packed her suitcase ready to fly from Peru to their new life in Ibiza. The morning that Connor had not just disappeared from her life for good, but had seemingly disappeared off the face of planet Earth too. Every attempt to locate him, to describe his green eyes and his rugged features, to unfurl the story of their hearts to the officers dealing with Lucie's arrest in Peru came flashing back into Lucie's mind. Of the futility of her tale about a man who had simply stopped existing. The man who sold her out and ruined her life and her faith in men. In humans.

The sympathy vanished in a heartbeat. Lucie could feel her venom rising. Connor and Ruby in love? Two people that she had once truly loved. Two people who had delivered the ultimate betrayal. She needed to know why even if she already knew that the sordid truth would break her beyond repair. If she wasn't already.

'What the fuck is he doing here? How do you know Connor? He's the man I fell in love with in Peru…'

As Connor began to stir from the slap, Ruby stared straight into Lucie's eyes and spoke. Her face was again painted with that look of someone who was enjoying being able to play vindictive storyteller. As if the words had been brewing just below the surface and were finally euphoric at release.

'You know Connor?' The words were drizzled with sarcasm. 'Of course you do. He's the man you fell in love with, the man you fell into bed with, the man who fell out of sight when you needed him most. Because he needed other things a whole lot more, including me.'

Lucie stared across at Connor, unable to comprehend what was being said. As Connor regained his vision and stared over at Lucie, there was no compassion in his eyes. The eyes that she'd stared into a thousand times all those years ago now contained nothing but duplicity and treason.

He spoke. 'Will you please untie me, Ruby?'

'You promise to behave and not kick off again?' Ruby's tone was school-like. Dictatorial.

'Yes, I do. I've learnt my lesson. You just surprised me, that's all. I didn't expect things to happen so soon. You won't need to punish me again.' Subservience echoed through every word.

Ruby nodded. But before she began to untie Connor, she walked over to a table on the far wall and picked up a small gun that was lying there. Lucie watched in horror at the sight of her mother holding such a dangerous weapon again, the two things at contrast with each other. It was the gun Ruby had used minutes earlier to kill Terrance.

Ruby tucked the gun into her pocket and walked towards Connor. 'I'll untie you, darling, but any more nonsense and I'll be forced to take action again, won't I? You don't want me killing two members of the same family in one day, do you?'

'You can trust me, my love,' smiled Connor.

As she watched her mother untie Connor, Ruby's words hit Lucie like a freight train. 'The same family...what do you mean?' Lucie's brain was struggling to piece all of the information that was firing towards her together. 'Terrance and Connor?'

Ruby's smile spread from one side of her face to the other as she let loose the ropes confining Connor and pulled his head towards her chest as he sat there. Like a baby to a bosom. The blood that still sat fresh on his forehead left a puddle of colour on her clothes as she did so. 'Oh Lucie, I've been dying to tell you for so long. Meet my boyfriend. You know him as Connor Perkins of course but that's not his real name.'

He stood up as Ruby continued. 'Meet Steven Allen, Terrance's son.' She turned to Steven. 'Say hello, darling.'

Steven rubbed his wrists as he spoke, the redness from his constraints still evident. 'Hello Lucie, nice to see you again.' A grin of conceit.

Lucie screamed in anger, a blinding rage blurring her vision for a second at the strength of his deceit. At the realisation that nearly everyone in her life that she had cared for had let her down. On a catastrophic level. As Steven came back into focus, she heard herself ask. One simple word. A need to hear. 'How?'

Chapter 49

Now

'That's quite some force you have there, Ruby,' said Steven, touching his temple as he leant over to kiss Ruby fully on the lips. She reciprocated, an unnecessarily overly urgent display of affection coming from her. Lucie knew it was for her own benefit.

The kiss dispensed with, Steven moved towards Lucie. He knelt down in front of her so that his eye level was the same as hers. Lucie wanted to cry. She wanted to spit. Determined not to show weakness or anger, she refrained from both and let him speak.

'Hi, Lucie. Yep, my name is Steven Allen and not Connor Perkins. My dad is…*was* Terrance Allen. He was the man who had been with Ruby for the longest time. Until a better man came along.' He turned to Ruby and winked. Suddenly, his flirtations seemed so ugly to Lucie, at extremes to how she had found them in Peru.

He continued. 'We've all worked together for a long time. The family business I guess you can call it. Drugs. Your favourite thing. All of Ruby's tales of property developing are a bag of lies.' His grin was unwelcome. 'My dad started supplying drugs years ago. It's how he met Ruby. People never seem to tire of them, do they? So when I came along and reached an age where I could see the attraction, I proved to dad that I would be a worthy addition to the business. That I wanted to become part of the family empire. To show my allegiance. Now, thanks to Ruby, the business is mine…' He hesitated before changing his words to "ours" as he stared back at a grinning Ruby again. He stood back up and walked over to Ruby, placed his hand in hers and stood united.

The two of them faced Lucie. Two people she had loved. Yet somehow, Lucie had never felt more alone. More abandoned.

Lucie needed further answers an attempt to comprehend. 'You all work together selling drugs? Is that why you packed my case in Peru with drugs. You wanted me to smuggle them through to Ibiza for you? Those were Terrance's drugs?'

'Got it in one. I had been hiding them into the lining for weeks and I packed a load into your case itself whilst you showered and sang tunelessly if I remember. You made a right racket. Except I didn't want you to smuggle them through to Ibiza. I had to make sure that you were caught,' sneered Steven. 'We all did.'

'I don't understand,' stammered Lucie, a grim cognisance that her two worlds were colliding horribly – the life she had experienced in Peru and her family life back home in the UK.

Ruby took up the story, her words quick and loud, again in a hurry to leave her mouth. There was a horrid sense of pride in her words. 'Doesn't it all make sense yet? I wanted you caught. Steven told me to tip off the airport that you would have drugs on you. An anonymous call from someone will always be investigated, won't it? It'll never be ignored and we knew you'd be banged up red-handed as Steven had told me what he'd hidden in your case. The whole thing was a set up. I wanted you found guilty.'

'But you didn't know that I was going to be in Peru. You didn't know that I would fall in love with Connor…' She shook her head at her mistake with his name but left it uncorrected.

'Oh Lucie, I did. I was behind it all. Every inch of your downfall was masterminded by me. To get you back for your dead brother and the misery you've caused me. I've felt trapped all of my life because of you. Because of losing my son. Because of you killing him. You may not have done it with your bare hands but the moment he stopped breathing was the moment I stopped living too. The drugs were an escape, a way to not think about what had happened. A way to escape you. I was glad when they took you away from me, but I couldn't stop thinking about what you'd done. About how you had killed Ashton. That was his name, you know. I chose it and had it engraved on a plaque on his coffin. It was the name Steven used for your supposed contact in Ibiza, wasn't it? I told him to. It seemed like a kind of perfect revenge. That he could be involved from beyond the grave. I wanted you to be as trapped as I have been all my life. I wanted you to realise that sometimes there is no escape from misery. You'd gone off to your happy new life with Roger and Tanya, Mr and Mrs Fucking Perfect, and I was still left with my memories. With that heartache. I needed to make sure that you suffered. Believe it or not, I hate the drugs deep down. I hate that I was unable to stop. Had no willpower. But I needed them. To take me away from my waste of a life. From the rejection and the death and the hurt.'

'But I always loved you. Why would you do that to me? And how...' The tears came now, silently down Lucie's cheeks as she soaked up Ruby's rage. Steven moved behind Ruby and held her in his arms, a welcoming cocoon, as she carried on speaking.

'I wrote to Tanya and Roger after you were rehomed. I was in constant contact but I kept it secret. I wanted you to think that I'd abandoned you. I wanted you to hurt, but I needed to stay in contact as I'd not finished with you yet. I needed to work out my revenge. For years, I wrote to them in secret every few months or so to find out what was going on in your life. They were even kind enough to suggest that perhaps I would like to re-establish contact. Fools. I had no intention of doing that. Not until I knew what I needed to do. I told them I wasn't emotionally ready. Fuckwits. That only came years later when I was truly with Terrance. The drugs business was booming. We were watching a news story about a girl who had got done for drug smuggling and sentenced to a long spell in prison. I joked that that's what we should do to you. Imprison you in just the same way that I'd felt imprisoned by you all of my life. He said it would be easy to do and that his son, Steven, was travelling in South America – a haven for drugs – and that it would be simple to unconsciously fool a girl into smuggling.' Ruby turned to Steven and stared. 'Especially when his son is so good looking, eh?' He nodded in approval of the compliment. 'Steven was working at this bar in Peru and was keen to be a bigger part of the business – he's an empire builder – so it seemed the perfect thing to do. Bar Dynasty was owned by one of Terrance's friends. He's been part of the *business* for years. I had found out from Roger and Tanya that you were at college. It was very easy to do a bit of detective work and pay one of your classmates, Jess wasn't it, to spin a tale of a fabulous job in Peru and dangle that carrot. You snapped it up, I knew you would. You loved the beach. That's one of the few things I do remember from when you were living with me.'

'The whole trip was a set-up?' Lucie was finding it hard to believe.

'Totally,' replied Ruby. 'Terrance loved me enough to keep me happy and give me my perfect revenge, even if it meant him sacrificing a couple of million on the drugs in your case. If you were going to go down, I wanted you to go down for a long time. I was rich way before you came back here, Lucie. Being left this cottage was a bonus. Terrance and I didn't need it. We already have a huge house in London and another in Brighton, a life you've never known, but I wanted you to see this. To see where my misery started when yours in Peru finally ended. I was keeping tabs on what was happening over there. But this cottage is where your misery will end. I wanted you here to play with you a bit before telling you what you needed to hear. I wanted to see what being imprisoned had done to you. If it had damaged you in the same way it damaged me. You're easy to manipulate. You're weak and vulnerable. That's why I fixed the mirror to break in your room by weakening the frame and why I trapped you in the attic after you'd told me about getting freaked out in the lift at the shopping centre. That was a stroke of luck. So I thought I'd concoct my own piece of luck. I told you I was going out, hid in the house, watched you put your washing on and then saw you go into the roof space. I knew you would after I'd said about the paintings. It was the perfect opportunity to add to your madness. I slipped out of the house after shutting the loft with you in it. I knew Drew wouldn't see me. He's as stupid as anything and besides, I could sneak off down the path without being seen. He'd never have seen me from where he was working on the well. It was all so easy to manipulate. You're my puppet, but now is the time to finally cut the strings. For good.'

Lucie felt any colour that was left in her face drain away as she took in the words. Madness. She was staring into the face of madness, a psychotic woman who had lived a life hell-bent on revenge. Every moment up until now had just been a sentence building up yet another paragraph in the final chapter of Lucie's life. A cursed life unknown for so long. But now, she was finally seeing it clearly. Every rotten strand of it. Clearer and darker and more twisted than ever.

'When the police arrive here, I will be hysterical. Steven will have long gone, back to the house in London, and all the police will find is the dead body of my poor darling Terrance, shot between the eyes with a gun fired by my dear daughter, Lucie, who couldn't cope with life outside prison. Who was so damaged by her ordeal that somehow, she went on the rampage and killed poor Terrance before turning the gun on herself. Ashamed of how she has wasted her life. We can make sure your fingerprints are all over it. I will be hysterical and crying my eyes out, inconsolable about the fact that I have just witnessed my daughter, the daughter who I have finally managed to reconnect with after all of those years of cruelly being torn apart, kill my man and then kill herself after hearing about how she isn't coping with anything anymore. A tale of tragedy where I can play the perfect victim. And know that the right person finally got what they truly deserved. Justice and revenge for me and for your dead brother. And a fitting finale for you.'

Ruby reached into her pocket to pull out the gun, ready to commit her final revenge. A puzzled look crossed her face as she found it empty. Steven had already removed it. She span around to face her younger lover. She had barely registered the gun in his hand when she felt the force of his blow as he smashed the gun across her head. She blacked out.

Lucie looked on in surprise as Steven spoke.

'That's for killing my father you crazy bitch.'

A second later, he stepped over Ruby's body and hurried towards Lucie.

Chapter 50

Now

Lucie was sure that her final moments had come as Steven, the man she had known as Connor, rushed towards her. But she was surprised when he began to untie the ropes that bound her to the chair.

'I thought you were on *her* side,' stated Lucie as she felt her wrists finally free. She stared down at the scar on her wrist, now clouded in a soft poppy-coloured bruise from the restraints. A scar so much smaller than the ones that now lacerated her insides. The scars of betrayal.

'I was, until she murdered my father. I didn't sign up for that. Drugs are one thing, moving up the family business and impressing dad is one thing, but fucking murder is quite another.' Lucie was waiting for an apology but one didn't come.

'What now?' asked Lucie. 'Is she dead?'

'No, I didn't hit her hard enough for that, but she'll be out for a while. We should tie her up. She can take the wrap for all of this. Then we'll phone the police. Tell them she went crazy.'

Lucie moved towards the body of Ruby lying on the floor. A fleshy mess of blood oozed on her forehead. At the sight of it, Lucie clamped her hand to her mouth and began to convulse. A gagging noise started in her throat.

'Jesus, are you going to be sick? Go throw up in the loo. I'll tie her up.'

Lucie kept her hand over her mouth as she bolted from the room, the image of her mother's injuries still in her mind. When she returned minutes later, she found Steven bent over Ruby, her hands and feet now tied behind her back. She was still unconscious.

'She's not dead, there's a pulse. She'll say we did it, but if you and I stick together in front of the police, we can make sure that she takes the blame. Just leave me out of it, eh? Let me be the victim too.'

Lucie didn't know what to think. To look at Steven now he was still the same Connor she had fallen in love with in Paradise Cove, the green-eyed god from behind the counter at Bar Dynasty, but his words and actions now seemed to strip him of any deific quality. There was an ugliness behind his ways.

'Why did you do it? Why did you let them use me?'

'I've always wanted the business to flourish and be successful in it. It's piss-easy money and I get to travel the world, stay in nice places and have a good time. I knew I'd take over from dad one day. He was grooming me. I didn't think it would be so soon though, but Ruby seems to have decided that. But I'll do a good job.'

'On other girls like me? You left me to rot? I loved you.'

No reciprocation came.

'I'm sorry. But your mum and my dad set it all up. I couldn't let them down. I liked you, I really did. You were fun to be with I guess. But I was doing a job, playing a role. I was acting if you like.'

'In bed too?' Lucie felt a harshness in her words. It suited her.

'No, that came naturally.'

'You just disappeared. Left me to hang. So did Kara and Tina. I had such a great time with you guys. For the first time in my life, I felt that I was really making good friends. Found something that was mine and had been missing in my life. They let me down too. They were *my* girls.'

'I paid them to disappear. It was all part of the plan. They weren't in on it, so they were genuinely fond of you but I scared them into thinking that they would be associated with you when you were arrested so I told them the owner of the bar wanted them out of the picture and was happy to pay them off. They packed up and cleared out as soon as I paid them off. I told them never to contact you. It was touch and go. They only left a few hours before the police came to the flat apparently. '

'You wiped everything off my phone, didn't you?'

'Yep, easy to do. Plus I made sure that I hardly ever posed for photos with you. I needed to be as anonymous as possible. That's how it was. I was virtually out of the country before you hit the police station. Nobody was looking for Steven Allen's passport, you just told them about Connor Perkins.'

'Why are you telling me this? You don't need to?'

'No I don't, but I do feel that you deserve some kind of explanation. Your whole adventure that summer was planned to see you imprisoned. Because your mum wanted it. I might not agree with it, but it had to be done. It was business.'

'That was all that I was to you? Business. Unfinished business for my own mother to deal with.' Lucie chewed over the total hurt for a second. 'Why did you fall in love with her?'

'That was unplanned and I'm not sure I would call it love. Not from me, anyway. That only happened over the last twelve months. We all went out one night – me, Ruby and my dad. We'd been partying and went back to the house in London. Dad went to bed as he was bushed. Ruby and I stayed up drinking and one thing led to another. She's an attractive woman and she knows what to do. What man wouldn't want that? She said I was like her son. She fixated on that a bit. Bit weird but I was happy getting my end away and it was useful to always know she was on my side.'

'Did your dad know?'

'No way. He'd have fucking killed me. She wanted to tell him once, so that we could be together. But I insisted we keep it out of sight. I'm ambitious but I don't have a death wish. We made up trips to go on for work. I'd go away with dad so it seemed logical that sometimes I should go away with Ruby. We've just been to Spain together.'

'Terrance was there too, wasn't he?'

'No, it was just me and Ruby. Spain's a good gateway for drugs so we said we were doing business but it was an excuse for her to be with me – to be together.'

Lucie remembered the male voice that she had heard on Ruby's message to her. It hadn't sounded like Terrance, a little too high-pitched, and now she knew why. It had been his son. Suddenly, everything was piecing together. Well, nearly everything…

'So if you and my mother are together in her eyes, then why were you tied to a chair and bleeding from your head when I came around? Why did Ruby do that?'

'Because she's a fucking psycho who killed my dad and when I turned up here, that's not what I was expecting to find. Ruby's gone too far, which is why she'll have to pay. The whole plan was to get revenge on you for what Ruby said ruined her life, but nobody ever said that my dad would be the casualty. He loved your mum, I know that. I flipped out and threatened to shop her to the police. I don't know if I would have done it, but the next thing I know is that she'd whacked me around the head and I woke up tied to a chair, so that made my mind up. She's a fucking psycho. She's a murderer. She said that she was behind the death of your foster parents.'

Another deadly blow, yet somehow Lucie was becoming immune. 'What? Why would she do that?'

270

'I've got no evidence and I have no idea how she did it but she bragged one day when we were high that it was very handy that they were out of the way and that it was so easy to run people off the roads these days. She needed them to be so that she could orchestrate her revenge on you when you came back to the UK. She said she knew you'd have to come back here even if it was merely to pay your respects to them and sort out any wills. Plus, she wanted to make sure you came to this place. To the cottage. She's a killer. We know that. That's why I was nice to her when she slapped me back awake. I had to pretend I was still on her side or else I thought I'd be next.'

Lucie had no more questions. She had asked all that she needed to know. Done all that needed to be done.

'You need to leave. Go now. Nobody has to know that you were here.' Lucie's words to Steven were cold and devoid of emotion.

'What? We need to phone the police.'

'Why should you get involved? Your drugs contacts will be shocked enough to know that your dad has been killed. Why associate yourself with it too. People will think you killed him to gain control of the business. People don't have to know that you were here.'

Steven looked confused. 'What will you tell the police?'

'The truth. That she did it. She might try and blame you, but the truth is that she did it. My mother killed your dad. We'll both be losing parents. I'm kind of used to it lately.' Lucie's voice was monotone and pragmatic.

'But after everything I've done to you, you'd just let me disappear again? That doesn't make any sense. Why would you do that for me?'

'I'm not doing it for you, Steven Allen. I'm doing it for the memory of Connor Perkins. For the memory of the man I fell in love with. The man who I thought loved me. That memory is tarnished enough without adding more to it. Now just go, get out before she wakes up again. Leave the gun here and run. Run for your life. A new one without her. Without your dad. Without any parents. Welcome to my world. To my life.'

It was seconds before he had wiped the gun on his T-shirt in an attempt to remove any fingerprints, left it on a table in the front room and vanished from the cottage. Vanished from Lucie's life again. Just has he had done all those years ago in Peru. A different time zone but history was repeating itself.

The Final Chapter

Lucie stared down at the body on the floor. It was unrecognisable. The body was that of Ruby Palmer, but any semblance to the woman that Lucie had once loved – her mother – was now gone. Any last shred peeled away with the final revelation about Roger and Tanya. She knew that her mother had done it. Somehow. It didn't matter how. But her gut told her that Ruby was to blame.

She walked over to a table near the door of the front room that led out to the hallway and to the toilet where she had gone to be sick. She hadn't been of course. Why would the sight of blood make her want to vomit? She'd seen enough of that in her life. She knew every shade and every hue of it. She knew exactly what it looked like.

No, that had been an excuse to leave the room. To sneak upstairs and grab her mobile phone. To try and salvage some kind of justice from all of this. From the mess of her own life.

She picked up the phone from where she had placed it on the table. She pressed the stop button. It stopped recording. The app she had downloaded just a few days before thinking that it might be useful for when she was meeting with Sarah. Recording facts about her dad. Things that she would never want to forget. She hadn't used it on Sarah, maybe she never would, but today it had captured every word of her conversation with Steven. With her Connor. She pressed the play button just to make sure. His voice detailing his part in her downfall in Peru was clear to hear. The evidence was there that would finally clear her name. Would she use it? She'd been unsure, right up until the moment that it became clear that he was happy to send Ruby to prison for life. The woman that loved him. Even if he hadn't loved her. Another rejection that eventually she would have faced. How many did one woman deserve? Selling her in the name of business. Losing her, losing Terrance, yet gaining a business. Just as Oliver and Sarah had chosen to lose Ruby and her unborn child. Children. The pattern was there. Maybe that was what Ruby deserved. Lucie wasn't sure. But she knew what Steven deserved.

Ruby began to stir. Lucie heard her moans but remained expressionless as she stood over her.

For a second, she thought of how similar they were. How they had both been abandoned by their own family. That they were closer than they realised. Maybe closer than Lucie wanted to be. Ruby so angry that she had been left with children, one dead and one to blame, at such a young age. The similarity to Ruby's own mother and her want to abandon her child before her.

Perhaps it was in her genes. Perhaps it was inevitable that Lucie was born to suffer. That the suffering of her twin in the womb had stained her existence for forever. That it had mapped out her own life. She felt close to him. To Ashton. Somewhere deep inside in a long forgotten corner she always had.

Ruby was damaged. As was Lucie. Could she really blame her? For a moment there was sympathy. It didn't linger.

Love had nearly been hers for the taking. It had come so close. She thought she had regained it with Ruby. She once thought that she'd had it with Connor. She thought it would always be there from Tanya and Roger. But now, it had all been snatched away. For good.

Ignoring Ruby's cries, she walked out into the kitchen, past Terrance's dead body on the floor, out into the garden and into the cool late night air. She continued walking until she reached the well. It was her favourite spot in the garden. Drew had done a good job there. It was the perfect place to think. About her life. About what, and who, had shaped her into who she now was. She stared down into the darkness of the well, into the void, then looked at the screen of her phone and contemplated her next move. In the distance, she could still hear her mother's desperate cries. Behind the prettiness of the wisteria-covered cottage and the bright red door, she could hear the sound of ugliness.

She knew what to do. Her mind was made up. Lucie was a damaged girl. A girl alone. A girl unknown. Until now. She dialled the number she needed and waited for it to connect…

CPSIA information can be obtained
at www.ICGtesting.com
Printed in the USA
LVHW041725280819
629267LV00011B/243/P